T0267635

The Sticky Note Manifesto of Aisha Agarwal

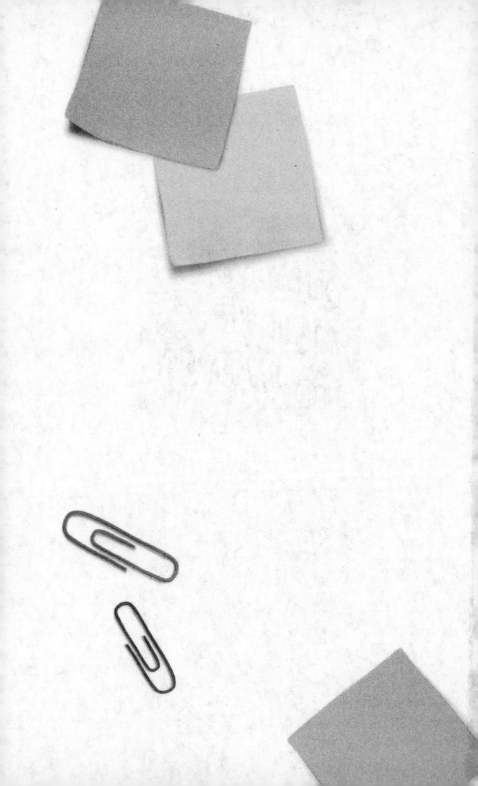

AMBIKA VOHRA

The
STICKY
NOTE
MANIFESTO
of
AISHA
AGARWAL

Quill Tree Books
An Imprint of HarperCollinsPublishers

Quill Tree Books is an imprint of HarperCollins Publishers.

The Sticky Note Manifesto of Aisha Agarwal
Copyright © 2024 by Ambika Vohra
All rights reserved. Printed in the United States of America.
No part of this book may be used or reproduced in any manner
whatsoever without written permission except in the case of brief
quotations embodied in critical articles and reviews. For information
address HarperCollins Children's Books, a division of HarperCollins
Publishers, 195 Broadway, New York, NY 10007.
www.epicreads.com

Library of Congress Control Number: 2023944489
ISBN 978-0-06-334716-8

Typography by Molly Fehr
24 25 26 27 28 LBC 5 4 3 2 1
First Edition

To the brilliant teachers who shaped me—
including Ms. Jane Taylor, Ms. Julie Kuslits, Mr. Chad
Zwolinski, and Dr. Kentaro Toyama—and to every teacher,
author, and librarian who spatters our little corner of the
universe with joy and empathy every day.

The Sticky Note Manifesto of Aisha Agarwal

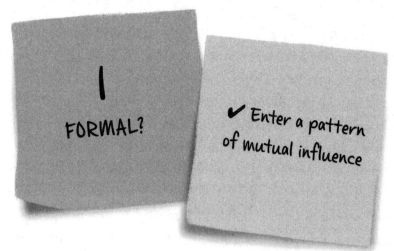

1
FORMAL?

✔ Enter a pattern of mutual influence

The Polaroid is missing.

From March of last year until today, the inside door of Brian Wu's locker displayed a Polaroid of his girlfriend, Riley, held up by two magnets that look like mini vinyls. In the photo, Riley's sitting cross-legged on a picnic blanket in front of a red-tipped barberry shrub, her hair gathered in a loose topknot. She's covering her eyes with her hands like she doesn't want her photo taken, but we all know that she probably did. If I looked like Riley does in a topknot, I'd turn all my walls into mirrors.

But now, all of it's gone. The magnets, the Polaroid.

Brian shuts his locker with a *wham*, and I jump, leaning into my open locker like I was very busy filing away very important senior year things. I have an opera box view of him from here, thanks to the esteemed Order of the Alphabetical that put our lockers in the same row. I have it all colored and labeled in my head like paint chips—where Brian sits in every class, where his locker is, even when his basketball games are.

I'm about to shut my locker, but I notice Brian's not rushing past me like he usually does when the warning bell sounds.

His footsteps are getting slower; his shadow's getting bigger. He must have dropped a pencil that rolled all the way here because there's no *way* he's about to stop in front of—

"Hey, Aisha." Brian gives me a small smile, little dents forming in his cheeks. His school uniform looks crisp and ironed, while mine looks as if it's been yanked down from a flagpole.

For the past four years at Arledge Preparatory, I've mostly seen the zoomed-out version of Brian's face from across assemblies or classrooms or hallways. I'm used to him asking me in passing what score I got on my test, like a drive-through for grade inquiries. We've spoken here and there outside of comparing GPAs, but only for a specific need, like freshman year when he asked me where I got my pencil pouch, junior year when we were in a group project for AP Physics together, or a few months ago when he asked to copy my notes because he forgot his glasses. But now, he's in 4K Ultra HD at my locker. And there are no worksheets or desks or pencil pouches between us.

My eyes move to my scuffed shoes. "Wh-What's up?"

"I know this is a weird question, but . . ." He points to the door of my locker, which is covered in blank yellow sticky notes, with a few filled ones peppered in. "Can I have one of those stickies?"

I blink at him. He towers over me now, not like in middle school when I had a few inches on him still. His straight black hair is lightly combed back with some loose strands framing his eyes like apostrophes, and while his lips are moving, all I can focus on is how *moist* they look.

"I need it for something," he goes on, "and I remembered you have a bunch stuck on here . . ."

I never realized that the whole locker visibility thing was a two-way street.

The sticky note sculpture is courtesy of my friend Marcy. This summer, she read a piece on how sticky notes foster innovation, and she convinced me to create a "lightbulb-moment space" in my locker to capture breakthroughs. Mine's unused except for the ideas Marcy donated, but her locker's lightbulb-moment space is thriving. It has to-do lists, wish lists, vegetables-to-grow-in-her-backyard-garden lists. She even gave me a sticky-note pad to keep in my bag in case of an *idea emergency.*

That's Marcy. She can freehand-draw perfect circles. She's never slouching, even when sitting on those annoying stools with no backs. She's president of the yearbook club *and* managing editor of the school newspaper. She's also basically my only close friend at Arledge Prep, but that job requires no tree killing.

"Oh!" My voice goes high. "Of course! Peel away!"

If I look into his eyes, all the words will evaporate from my brain, so I focus on his backpack straps instead. Marcy once told me if I looked closer, I'd see a Japanese brand name stitched into the leather that puts the bag at $549. Pretax. Considering I've had the same faded JanSport backpack since freshman year with shoulder padding that could double as a bowling lane bumper, I might as well stitch FINANCIAL AID onto the front. Pa pretended that he bought it out of practicality—it would last through high school *and* protect my shoulders from strain. Or he saw the buy one, get one free deal and looked no further.

"Thanks, you're the best!" Brian says, and after he carefully peels off a note, he walks away without another glance. His steps are self-assured, like he's walking to the beat of a song.

One, two, three—everyone wants to be me or date me!

The bell rings, and I pull my composition notebook from my locker and stuff it into my backpack. Brian could've waited for me, considering we're going to the same place, but he probably forgot we're in the same class.

When I get to AP Lit, he's already at his desk and riffling through his $549 backpack, eventually pulling out his copy of *The Great Gatsby.* As I sit down, I see a folded note on my desk. I turn to my right to throw a curious look at Marcy as I open it, but she pretends to be busy arranging her pencils. Her straight brown hair is gathered into a French braid, and she's wearing a monogrammed Arledge Prep sweater over her uniform blouse today.

Arledge Prep has a strict no-phones-except-during-lunch rule, so Marcy passes me notes sometimes. Her handwriting is like decoding hieroglyphics. After much squinting and head tilting, I get the following:

Winter formal top 5 date options:
Alex Currant
Connor Belle
Kenji Tanaka
Jerome King
Sean Truwald

Wild card option:
Brian Wu

I grin. Another listicle from Marcy, though this one feels more thought out than usual, since each name is written in a different gel pen color. She's been trying to get me to ask someone (read: anyone) to tomorrow night's winter formal. She was supposed to go with me as my platonic date as usual, but last week she got asked by Kevin Wright. I can tell she feels bad about leaving me behind, so I've been kind of milking the whole thing. My lonely eyes drove her to buy me a Snickers bar from the vending machine yesterday. She said it was *just because*, but I know better. Her guilt must've driven her to write this listicle, too.

She wouldn't have added Brian as an option if she knew what happened between him and me, but I haven't told anyone at Arledge Prep that I was friends with Brian. Sometimes I want to reveal that he used to be My Clumsy Neighbor ft. Pokémon Card Collection before he became Chiseled Private School Senior ft. Dumbbell Collection, but then I think better of it. It'd be betraying his secret past. Like revealing to 1920s society that Gatsby was a farmer's son. Besides, I'm not jumping at the opportunity to tell everyone how Brian forgot about me like the bunches of cilantro wilting at the back of my fridge.

"Put away your pocket-sized dopamine devices, or they're mine." Ms. Kavnick uncaps an Expo marker with the gusto of a knight unsheathing a sword, her owl earrings spinning. She always knows when students are texting. The owls must tell her.

"Since we just finished discussing *The Great Gatsby*, I'd like to use some of class today to reflect on F. Scott Fitzgerald. When he died of a heart attack in 1940, he'd sold fewer than twenty-five thousand copies of *Gatsby*, and it was only years after his death that the novel became so well-known. He died never seeing the extent of his success." She paces from one side of the board to the other. "Isn't success an unreliable measure, then? And because it's so difficult to define, we often mistakenly equate it to external achievements. Gatsby equated success to winning Daisy's affection. For others, it might be the amount of books we sell in our lifetime, how much money we make, what college we attend . . ."

I swear she's looking right at me. She probably knows I've been a member of the sell-your-soul-for-college-acceptance coalition since freshman year.

"This is what I want you to write about in your journals today." Her marker squeaks across the board. "What do you think Jay Gatsby *lost* in his quest for success? And how could he have defined success differently?"

In my notebook, I pretend to respond to these questions, but I'm brainstorming ideas for the Stanford application essay question that's due next month. I talked to my college counselor for weeks about whether I should apply to Stanford restrictive early action or regular decision. We decided regular decision would be better for me, since I could use the time to retake the SAT and write a stronger personal essay. I raised my SAT score to a 1510, but the essay remains. Undone. Mocking me.

When the bell rings, all I've written down in my notebook is a few bullet points, none of them promising. Students are already stuffing themselves through the doorway to get to the cafeteria, and Brian lifts his backpack over his shoulder, creating a sizable bulge in his forearm. He laughs at something my chem lab partner, Alexander Currant, says, and then walks out without a glance in my direction. There are always people accessorizing his existence wherever he goes now, like a collection of rotating scarves.

It wasn't always that way.

Brian Wu has a *past*. A past full of crimes, to be exact. And there's no Colonel-Mustard-did-it-in-the-study-with-a-candlestick way to summarize them, but I'll try.

In middle school, there was a force field around him that repelled all signs of life, including me. The only time we talked was at the monthly bagel breakfast for the young readers' book club. He would tear his bagel to shreds and stick the pieces into the cream cheese like it was dipping sauce for mozzarella sticks, leaving blueberry bagel crumbs in the container. In hindsight, it probably wasn't the whole sloppy-cream-cheese thing that set me off. It was being a few percentage points behind him on every test, and along with him disrupting the class with unfunny jokes and waving his perfect score papers around for everyone to see, there was one *very* important thing that made Brian impossible to ignore.

We were neighbors.

There aren't many Asian families living in Arledge, Michigan, so ours stuck together like Mrs. Wu's sticky rice cakes. She'd tweeze the sesame seeds into a smiley face for us, and Ma would send foil-coated burfi that beamed back. The trade of rice cakes and burfi went on for years, with Mrs. Wu sending Brian to drop the cakes at our doorstep every few months, and Ma sending me to drop burfi at Brian's. I always looked forward to it since Mrs. Wu would come to the door gushing about how precious and well-behaved I was, as Brian stood by the railing and scowled.

Scowling is how I found him sitting at my dining room table one fourth-grade afternoon when I came home from school. No rice cakes to be seen.

7

"His mother works late now because of her promotion," Ma explained to me in hushed tones. "So your pa and I offered to help watch Brian. I'm relying on you to serve him some snacks and juice, okay?"

"*What?*" I thought of our everything bagels lying next to the toaster, stacked neatly like a roll of quarters. Our bagels must be protected. "But after school is my ME time, to watch cartoons and eat salt-and-vinegar chips and—"

She was already gone.

I begrudgingly offered my chips to Brian that day, and he only took one, probably because he knew Ma made me offer them. But as he spent more afternoons at my house, the silences got shorter, and the half waves and shrugs between us turned into high fives and giggles. I realized that behind all the loud sound effects, boasting, and annoying did-you-know facts was a kid who needed a friend, like I did. I started saving him a seat on the bus ride home. I let his poor bagel etiquette slide. I didn't mind so much when I misspelled *imperative* on a spelling test and he didn't, or when he unabashedly ate all my chips.

The rest of fourth grade took on this new best friend glow, and when the school year ended, we spent summer evenings catching fireflies in old mango pickle jars (although we never kept them too long since Pa would lecture us about "respecting each atma on earth"). By the time fifth grade started, we were eating lunch together, doing our Kumon worksheets together, and even cleaning my landfill of a room together if Pa made me.

A clean room means a clean mind, he always said.

I'd made my own proverb—when a friend helps shove everything you own under your bed, that's when you know the friendship will last.

But then sixth grade hit, and that's when I started thinking of Brian as more than a friend. I doodled his name next to mine in the margins of my notebooks. I drew hearts in the corners of my foggy bathroom mirror after a shower. I imagined what it'd be like to go to the eighth-grade Spring Fling with him.

Turns out, I never went to the Spring Fling at all. Mrs. Wu's late nights at American Axle paid off, and she became senior director of finance. The summer after seventh grade, Brian moved out of our quaint neighborhood and transferred to West Middle. I never got the chance to tell him how I felt, and along with the sticky rice cakes, he wasn't at my door anymore. Firefly jars reverted to pickle jars. Brian stopped being my friend.

Marcy follows my gaze to Brian and then starts violently poking my arm. "What about asking, er, *wild card* to formal? I know he's your competition for valedictorian and everything, but look." *Poke.* "At." *Poke.* "His." *Poke.* "Arms."

"Hey, remember Kevin? Your new *boyfriend*?" I cover my arm with my hand, but she keeps poking my fingers until she gets a smile out of me.

"Just because I'm going to the dance with Kevin now doesn't mean my eyeballs fell out. Also *boyfriend* is too far. We're not official yet."

"Ten bucks you will be by next week," I say, trailing behind her into the hallway. I'm not one to gamble, but Marcy and Kevin fit too well for them not to be together. They're the traffic cones of the world—they're meant to be seen. Kevin is student council president, and Marcy's part of every student publication. She's known she wants to major in journalism since freshman year. She's always been sure of herself, like a newspaper that's already gone to print.

"Please, *please* come to formal tomorrow. Just think of how disappointed Gatsby would be in a young woman like you saying no to a party." Marcy points to Principal Cornish whacking his dead microphone on the cafeteria stage as we sit down at a table. "*He'd* be especially disappointed."

In the weeks leading up to winter formal, Principal Cornish has been recounting to unsuspecting victims the tale of how he met his wife at a winter formal. There are probably more important issues he could be focusing on, like the cost of private school tuition or the rampant cheating that's been happening on calculus tests, but I digress.

"I don't feel like going this year." I dig into my backpack for a browning banana and a vending machine Snickers bar.

Marcy watches me. "Is it that you don't feel like going or—"

"Before you say it—it's not only because I don't have a date. The tickets cost a hundred dollars. What is this, Coachella?"

"I told you I'd cover you. Or you can use your nest egg of Antelope bucks. . . ."

Principal Cornish calls the money in our student accounts "Antelope bucks," but I refuse to acknowledge a currency that can only be used for school lunch, school store merch, and school-sponsored events.

"Or I can catch up on college applications. And crochet on my couch in between."

At that, Marcy presses her lips together and gets this look like she's trying not to laugh, which is somehow *worse* than her laughing. I joined crochet club last year, after reading that crochet uses a single hook to combine loops, which is supposed to make it easier than knitting and meant that I'd become a yarn whisperer in no time, but I haven't. It's more of a shout-at-my-tangled-mess-of-yarn situation, and usually I'd laugh with Marcy about my wonky crochet animals. I even named the collection Graveyarn. But there's something about Brian asking me for that sticky note that set me off. It's like everyone has *I'm better than you* painted on their foreheads.

Realizing I'm not laughing with her, Marcy looks down, suddenly very interested in her sandwich. I think she can tell that I'm in a mood. Both Marcy and Pa are good at discerning that. When Brian and I stopped being friends, Pa comforted me by saying that maybe Brian and I weren't meant to stay friends in this life—that in a future life, we might come together again. I imagined us centuries later as two cherry trees planted next to each other in an orchard. But our reunion came sooner than I thought. I got a full-tuition scholarship to the same high school as Brian: Arledge Preparatory, one of the most prestigious and expensive private high schools in Michigan. A school with a customizable course catalog for grades nine to twelve, rigorous advanced placement classes, college counselors, a focus on nurture, college readiness, and resilience . . . and admissions committees all over the world know the Arledge difference! (The website's words, not mine.)

But even though we go to the same school, Brian and I didn't come together again like my dad thought we might. I'm just a sticky note vending machine to him. At best.

"Maybe you won't need to ask anyone to the dance," Marcy says. "Someone might ask you."

"Doubt it. Here I come, twenty-five-minute Pomodoro blocks."

She gives me a blank stare.

"To work on my Stanford essay."

"There it is," she groans through a mouthful. "And here I thought we were going to get through lunch without you mentioning Stanford."

I bite my lip. I get it. I irk *myself* with how much I talk about Stanford sometimes, but mentioning it makes it feel like it's all possible—for me, and for Ma. She got admitted to Stanford a few years after immigrating to the United States, but never graduated.

"Just imagine us in *Californ-i-a*!" I sing. "The land of movie stars. Ocean views. Redwood trees. Year-round sunshine."

"Hard pass. You forget I'm white."

Marcy's pale skin is extra sensitive to the sun. I used to be confused by the kids around me lathering on sunscreen during elementary school field trips to Houghton Lake, but it all made sense later when I found out that Arledge, Michigan, is 81.4 percent white. Forget lemonade stands—I should've been selling Sun Bum during my summer vacations.

Ma never gave me any sunscreen. She thought that with our darker skin, we don't need sun protection, so I'll probably look like a raisin sooner rather than later.

"What's the Stanford essay question again?" Marcy asks, poking drooping tomato slices out of her sandwich, which means that she was at her dad's yesterday. He never remembers that she hates raw tomatoes. "Tell us about a time you fell off a cliff and totally almost died but then didn't, and then tell us how it was actually the best thing that ever happened to you and what a deeply precious growth opportunity it was to snap all your limbs in half after all?"

I chuckle. "Close. It's *share a time you left your comfort zone.*"

"The irony. College admissions criteria is the reason we've been glued to our desks for the past four years. I have back pain already. I can barely bend far enough to help my grandparents plant zucchini."

Marcy's backyard garden has stepping stones that lead to a wooden arch covered in snaking vines, and when I first saw it, I remember thinking that the space was bigger than my whole apartment. Marcy's grandparents live nearby, so they usually come over to trim overgrown shrubs. I'm fascinated by how often they visit. I've only seen my nani and nana a handful of times—once when they visited Arledge and spent every evening at the Jai Ho Indian grocery store, and again the summer of eighth grade when my family visited India for a month. I remember Pa packed *The Peterson Method®: An SAT Vocabulary Workbook* in his suitcase for my older sister, Seema, to review, and he'd plop it on her lap every time he'd catch her watching an Indian drama.

"You might have back pain, but at least you have *direction*," I tell Marcy. "I still don't know what to put down for my major. My counselor said she doesn't recommend going in undecided."

I've been doing well in AP Computer Science, and majoring in it makes sense since I've loved math and puzzles for as long as I can remember, but I'm not sure I want to spend eight hours a day coding. After my counselor told me to think about what I do that makes *time fall away*, I remembered painting, but the only things I've had time to paint in the last four years are the decorations for our school dances. Besides, if I told Ma and Pa I'm majoring in fine art, they'd hear that I'm majoring in instability. Which might not be wrong.

"I think it's okay to take your first year of college to explore. Better than choosing a major you might hate. Besides . . ." Marcy's shaping her sandwich crust into a heart. Based on her general disdain for all institutions, I can guess what she's about to say. "No matter what major you put down now, those admissions gatekeepers are gonna expect stellar grades, leadership experience, a bazillion volunteer hours, and in your spare time you better be listening to mindfulness podcasts to work through your trauma that you can spin into a heartfelt application essay while raising money for multiple scleros—"

"Marcy, may I borrow you for *just* a moment?" Principal Cornish is shuffling toward our table with this big smile that looks permanently stapled to his face; his cheeks a splotchy red and forehead beaded with sweat. The polka-dot tie he's wearing is knotted so tightly around his neck that I wonder how he ever looks down. "It seems I need your expertise on AV equipment! My microphone isn't working, I'm afraid."

Marcy and I exchange looks. "I'm president of the yearbook club. I think you're looking for Mari, president of the theater club? She can probably help you fig—"

"Oh dear, right you are! My deepest apologies for the mix-up!" His smile doesn't waver. "But it's a happy accident, considering I was just thinking about checking on the yearbook this morning to make sure everything's going swimmingly. This is the butterfly effect at its finest—even if two things collide just once in space and time, they enter into a pattern of mutual influence forever. I guarantee, I was meant to run into *you* today!" He winks and holds up his hand for a high five, and when she reluctantly slaps it, he asks, "How're things coming along? Is the cover design all set?"

"Uh, yeah—yes. The students voted and Aimee's design won—the one with the Antelope emblem in the center."

"Wonderful." He looks distracted, no doubt combing the cafeteria for Mari. "I better go, but keep up the great work, Marcy!"

He shuffles away, and Marcy turns to me as soon as he's out of earshot. "What the heck did he say earlier? *Butterfly effect? Space and time?*"

I laugh. "He can talk his way out of anything. How do you think he deals with all the nightmare Arledge parents?"

Her shoulders droop. "Lucky Mari. No one ever comes lookin' for the president of the yearbook club."

"*I* do."

I've been pestering Marcy all month for a peek at the yearbook draft. I love yearbooks, for the glossy pages and hand-written messages on the inside covers. I'm buying one knowing I'll hardly be in it, unless I get valedictorian or they dedicate a spread to Seniors Who Started a Bullet Journal but Then Decided It Was Too Much Work.

At that moment, presumably with Mari's help, Principal Cornish gets his microphone to work.

"Arrrrrledge Antelopes!" The microphone screeches as his voice booms across the cafeteria. "This is a reminder that winter formal is happening tomorrow night at our beloved Conservatory of Music in downtown Arledge. Tickets are being sold until three in the West Pavilion. If you have any questions, you can ask your friendly student council vice president . . ." He gestures to Brian, who gives the crowd a wave and gets a few whistles in return. I swear that boy is everywhere at this school. Sometimes I question if I'm trapped in one of those old Bollywood films where one actor plays multiple roles by switching wigs. "Brian Wu," Principal Cornish adds, although I doubt he needs the introduction. "You can direct questions about logistics and parental chaperone sign-ups to him."

"What's that shiny thing on Brian's sweater?" Marcy asks, squinting.

I pretend to squint, too, even though I already know. "I think it's his honor roll pin."

Arledge is strict about altering our uniforms, but wearing small brooches or enamel pins is allowed. Brian wears that gold antelope pin almost daily, so I suppose he likes displaying his Principal's honor roll status in a subtle way.

Marcy snickers. "Of course he's wearing that."

Okay, maybe not *that* subtle.

A 3.4–3.8 GPA makes the regular honor roll, and anything higher puts you on the Principal's honor roll with a capital P, which means you get a gold antelope pin and early registration for special courses like metalsmithing and fiber arts. I'm on the Principal's honor roll, too, but I lost my pin a month after I got it.

Principal Cornish clasps his hands behind his back, leaning so close to the microphone that he's practically kissing it. "As some of you might know, I met my wife at my school's winter formal. We had our first dance in the gymnasium there, and this could turn out to be an equally special time for you."

"Kill me," I groan, turning back to Marcy.

Everyone I know has a date to formal, or at least has *been* on a date before. Given that I spend all my time studying and pining for a boy I'll never have, it makes sense that there isn't an avalanche of love notes falling out of my locker when I open it. Still, a part of me hoped a good thing would magically come knocking for once, instead of me plotting everything like a mystery novelist. Take eighth grade, for example. In order to get Ma and Pa to let me go on a camping trip with my environmental club, I started sending them articles with titles like "Green Surroundings Linked to Higher Attention Spans" weeks in advance.

"Did you and Kevin decide what you're going to wear to formal?" I ask.

In addition to being student council president, Kevin Wright is editor in chief of the *Antelope Times* and, from what I gather, Brian's best friend. He's one of the few Black students at Arledge Prep. He's also a trifecta of friendly to everyone *and* popular *and* attractive, so it figures he was crowned best friend, while I got thrown out like an old sock with toe holes.

"Kevin's grandma advised us both to wear red. She said it's the color of *passion*."

I can't imagine my nani saying something like that. She'd probably say red is the color of dried chilies.

The lunch bell rings, and I head to my locker. I used to have a track on a loop in my head leading up to all school dances: *at least Marcy doesn't have a date, either!* But now she's planning cute matching outfits with the blessing of Kevin's grandma, while my entire life's yearbook has been stuck on the same page since freshman year. I can't even remember the last time I didn't rush through dinner to get to the chimney stack of AP homework waiting for me. Maybe it was years ago, when Brian and I were still neighbors. He used to stay for biryani and always brought me a piece of Chinese milk candy. If he forgot, he'd bring me two pieces the next time.

And now we barely talk.

As I approach my locker, Principal Cornish's voice rings in my head. *Even if two things collide just once in space and time, they enter into a pattern of mutual influence forever.* I have my doubts about the butterfly effect. I can't imagine Brian and me existing in a pattern of influence again. The only pattern we share now is competing for valedictorian, so I'd be surprised if we ever—

That's when I see it.

There's a sticky note on my locker that says *FORMAL?* in black pen, and what's more is that I'd recognize that handwriting anywhere.

"Hey, Aisha."

I spin around. Standing there, hands by his sides, is Brian Wu.

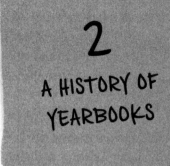

2

A HISTORY OF YEARBOOKS

✔ Memorize what Brian wrote in every yearbook I bought

GRADE 4

Aishaaaa—

Thx for letting me eat all your chips this year. At least we don't have to be sad about school ending because I'll cya in probably 5 mins when u come over.

Brian

GRADE 5

Aish,

I know you love my fun facts sooo much, so here's another: did u know Q is the only letter that doesn't appear in any US state name?

Brian

GRADE 6

Yo Aish-slice!

I'm writing this super tiny because it's top-secret: as of yesterday, a new fro-yo place opened downtown in place of that closed watch repair shop. First 100 customers get free cereal toppings. We gotta bike there ASAP!!!

—Brian Wuletthedogsout

GRADE 7

Dear Aish,

I'm going to miss you so much when I move!!! Thank you for letting me win at Connect 4 sometimes :P, and for the assortment of turtle drawings. They kept me awake during all of Mr. Clark's boring history documentaries (I still don't understand how your ~~handwritting~~ handwriting is so neat). I saved the drawings for when you become a famous artist. I still won't sell them if you do, though, so don't worry. Can't wait to hang out this summer!

Sincerely, Brian

GRADE 8 (NO YEARBOOK)

"These yearbooks are too expensive and a waste of money. You can buy one next year."

—Ma

GRADE 9

h.a.g.s
—brian

GRADES 10 & 11

See Grade 8.

GRADE 12

TBD

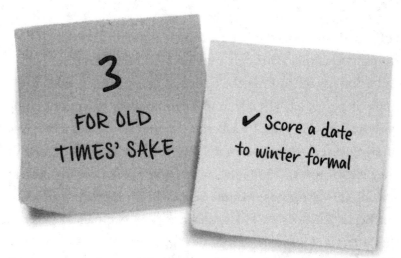

✔ Score a date
to winter formal

"Sorry to startle you." Brian has this mischievous twinkle in his eyes, the same look he used to get when telling me stories about Rooney the witch, who lived in the woods behind our apartment building. She was actually a mechanical engineer who lived in unit 109 and had a tarot card deck. "I come in peace. I'm here to ask you a very important question"—he points to the *FORMAL?* sticky note—"with the aid of the sticky you provided this morning."

"Y-You mean—"

"I was wondering if you would accompany me to winter formal tomorrow night." His voice goes low on *accompany*, like he's the governor inviting me to a gala. He's always had a proper way of speaking—he says *doing well* instead of *good*, or *may I* instead of *can I*.

I breathe in. This is *real*. This is not a drill.

"I know it's last minute. The thing is, my girlfriend and I broke up last night."

My expression remains blank because I know all about Polaroid Riley already. She goes to a different school, is some sort of volleyball star, and she got a puppy last month. Border collie, I think. I've scrolled through a zillion pictures of her.

"I don't want to miss the dance or go by myself. Everyone I know is paired off already, and Kevin told me you're not going with anyone. He said if I ask you, I better do it with some sort of sign or something, so that's how I thought of using one of your sticky notes." He smiles at me, and I look away to prevent melting into my shoes. Middle School Brian used to smile a lot, but Brian 2.0 doesn't. His smiles are rare, like pancake day in the cafeteria. I just earned a smile with *teeth*. "So? What do you say, Aish?"

Aish. My nickname in his deep, buttery voice.

The antelope honor roll pin on his sweater glints as he folds his arms across his chest. "No pressure."

AishAishAishAish—

"I was just thinking we could go together for old times' sake," he adds, watching me.

Doesn't he remember how things left off, back in the *old times*?

It was when Brian was moving out of our Coral Tree apartment complex. Seventh grade had ended a week before, and we were sitting in the trunk of Pa's old station wagon like we often did, admiring the sunset, our legs dangling over the back bumper. The orange sky was bleeding into pinks and purples, and my cheeks were wet with tears. Usually, I'd be embarrassed crying in front of anyone, but not Brian.

"You're still going to come over, right?" I'd asked him.

He nodded, tufts of his pin-straight hair lifting in the wind. "Of course."

"Who's going to untangle my necklaces for me?"

I'd always let the chains of my Claire's necklaces fold into each other until they became one evil Pangaea that could not be separated. Brian would come over with a safety pin and magically pry them all apart.

"Maybe you could stop dumping them into your nightstand drawer. Just a thought."

"It's gonna be so boring without you." My voice was cracking from the effort of not crying harder.

"Maybe change will be good. My house is going to be way bigger, so we'll have more room to—"

"No change allowed. We're staying best friends."

I said it like it was the thing I was most sure of in the world, but I knew it wasn't true. I'd already felt him slipping away into someone new, someone who wanted to be different. Brian's comic books and "Be Water, My Friend" poster were thrown in the trash instead of tucked into his Things to Keep box. His square glasses had been replaced by trendy round frames, and he started walking by the pond a few blocks from our apartment complex without looking for tadpoles. I hoped he'd put me in Things to Keep last minute, but he didn't. After he moved, he kept telling me he was too busy to hang out. After three weeks went by, I knew what he meant, but I didn't want to believe it.

I rode my bike to his new house one sweltering August morning in hopes of salvaging our crumbling friendship, and when he opened the door, I barely recognized him. His mop of straight hair had been cut and styled into a tapered fade. Instead of a graphic tee, he was wearing a plain collared shirt with a logo I couldn't place. It was jarring, like the time I'd gone back to visit my old elementary school to find that the library had a new computer lab where the reading corner used to be. He looked at me different, too, like I was a moth who had whizzed into his house by accident, while I joked about how many rooms his new house had.

"You'd have to skateboard to get from one end to the other," I said.

He shrugged. "It might look big, but my mom is so afraid of me breaking things that I'm barely allowed to touch any of it."

At the time, Mrs. Wu was focused on Brian behaving properly and losing some weight, believing those to be the last steps in her Five Steps to a Flawless Son program. By the evening of my visit, Brian had bulldozed over the bridge I'd tried to build between us. He sighed when I wound up his music box for the fifth time, and he looked away when I asked about his new school. Finally, I gathered the courage to ask him what was wrong.

"I feel like I've outgrown the stuff we used to do together," he said, and my heart dropped to the floor.

That was that.

I never asked him to hang out again, and he never asked me. We didn't run into each other until freshman year, when we both started at Arledge Prep. Even then, I didn't find the loud, comic-loving kid I knew—the kid who always got his sundae with whipped cream and an extra striped paper straw. He had a certain smoothness now, like someone had taken a knife and sheared that whipped cream straight off the top.

"Um . . ." I clear my throat, returning my eyes to my shoes. I'm afraid if I look at him, he'll see a billboard flashing my secrets. That there are more than a few sketches of him in my sketchbook. Or that I play reruns of our moments together in my head. Or that for my birthday, I wished we'd be in all the same classes this year.

Brian steps in front of the FORMAL? sticky note, covering it entirely. "I didn't mean to make—I mean, if you don't feel comfortable—"

"I— Yes," I blurt, my eyes meeting his. They haven't changed. They're the same dark eyes of the boy who loved card magic, skipping rocks across the Clinton River, sticking maple tree whirlers in my hair . . .

"Oh." His furrowed eyebrows suddenly relax, like uneven grass being mowed to a straight edge. "You sure?"

"I'm sure," I say, nodding vigorously to show *just* how sure I am.

I feel like a new woman, like that time I took an hour-long bath and filled out one page of a bullet journal. This kind of stuff doesn't happen to people like me—the extras in the film. The universe must have promoted me to main character, pushing me through a wormhole to an alternate dimension where the yearbook of my life could finally be filled all at once: my first and only crush asking me to winter formal, my first slow dance, my first corsage, my first date . . .

Could Brian Wu and I be in a pattern of mutual influence after all?

4
DUELING PIANOS

✔ Attend winter formal

I'm sitting cross-legged on the floor of my bedroom wearing a sequined white dress, shaking my right thigh to dispel nervous energy. My sister, Seema, is kneeling on the ground in front of me, peering at my fresh chin pimple. I call them *chimples*. This one looks like Mount Vesuvius minutes before its eruption in AD 79. Unlike me, Seema has long, straight hair. Soft, blemish-free skin. She got Ma's genes. That's why I half believed her when she used to tell me I was plucked from the dumpster.

"I can't believe you made me drive home for this. It's not even that bad." She's dabbing a dime-sized dot of her crusty foundation on my chin, but in *Volcano v. Foundation*, I know volcano always wins. "It's like the time you made me drive home to kill a spider in your room when Ma and Pa were in India."

"Not my fault you chose a college so close by. Besides, I was going to vacuum the spider myself, but then I imagined it escaping and laying eggs all over my room."

"Think about it, Aish. Is the spider in *your* room, or are you in the *spider's* room?"

I roll my eyes.

"Just giving you a preview of the hippie-tie-dye-crystal crap you'll hear in California. . . ." She squints at my chin. "All righty, my foundation is kind of light for your skin, but at least the chimple looks covered."

"You really cured it?"

"You're looking at me like I'm a vet who saved your sick hamster. I just slapped some foundation on your zit, man."

"ThankyouthankyouTHANKYOU."

Have you ever noticed how the Mega Million jackpot winners only get interviewed on the day they find their winning ticket? No one interviews them on day two, when they're crouched under a desk, sobbing about how they're woefully unprepared to handle the responsibility of managing the money.

I'm on day two.

"Yeah, yeah. And by the way, it's super obvious you're going with a boy tonight, but I don't want to know anything. Or else Ma will hold me responsible."

It already took a lot of work convincing Ma to let me start going to school dances in the first place. I had to explain the landscape: kids flailing around to music, surrounded by hand-painted leaves, flowers, or snowflakes (depending on the season), and chaperones patrolling for any *unseemly* behavior. With a little coaxing from Seema, Ma agreed, but there's no way I'd get away with adding a boy to the mix. Even if it's golden boy Brian.

My parents are the kind of loving parents who fret over you when you're sick and take your temperature constantly by pressing the backs of their hands to your forehead (very scientific), but they're also the kind of parents who make you wear knee and elbow pads even if biking only a block. There's this jumpiness about them, like they're expecting a vortex to open in the center of our street and suck Seema and me into the earth. Sometimes when I go over to Marcy's and see how relaxed her mom is, I wonder what life would've been like if my parents gave me space. Like Marcy's-vegetable-garden amount of space.

My cheeks redden. "Okay, so I might be going with a boy, but the dance is also, er, research for my Stanford essay. Share a time you—"

"Left your comfort zone. We all know. Maybe if you'd killed that spider yourself, you would've had content for your essay already." She caps her foundation, helping me get to my feet. "And why are your eyes all red? Please don't tell me you were crying over your pimple."

"Sounds plausible, but no. My contacts are bothering me."

Probably because my eyes were shut for a whopping seven minutes last night. I was up brainstorming what I'll talk about with Brian at the dance. Versions of *How's student council going?* or *I've missed talking to you all this time* or *insert inside joke here*. Add to that an hour of research on how to slow dance and another half hour practicing walking in Seema's four-inch pumps, which I snagged from her closet. I couldn't leave tonight up to chance.

"You should've just worn glasses. Contacts are *very* drying for your corneas, you know." She sighs, dusting my dress as I stand. "Not that you listen to me. Now get going. Pa's waiting outside."

"Don't worry, I got it all under control," I say, and then I proceed to ransack my room to find the rose boutonniere that I bought for Brian yesterday after school.

By the time I find the rose and rush out of the apartment building, Pa has defrosted the car and is watching from the driver's seat as I hobble toward him in Seema's heels.

Pa puts an affectionate hand on my head as I slide into the passenger's seat. "Tum kab itni badi hogayi?" *When did you get so grown-up?*

I'm clearly not all that grown-up because I immediately start rockin' out to "Jingle Bell Rock." It's only the end of November, but 100.3 FM starts playing Christmas songs on November first every year, like clockwork. Seema says they start early to fuel consumerism.

As we drive into Marcy's neighborhood, Pa turns down the radio every so often to point to houses blanketed in blinking lights and reindeer inflatables.

We roll to a stop in front of Marcy's, and I turn my head toward the snowcapped pine trees as I wait for her to come outside. I've learned to avoid resting my eyes on the brick driveway, the pruned bushes, or the gated garden. If I look too long, I'll start comparing my tiny apartment to all of it.

The car door opens, and Marcy settles into the back.

"Hello, Mr. Agarwal!" She's wearing a red floor-length dress with a square neckline, and her hair hangs in soft curls around her face.

"Don't you clean up nice," I say, reaching my arms up like I'm on a roller coaster. As she bends forward to slap both my hands, Pa nods at me. "Go sit in the back. I don't want you girls breaking your arms."

Good old Pa. I like that there are nights he lets me be. He must know that Ma asked six parents' worth of questions about this dance already. After he hears the click of two seat belts, he adjusts his rearview mirror and starts rolling down the snowy street.

"You look super pretty," Marcy says, which makes me feel a little better about my chimple. "And thanks for the ride. Driving in these heels would've sucked, and Kevin had to get to the conservatory early because his grandma needed a ride there, too. She practices with her band on Saturday evenings." She lowers her voice. "Why didn't Brian pick you up?"

I press my lips together, glancing at Pa. The radio commercials seem to be loud enough, so I whisper back, "My parents would flip if they knew I was going with a date, so I asked him to meet me there."

"Is he there already?"

"I texted him to check if he's on his way, but no reply yet."

The more I look at my phone, the more I start to wonder if Brian regrets asking me. I know he must've really been scraping the bottom of the barrel if he's okay bringing me as his date, with all his gorgeous and popular friends looking on. It's like serving lobster with a side of Cheez-Its.

I'm the Cheez-Its.

"I still can't believe he asked you to formal ten minutes after I joked about it. . . ." She leans closer, tugging on her seat belt. "It was out of left field. You haven't really hung out with him outside of school, have you?"

Brian felt embarrassingly out of reach before, like having a cardboard cutout of a celebrity crush I'd never meet, but now that he asked me to winter formal, I feel like I can finally tell Marcy. I'm invited to the meet-and-greet now, so to speak.

"Actually, I have. In middle school." I bite my lip. "We were . . . good friends."

Her mouth drops open. "You're *kidding*."

I shake my head.

"*How could you not tell—*"

"*Shhh.*" I put my finger to my lips, looking over at Pa to make sure he's still humming holiday tunes. "I know, I know. It's just, he totally dropped me as a friend back then, so I didn't like talking about it. Plus, I felt stupid for still liking him."

"Half the student body likes him." She turns her face to the window. "Of course. You always pick him for popcorn readings in AP Lit, and he comes up a weird amount in your conversations. I just can't believe you didn't *tell* me before."

"Hey, I pick him because he's one of the few people who doesn't hate reading aloud. It's a favor to everyone else in the class. And I talk about him because he's my competition for valedictorian, remember?"

"You don't let me forget." She's blinking a lot, which I know means that she's starting to get upset.

I scoot closer to her. "I'm really sorry, Marce. I should've told you."

Her eyes stay on the window. "*Sorry* won't cut it. After this, you're buying me an apology brownie sundae from Wooly's to discuss in more detail."

I knew this would happen. Marcy likes being in the know. Whether it's an *Antelope Times* article or her life, she can't stand when facts are omitted. Pa parks in front of the Conservatory of Music. I recognize a few Arledge students, arm in arm as they ascend the cement steps.

"What smiley should I expect tonight?" Pa asks as we get out of the car, his eyes crinkling.

Whenever I'm not home, Ma and Pa make me text them every few hours to let them know I'm okay. Instead of typing out *I'm alive*, I periodically send an emoji. Last week, it was a turkey in honor of Thanksgiving.

"Red lady dancing?"

He gives me a thumbs-up. "Have fun, girls! Call me if you need, I won't be far."

This means he'll be at Costco stocking up on discounted gas and the Kirkland holiday cookies he dips in his chai. Pa believes Costco is America's crown jewel.

We wave as he pulls away. My hands are turning to ice, but I still pause to admire the brick facade of the conservatory before climbing the steps. The shape of the sculpted bushes lining the railing reminds me of erasers on brand-new pencils, and warm-toned lights hang from the conical roof, with trees curling over either side of the building like bookends. Pretty, but still not worth one hundred dollars a ticket. I was relieved Brian bought mine, because the four Antelope bucks in my account would've scored us a four-ounce juice cup from concentrate.

I hear the roar of the crowd as soon as Marcy opens the door. Paper snowflakes hang from the ceiling, and there's a cardboard snowman at the entrance wrapped in a string of red and green bulbs, a glittery carpet runner that looks like snow, a refreshments table, a photo booth, and a hot cocoa station with a *Co Co Co* sign painted above it. The dance floor is crowded with students bobbing to the holiday hits.

"I'm gonna find a bathroom," Marcy shouts at me over the

music, handing our tickets to the parent volunteer at the door. She always drinks copious amounts of liquids at the worst time. On our AP Physics field trip to the Cedar Point amusement park last year, she drank two Cokes in the first hour of the four-hour bus ride.

"I'll wait here," I call back, wriggling out of my coat and draping it over my arm. I'd usually accompany Marcy, but these heels make walking feel like snowshoeing. As soon as she's gone, I check my phone. Still nothing from Brian.

"Hey! Agarwal!"

There's only one person at Arledge who calls me by my last name. Sure enough, Kevin is waving emphatically at me from the refreshments table. It's like he's trying to flag down a taxi. I have to admit, his tuxedo looks sharp, and his big smile is charming as usual. As I wave back and make my way toward him, I spot more familiar faces: Alexander, my chem lab partner, and Lily, president of crochet club. After I see her strapless velvet dress with cutouts, the long-sleeved, high-neckline dress I'm wearing suddenly feels plain and childish.

"Thanks a million for bringing Marcy. My grandma is rehearsing here tonight in one of the soundproof rooms upstairs, so I came early to drop her off."

"Of course." I look up at the snowflakes dangling from the ceiling, and Kevin follows my gaze.

"You like the decorations, huh?"

"I'm . . . on the decorations committee." I say it in the same forlorn tone I use to tell people I'm sensitive to gluten now. Those student council reps got me by advertising it as a leadership position, but I'm really just Snowflake Painter #6.

"Me too! I cut the cardboard for the snowman sculpture."

Of course. I bet he also bakes the school cafeteria muffins and mows the soccer field himself.

"Hey, Aisha," Alexander says, giving me a paltry half wave as I slip my phone into my bag. Marcy said it best—he has the makings of a white Abercrombie cashier, with his thick sand-colored hair and striking blue eyes. Too bad he always pronounces my name *ay-shuh*. It's *eye-shuh*, but I gave up after correcting him a few times. If it makes AP Chemistry go a minute faster, *ay-shuh* it is. "I wrote my half of the chromatography report. I'll share it with you tomorrow."

"Thanks," I say, but we both know I'll have to rewrite all of it. Alexander and I were assigned as lab partners freshman year, and he asked me to be lab partners again in AP Chemistry this year. When he did, I was thinking something like, *I'm better off with a Tater Tot.*

I said yes.

As I grab a cup of orange juice to give myself something to do, I watch the entrance for a Brian-shaped silhouette. I was thinking Kevin would go and fluff up the cardboard of his snowman or something, but he stays next to me, munching on a snowflake sugar cookie.

"So," Kevin starts, biting off another arm of the snowflake, "Brian's your date tonight, huh? He told me at basketball practice yesterday. I was glad to hear he asked you."

My eyes snap from the door to him. ". . . You were?"

"You're Marcy's best friend, so you're vetted. And no one can be worse than his ex. Riley was pretty toxic. She equated having a boyfriend with going to Build-A-Bear." He must notice my confusion because he explains, "I mean, she kept telling him what clothes he'd look better in, what kind of haircut he should get, that sort of thing."

Oh. Indian parents don't take their kids to Build-A-Bear. I remember Ma saying something like, *It's the same as going to a restaurant, and then paying to go to the kitchen and make my own naan!*

"She even told him to wear contacts instead of glasses," he adds.

I pause, trying to imagine someone giving appearance-related pointers to *Brian*. I'd never tell him what to wear. I'd tell him he can wear anything.

Or nothing.

"Contacts are very drying for the corneas," I say finally, channeling Seema. "So how'd you and Marcy happen? Last I checked you were always snapping at each other."

"Newspaper deadlines bring out the worst in everyone, as I'm sure you know. You were in it for a few months, right?"

Newspaper was where Marcy and I first met. She spoke up about everything, like how menstrual products in school bathrooms should be free, while I watched and ate vending machine Skittles. But after we got paired to write an article, we found we had more in common than we thought. I helped her manage her short temper, and she encouraged me to pick bolder topics for my pieces. In sophomore year, she took up journaling and came out as bi, while I took up more of the couch and realized lime Skittles are the worst flavor. I say we both grew. And even if we don't always agree, we have an understanding. She knows that I'm the person who rewrites Alexander's part of the lab report for him, and I know that she's the person who would sit with Alexander and make him fix each mistake on his own, but we don't try to change each other.

"Wait!" Kevin snaps his fingers. I don't know how he always has energy for all this hand waving, exclaiming, and snapping. "I remember one of your op-eds! You quit social media for a month, right?"

That was a wondrous month. Who knew that scrolling through every Arledge student eating pie at Orville's pumpkin patch from different angles wasn't essential to my existence?

"You should write a guest op-ed for us. We need fresh stuff. We were thinking a new comic strip, and Marce was telling me you draw these one-panel comics about a turtle and a shark that become friends and go on advent—"

I jump as my bag vibrates.

Brian?

Compact mirror. Wallet. Instant camera. Sticky-note pad. Finally, the bag monster regurgitates my phone, and I see that it's a message from Marcy.

Eyeliner emergency, help!!! In the bathroom up the stairs to the right.

I motion to Kevin that I'll be right back, although I'm not sure *I'm* the best person to call on during an eyeliner emergency. As I clomp up the stairs to the second floor of the conservatory, I hear jazz music ringing faintly from the practice room across from the women's bathroom. The room's door is shut, but I peek through the square window.

A band.

I see drums, bass, saxophone, guitar, and clarinet. All the players are Black, and there's only one woman, wearing a knee-length white dress and purple pumps, her lips stained a cherry red and her eyes shut. She appears older than the rest of the members, but she's playing with more energy than everyone else combined. Her hands dance across her clarinet, and the way her whole body is swaying reminds me of a daisy waving to and fro in the wind. It's like she's not in this world anymore, like she's somewhere safe.

"That's Kevin's grandma," Marcy's voice announces, and I jump, spinning around to see her standing behind me. "If you're wondering, the musical talent isn't genetic. You should hear Kevin on his drum set."

They must be hanging out a lot if Marcy has heard him play. The only male student's house I've been to in the last year was Alexander's, and I only stopped by to retrieve my chem textbook, which he'd accidentally taken.

"I'm jealous," I murmur, imagining Marcy and Kevin lying on the shag rug in her room, giggling and doing homework together.

"Huh?"

I feel a stab of guilt. I'm supposed to be happy for Marcy's budding romance. Clearing my throat, I point to Kevin's grandma poking her clarinet in the air as the rhythm quickens. "I mean, I'm jealous of her. I wonder what it's like to enjoy doing something that much. And in front of people. I bet *she'd* have plenty of stories to tell for my Stanford essay."

"Uh-uh, no Stanford talk today. You're here to dance your socks off with Brian and eat pizza . . . well, gluten-free pizza."

I laugh. "Thanks for specifying. And your eyeliner's perfect."

"Sure?" She smooths her hair. "I couldn't tell if I fixed the smudge."

I've never seen Marcy concerned about how she looks. She has this unapologetic *take it or leave it* attitude, so now I know she really likes Kevin. Earlier I wasn't sure if she had a case of Senior Musical Chairs Syndrome, as Seema calls it, where seniors pair up since prom is nearing and the song of high school is about to stop. But this seems real, and now all I can think about is how I don't want to be left standing when the song ends.

"It's fixed," I assure her. "Now, c'mon, lover boy has been waiting for you."

We start back down the squeaky wooden stairs. My eye catches on a framed vintage poster of a 1942 dueling pianos concert hanging above the railing. Dueling pianos are crashing in my *head*. One of them is playing "Go Home Before It's Too Late" and another is playing "Brian Wu's Arms." I check my phone, sigh, then weakly toss it back into my bag.

"Don't worry, he'll be here soon," Marcy murmurs, draping an arm over my shoulder. But a pit of dread is forming in my stomach. Brian's usually early, or at least on time. Even when he came down with food poisoning, he still arrived early to rehearse for the premiere of our fifth grade's production of *The Sword in the Stone*.

When we get back downstairs, it's so packed that the chaperones have started patrolling the dance floor, including Ms. Kavnick. I don't know how she has the energy to teach *and* chaperone after-school events, but she claims that spending time away from her husband helps her to not murder him. Marcy and I are wading through students toward the refreshments table when I feel a light touch on my shoulder. For a moment, the pianos in my head stop.

Brian?

Kevin. His eyes catch on Marcy. I'm about to nudge her forward, so he can whisper into her hair how beautiful she looks and twirl her away to his horse-drawn carriage or whatever, but my bag starts vibrating for what feels like the millionth time tonight.

BRIAN?

Brian's mom.

I don't remember ever saving her number. I must've copied it from Ma's contacts when I first got my own phone. Maybe she drove Brian here and is confused about which entrance to come through. I immediately answer, plugging one of my ears with my finger and pressing my phone into my other ear as I beeline toward the *Co Co Co* station, where the crowd is thinner.

"Hello, Mrs. Wu?"

"Aisha? Is that you?" It's a voice I haven't heard in years. It's so familiar that it should be comforting, except tonight, her voice sounds panicked.

"Yeah—I mean, yes. Is everything okay?"

"Aisha . . ." Her voice cracks. "I'm so sorry. Brian won't be coming tonight."

5
LEFT IN THE LURCH

✔ Get stood up for winter formal

Marcy says that because her parents got divorced when she was seven years old, she senses bad news from a mile away, but even *she* didn't predict that Brian would end up being sick tonight.

It's okay, I tell myself, *it's not Brian's fault for getting the flu, and his mom wouldn't lie to me.*

Or.

Or was Brian asking me to the formal like the plot from *She's All That,* where popular Zack Siler asks awkward Laney Boggs out because of a bet? Or did Brian realize he missed his Build-A-Bear ex too much? Or did he decide he can't be seen with me?

It is *flu season. And exam season, which means no one is showering nearly as much as they should, which means germs multiplying at alarming rates . . .*

Tears are pricking at my eyes, but I can't cry in front of this hot cocoa station. My Conditions for a Good Cry include total solitude. I know I should find Marcy and Kevin to tell them what happened, but the thought of pitying pairs of eyes looking back at me makes me sick.

I put on my coat and dissolve into the crowd of students dancing and singing along to the music. I linger there for a few extra beats, the loudness enveloping me like an emergency blanket. As soon as I get through the crowd, I scurry toward the back doors. The red glow of the exit sign has never seemed more inviting, and without looking back, I slip out into the cold night.

Outside, I shiver from the frosty air, checking my phone again and hating myself for it. Still not a peep from Brian. A part of me wants to text Pa, asking him to whisk me away to Costco to eat free samples together, but instead, I send him a red lady dancing emoji and then stuff my phone as far down into my bag as I can.

Take note of two things you can see, and one thing you can hear.

I learned that relaxation trick from a poster at my dentist's office. I watch a nearby streetlamp blinking in Christmas lights, illuminating the parking lot I'm standing in, and then I listen to the muffled music blaring from the door, the bass mixing with the hum from the streetlamp.

This trick isn't working.

Suddenly, the door swings open with a screech, and I jump. I think Marcy has somehow found me, but then I see an elderly Black woman emerging. I recognize her cherry lip and silvery hair.

Kevin's grandma.

"Oh! Hello there." She smiles at me, hauling an instrument case behind her. It must be her clarinet. "That's a beautiful dress." She smooths the skirt of her own white dress, and from its shine I bet she separates her darks and lights in the laundry. "The lace is especially beautiful. It reminds me of my wedding back in—well, I won't tell you what year. Even saying it ages me."

"Thank you," I croak, trying to stop my teeth from chattering.

Maybe my dress *is* her old wedding dress. After all, I thrifted it from Moody Vintage.

"My grandson told me there's a special dance happening for y'all tonight?" Her gaze is bright, as if she's remembering her own days of sparkly gowns and cold evenings. "It's nice to see the conservatory so full of young people."

"Winter formal." I should tell her I know Kevin, but I don't. Instead, I point to the black case resting on the pavement behind her. "Is that your instrument?"

"I play clarinet for a jazz band. We perform all over town, mostly at the Blue Llama. We were rehearsing our new holiday set tonight, which means *lots* of Ella Fitzgerald." Propping one hand on her case, she twiddles the fingers of her other hand as if missing a cigarette. "Your coat isn't hefty enough for the snow, hon. You should go back in and join the party."

"I'm actually going home," I lie. "My friend's coming to get me soon."

My friend the Grim Reaper if I stay out here too long and get frostbite.

"I'm waiting for a ride, too. My grandson usually drives me home, but since he's busy with the dance tonight, a good friend of mine offered up his own grandson's services." She taps her wrist. "Seventeen minutes late and counting. I'd give the boy a call, but I don't have his number. My friend's one of those old geezers who believes cell phones are the government's strategy to control us—Big Brother and surveillance capitalism and whatnot. He's so serious about privacy that he refused to give me a phone number, no matter how much I asked. He claimed his *gem* of a grandson is always on time." She sighs. "I hate to be one of those 'back in my day' folks, but back when my husband was alive, he picked me up on the dot. Not a minute later. Common courtesy was more common then, I'm afraid."

"I—I actually know what you mean." I pull my coat around me, shivering. I'm usually not one to bare my soul to a fellow student's grandma, but I can't pass up the opportunity to revel in our tragic likeness. "My date for winter formal actually stood me up tonight." The words tumble from my mouth like bags catapulting into a garbage truck. I let the sentence hang in the air for a moment, but there's no reaction, so I reflexively tack on a short chortle, like, *ho, ho, 'tis all but good fun!*

"Oh, *Lord*. So we both got left in the lurch by teenage boys tonight?"

I'm deathly afraid she's going to offer me a lint-covered lemon lozenge from her purse or something. The good cry would commence for sure, notwithstanding the Conditions.

She only shakes her head. "Look at you glowing in that dress. He missed out."

I'm pretty sure Brian Wu is in bed playing Tetris on his phone and cursing those S blocks right now. For someone who's always in the spotlight, missing one dance because of the flu must be nothing of note, but for me, wearing a dress and feeling like I look half-decent is a rarity.

"I give up. I'm calling a cab." She hoists her instrument case from the cement. I catch a name etched along the side in golden ink: *Sophie*. "Don't stay out here too long, dear, or you'll turn into an ice pop." Sophie hesitates mid-step on her way back inside the conservatory, her piercing eyes meeting mine. "May

I offer a small piece of advice before I go, though? As a woman who took life too seriously for most of her years?"

"Oh." I clear my throat. "I mean, yes. Of course."

"I know when you're young, getting stood up can feel like the end of the world, but trust me. Boys come and go like buses. The only thing that remains when you cut through the noise is yourself. And if you can take the time to truly know yourself, to go on adventures and push a little past what you think you're capable of each time, hiccups like these won't seem as big anymore in comparison. There's even a saying—*fortune favors the brave.*" She smiles. "Promise you'll remember that for me?"

"I promise."

She winks and turns again, her small figure slipping through the door. As soon as she's gone, the halo from the streetlamp warps, my eyes blurring with tears. I don't know *how* to be brave right now. Walking home is not an option with these torture devices strapped to my feet. Calling my parents or Seema means they're going to ask questions about what happened, questions that I don't want to answer. Asking Marcy and Kevin for a ride home means ruining my best friend's winter formal. It's funny how you can know a lot of people, but it still doesn't feel like enough people.

That's when I see a car with blindingly bright headlights snaking through the parking lot so slowly that I could probably outwalk it. Someone's arriving an hour into the dance. I expect the car to park, but it pulls up to the curb in front of me, its hazard lights flashing. For a moment, I think it's Brian making a heroic appearance for me, but I know Brian's shiny Jeep Wrangler from seeing him drive to school. This is an old

Volkswagen Jetta, practically a fossil. My chest tightens with is-this-a-kidnapper-with-a-handlebar-mustache fear as the window rolls down, but I relax when I see the friendly face of a clean-shaven boy.

He looks around my age, but I'm terrible at guessing ages, so I can't be sure. I note deep-set eyes shaded by thick eyebrows, a square jaw, and a mop of dark brown hair that's trying to stay combed over but is clearly going through a rebellious phase. The orange hue from the streetlamp makes his hair glow like an angel's curls in a Renaissance painting. And the thing that stands out most about him is that he's positively *beaming* at me. His smile rivals the brightness of Michigan's entire power grid. Seriously, no one has looked this happy to see me since my nani visited from India five years ago.

He waves. "So sorry I'm late. Hop in!"

I squint and take a tentative step closer. I don't see any bones, rope, or bleach in his car, so that's a good sign. Maybe he's lost.

"I'm Quentin Santos." His breath makes clouds in the air. "Shelly's grandson?"

I squint some more.

"I swear I'm never late." He looks sheepish as he retreats in his seat, half his face in shadow. "I was waiting at the front entrance. In case you wanted to know, there's *two* entrances for this old conservatory. Speaking of old, though . . ." He leans out the window again, and I notice his eyes turn a golden brown when they catch the light. "You're a lot younger than I thought you'd be, for being in a jazz band." He seems pleased with himself, ready to accept his Observation of the Year award as he fiddles with his car's radio tuner. The moving magnets in my mind snap together.

My grandson usually drives me home, but since he's busy with the dance tonight, a good friend of mine offered up his own grandson's services. . . .

He's mistaking me for Kevin's clarinet-playing grandma. He probably wasn't told what she looks like.

Well, I guess this isn't the *most* humiliating thing that has happened tonight.

"Not doubting your talent, of course," Quentin adds, his wide smile shrinking as he watches my blank expression. He removes his hand from the radio tuner and glances at the wooden watch on his wrist. "Sorry, you *are* Sophie, right? I could swear my grandpa said nine p.m., conservatory entrance, white dress. He refused to send me a picture. He doesn't support the cell phone industrial complex or whatever he calls it. All he told me is there'd be a woman who needs a ride home from—what was it—trumpet rehearsal . . ."

Clarinet.

The square of cement I'm standing on is a crater, and the warmth of Quentin's face is an outstretched hand. He has a pizza plushie resting on his dashboard, and he's giving me a real I'd-water-my-neighbor's-plants-while-they're-on-vacation vibe. And the bite of this frigid air combined with the seven minutes of sleep I got last night has vaporized any complex thoughts about stranger danger that could've been. All I see in front of me is an enclosed, warm box. Its steaming exhaust pipe means it's a *breathing* box—a box that's in motion, a box with the promise of going somewhere. Anywhere but here.

If Arledge Prep's student council president's grandmother

was going to get into this car, it's good enough for me. Quentin's hair *is* glowing in the light like an angel's—maybe he's supposed to be my savior.

Maybe fortune favors the brave.

6
CONFESSION

✔ Get into a stranger's car

I'm in a complete stranger's car, it's *moving*, and I'm not in prison yet. In my world, you can't do things like this. You can't sneak into a concert or steal gummy worms from the plastic containers at the grocery store. The universe implodes when you break the rules.

Yet I'm coasting in this guy's Volkswagen Jetta, and the universe is very much intact. The radiating heat is defrosting my face, the streetlights are whipping past the window, the wheels are bumping on the road. Instead of feeling guilty that I'm currently taking advantage of this stranger and stowing away in his car, I'm drunk on adventure. I'm not a puppet on strings doing homework, I'm *brave*! I am—

"Uh, Sophie?"

I flinch. I am definitely *not* Sophie.

"Sorry—didn't mean to startle you."

"It's fine," I squeak. It's wise to say as little as possible in this incriminating situation.

"Can you navigate to your house for me? You can pull up the map and pop your phone into the cradle."

Cradle? I look around, half expecting to see the doe eyes of a baby peering at me. "Um, your cradle?"

"My phone stand." He gestures to a clasp mounted near the steering wheel.

"*Oh.*"

"Sorry, my grandpa's way of saying stuff rubs off on me sometimes." He continues whistling to some Beach Boys song on the radio, and he's confidently shifting gears as he drives, which makes me realize he has a manual car. I don't know anyone with a manual transmission. Then again, I also don't know anyone with a car this clean. No crumbs, receipts, wrappers, or plastic bags—just an empty burlap grocery bag in the back seat. I'm glad Pa isn't here to see this. I've been using the *all teens are messy* card for years.

As I fish my phone from my bag and type my address, my hands tremble.

"So, which neighborhood do you live in, Sophie?" His voice is cheery, and he's leaned back in his seat, shoulders relaxed like he's lounging on a pool chair.

"Coral Tree." I peek at him, but there's no reaction.

Coral Tree is one of the shabbier neighborhoods of Arledge, but I like it. Our neighbors bring us candied ginger cake for Christmas every year, and now that Seema is in college, I have more space. I bet Brian's and Marcy's neighborhoods have canceled refined sugar and hand out organic kale chips on Halloween.

Thinking about my neighborhood makes me think of Ma and Pa. They were right to be skeptical of school dances. I should've spent tonight focusing on Stanford. I should be forgetting about silly childhood crushes and winter formals.

I should. Theoretically.

The rush of being in a stranger's car has waned. There's no avoiding the fact that I'm here because there was no one else I could turn to tonight. I'm alone, and winter formal is another addendum to the scroll of Things I've Never Done.

"You're welcome to change the music if you want; they're doing an hour of Beach Boys. I'm an old tunes kind of guy. And I know I'm a slow driver, but this car's so ancient that if I drive faster, pieces will fall off." He throws me a glance. "So, how do you know my grandpa?"

Oh, golly. I close one hand over the other to keep my fingers from quivering. "I don't exactly—"

My phone vibrates, and my eyes flick to the cradle—er, phone stand. Marcy. The message preview reads **WHERE ARE YOU?** I glance at Quentin before shrinking back into my seat, hoping he didn't have time to read the message before it disappeared.

"Sorry." He snaps his head forward. "Didn't mean to look."

"It's okay." I watch the park whip by, then the stationery shop and the plaza of restaurants. I may be in a stranger's car, but the streets of Arledge haven't changed. How many days have I had that are so similar that they're forgotten?

I thought tonight would be different. I was going to poke a rose boutonniere through Brian's suit jacket and collect photo strips from the photo booth. I was going to be *seen*, and not just by anyone, but by Brian. It was going to be like a movie. That's why I spent so much time on my hair and wore lipstick even though I hate the chalkiness of it. I was film ready.

You're pathetic, Aisha.

Fat teardrops inch down my cheeks, breaking all my Conditions for a Good Cry. I angle my face toward the window, until I'm basically peering over my shoulder, praying Quentin won't notice.

Of course, he *instantly* notices.

"Holy sh— Crap, are you crying?"

I never understood why people think it's a good idea to ask crying people if they're crying.

Without warning, Quentin pulls over, one block south of my house. The headlights dim as we slow in front of a sky-blue mailbox with clouds painted on it. He pops my phone from the stand, exits navigation, hands it back to me, and twists the radio tuner knob. The Beach Boys track is sucked from the air.

"Sophie, what's going on? Did something happen at rehearsal?"

I look at Quentin—*really* look at him for the first time since I got into his car. He's no longer wearing that big smile. Instead, he looks concerned, his forehead creased and his gaze soft and searching. He'd clearly be one of those grocery store cashiers who hands you your gum instead of letting it drown in the bag. He doesn't deserve this.

I wipe my snot on the sleeve of my coat, clutching my phone in my hands. I might as well make this night worse. Besides, I'm only a block away from home. I can walk it.

"I-I'm." I heave a breath, trying to stop the shoulder-shaking sobs threatening to rattle me. I can't look at him as I say it, so I focus on the glow of the Jetta headlights instead. "I'm not Sophie."

His eyes widen. "Wait, you're not . . ."

"N-No." The sobs are coming now. "I d-don't p-play the c-clarinet. I l-lied to you. I'm s-so s-sorry."

"I see . . ." He's looking around, as if he's hoping a handbook on how to talk to crying criminals is somewhere in the car. "Should I— I mean, would you like to talk about it?"

I take a few deep breaths to stop shaking, wiping my tears with my hands. "No."

He nods with enthusiasm, like my *no* was an opinion he really agrees with, but the creases on his forehead deepen. "No worries. I mean, uh, no rush. Take your time."

After a few beats of silence, I peer up at him with bloodshot, tear-filled eyes. "Take my time?"

He nods again, but with more reluctance.

"*What* time?"

"Oh." He cringes, like he's a bomb defuser who might've just cut the wrong wire. "I'm not sure I—"

"There's no *time*. We don't get recess anymore. You know what we get? *Recession*. After extracurriculars and homework, you're lucky if you have enough energy left to scroll through your phone. No one's hanging with their friends after school being all, 'Thanks for the fresh-baked cookies, Mom! You're the bestest!' No one's mom even has *time* to bake. Or dad. Dads can bake cookies, too. And something like *Ferris Bueller's Day Off* could have never happened to me, and not because my dad doesn't have a Lamborghini to crash. Or a Ferrari or whatever. It's because Ferris stays home from school for a whole day pretending to be sick. I go to school ESPECIALLY when I'm sick!"

He raises an eyebrow. "What?"

"I know it's a public health hazard, and I feel bad about that, I really do, but if I missed a day of school, I'd spend all week catching up. We're all grinding out here. Even some students at the dance, if you know what I mean, which, *why*? Who wants to see that? And guess what else?"

He clears his throat. "I—"

"Actually, don't guess, I'll just tell you. What's worse is, if I tried to tell Ma that I'm exhausted from school, or even that I got into a total stranger's car tonight because I was so sad and it was SO cold outside, she wouldn't be like, 'You got into a stranger's car?! What were you *THINKING*?' Nope. She'd be like, 'You wouldn't have been cold if you wore the thicker coat I told you to wear!'"

He waits, and after I don't add anything more, he says, "Uh, you've raised some very interesting points. If I may ask one question . . ."

I sniffle. "Please."

"Can you back up and start from the beginning?"

Quentin's tapping his fingers on the steering wheel. I just unloaded the play-by-play of the full night's story onto him.

"So . . . let me get this straight. This jerk—what's his name again?"

"Brian." I'm oddly mollified that this random stranger called Brian a jerk. It's a pledge of allegiance.

"Brian didn't text you before the dance?"

I shake my head.

"So he had his mom tell you he wasn't coming?"

I shrug.

"Not to sound insensitive, but . . ." His steady gaze makes me uncomfortable, knowing that my mascara has probably run black rivers across my face after crying. "Maybe it's better he didn't show. I mean, I get he's sick and all, but our phones are basically glued to our faces. A message is the minimum." He brushes the sleeves of his beige coat the way I'd imagine a medieval prince would dust his trousers. "I believe the lady is in much better company now, if I do say so myself."

I hug my arms to my chest. "I dunno, maybe he was passed out from a high fever or something."

I know I probably shouldn't be defending Brian, but I can't help it. Even with all the tragic history between us (tonight included), he's part of the reason I got the scholarship to Arledge Prep. His mom always talked about wanting to send him there and how selective admission is, and even though Ma was suspicious of the lengthy application process—parent interviews, transcripts, student essays—she eventually was convinced that it'd be a good place for me to apply, too. It's hard to forget all these strings connecting Brian and me, tying us together in knots.

"You both are friends, I take it?" Quentin asks.

"Er, well, we're not really friends anymore. We talk occasionally, but only to compare grades or the answers to tough assignments. We used to be close in middle school, though."

"Ah." He rubs his chin. "So there's *history*."

"Where do you go to school?" I ask. I think I would've noticed Quentin if he went to Arledge, despite me making like an ostrich and burying my head in textbooks.

"Kresge High. I'm a senior, too."

Kresge is the town adjacent to Arledge. I haven't been there much despite growing up so close to it, but it's similar to Arledge, except with fewer retirees and a better cider mill.

"Wow, what are the odds?" I murmur. "Of all the cars I could've gotten into, you happen to be in high school *and* a senior."

"I'd say the odds are actually pretty good. Lots of parents move here to send their kids to the reputable public schools, right? Or the crazy expensive Ivy League feeder prep schools where kids probably wear those ridiculous Canada Goose jackets and drive their parents'—" He notices color draining from my face and stops. "Um, where do you go to school again?"

"Arledge Prep."

He winces. "Sorry. And Jesus. If I had known earlier, I would've kept the meter running here or something."

I start to smile. "It's not like that. I'm on scholarship."

After he sees me blow air into my hands, he immediately reaches over to turn up the heat. Fifteen minutes ago, he didn't even know I existed, and now he's concerned about his hijacker finding the temperature of his vehicle comfortable. Okay, *hijacker* sounds bad—how about *stowaway*?

"Golly, I need my Canada Goose jacket," I deadpan.

"C'mon, you have to admit those jackets are stupid expensive. I bet if I stuffed my coat with one thousand dollars in cash, it'd be warmer."

"What'd you say earlier? The way your grandpa talks rubs off on you?"

He laughs, and involuntarily, my lips curl up, too. He has one of those full laughs that compel you to laugh along no matter what the joke was in the first place.

"I forgot to ask, what's your name?"

"It's Aisha."

"Come on. In that dress, I expect a full name and a British accent at least."

I put a hand to my chest, bowing my head, and give my best attempt. "Lady Aisha Agarwal, er, of the Arledge Colony."

He bows his head in return. "Pleasure to meet you, Lady Aisha."

"And you are Sir Quentin of the Kresge Village."

His face brightens. "Hey, you remember my name after one mention. Although I figure most students of the . . . er, Arledge Preparatory probably have a good memory."

I notice the time: 9:47 p.m. Twenty minutes have already passed. Poor Sir Quentin has done enough—certainly enough to be knighted. I'm about to tell him that I can get out here and let him go home when he snaps his fingers.

"So how about some dessert? You're all dressed up, you shouldn't just go home."

"Oh . . ." I look down. He's probably offering out of pity. "Thanks, but that's okay. I feel bad for taking up so much of your time already. And for, um, lying. Sorry about that. I hope you won't be in too much trouble with your grandpa."

"I'm in trouble with him by default, so don't sweat it." He leans his head against the driver's seat window, and I notice his ears slightly protruding outward like they're saying hello, poking through his curls, which have a mind of their own. "Besides, who says dessert is for you? *I* want something sweet to help me recover from you scaring the pudding out of me."

"Um . . ." I'm protected in this car, like everything I said tonight is sealed in. If we go somewhere else, it'll be like a pressurized can exploding.

"How about some ice cream?"

Maybe it's because I figure I'll never see him after this, but talking to Quentin tonight doesn't make me feel like hiding in a closet or bringing up the weather, like most conversations do. And drowning my worries in hot caramel fudge sauce *does* sound good.

Then again, I'd be in a public place with a boy. What if Ma and Pa happen to be there by some strange turn of events? Or worse, what if we have nothing more to say to each other as soon as we get out of the car, and then we're stuck talking about the weather after all?

Unbidden, the Stanford essay question pops into my mind in the booming voice of a sportscaster.

Share a time you left your comfort zone.

It's one night, one stranger. I can forget it all happened tomorrow.

"I do know a place," I say. "My treat."

7
THE NEW DEAL

✔ Cut a deal
with a stranger

I snuggle into the booth at Wooly's, hoping it'll hide how overdressed I am. Soft jazz music plays through the speakers, crackling occasionally. As Quentin slides in across from me, I notice there's a tiny pear-shaped birthmark on his neck the size of a pumpkin seed, barely visible over the collar of his coat.

"So, you've been here before?" he asks.

As a kid, I made my family come here for every birthday. To this day, I'm convinced Wooly's has the tastiest sundaes and sweet potato fries the universe has to offer, alternate dimensions included. As Quentin peels off his coat, I notice that his plaid red-and-green hoodie matches the Christmas tinsel hanging around the diner walls. It almost makes me want to snap a picture.

"I live at Wooly's. They have the best ice cream, and, bonus—word searches and coloring pages for kids." I hold up the transparent cup of crayons on the table and the blank activity pages underneath. Seema and I used to compete in a self-organized Coloring Activity Olympics back in the day.

Quentin takes a blank snowflake page from the top of the pile. The sleeves of his oversized hoodie go past his wrists, which makes it look extra cozy. "Crayons were a revolutionary invention for the food service industry. Kids are busy, parents are happy, and the other diners are undisturbed."

"Grandpa, is that you?" I push my invisible glasses up the bridge of my nose. Quentin chooses a crayon and starts coloring. From ninety to four years old in under a minute. Impressive.

As the waiter nears our table, I wipe under my eyes with my fingers. I forgot to use the car mirror to check how much my makeup spread over my face.

Wooly's staff is mostly composed of old ladies ready to fire extra butter squares from their apron pockets at any moment, but there's one cute boy who works here. His eyes remind me of freshly cut grass catching the sunlight. He sets a pair of menus on our table, and as I hand one to Quentin, I remember Marcy must be worried sick.

I reach into my bag for my phone, emptying its contents onto the table. Rose boutonniere from the florist. Compact mirror. Wallet. Instant camera. Sticky-note pad.

Quentin eyes me from over his laminated menu. "Mary Poppins, is that you?"

"I have a lot in here, I know. But I like to be prepared. It's all stuff that was originally necessary for the dance."

"Right, like *sticky notes*?"

"My friend Marcy gave these to me to carry everywhere. She says you never know when you might need to write down a good listicle." I look at my phone and see walls of messages from Marcy, progressing from an all lowercase **where'd u go?** to all-caps shouting. I type back **I'm really sorry, I'm okay, will explain later!!**

I look up to see Quentin scrutinizing the to-dos scribbled

in pen on my sticky-note pad: *Essay draft!!!!, AP Lit journal entry, AP Chem chromatography report* . . . "Wait, does that say *save turtle*? You have a turtle?"

I laugh. "I wish. I meant save my crochet turtle for crochet club. I'm going to try to undo the stitching and rescue the little guy."

"Crochet club? And *I'm* the grandpa?"

I shrug. "Yes, I crochet animals in my free time, and no, I don't keep count of all the people fainting from how deeply cool I am." He grins. "I would've joined art club, but all the leadership positions were filled, and I needed a club leadership position for my college apps. I thought I'd have the president position in the bag, despite my uninspiring speech . . ." I sigh. "Lily Perez ran against me. She won, and I got stuck being in the club. But it grew on me. And the meetings don't clash with my after-school volunteer gig. I try to help at the Sunrise Retirement Home on Mondays."

"Speaking of Mondays, are you gonna be nervous about seeing Brian at school?" Quentin asks, choosing a turquoise crayon from the cup.

"He still might be out sick, and honestly, I wasn't crying because of him. He was just . . . the last straw."

He leans in, like we're sharing a secret. "What were the prior straws?"

My life's yearbook flips through my head. School, bedroom, homework. It's the grayscale "before" portion of an infomercial.

"Haven't I scared you enough tonight?"

"Nope." Quentin begins scribbling on his snowflake, alternating between turquoise and shamrock green. He keeps stopping every so often to lean way back and get a big-picture view of his progress, which reminds me of Pa, who is terribly farsighted and does that when he needs to read a menu without his glasses. "This is the most amusing thing that's happened in my life in a while. And talking to someone will make you feel better. We go to different schools, so you'll have automatic confidentiality."

That's true, but a part of me feels ashamed for complaining to Quentin, like a sinner in a confessional box. Quentin is no priest, but his default expression is a slight smile, his voice is measured and slow, and I notice he puts down his glass of water gently after every sip instead of with a *clack* like me. I can't imagine him yelling at anyone or cutting someone off in traffic. He seems like a Zen proton. Like someone who saves you half a muffin. Like someone who keeps a gratitude journal. I look at my blank coloring page. I am most definitely a disturbed valence electron that'd eat the whole muffin and use a gratitude journal as a coaster.

"I feel like I haven't *done* anything with my life. I didn't even go to winter formal tonight. I bet if you guess it, I haven't done it before."

He gets this sly look as he asks, "Is that a challenge?"

I shrink in my seat. "I mean, the 'guess' thing was *rhetorical* . . ."

He plucks my sticky-note pad from the table and peels the top note away. I watch as he writes, covering the pad with his hand like I might cheat off his multiple choice test or something. He writes *slowly*. After a few beats, he holds the pad up. His letters are neat and evenly spaced. "Have you done this?"

Sneak out of your house at night.

I shake my head.

"All right, point for Team Aisha." He peels the note away and starts writing another. I notice he's left-handed. I keep craning my neck to see, but his little hand dungeon is impenetrable.

Not turned in your homework.

I shake my head again. "Well, once I forgot my social studies poster at home, so I called my—"

"Respectfully, we're not counting that. Another point for Team Aisha."

"I don't exactly feel like I'm *winning* here," I grumble, holding out my hand. "Give me that."

Once I start writing with his now-stubby crayon, the words spew from my hand like I've been waiting years to document the festering list of Things I've Never Done.

Go to a typical high school party.

Go on a date.

I'm about to write *kiss someone* as a continuation of the theme, but my lack of sexual experience can be inferred through context clues, and there's no implicit way to write it on a sticky note. *Call me olive oil, because I'm extra virgin*? Actually, that's not too bad.

Dance with someone.

"Okay, okay, point taken," he says, and I stop writing. "So what was stopping you from doing all this?"

"It takes guts and time, both of which I don't have. I was too busy trying to get the grades. To get into my top choice for college."

"Let me guess, Harvard?"

"Stanford."

"Ah, much better. That's a one percent acceptance rate, is it?"

I fold my arms. "It's 3.95 for undergraduate students, thank you very much."

Two tiny worry lines appear between his eyes. "That's still a ton of pressure to put on yourself."

"Yep, and being Indian, I have to compete with throngs of other Indian kids in my AP wheelhouse." I figure Quentin will mention his ethnicity eventually, too, without my having to ask. "But I have to try because . . ."

I don't want him to think I'm shallow, but Stanford feels like my ticket to a higher echelon of society. Goodbye, leaky apartment roof; hello, apartment in the city. Extra hello for being able to add jack cheese and guac to my burrito.

And more than that . . . Ma.

"My mom went there for a PhD program and she finished around two years, but she dropped out before starting her dissertation because she got pregnant with my sister. Not that it was an accident," I add on quickly. "My parents wanted a kid, but once my sister was born, it was harder to afford childcare than they thought, since PhD stipends aren't a lot. So my mom dropped out. She doesn't say it, but I think she regrets not finishing. I know it'd mean a lot to her if I went." I point to his snowflake. "Plus, California wouldn't have any of *that*. And accomplished professors teach there. Tech pioneers."

"*Tech pioneers?*" He looks like he's trying not to laugh. "Did you get that off their website?"

"Maybe." I smooth the skirt of my dress. "Probably. I've been on their website *a lot* looking for inspiration for my application essay. The prompt is *share a time you left your comfort zone*, and as we've established, I have zero such times."

"Can't you make something up? You seem . . ." He points to the pile of stuff from my bag lying on the table. "Resourceful."

"I don't want to write a cheesy essay about camping for the first time and becoming one with the land or whatever. I want to give my best."

His eyes stay on the blinking Christmas tree in the back corner of the diner. Something inscrutable passes over his face. I can't quite place it. Ridicule? Boredom?

I place my bag over our scrawled sticky notes, out of the waiter's sight. "But enough about me. What colleges are you eyeing? Or are you taking a gap year?"

"I applied early decision to Northeastern." He continues coloring his snowflake like it's no big deal, but I know better. Northeastern is a fairly selective private university in Boston.

"*And?*"

"I got in. I heard back a few days ago."

"Hey, congratulations!" My slap on the table shakes his hand, creating a few jagged lines on his snowflake. "You can relax for the rest of senior year."

He's pressing down with his cadet-blue crayon so hard that I'm sure we're going to have to hold a funeral for the brave cadet pretty soon. Right as I'm about to ask him more, his phone vibrates on the table. I don't mean to look, but it's instinct.

Grandpa.

My eyes go wide. "*Omigod*, he's probably calling about Sophie. She probably told him that no one showed to pick her up. . . ." Quentin's squaring his shoulders like he's gearing up to fight a zombie army. "I'm so sorry. If you want, I can explain to—"

"It's not your fault." He slides out of the booth. "He lives a couple hours up north, so he can't do much damage from there. But I'll take this. I bet it's important if my grandpa decided to use his phone, even if it is his *cutting-edge* landline."

"Your coat . . . ," I start, but he's already shuffling away, his phone grasped so tightly in his hand that his knuckles are white. I'm gathering that Quentin's grandpa is bad news for Quentin's positive-as-a-proton nature. *Ol' gramps is Quentin's radioactive decay*, I think as I watch him from the window. He's pacing, and he kicks at the frosted ground every so often. Based on how he's hanging his head, the call isn't going well. Finally, the bells above the door jingle to announce his return. I snap my head back down to my blank coloring page.

As he sweeps into the booth with a strained smile, the cute waiter comes to our table. I ready the enthusiastic voice that I used at the seasonal Arledge club fair this fall to recruit new crochet members. (It didn't work, for your information.)

"I'll have the s'mores sundae with caramel. Gluten-free, please."

The waiter nods and turns to Quentin, but he's lost in space.

"Uh, make that two," I add. "Except gluten's fine for him."

I poke Quentin's hand as soon as the waiter is out of earshot, and then I recoil. His skin is cold as ice. "Hey, are you—"

"Can I tell you something?" He's looking down at his snowflake. He feels so unlike the person who was sitting here minutes ago. It's like his gloomy doppelgänger kidnapped the real him, and then crept back inside to replace him. I've seen enough Indian dramas with that trope, so I make sure that this Quentin still has the tiny pear-shaped birthmark on his neck. He does.

"Of course." I scoot forward. "Anything."

I don't know why I said *anything*. What if he sells weed out of his garage or something? Although it's probably much more underwhelming. Like "I'm sensitive to gluten, too."

"I'm failing math."

"Huh?"

"I'm failing math at Kresge High." He looks at me. "If I don't pass, my admission to Northeastern next fall could be revoked."

So I was wrong. *This* is Quentin's radioactive decay.

"I've always barely scraped by in math. I've gone through tutors, books, everything. And it's not that I don't try. I got AP History and Government down, and I really enjoy them, but I can't do math. It killed my grade point average, which my grandpa so kindly reminded me of just now, along with the fact that my admission could hang in the balance. And before you ask why I didn't stick to lower-level math, it's because if I didn't graduate with precalculus at the least, I knew I wouldn't get into the colleges I want to go to. You know they look at the classes you take. And my mom pushed me to take more advanced classes, too . . ." He looks away, mumbling, "I doubt this is relatable to you. With the school you go to, you're probably good at everything."

"Are you *kidding*? I'm terrible at history. I can't swim. Can't cook. And math is one of those subjects that builds on itself, so you probably fell behind somewhere, but you can still catch up. Besides, the likelihood that a college revokes admission after acceptance is very low. Your grandpa probably told you that to scare you."

"It's not only about college admissions. I wanted to be able to pass with a better grade for *me*. Like you said, to know I gave my best. But it's too late." He reaches over and crumples the snowflake he spent so long coloring.

I gasp, snatching the crushed wad of paper from his hands, but I can understand how he feels.

It's like when I first learned how to read. Seema would sit with me and enunciate the words, and I envied how they came to her, while I only saw marks on a page. It was the worst feeling. I had to bribe her with my turtle erasers to get her to keep teaching me, even though I'd planned on trading them with a kid at school for Hello Kitty sticky notes . . .

Sticky notes.

Trade.

Eureka.

"Quentin." I jump like a cartoon cat struck by lightning. "You said you'd trade anything to understand math, right?"

"Um, yeah, I think that's kind of what we were just discussing—"

"I need a tandem jumper."

He tilts his head. "A what?"

"A tandem jumper is the instructor who jumps with you when you go skydiving." I shove my bag aside, revealing the stack of sticky notes we wrote. "I need someone who'll push me to get out of my comfort zone because I'm too much of a chicken to do it myself. If I try some of these things that scare me, I'll have material for my Stanford essay." I look at him, my eyes alight.

"You help me do that, and I'll help you pass math."

If I have adventures, as Sophie suggested, I'll become more confident. Then I'll be impossible to ignore. Stanford will notice me. I'll be the bee's knees, the best thing since sliced everything bagels. And what better person to help me than Quentin? I can experiment and mess up around him all I want, without worrying about leaving a good or even average impression. Considering he's already seen both my ability to ruthlessly steal someone's identity and my snot bubbles in one night, that ship has sailed. And he doesn't go to my school, so I don't have to worry about anyone finding out about our arrangement. It's, dare I say, perfect.

Except that Quentin doesn't appear to share my enthusiasm.

"I already told you," he says. "I've tried tutors before. Nothing worked."

"If there's *one* thing I know how to teach, it's math."

"I'm sorry. I'm gonna have to pass."

"That's the idea."

Quentin's looking at me like I'm a flat-earther, but I don't want to give up yet. I *want* this. I've tutored plenty of kids in math before, and Quentin can't be harder to teach than that fifth grader who kept licking my scented highlighters. I could ask Marcy to help me complete my list of Things I've Never Done, but there's comfort in asking someone who doesn't know the extent of the *Nerd Here, This Side Up* box I've been living in. Someone who doesn't have a box for me at all.

"Every good film starts with a deal. And you said you like history, right?" I unfold his ball of a snowflake, smoothing the creases. "This is like Franklin Roosevelt's New Deal. You know, with the three *R*s? Recovery, renewal, and . . . uh, resilience.

Except it's for our *lives*." I draw rainbows in the air with my hands, imagining glitter raining from my fingers. I hope that's how it's coming across.

"It's recovery, relief, and reform. And you're comparing tutoring me to a deal that reformed the government and saved the country from the Great Depression?"

I drop my hands. "Yes, I am, and I didn't have time to take AP History last year, okay? That's the *one* AP that eluded me. I needed time for my independent research project."

"Naturally. *Designing AR glasses for fish so they can avoid plastic in the ocean themselves* isn't going to write itself."

"Har har. If you must know, my project was on fractals found in nature. They're the basis for recursion that we use in algorithms today. There's even a wrapping paper company that uses fractals to create their geometric prints, so I used their—" I swallow the rest of my sentence, my cheeks reddening. "It's probably not that interesting."

I usually babble only around my family, since I view listening to my babbles as part of their job description. Around everyone else, I measure my words out carefully like vanilla extract, by the quarter teaspoon. I don't accidentally dump out a whole cup of them. There's something disarming about Quentin that makes me stop measuring.

He stares at me for a minute, so I'm sure he's about to make some joke about how he didn't follow any of that, but instead he asks, "What are fractals?" The way he's looking at me makes me think he truly wants to know.

"Fractals are geometric shapes that can be split into parts, each of which is a smaller copy of the whole. Like broccoli, for example. Every broccoli branch is identical to its parent stem.

And that six-pointed snowflake you crumpled . . ." I hold up the wrinkled paper in my hand. "Each subsection is identical to the whole."

He's nodding. "I think I know what you're talking about. Like that infinite pattern on seashells, too, right?"

"Exactly! See, you're a natural. Fractals are pure math, y'know. If I tutored you, these are the kinds of things we'd discuss. I could show you that math can be fun."

He's not reacting. I'm starting to think all hope is lost, but after a few beats . . .

"You really think you could help me?"

"I do." I'm almost holding my breath. "Are you in?"

He grins.

"Omigod, yes, yes, *yes*! You will not regret trying this, Quentin. I promise, we're going to—"

I stop as I see the waiter approaching with our sundaes on a tray. With my gaudy earrings, overcoat, and shifty eyes, it probably sounds like I'm roping Quentin into a pyramid scheme.

"Here you are, y'all. Two s'mores sundaes." The waiter smiles as he sets a tulip-shaped dish in front of me. "Gluten-free for the lady."

"Thank you," I murmur, watching dreamily as he walks away.

"Well, well," Quentin realizes, his eyes moving from my flushed cheeks to my stiffened shoulders. "Maybe asking for the waiter's number should be on one of these sticky notes."

"I basically stowed away in your car. That was my first and last comfort zone breach of the night."

And I'd never ask the waiter out with this chimple on my face.

He takes a spoonful of his sundae. "Fudge nuggets. This is *good*."

"Right?" I've been trying to convince Marcy for ages that Wooly's has the best sundaes. "Also, *fudge nuggets*? What are you, seven?"

"I babysit an eleven-year-old, and his dad says I'm not allowed to swear in front of him. So, I have workarounds. Fudge nuggets. Shiitake mushrooms. Frackin' crackers."

"Frackin' fractals," I say, and he lets out a chortle that makes an older lady from the next table look over. I like that he doesn't measure out his laughs.

"He'd love that one. He's a math guy, like you."

"Math isn't everything. Electives are underappreciated."

"Funny you say that, because I'm taking this great Buddhism for the Modern World class as my elective right now. We're learning about how giving is better for the giver than the receiver, and although that might be true, I have to ask: What's *really* in it for you with all this?"

I stare at him. "I told you already. Stanford."

"Can't you just get out of your comfort zone on your own? What am I gonna do, wave pom-poms as you go on your first date and scream '*Keep those conversation starters coming, Aisha! You can do it!*'?"

I scowl. "It's a demanding job. I'll need someone I'm comfortable with to support me as I do uncomfortable things. And someone holding me accountable. You'll be my one-man hype crew." As I shift in my seat, my elbow bumps the rose boutonniere I was going to give to Brian. I hold up the plastic box to the light—the petals are a bit droopy but intact. "This poor rose.

Maybe I'll just leave it here next to the crayons for some kid to destroy."

"No way." He holds out his hand. "As your one-man hype crew, I'll take it. Wrong boy gets the flower, but a boy nonetheless."

"Fine, but there's a catch."

"You love making deals, don't you?"

"You're looking at a fully indoctrinated capitalist right here. The deal is: if you take it, you gotta wear it."

I don't think he's going to do it, but then he lifts the rose from its box. As he tries to pin it to the front of his hoodie, chin pressed to his neck and eyebrows joined in concentration, my chest warms. It's nice seeing the rose being worn, even if it's not on Brian's lapel.

"Thank you for everything today," I say, my voice soft.

"Thank *you*. You bought me ice cream."

"Um, it was four dollars. With tax."

"Four of *your* dollars. Plus, you threw in a rose."

I grin. "Seriously. Thank you. This might just be the most eventful night of my life."

"It was eventful for me, too. I did a bangin' job coloring that snowflake."

I roll my eyes, and as he gives me that thousand-watt smile of his, I take a mental picture. For the first time in a long time, I have a new addition for my life's yearbook.

I approach the door to my apartment like I approach a spider with a tissue. I must be slow and stealthy if I don't want Ma hearing—

"Aisha?"

"You're still awake?" I shut the door behind me, squinting to find the source of her voice. It's almost dark in the living room with only a reading lamp on. Ma's hair is piled in a loose bun atop her head, and she's nestled on the couch, a book in one hand and a mug in the other. The house smells of warming spices, and my stomach rumbles. My dinner was ice cream. I left before they served any real food at formal.

Usually, I look around our living room, at the worn couch and peeling paint, and I pray we get chosen for one of those home makeover programs. Tonight, seeing our cozy apartment and the arranged idol statues on the mantel is a relief.

"Your papa is asleep, but you know I can't sleep until you're home. And I wanted to see how the dance was." Deep-set lines that run like valleys from her nose to her lips and a few streaks of gray in her hair betray Ma's age, but people often mistake her for Seema.

I once tried grilling Ma about the boys who liked her in school because I'm sure there's a list longer than a dictionary, but she gave me a coy smile and said, "There's no one else for me except for your papa." That's code for, *I had a lot of offers*. I always wondered what school was like for Ma. What's it like to be so beautiful that people notice? With my frizz and chimples, I'm not going to find out. Besides, my mother went to school in India. Even someone as stunning as her could blend in. When people see me, they don't think, *What a beautiful girl*. They don't even think, *Oh, a girl*. Instead, here in Arledge, where the ethnicity breakdown looks like a tub of white rice with a few stray brown grains, they think, *Indian girl*.

"Winter formal was, uh, fun." I kick off my heels and sigh with pleasure as my toes sink into the carpet. I've never been so grateful for level earth.

"You begged me for so long to go to the dance, aur bas itna hi?" *And that's it?* Ma pats the seat on the sofa next to her and hands me her mug of saffron milk. I sit, gathering my knees to my chest. It's comforting to hear that mix of Hindi and English. There are always two languages per one sentence in my family, but I answer in English because my Hindi pronunciation is shoddy at best.

"Nothing much happened. Marcy and I ate dinner and danced, and then her mom gave us a ride home."

If my parents knew I got into a stranger's car instead of going to a parent-chaperoned school dance, I'd be the Indian version of toast. I'd be skewered tandoori paneer. Even mellow Pa would be more than happy to roast me over the open flames.

"What about your other friends? Brian and Lily? Riya?"

Clearly, Ma's friend database hasn't been updated in a while. And Ma only asks about Riya because Riya is Indian and goes to my school. I've never even hung out with Riya. I tried to once, but she kept insisting I join her kathak dance group at the temple.

"They're good." I rub at the lipstick print left on the mug's rim. "Ma, I never asked, but whatever happened between you and Mrs. Wu? You used to be close, right?"

She nods. "From the day we moved to this neighborhood. We understood each other's struggles moving to a new country. Trying to raise our kids right, making sure our babies don't get into the wrong crowd." She pinches my cheek.

"But then what happened?"

Ma's hand drops, her smile thin. "Nothing. She moved out of our neighborhood, that's all. She runs the whole finance department of her company, beta. Friendships are hard to maintain as you get older. Apne apne lives main hum busy hojate hai." *We all get busy in our own lives.*

I know that's not true. She talks on the phone for hours with her friends from college. I'll have to ask Pa. Ma never says anything negative about anyone. I bet she'd even find something nice to say about a serial killer, like, *At least they're dedicated to their line of work.* While Ma is a gentle creature, she's still an Indian mother—a puffer fish that inflates into a protective ball at the first sign of her daughters "going astray." And by *sign*, I mean mentioning the male species, studying with members of the male species, and going anywhere there is any chance alcohol and/or the male species is present.

She pokes her reading glasses into her hair. "I'm going to sleep now that you're back. Aur ye ankhon main makeup mereko dhikraha hai. You know my rule about not wearing makeup until college. And your eyes are all red, so go to sleep soon."

I sigh. "Yes, Ma."

When I get to my room, I walk straight into a mountain of bras. Before I left tonight, I was trying to find the bra that would be least visible under my dress. I have no recollection of taking out *this* many from my closet. That's how it is with my room. I find wrappers without remembering when I ate the contents. My socks disappear. My bobby pins reproduce. My parents aren't too happy about it, but I tell them that I'll fix my messy ways once I graduate. I sit down at the edge of my bed, holding my breath as I unlock my phone to blocks of texts from Marcy. There's also, to my surprise, a text from Quentin. We exchanged numbers after he drove me home, but I didn't think he'd text so soon. **I forgot to ask, when exactly do our deal's terms take effect, Lady Aisha?** I smile, and right as I'm about to suggest next weekend, my phone rings.

"FINALLY. WHERE HAVE YOU BEEN?" The octave of Marcy's voice almost cracks the window in my room. "ARE YOU OKAY?"

"It's a long story—are you comfortable?"

"In bed. Holding phone to ear. *Waiting.*"

When I finish the entire night's story, Quentin and sticky notes and fractals and all, I hear her heavy breathing through the receiver.

"This is worthy of being front page in the *Antelope Times,* no doubt."

"So you forgive me? And you promise not to tell Kevin I stole his grandma's ride home?" I flop onto my bed, my hair splaying over my pillow. I gaze at the fading paper stars on the ceiling, hand-painted golden. I taped them up there years ago, but I can't bring myself to take them down. During late nights studying, they make my room feel bigger. Until I look back at my notebook full of conjugated Spanish verbs, that is.

"Of course. I'm just sad you missed out on the mini fried samosas."

I laugh. Luckily my room is far enough away from my parents', so I don't have to be too quiet. It's my oasis of privacy. "I have fresh samosas at home for the taking."

"I'd take some if you ever invited me over."

I've been protecting Marcy from the stained carpet and creaky doors at my apartment. Why not hang out at her house, where the gardens are full of tomatoes and the shag rugs feel like puppy fur?

"You wouldn't like my house, trust me," I say. "And my sister comes home from college a lot, so it might be cramped."

"But I love your sister."

That's the problem, I want to say. Everyone ends up liking her more than me. It happened more than a few times when we were younger. With much difficulty, I'd make a friend at school, and then when they met Seema, they'd forget I was in the room.

"Man," Marcy says, "you're just chock-full of surprises today. You get into a stranger's car. You become his tutor. *And* you know Brian from childhood." A beat of silence passes between us. "What was he like back then?"

"I can send you a picture from our fifth-grade yearbook. He gave this speech about wanting to own an animal shelter on Dream Career Day."

She gasps. "*This* is why I'm in yearbook. To document change. Now he'd probably own an animal shelter just to whisper in the ears of all the little hamsters and cats that he's on the Principal's honor roll."

I laugh and set my phone on the carpet so I can pull the dusty fifth-grade yearbook from the bottom of my bookshelf. The yearbook always flips to the same page when I crack it open, as if the spine's binding has muscle memory.

It's a glossy page, with Brian smiling so big you can see the edge of his gums. His cheeks are flushed and full, and his two front teeth have a gap the width of a Popsicle stick. He's holding up the blue ribbon he got for his Dream Career Day speech.

And there's Brian's mom. She's facing away from the camera, but she has her hand on Brian's shoulder, looking the happiest I've ever seen her. When I was a kid, I forgot Mrs. Wu had teeth. Her mouth was always set in a line.

My eyes move to a tiny me. Half my face is cut off, and I'm in the background wearing a cartoon paintbrush T-shirt. If you follow my gaze, you can see who I'm looking at, in admiration for his first-place win.

"Aish, I know you had a rough night, but on the bright side, this is all perfect for your manifesto."

I almost drop my yearbook. *Manifesto* makes it sound like I'm going skydiving and losing my virginity. At the same time. "My what?"

"Your manifesto to get out of your comfort zone. To do all that you haven't done. Go on *adventures*. Dye your hair, crowd-surf, etcetera."

"It's more of a to-do list. And it's not only for fun, it's for my essay. Fun is more of a desired side effect."

"*Side effect* is the saddest description of fun I've ever heard. You gotta think short-term—what if you die before college?"

My throat tightens. "I do eat pretty unhealthy."

"Uh-huh. You had two Snickers bars for lunch on Thursday. . . ."

I stopped bringing Ma's dal for lunch in third grade, after a kid asked me if I don't eat "regular" food because the elephant god in my religion would punish me. I should've told him that my elephant god was about to inflict a peanut allergy on him and blast all his Reese's Pieces into the ether, but instead I mumbled back, *No*. Bet that showed him.

"So the time to have fun is now. In fact, it's yesterday."

"Gee, thanks for that mild existential crisis."

"Besides, *manifesto* sounds official. Like you're making a pact with yourself." I hear her covers rustle. "What are you going to try first? Going on a date maybe?"

I'm pretty sure I know where she's going with this.

"What about a little revenge date with Brian? You can ask him out and then say you're sick, too. Or just make out with him—*after* he recovers from the flu, of course."

I moan. "Stop. I don't want to think about Brian any more than I have tonight."

Marcy goes quiet, which means she's brainstorming. That's never good. "Oh my—wait, how could I not think of this? Is this math boy cute? Quentin?"

"Don't start. He might have a girlfriend. Or he could be gay."

"Or bi like me."

"Whatever he is, I refuse to think of him like that."

"Why not?" She sounds like an exasperated publicist.

I considered this at Wooly's. *What if I could just go on a date with* this *guy?* I've always hated those movies where the girl wrinkles her nose and goes, "I never considered Raju that way . . ." even though Raju has been there the whole movie, hiding his attractiveness beneath a bowl cut, and is clearly perfect for her.

"It'd be super weird because I'm his tutor now. And he didn't make me feel that jittery crush feeling, and I know this sounds bad . . ." I pause, my cheeks going warm as I try to choose my words carefully. "He's the same height as me. Inch taller, tops."

"You mean . . ."

"Ilikeboyswhoaretallerthanme." Saying it faster makes it sound less terrible.

"Okay, okay. Preferences are allowed. I guess he can kind of be like boy exposure for you. You can get more comfortable talking to boys, while making a new friend . . ." I hear a pen scratching against paper, and I press my phone closer to my ear.

"Marce, are you *crossing his name off*?"

"Maybe."

"Okay, that's it. Bedtime. No more listicles."

As soon as she hangs up, I turn my lights out and crawl into bed, leaving the yearbook open on my desk, Brian's face smiling up at the painted stars on my ceiling.

It has a ring to it. *Manifesto*.

8

STANFORDESSAY.
DOCX

✔ Write my
Stanford essay

Stanford Essay.docx
Last Modified Sunday, Dec 1, 12:46 p.m.

Share a time you left your comfort zone. (600 words)

~~"Leaving your comfort zone" is rather subjective. For a professional rock climber, it might be climbing up the Half Dome in Yosemite National Park. For me, it's ordering anything other than my usual sundae at Wooly's. But this doesn't make my experience any less valid, of course. My experience is~~

~~I have never been one to get out of my comfort zone. Until yesterday, when I stowed away in a stranger's car. But don't worry, I gave him ice cream in exchange, so it's not~~

asdsdkasdkjsadlksef;l

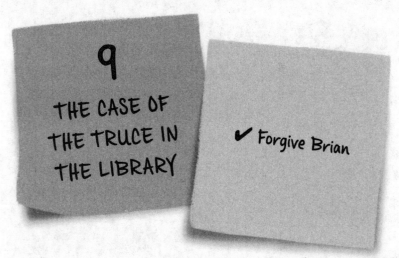

9

THE CASE OF THE TRUCE IN THE LIBRARY

✔ Forgive Brian

On Monday morning, I settle into my usual window seat in Ms. Kavnick's class. I wait for Brian to walk in so that I can lock eyes with him and then look away, unbothered.

Only he never walks in.

A part of me is relieved, thinking it proves that Brian *was* really sick. But then I remember that this is Brian Wu we're talking about. Even if he was at death's door, his mother would probably still drive him to school, wheeling his IV pole behind him so he could maintain his perfect attendance record "during this minor bump in Brian's academic road."

I head to the library after class. Marcy has yearbook stuff to work on, and whenever that happens, I eat by myself at the open library tables across from the computers.

I've always loved the Arledge Prep library. The rest of the school is constantly being waxed and painted, but Principal Cornish leaves the library alone. The lighting is soft and yellow, a welcome departure from the fluorescent tubes in the lunchroom. My favorite part is the stained-glass lamps whose silver chains you have to yank multiple times to turn on. I often see

Brian, Kevin, and the rest of the basketball team perched on the armrests of the faded couches after school as they wait for practice to begin.

I sit down at an empty table with a sigh, scavenging for the family-sized Snickers bars in my backpack, when I see a looming shadow wash over the carpet. I half expect it to be Marcy holding a scroll containing her plan for my *manifesto*, but there he is. His eyes are a bit puffy, but his uniform is ironed as usual, and his hair is gelled in place. He's holding a late pass and a Tupperware container. He looks like Brian. Sharp jawline. Prominent Cupid's bow. No IV pole.

"Aisha, these are for you." He sets the Tupperware container on the table in front of me, and the plastic makes a *thump* against the wood. "My mom sent these almond cookies for your family as an apology. She baked them fresh. She usually makes them on Lunar New Year, but . . ." He looks like he's expecting me to chuck hard-boiled eggs at him any second. A part of me wants to as I think about how many times I checked my phone this weekend.

"O-oh," I manage, trying to breathe. "Um, thank you."

I have won Conversationalist of the Year. I will be approaching the podium to accept my award.

"Listen, do you have a minute? I want to talk to you about formal, but then I thought maybe not here." He nods toward a group of students playing DnD at the next table, also regulars at the library during lunch. "It's kind of private."

Right then, Lily Perez, official president of crochet club and unofficial president of snooping club, ambles by. Her eyes rest on me for an extra moment as she breezes toward the computers. She's either wondering what academic rivals competing for valedictorian are doing together, or she's fascinated by the astounding radius of my chimple.

"I, um . . ." I glance up at him, and then back down to the brown fistful of Snickers I'm squeezing like a javelin. "I know a place."

I get up and lead Brian through the shelves, passing through Fiction, Comics, and Autobiographies until I arrive at the spot always deserted at Arledge Prep during lunch periods: Biographies. I guess no one wants to hear from people writing about other people.

"This is a nice find," Brian remarks as he drops onto the carpeted floor between two shelves, pulling his legs to his chest. I can't fully process the sight of Brian's immaculate Arledge uniform touching the carpeted floor, which probably has years' worth of accumulated fuzz balls. I settle across from him, pulling one ankle over the other and watching, rapt—the way I watch nature documentaries. Even though we're on the ground, his back is straight as an arrow. Mrs. Wu always used to tell him to sit up straight, so I guess all those reminders worked.

"I'm going to open with, 'Please don't hate me.'"

"I don't," I immediately proclaim, and it's true. I tried hating him after that summer of seventh grade, but it never worked. Sometimes I told myself I'd throw away everything that reminded me of him—the ticket stubs from all the movies we'd seen together, the San Francisco souvenir key chain with an "interesting shape" that he didn't realize was a bottle opener. But I still have it. All of it. "I understand if you were sick. I hope you're, uh, feeling better. You seem to be doing better, I mean."

I nibble on my Snickers, careful not to let the caramel strings stick to my lips. I hate eating in front of people I don't know well, especially hot people. I imagine the crumbs around my lips drawing attention to the acne scars on my chin, and even chewing small bites makes me wonder about how my cheeks are contorting.

"Honestly, Aisha . . ." His eyes lower to his shoes. "I wasn't sick."

I was wondering how he looked so well rested after having the flu all weekend.

"I know my mom told you that, but the truth is, she and I got into a big argument on Saturday afternoon."

I think back to my memories of Mrs. Wu. She's one of those people you want to please—someone who could ask you for your spleen and you'd readily agree to it, and years later, if the situation repeated itself and she asked for your pancreas, you'd say yes all over again. Brian has the same effect on me, but luckily *he* doesn't know that, so all my organs are intact. For now.

"What was the argument about?" I ask, my voice soft.

He takes a deep breath, picking at the carpet fibers with his fingers.

"You don't have to explain," I add. "I understand if it's personal or if—"

"I want to. And it's easier because it's you. I think you'd understand, since you know my mom." He's blinking a lot, so I sense he's gathering his words. I wait.

"The morning of winter formal, I got an email from a supposed connection of my mom's. She introduced herself as a college application mentor, and then she asked me to reply to the email describing some of my life experiences in detail. The more I read the email, the more I realized *mentor* is more of a euphemism." The black dress shoe that he was tapping on the carpet to some inaudible song goes still. "She's a Harvard grad my mom hired to write my essays for me."

My whole body stiffens. I've heard of helicopter parents at Arledge revising college essays, but parents hiring professionals? That's unethical. *Unfair.* Unlike what I'd expect from Mrs. Wu, who always encouraged hard work.

"Before you jump to any conclusions, I was against it completely. I'd already insisted months ago that I'm going to write the essays myself. My mom promised me she'd drop the idea of the essay mill, and I thought she did." His jaw pulses. "Evidently not. She said that if we have the resources to make my application better, we should use them. And she was in denial about this being against the rules. She insisted that I can use the essay as a guide and then *make it my own*, but I know moving commas around and paraphrasing doesn't make it mine."

I can't imagine what control of that magnitude feels like. Forget hiring an essay mill on my behalf, my parents barely know how to text. Ma sends me a letter *a* sometimes. An accidental, stand-alone *a*. Still, I'd take that over this any day. If my parents offered a way to have my Stanford essay written, I'd be at least a *little* tempted. I'm almost glad the option doesn't exist for me.

"There were hours of arguments. Even my dad came downstairs from his cave of solitude to defend my mom. I guess they think I can't get into an Ivy on my own." He swallows, and I notice his prominent Adam's apple dipping and rising. "Even if I can't, I don't care."

My heart squeezes. "I'm sorry, Brian."

"No, *I'm* sorry." His eyes meet mine. "I really wanted to go with you, but it was all too much. I couldn't even bring myself to text you because I felt so bad about ruining your night. It was like I was . . . paralyzed."

"I understand. I didn't realize . . ." My remaining hurt from that night is suddenly hosed down to smoke.

"And to top it off, Riley broke up with me two *days* before winter formal." He shrugs. "But maybe it's for the best. A relationship would be another thing for my mom to pick apart."

I'm dying to ask why smokin' hot Riley broke up with him, but I know that'd cross an invisible line. "*Would* be? So you never told your mom about Riley?" I ask instead.

"No way. I knew it wouldn't go over well, so we always hung out at Riley's."

"I get it. I told my parents I was going to formal with my instant camera."

"My mom knew I was going with you. That's how she knew to call you that night." He looks almost proud of himself.

My eyes go wide. "She was okay with it?"

"I told her I'm going with you and that's that." He rakes his hand through his hair. "She was surprisingly cool about it. You know how much she liked you."

Liked. Ouch for past tense.

As if reading my mind, he corrects himself: "Likes, I mean." He picks up my candy wrapper from the carpet with his thumb and index finger, studying it like it's an amoeba moving under a microscope. "Side note, but my basketball coach would probably kill me if he saw me eating these for lunch."

"And eating these for lunch will probably kill me."

He gives me one of his rare half grins, one that creates a slight dent in his left cheek. His teeth are straight, no gaps like before. At the end of fifth grade, he got braces to fix his overbite. As I zip open my backpack to take out my notebook from Ms. Kavnick's class, my mind sings, *I'm going with you and that's that.* "This is for you. It's what you missed in class today."

He reluctantly accepts, eyebrows raised. "You're sharing notes with *me*, your rival? I hope this isn't out of pity."

"It's payback. You gave me your calculus notes when I was out with the flu last year."

"I remember you asking the four other people in our row before me."

I laugh. I was too shy to ask him first. "No one else's notes were legible. Marcy's were like a series of doctors' signatures."

He thumbs through my notebook. "Look at all this sectioning and highlighting. They're almost *too* nice to study from."

I've heard the compliment "nice notes" a lot, but coming from Brian, it feels like it's been covered in buttercream frosting and sprinkles. "Whether you use them or not, I'm still getting valedictorian."

"Oh, we'll see about that."

We smile. I'm relieved by the return of our competitive dynamic. It's like a book returned to its rightful place on a shelf.

The bell rings, and Brian stands, slinging his backpack over his shoulder. "Thanks for hearing me out today, Aish. And for the notes. I've been in a dark place, and I haven't been able to talk to anyone about it. Even Kevin."

Aish.

I feel like I've been chosen for something special, like I'm the one performing with my clarinet at the Blue Llama jazz bar. "I have experience listening. You used to practice your squire lines on me, remember?"

Brian auditioned for the part of Arthur in our fifth-grade production of *The Sword in the Stone*, but he got cast as Squire Two. He had seven lines. He made up for that by reading them with so much gusto that his opening night performance was a little *too* theatrical.

He groans. "Don't remind me."

Standing there with him in the narrow corridor of Biographies, it feels like a marching band has paraded in, drums reverberating in my chest. It's frackin' crackers *hard* to stop liking Brian. It's like those parents at park playgrounds who have distracted conversations with each other while keeping one eye on the swings where their kids are. I will always keep an eye on Brian.

"I should get to class," I murmur, tucking the container of cookies under my arm.

There's a light shining in my mind's attic—the creaky, musty attic overflowing with things I wished for but haven't dared revisit in years. It's late to be admitting this to myself with months left of senior year, but it's not *too* late. I've been focusing my deal with Quentin around my Stanford essay, but maybe Marcy's on to something with this manifesto idea. Maybe I should think bigger. Senior year is my chance to explore. With Quentin helping me, and with Brian newly single, maybe I can have it all. The admission to Stanford, the soul-searching, and even the guy.

The thought makes me feel light, like a hot-air balloon rising into the sky. I fling open the library doors with the determination of an astronaut closing her visor.

Goodbye, comfort zone.

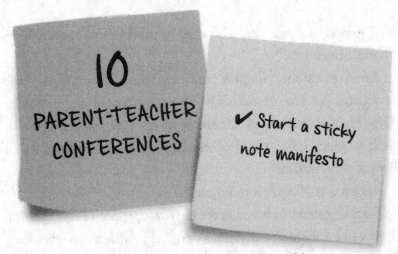

10
PARENT-TEACHER CONFERENCES

✔ Start a sticky note manifesto

I spend a few extra minutes insulated in Ma's old station wagon. Quentin asked me to come over this weekend for our first tutoring session, so I struck a deal with my parents to lend me the car sometimes for a "volunteer tutoring project." There was no suspicion because I've been tutoring kids for a while. I just left out the part that this "kid" is my age and male.

The darkness made it easier the night of formal, but in the harsh light of the winter sun, my deal with Quentin feels like a faraway dream. I get out of the car, my old precalculus mathematics book in my hands.

As the doorbell sounds, I pray to the lucky stars on my bedroom ceiling that Quentin will open the door, but there's a blob of neon orange swimming toward the frosted glass. When the door swings open, I see a small-framed woman's face light up. Her black hair is gathered into a loose ponytail, and she's wearing tangerine joggers and a silver Catholic cross pendant. "You must be Aisha! I'm Quentin's mother."

"Nice to meet you," I blurt. "I'm here to tutor Quentin?" I say it as a question to myself, like, *Am I here?*

"Of course. Come in, come in, it's cold." As soon as she ushers me inside, she extends a hand, and I take it, hoping she won't notice my palms are sweaty.

While standing in the foyer, I smell chocolate. It's the scent of either heaven or Willy Wonka's factory. The walls have floral wallpaper that matches the salmon-colored furniture, and there are twill rugs laid on the wooden floors. There's a big Christmas tree already up in the living room, with tinsel and tiny glass ornaments. It's a stark contrast from my apartment, which smells like butter chicken and has expired coupon books drooping all over the counters like melting clocks from a Dalí piece.

She stands with her hands propped on her hips, and we exchange awkward smiles. I get this feeling I've seen that exact lopsided smile before, and after a few moments, I realize it's identical to Quentin's. "Well, I'll get Quentin. You can leave your shoes there."

"Thank you . . . er . . ." For a second I forget Quentin's last name, but then I remember. ". . . Ms. Santos." As I bend to unzip my boots, I notice the framed photos of Quentin and his mom dotting the wall. There's one of Quentin as a kid lying on the beach, squinting from the sunlight. He's covered in sand. When *I* used to go to the beach, I was paranoid about crabs, so I'd plop into a beach chair and keep sand from getting on the pages of my book.

"Anaaaaak!" Ms. Santos sings up the stairwell. When there's no answer, "Quentiiiin, come downstairs right now!"

"Coming Nanay," I hear Quentin's weak, muffled voice call back.

After some clattering, Quentin emerges. His hair is disheveled, but he makes it look purposeful. When I know someone's coming over, I can't roll out of bed. I spend an hour straightening my curly hair and another hour preparing to dodge awkward silences.

I did that this morning anyway, though.

"Sorry, Aisha." He rubs his eyes as he trots down the carpeted stairs. "I slept through my alarm. You know how alarm clocks can be. Not always alarming enough."

Ms. Santos rolls her eyes and links her arm through mine. I look up with a start, and Quentin stares at our arms for a moment as if he, too, can't believe that some girl he just met a week ago is intertwining arms with his mother.

"Ay nako, you're just waking up? Go wash your face. Show some respect to your teacher."

Before I can give Quentin a gloating, yeah-show-me-some-respect smile, she pulls me to the kitchen and sets a steel slow cooker on the table. Terra-cotta flowerpots line the window above the sink, and there are a few star-shaped decorations hanging from the ceiling. It's nice to see some color. By this time of year in Michigan, the trees look like little freezer-burned broccolis, and even the days die early.

"I've made champorado. It's a Filipino breakfast dessert I grew up eating that's like sticky chocolate pudding. When I visited my mother in Dumaguete a few winters ago, she showed me how to make it from scratch."

Aha! So Quentin is Filipino.

She hands me a bamboo bowl filled to the brim. "No gluten. Quentin told me no wheat."

Quentin must've remembered my sundae order from Wooly's was gluten-free. Impressive. I can hardly remember which of my cousins are vegetarian.

"Take a big bite. That's how you'll get all the flavor."

I take a spoonful and lick the chocolate from my lips, careful to stop it from dribbling down my chin. "This is *amazing*. And your home is beautiful. My mom would love the flowers you have on the windowsill."

"Thank you." She smiles. "I'm a plant person."

I'm curious about where Quentin's dad is. When I came inside, I didn't see prototypical dad signs like giant shoes placed near the welcome mat or big coats curled over a hanger.

She sits next to me, resting her head on her hand. "We've lived here for many years, so I kept thinking it's about time for a move, but we stayed for my work. And I became strangely attached to everything here, even the old wallpaper in the living room."

I give her a nod. "We live on the first floor of an apartment building, and we have a hideous orange door we haven't painted over, even though the landlord said we could. It's like a year-round Halloween decoration. On the bright side, no one had any trouble finding our unit for birthday parties." My *sister's* birthday parties, rather. I had two friends.

Ms. Santos smiles, and I'm reminded of Quentin again. Speak of the devil. Quentin yanks out the chair across from me and sits down. The tips of his hair are damp, and the smell of pine trees wafts through the air. As the scent mixes with the chocolate, I'm reminded of a mint chocolate chip sundae from Wooly's. He looks at his mom from behind his thicket of hair. "I missed this,

Nanay. In honor of the return of champorado, I will grace you with my enchiladas for dinner."

I'm expecting her to wrinkle her nose and retort *no one wants your microwaved frozen enchiladas*, but she looks delighted. "Really?"

"Aisha can judge whose dish is better."

He already made plans for me to stay for dinner. What's more is he is going to *make* the dinner. The only time I use the stove is for boiling water for tea. If my parents aren't home, I only eat stuff that comes in plastic wrapping.

Man, Marcy is right. I *am* going to die early.

After Quentin's done inhaling his pudding in record time, he leads me through the hallway and scales the stairs, taking two at a time without touching the railing—a giveaway of having lived in a place for years. I'm about to follow when his mom's hand grazes my shoulder. I'm thinking she's going to tell me to leave the bedroom door open while we work, which is definitely what Ma would do.

"Thank you so much for doing this, Aisha. He just about gave up on tutors."

"Are parent-teacher conferences over yet?" Quentin waves from the top of the stairwell.

"I'll leave you two be, then. And, um . . . leave the door open, please."

There it is.

His mom nods at me and disappears back into the kitchen, and as soon as I'm up the stairs and in Quentin's room, I have to say it. "Your mom is *so* nice." It's always been easier for me to interact with adults instead of Arledge students my own age.

I can talk about plants, books, nature documentaries, granite countertops, home improvement projects . . .

"It's genetic."

"Please. Also, you never told me you're Filipino."

"Must have slipped my mind when you hijacked my car."

"Touché."

"Kidding. But yeah, my dad's Italian, and my mom's Filipino."

I look at him with new respect. Being Indian is hard enough for me to figure out, so I wonder how Quentin reconciles all those layers. And my romance-starved self must ask . . .

"How'd they meet?"

"My dad was a chef making pizzas back in Italy, and my mom visited his pizzeria as a tourist."

"Omigod, that's *so* adorable. It's like a movie."

"Then my mom asked for an extra layer of cheese, and he was like, *Now that's a real woman.*"

"Aw, that's—"

"Then he picked her up and spun her around and they made out in the middle of the Italian street."

"Wait, are you—"

"And they got married that very day, and their cake was made of adorable little stacked pizzas with mozzarella cheese and sun-dried tomatoes in between the layers."

"I hate you."

He laughs. "They met in grad school."

As I look around, I put on my forensic scientist hat. I like analyzing room decor, but from Quentin's room, I can't glean much. There's an alarm clock on the nightstand, a bed with gray sheets, a few sticky-note pads on his desk, one plant, some candles, and a matchbox. I think of my room, with rainbow stripy sheets, a mass of clothes on the floor at all times, and golden paper stars on the ceiling.

"Whoa, you have an alarm clock? How retro. You know there are these nifty clocks called *phones* now."

"I like old stuff."

"What stuff? Your room has . . . *nothing*. No knickknacks. No wall art."

"Keep looking."

I spot a star-shaped paper decoration hanging from the ceiling. "Hey, I saw a few of those downstairs!"

"Yeah, it's called a parol. It's a lantern Filipinos usually put up at Christmastime. There are ones tricked out with LEDs, but my mom likes making simpler ones together every year out of bamboo and paper. That being said . . ." He grins. "It's actually not the wall art I was referring to."

I keep searching, and my eyes catch on a handful of yellow sticky notes stuck to Quentin's wall, right above a power strip on the floor. "*Wait*, are those . . ."

"I found the sticky notes we wrote at Wooly's in my coat pocket the other day, and I stuck them to the wall so I wouldn't lose them." He looks pleased with himself, like a film director about to make a frame with his fingers.

"And you decided that's enough decoration for your entire room?"

"I like having less things to keep track of. And that Buddhism elective I'm taking had a whole unit on using only what we need to survive."

I smirk, holding up a three-wick candle from his nightstand by the rim. "Why, of course. The threatening scent of pine mist certainly repels wilderness predators."

"We haven't gotten to the class on hypocrisy yet."

I put down the candle and raise my tattered precalculus textbook above my head like I'm King Arthur brandishing Excalibur. "So who's ready for some M-A-T-H?"

"I may not be able to do math, but I can still spell, okay?"

"I thought we could start with some probability."

"One hundred percent chance of me not getting this."

"You clearly already get some of it." I lower myself onto the edge of his bed, careful not to wrinkle the leaf-patterned bedspread. "Don't worry, I'll go slow with you."

He cocks an eyebrow, and my cheeks flush.

"Okay, that's *not* what I—"

"Slow's probably best. My mom's outside, and the door's open."

As I pop from his bed like a jack-in-the-box, he grins with this distinct slyness I'm starting to pick up on. Then he walks out and returns moments later, rolling in an extra chair. His desk faces the window, which means maximal light will be illuminating my acne and stray eyebrow hairs. This makes me fix my gaze to his three-wick candle instead of him, but after I start explaining sample spaces, I relax. Math is my thing. Fractals for fortitude.

Quentin jots notes and hangs on my every word, but when it's time for him to do problems by himself at the end of the section, he falters. He squeezes his pencil and stares at the blank page, but I can't tell if he's nervous or unsure how to solve the problem. I pretend to look through my phone to make him feel more comfortable.

"I'm not going to get it." He sounds like he's stating a fact. *The sky is blue.*

"Don't be so hard on yourself. It's day one."

"I'll try to work on it more after—"

I snatch the pencil from his hand. "Give me your notebook."

He obeys, and I solve the problem while talking through my process. I circle the answer and watch as he carefully scans the page.

"Wait, if you already pulled one of the red socks out of the drawer, I thought you were supposed to subtract the probability of pulling—"

I clap. "Knew it! You do get it."

"So you just solved the problem incorrectly on purpose? That's, like, evil."

"Be quiet and try the next question."

When I leave to go to the bathroom to give him some space, I linger inside, reading the names of the products Quentin has on his sink counter. Dior pine aftershave, Degree deodorant, Mrs. Meyer's lavender soap. I used to be curious about boys' bathrooms. It was a hot-button topic in middle school, but the reality is not nearly as interesting as my theory was. I thought there would be algae and creepy-crawlies everywhere, but his bathroom is neat.

When I return, I sit down and check his notebook, spinning slightly back and forth in my chair.

"*Correct!*" I wave the notebook in the air like it's a full bingo card.

"What's my reward for all my progress?" He shoots me a winsome smile that I bet has gotten him out of trouble with his stickler grandpa more than a few times.

"After a sunny morning filled with math, you get to now"—I flash him a double thumbs-up—"help me with my *manifesto*!"

"Your what?"

"Manifesto. Marcy coined the term, and I've decided to use it. It sounds way more official than a to-do list."

"Um, never thought I'd say this but, can we just do more math?"

"Very funny." I slide from the chair to the floor, choosing a patch of carpet *not* in unflattering sunlight. "So I need your advice. I talked to Brian on Monday. He wasn't sick the night of formal, but he had a good reason to not show up, so I forgave him. He also gave me a container of homemade apology cookies that his mom baked, which was—"

"I thought you said parents don't have time to bake cookies anymore."

I grin. "I guess she made an exception for me. I'd have saved you some, but I already promised them to Seema when I realized they probably have gluten. You should try the Indian dessert that's going to replace them, though. Ma will probably make me refill the container with some burfi before giving it back to him."

"Ah, the Asian Tupperware War of Gratitude. I'm all too familiar."

I didn't realize that Asians feeling the need to add food to a container before returning it is a *phenomenon*. I thought it was just Ma.

"So what do you need advice on? And don't worry, my mom won't come upstairs. She's probably glued to the couch, shopping online for Christmas gifts for the fam." Quentin bends forward in his chair. I notice that his long, striped socks peeking out from his joggers match the tie-dyed Kresge High tennis team hoodie he's wearing. Unlike Brian's stiff, upright posture, his shoulders are relaxed.

"Well, I . . ." I look down.

"Let me guess. You want Brian."

"What the fu—" I cough. "I mean, fudge nuggets? How did you—"

"Hey, *you* just taught *me* the concept of sample spaces. In a set of outcomes, that was the most likely one. So what's the goal? To get asked out on a date?"

"I think so. I'm tired of liking him from far away. I want to finally do stuff about it."

"Oh, you mean . . ." He lifts an eyebrow.

"No! Wait, not, like, do *stuff*. I mean just hang out with him. Maybe make out, tops. PG-13 stuff . . ." I groan, feeling my cheeks starting to burn. The whole point of striking this deal with Quentin is being able to freely embarrass myself in front of him, but I still can't believe what I'm divulging to an almost stranger.

"Hey, hey, was just messing with you." Quentin rises from his chair and sits down beside me, his hoodie drawstrings jumping about. "Go on."

"I . . . don't know what dating means. I do want to"—I lower my voice—"*kiss* someone in theory, but it's not like I've ever tried. I'd die if anyone came that close to me."

"You need a surprise kiss. No time to think."

I snap my fingers. "Exactly." He's quiet for a moment, and I jerk my hand up to my mouth, my eyes widening. "Don't you dare."

He chuckles. "C'mon. I'd never."

Never? I'm almost insulted by his sureness, but it's all for the best. I'd probably fall for Quentin if he kissed me, out of sheer lack of comparison, and then our differing opinions on math's value as a subject would tear our relationship apart until we're old and eating pancakes at a diner in silence.

"Well, you're not wrong." My hand drops. "I wouldn't freak out if I couldn't *see* the person getting closer to me. It's that whole *before* process that freaks me out."

"How are you not going to see the person as they get closer?"

"Total darkness. Or I can look at the sun right before the kiss, so I'm totally blinded."

"Yeah, you could temporarily blind yourself, not crazy at all. Or . . ."

"I was hoping you'd say *or*."

"Or you can just wait until you're comfortable enough with them. And let it happen naturally."

"That's a nice thought, but do I look like I'm capable of that?"

"Fine. Aim your phone flashlight into your eyes whenever you feel a kiss is about to happen."

"Gee, I should write that down." I pretend to look around for a writing utensil.

"That reminds me . . ." He gets up, nabs an unused stack of yellow sticky notes from his desk, and settles back down next to me, close enough so his knee brushes mine. The sunlight streaming in from the window makes his eyes glow like embers of a fire. It's pretty. Maybe direct sunlight doesn't make *everyone* look bad. "The more I looked at the notes from Wooly's, the more it got me thinking. Why don't we write your manifesto stuff on sticky notes and stick them to the wall? Way cooler than a spreadsheet."

"Those are fighting words. I'm a spreadsheet enthusiast."

He rolls his eyes. "You don't say. But this way, whenever we do a note, you can *cross it off*. How satisfying will that be?" He overlaps his hands and then separates them, like, *Abracadabra!* "We can call it the Great Wall."

"I think that name's taken already."

"Okay, Greater Wall."

"Your blank walls do make me sad, so I'm very on board with this. But isn't it kind of . . . extra?"

"You're calling this a *manifesto*, and the sticky note wall is extra?"

"Fair point, but wouldn't your mom see it? If this was in my room, my mom would find it in seconds."

"Nope. She always stands at the doorway when she comes to my room, out of respect for my privacy. And I do all the cleaning and laundry myself." He holds out the stack and a pen. "Before we start, ground rules. Whatever goes on this wall must be: one, something you genuinely want to do; two, something that scares you; three, doable before your essay deadline; four, within our, er, *conservative* budgets; and . . . five, safe for all parties involved. Anything I'm missing?"

I shake my head. Making up an essay about camping for the first time is sounding more and more appealing.

"I can tell you're thinking too much. Write whatever comes to mind, and I'll do the rest, as your one-man hype crew. I even have the perfect hype song."

He starts playing "Eye of the Tiger" on his laptop, and without another word, we form an assembly line. I scribble on a note. I slap it onto any exposed patch of his skin—wrist, arm, forehead, anywhere—and he sticks my notes to the blank wall across from his bed, under the hanging parol. I start with the notes I scribbled at Wooly's and rewrite them in neater handwriting, making small tweaks as I go.

Go to a typical high school party (with alcohol).

Try alcohol.

Dance with someone.

Make (gluten-free) holiday-themed macarons from scratch.

"*Macarons* scare you?" He's chuckling, but I give him a solemn nod.

"I've always wanted to bake in theory, but ever since I burned my mom's favorite steel pot to a crisp while trying to make rice, I've stayed out of the kitchen."

Sign up for a watercolor painting class.

Quentin turns when he reads this one, and my lips curl up as I notice a pen tucked behind his ear, swallowed by his damp hair. It looks dorky yet cute. "Didn't you say you paint already?"

"For fun, but I've never taken a class. Sharing my art with other people freaks me out, and calling what I make art *also* freaks me out." I tell myself the classes at the craft store around here are too expensive, and I can't ask Seema for a loan because she's a broke premed student, but I know those are excuses.

Get someone (anyone!) to fall for me.

Go on a date.

Kiss someone at midnight on New Year's.

"These three look suspiciously related, huh?" He rearranges the other notes on the wall to make room. "Although kiss on

New Year's from Brian might be difficult. You only have, what, three weeks to somehow make that happen?"

"I didn't say the kiss had to be from *Brian*."

I'm drawn to the time-sensitive part of a midnight kiss. It's the same thrill I got from timed multiplication tables. I hope my midnight kiss is from Brian this year, but as Ma always says, beggars can't be choosers. I just want to get my first kiss over with.

Change up my look.

He smooths the folded edge of the note. "Ah, yes. Which will it be, clear-framed glasses hipster girl with overalls or edgy crop top girl with black nails?"

"Neither. Crop tops are usually *too* cropped for my liking, and clear-framed glasses are too hard to find on white bed-sheets."

He laughs. "You've thought about this."

"I have. I hide in my crochet club hoodies on the weekends, and during school I get to wear my uniform. I play it safe with muted colors and plain tops, but I'm not sure if that's really me. I guess I always felt like if your style is more distinctive, it's more likely to be disliked. On top of that, Ma really hates me wearing makeup. She thinks I'm too young."

He presses the note to the wall, and I realize he's scary good at eyeballing straight lines. "What would you want your style to be, if you weren't worrying about any of that?"

"That's where you come in." I shoot finger guns at him. "You get to drive me to the Lakeshore Mall and be my clothes holder and provider of opinions whenever called upon. I'll also ask my sister to come because she has the best eye for fashion. Both of you will have to show me where everything is because I haven't been to Lakeshore in a year."

"*What?* A year without free chocolate samples from Godiva? Without Jamba Juice?"

"They rebranded to Jamba now, I believe."

He gives me a look.

"What? It's true, they dropped the *juice* part to be seen as more than just—"

He folds his arms.

"Fine. I hate shopping at malls, okay? Too much stimulation. And I was busy with school and my zillion other commitments."

"That's a new definition of commitment issues."

I laugh. "Hey, the arcade made me think of another one. I've never had the guts to skip school before . . ."

Skip school and go to the arcade.

Host my own dinner party.

"This one's easy-peasy," he says. "You can invite me and your friend Marcy over. Bam. Dinner party. What's scary about that?"

"Hosting means being the center of attention *and* opening my space to everyone. My apartment is small and old. And there's a big statue of Lord Ganesha in the living room."

"Okay . . ." He flips to the next. I wonder if he's thinking about what a scaredy-cat I am.

Learn to swim.

"I was afraid of water when I was young, so I never learned," I explain.

"I'll teach you." His eager smile makes me gulp.

Just wearing my bathing suit in front of Quentin would leave me unable to breathe, no deep water necessary. He has that tennis player body—lean yet toned. I'm flat as a plank of wood with legs as thin as wire. My body is basically a resistor. Every time I poked one into a circuit board during AP Physics last year, I felt a sort of kinship.

We write more notes, and before long, Quentin's wall is annexed by my handwriting. We stand together with our arms crossed, and I take a step back to admire the mosaic of yellow.

"Your wall has character now. My job here is done." I gather my bag and start cramming my notebooks and textbook inside.

His face falls. "Wait, you're not staying for my enchiladas?"

I don't know how to tell him that I've led my parents to believe I'm tutoring a little kid, so I decide to save that tidbit for another time.

"Sorry, I have to get back home for dinner, since my family usually eats together. And I should probably work on my AP Chem report." I tap on the *Change up my look* note. "But maybe we can do this one next weekend? I gotta take advantage of the Christmas sales going on."

That's half of why I need the new look to happen early. If I revamp my style, I'll be more confident. If I'm more confident, I'll be able to be myself around Brian. I'm not quite sure what happens after that, but it sounds like a good place to start.

"Of course. Lady Aisha must have her acai Jamba juice."

A week ago, I didn't know Quentin existed. Now, because of him, I'm starting over.

I'm on a sticky note manifesto.

106

11

MAKEOVER MOMENT

✔ Change up my look

Quentin and I are waiting for Seema next to the double doors of the Lakeshore Mall. It's been a week since we put up the sticky notes in Quentin's room. The mall is teeming with eager holiday shoppers swinging bags and cupping hot chocolate. I try not to look at the California Pizza Kitchen sign. California reminds me of Stanford, which reminds me of my unwritten essay. To be fair, a pine cone reminds me of my unwritten essay these days.

Tutoring Quentin has been keeping me from spiraling. We met twice this week after school at his house, and once I started explaining how to divide rational expressions, all else melted away. I liked how he used his phone to record voice memos of me explaining at some points. It made me feel like a college professor.

Ma and Pa still think I'm tutoring a little kid in long division. I know they'll find out the truth eventually, but I just hope Seema doesn't accidentally let it slip first. Secrets come out of her with the tiniest bit of prodding, the way snow falls from a branch with one nudge.

"Are you going to buy anything today?" I ask Quentin.

He buries his chin into his scarf, his ears poking out. "As you've probably noticed, I wear pretty much the same shirt in different colors every day."

I have noticed. His closet's palette is mostly shades of navy blue and dark green, and he seems to go for comfort over aesthetic—baggy hoodies, pocket tees, medium wash jeans, cognac sneakers. The only accessory he wears is a watch.

"That Buddhism elective is teaching you well."

"Nah, I'm still unenlightened enough to buy an almond pretzel."

"Cinnamon sugar's better," a familiar voice announces. Seema's standing there with a smile, and I go in for a hug, but she squirms and leans away. "You know I'm not a hugger." She gives Quentin a half wave. "Hi, you must be Quentin. I'm Seema, Aisha's sister. Also known as the favorite child of the family." She winks and draws an invisible halo above her head.

Quentin smiles. It's a sort of shy, blushing-Indian-bride smile I haven't seen from him before. Seema has that effect on people. Everyone falls in love with her thick, shiny hair and witty remarks, and then pines for her approval for all eternity.

She yanks off her knitted winter hat by the pom-pom. "So, where are these cookies you promised me?"

I pull out the Tupperware Brian gave me, shaking it like a maraca. "Almond. Freshly baked from Brian's mom. Er, well they *were* fresh last week."

She stuffs it into her purse. "I'll give the container back to you. Ma's probably gonna make you put some burfi in this before returning it."

Quentin and I exchange grins. He was right about the Asian Tupperware War.

"Anyway, I'm surprised, Aish. You wanting to meet at the *mall* of all places? Is there an extra credit assignment involved? Or wait, a crochet club scavenger hunt?"

I scowl. Yesterday I called Seema to catch her up on the manifesto, and she promised not to tell Ma and Pa. I already told her that changing up my look was part of it, but she probably stopped listening somewhere halfway through my story and started scrolling on her phone. "I'm trying a new look, remember? And then I'll write about how it felt to wear things I'd usually write off as too out there for me. For my Stanford essay."

"Ah, *there* it is." Seema eyes Quentin. "And he's here for moral support?"

"Yep. And I brought him along for a second opinion."

"Your friend wearing a plain tee, cropped pants, and long striped socks is providing the second opinion?" She flashes Quentin a winning smile. "No offense."

He chuckles. "None taken."

I clear my throat. "My plan is to get a few dresses, maybe a pair of printed pants. And some bold makeup."

Even if it's stuff I wouldn't normally wear, at least I'll be choosing. Ma and Pa don't believe in shopping for style. They drive thirty minutes out of Arledge to shop for cheaper bananas. They buy all my clothes on sale, sometimes from grocery stores, and throwing out clothing is never an option. Wear, tear, mend, repeat.

"And how're you paying for this?" Seema asks.

"My savings, from working at the stationery shop last summer."

"I'm surprised you didn't spend it already."

"I was . . ." I take a deep breath. "I was saving it in case I wanted to take that watercolor painting class at Crafterina."

"Oh." Seema had been tapping her foot on the tile to the beat of "All I Want for Christmas Is You" blaring through the mall speakers, but she stops swaying when she hears this. "I didn't know you still painted."

"I . . ." I sigh. "I don't."

Quentin's looking at me. He almost seems disappointed, but I can't say for sure. My readings of his imperceptible expressions are about as reliable as me using my $6 astrology book to read tea leaves.

"And not to derail this," Seema goes on, "but no way Ma will be okay with you wearing makeup to school."

I have a tube of lipstick that I've accidentally smashed into its cover (rest in peace). That's all Ma allowed. She thinks worrying about my appearance is a frivolous distraction, which is easy for someone with perfect skin to say. I'm nervous about hiding my makeup from Ma, but I want to stop obsessing over my skin every morning.

"I'll just put it on in the morning before class starts and take it off before getting on the bus. She'll never know. I'll only wear a little lipstick anyway. I kind of hate the texture. It turns my lips into prunes."

"Well, well, well. Aisha becoming a brave little rebel. Welcome to my world, sis."

Seema has always been the rebellious one. When I say this, people imagine a gum-smacking girl with hair dyed blue and report cards of straight Ds. The reality is, she once got her hair highlighted blond against Ma's wishes, got contact lenses against Pa's wishes, and brought home one B+. To me, however, she has a *legacy*.

She tousles my hair, and I duck away. "Stop! You know how long it takes me to straighten my hair."

Quentin's eyes go wide. He's looking at me as if I said I eat my cereal with water instead of milk. "Your hair isn't naturally straight?"

"Nope. It's more of a wavy-curly. Except not nice curls like yours."

I *have* to straighten my hair because my natural texture includes frizz that others can only obtain via rubbing their socks on carpet.

"Anyway," I say, bristling. "Can we look at makeup first?"

When we get inside Nordstrom, I see a group of older girls giggling over some lipstick swatches. I feel like how the Wizard of Oz would feel if he entered a room filled with actual wizards. I suppose my intimidation shows because a lady approaches us with a welcoming smile. She has piercing blue eyes lined with black liner and straight blond hair. I can only hope makeup will make me look half as good.

"Hi there, I'm Breanna. Can I help you find something?"

Seema drapes an arm over my shoulders. "My sister here hasn't used much makeup before and was looking for a bold new look. Can you get her started?"

I give my sister a grateful nod, and she nods back. Sometimes I wish I had a younger sibling to show the ropes to, but during moments like these, I'm happy to be the younger one.

Breanna claps like I've been awarded the Nobel Peace Prize. "Oh my goodness, that's *so* exciting! Can I do your makeup for free? That way I can demo the products and show you how to replicate the look at home."

Seema points to the perfume section. I know this translates

to, *We'll be waiting there*. Hanging out with Seema without getting my feelings hurt is tricky, but at least our nonverbal communication is solid.

Breanna wades past shoppers, stopping at a high chair that faces a mirror. I take an inward sigh of relief as I climb on—the mirror is not one of those magnification mirrors. I remove my glasses, and Breanna starts dabbing my face with a sponge. At first, my hands are sweaty since I see a pair of those eyelash-curling devices that look like embroidery scissors, but after a few minutes of Breanna chatting about how BB cream has a lightweight coverage, I relax. When it's over, she hands me my glasses. I almost fall out of the chair when I come into focus. My eyes look brighter, my lips are a matte red, and my skin doesn't look like tomatoes that have been stomped on. I'm having my makeover moment.

"Oh my . . ." I lean so far forward I probably look like I'm about to kiss my reflection. I'll get the cheaper drugstore versions of everything Breanna used, complete my makeup in the Arledge Prep bathroom on Monday morning, and then brace for compliments. From crochet club, at the very least. "This is *amazing.* I don't recognize myself."

"It's still you, hon. Makeup just accentuates your already gorgeous features."

I know that's what they tell Breanna to say during her HR training, but we all know makeup is there to cover your blemishes or distract from them. I thank Breanna and make a dash for the perfume section. Seema and Quentin are laughing.

"*Guys.*"

That's all I say. I wait for the *Wow, who is this mysterious and beautiful woman?*

Quentin points to the blue perfume bottle Seema's holding. "Aisha, you're gonna love this. That is $494 with the holiday discount, I kid you not. And look at that shape."

Seema shakes her head. "They were all, *Octahedral crystal? That's the perfect shape for our overpriced scented water.* You know, I bet it's a strategy companies use to give the appearance of a larger size, while in reality holding lesser volume."

The odd shape of perfume bottles *is* sensational, but I'm not having any of it.

"Yes, corporations are cunning indeed, but *hello?* Notice anything different about me?" I point to my face. "I can't believe I was too scared of Ma to do this earlier. Breanna fixed everything. She used concealer on the bags under my eyes, so I don't even look sleepy anymore."

Seema leans in. "Wow, yeah. You don't look sleepy. You look like you slept *forever.*" She waves her fingers at me, pursing her lips into an O.

"Huh?"

"You look like a ghost, Aish," Seema says. "She went way too light for Indian skin. Also, it flaked on your cheeks."

"It did?"

"Yep, it kinda looks like you face-planted on a white-sand beach."

Leave it to Seema to ruin everything. Even if her observations are true, would sugarcoating them be *such* a bad thing? Besides, it's not my fault I have dry skin. Michigan isn't exactly the most hospitable climate for my skin type. If Marcy was here, she would've gushed about how great I look. The only reason I didn't ask her instead is because I didn't want her to see how low my shopping budget is.

Seema notices my face clouding over and sighs.

"Hey, I'm not saying it looks bad. It's just, although I want to help you with your Manifest Destiny—"

"Manifesto," Quentin and I correct her.

She rolls her eyes. "Whatever. Although I want to help, I don't want you to depend on makeup to make yourself feel good."

"I won't. But you can't deny that I look way better than before." I eye Quentin, but he seems to be preoccupied with mining for more octahedral crystals. "What do you think, Quentin? Be honest."

"Um . . ." He's looking past me. "You look good either way."

"Did you also get the HR training here?" I grumble, and he gives me a quizzical look.

"What's next, Aish?" Seema asks, returning the octahedral crystal to its throne.

"How about Pressed Perfect? I saw that they have a sale on dresses."

"Their dresses unravel after, like, three washes."

"That's a price I'm willing to pay. Along with the low price of $7."

When we get to Pressed Perfect, Seema melts into the shoe section before I can ask her to help. To my surprise, Quentin doesn't take the opportunity to scurry off to the men's flannels.

"So what am I looking for here?"

I see a store attendant smile at us as she overhears him. I bet she thinks my boyfriend is helping me look for my size. My palms are sweating again. I don't know what I'm looking for. Anything that makes me look hot?

"Anything that's on sale and a size small."

"I'm going to see what you pick out first. Then I'll try to help find similar things."

He stands next to me as I thumb through dresses. His watchful gaze and faint pine scent are ruining my concentration. Is he thinking I can't pull any of these off? Is he thinking about how a woolly mammoth probably has less body hair than me? Indian women have a lot of hair. It's great when it's on top of our heads, but not so great when it's, well . . . *everywhere* else. A lot of these dresses are going to take some major razor to the leg.

I pluck a short black dress from the rack and hold it up to myself, trying to gauge how far up my thigh it will fall. Pretty high up. That means a lot of shaving. And what kind of bra do I need to wear under this?

"Hey, you okay?" Quentin asks, and when I look up, I realize he's been studying me. "You look kind of stressed."

I am. Somehow, I have gotten stressed by going to the mall. Leave it to me to get stressed by a recreational activity.

"I'm okay." I stick the black dress on the rack. "Can you help me choose?"

"Of course. Let's have you try on a bunch of different things you normally wouldn't." He pulls a top that has rainbow pinstripes off the rack and checks the size. "You said you tend to wear muted colors, right?" After a few minutes of putting tops up to my shoulders and *hmm*ing, he has an armful of clothes. He's even holding a few pairs of earrings—Indian-style filigree hoops, golden studs with pom-poms hanging from the ends. "To the fitting rooms?"

I squirm. Everything he's holding is so *noticeable*. That neon-yellow dress could single-handedly cure seasonal depression.

"We're going to the fitting rooms, not the gallows." His smile fades. "What's wrong? You don't like the clothes?"

I feel a strain in my chest, the strain that happens right before tears come. I can't wear this stuff out. What was I thinking? What's so wrong with my old wardrobe?

He touches my shoulder, lightly guiding me toward the back of the store. "C'mon. I think you need to sit down and take a break."

"There aren't any chairs."

He gives me a sly smile, and that's how I find myself sitting next to Quentin on the ledge of a Pressed Perfect ladies' fitting room, curtains drawn and our feet tapping on the tile. The clothes I was supposed to try on are hanging from a hook on the door. We're facing the mirror, and our reflections are slouching together. My puffy brown coat matches the stripes in his wool scarf.

"This is a really odd spot to take a break," I whisper. "And we're lucky there were no employees taking numbers in front of the fitting rooms like there usually are."

"I would've still charmed my way in."

Instead of facing Quentin, I watch his reflection. His cheeks are slightly flushed, and his eyes are catching the light of the Edison bulb hanging from the ceiling.

His shoulder brushes mine as he leans back. "Are you worried about blowing your savings on the makeover? I know you wanted to take that painting class."

"I do." I sigh. "I may not like sharing what I paint, but painting is the only thing that makes me feel like *me* sometimes." Unlike my AP Lit journal covered in eraser shavings and carets poking forgotten words into sentences, paint is final. It's a welcome stop sign on my expressway of overthinking.

"You shouldn't let that go, then, should you?"

His voice is gentle, and even though his questions are challenging me, they don't sound like accusations the way Seema's often do. I want to tell him about struggling with acne, but the words stick in my throat like honey. I've never pointed out my acne to anyone. I'm afraid naming it gives it more visibility, like Voldemort. But, seeing as Quentin is one of the few people I've cried in front of who isn't a family member, I have no dignity to lose.

"I guess it feels like I *should* change my look. As you probably noticed, I . . ." My gaze drops to my shoes. "I have a lot of acne. And because I'm so self-conscious, it makes being myself harder in general, especially . . ."

Quentin waits.

"Especially around Brian. So I have to *do* something about it if I have any chance of making conversation with him. Or anyone, for that matter."

I look down, wanting to shrink into the bench. Is he appraising my face for all the redness as we speak? Then I remember that luckily, a white-sand beach is covering my face at present.

"You don't have to do anything about it. And whenever you feel like you do, think about those fluffy Michigan red squirrels. They spend their days burying acorns, scaling trees, hangin' out. They probably don't even know what they look like. They don't question if they're beautiful or groom their fur to fit the newest squirrel standard. Being alive is enough for them." He scoots closer. "And sure, humans spend billions of dollars and hours on how we look, but at the end of the day, we're no different from squirrels. We're bags of bones and fur, too, and no one's gonna remember what our skin or clothes looked when we—*ka-blam*—die."

I stare at him. "'Ka-blam,' huh? How comforting."

"My *point* is that, ultimately, people remember you for how you made them feel. So if anyone thinks less of you for something as inconsequential as acne, it means they're not worth your time. That includes Brian."

If only *I* could stop thinking less of me. I usually would save prying questions for a tenth meeting, but I feel like asking now. "Can I ask you something personal?"

"Of course. A ladies' fitting room is made for that sort of thing." He gives me a small smile, resting his chin in his hands and propping his elbows on his knees. I spot a few freckles on his cheeks that I've never noticed before.

"Do you have a girlfriend?"

"*Really?* That's your question?"

I blush. "Yeah. I'm very curious. I assume you do because I feel like if a room of girls heard you recite that squirrel speech, they'd love you forever. Which leads me to believe you have a *source*. On the inside."

"I do have a source, but I don't have a girlfriend."

"Oh."

Maybe he's gay.

"And I'm straight, if that was your next question."

"Oh."

Maybe he's suffering a slow death by unrequited love, too.

"My source is my mom. She helped me through my am-I-really-not-growing-another-inch phase, when I measured how tall I was almost every week and kept hanging off monkey bars to get taller. She used to work as a cosmetic chemist after graduating with her chemical engineering degree, so she knows about the marketing that goes into making everyone insecure about how they look. And the toxins in makeup."

I know that frosting my face with makeup every day will not solve my issues, but at least it will brand me as something other than Smart Indian Girl. I'd be more widely known for my killer eyeliner.

I twist a strand of hair around my finger. "I'm probably going to die young from my overconsumption of processed food anyway, so I might as well add in some lead from lipstick, eh?"

"Pencil lead is more you." He suddenly springs to his feet. "Aisha, I have an idea. Let's think of the worst things someone could say about the stuff we brought in here."

"Huh?"

"It'll help you think more like a playful squirrel, less like a self-conscious human. Let me demonstrate." He turns to the mass of dangling clothes and jewelry and plucks the first one off. It's a bomber jacket covered in silver sequins. "Is this a jacket or a—or a . . . deflated disco ball?"

I giggle. "That was terrible."

He holds up a sheer, cream-colored fringe blouse with strings of crystals hanging from the bottom. "Your turn."

I think for a few moments. "Is that a blouse or a lampshade?"

He snickers and picks a short black dress with triangular cut-outs on either side of the waist. "This looks like someone cut a hole in the dress while it was folded."

"Is that a dress or were you trying to make a pop-up card for Mother's Day?"

We guffaw, and after a few more, I feel better. I finally shoo Quentin from the fitting room and try on *everything*. Even that bomber jacket that could be seen from space. It feels more like a game now, and less like *Aisha v. Clothes*. As soon as I'm done, Quentin comes back and helps me put everything back on the hangers. He's using the ribbon loops inside the shirts to make sure they stay put. I didn't even know that's what they were for.

"I'm not sure what mind trick you played," I say, "but I somehow just had *fun* trying on clothes. Usually, I criticize myself in my head the whole time. You should start a life coach brand. I'll draw you a squirrel logo and everything."

"I always wondered if life coaches give life-ruining advice so their clients keep coming back."

As soon as we finish gathering our things, I spot Seema plodding through the hallway, a blouse draped over her arm.

"Look, she has one of the lampshades," Quentin whispers, nudging me, and I giggle.

She freezes in her tracks when she sees us, giving me a stern look. "Were you guys in a fitting room *together*? Listen, I'm a cool sister when it comes to buying makeup, Aish, but there are some things I cannot—"

"*What?* We were just taking a break because there are no chairs!"

"I'm kidding. Relax." She snorts. "You're afraid that eating your baby carrots at the public library will disturb the peace, so I highly doubt you'd be capable of sucking face in a mall fitting room."

Sucking face? I groan at the same time Quentin chuckles. I can't look at him. The flush of my cheeks is probably apparent through the layer of sand—er, *makeup*—on my face.

"I'll see you guys outside." Seema gives me a Cheshire cat smile.

"Your sister likes messing with you," Quentin notes, and I grunt in response, storming toward the registers. That's always how it's been. I think she goes too far. She thinks I'm oversensitive. I was willing to overlook this in exchange for her expert fashion sense, but I didn't even get any help from her today.

Seema buys the lampshade blouse, and I buy a corduroy skirt with an embroidered chili pepper patch, a rainbow pin-striped top, red jeans, a polka-dot sweater, and the cutout dress. I wasn't sure about pulling off that dress, but ever since thinking of it as a pop-up card, I feel better.

"Now that shopping's done, snacks on me," Seema says, and I realize that'll be pretty much the only helpful thing she's said all day. As we wait in line at Jamba, I watch kids snap photos with a seven-foot cardboard Santa.

"Wait, I almost forgot." Quentin reaches into his messenger bag and hands me a black Sharpie.

"Is this supposed to save me from buying eyeliner?" I ask.

"No . . ." He pulls a square of paper from his bag, holding it out to me. It's the *Change up my look* sticky note I pasted on his wall. "I brought it for you to do the honors of crossing it off."

I rest the note on my thigh, drawing a shaky line through my handwriting. As I give it back to him, I feel kind of proud of myself, dare I say it.

After we get our drinks and snacks, we find a spot on a bench in front of a stone fountain. Seema and Quentin sit on either side of me. For a few minutes, we kick our feet back and forth and take in the dull roar of mall chatter. I notice pennies glinting on the fountain's floor.

"What do you think people wished for?" I ask, taking a slurp of my watermelon smoothie.

"I've seen an obscene amount of awkward teenagers today, and I believe they all wished for their crush to notice them." Seema rips into her cinnamon pretzel with her teeth. As she does, the powdered sugar rains onto my shoes, but she doesn't seem to notice. I shake my head, brushing the sugar off, and Quentin stifles a smile as he looks on.

"Maybe they wished for a solution to climate change," I offer, but as I do, I know it's not true.

"Unlikely. But I don't blame 'em for wanting some love. High school is a hard time, especially for Indian kids, since we're all unequivocally hideous during our adolescence."

Quentin almost chokes on his Veggie Vitality juice.

"Oh, c'mon. It's a straight fact that our prime comes later. I bet even Priyanka Chopra's high school photos came out terrible." She rests her half-ravaged pretzel on a napkin placed on the granite ledge, dusts her hands off, and looks at me. "That's why I came along for your thing today. I know you've been struggling to feel normal at school. I did, too, and I wished I had someone. Not even to talk to necessarily, but to just be there."

I nod. "Yeah, and that's about all you were today. There."

She slaps my arm. "Shut up. You know I'm that person who comes late to the party and signs the card of another person's gift, but I still care. And I know school is hard. It can feel like home and school are separate lives. We don't have enough space to express the duality of our lives all at once—the macaroni-and-cheese-loving parts and the biryani-loving parts." Seema nudges Quentin. "You get me, right?"

"I do." He nods. "It does feel like I have to choose sometimes. Like I can't be both Filipino and Italian. It's almost too hard for people to get that you're many things."

"And I've realized you shouldn't make yourself smaller so that people get it." She shrugs. "But hey, change is afoot. People are adding turmeric to their lattes now. It's only a matter of time before Jamba Juice jumps on board."

"It's Jamba," I murmur, and Quentin gives me a look.

"You're right," he says. "My mom puts turmeric in her face masks now."

Seema gives me a delighted smile. "See? We're taking over the world, Aish, one teaspoon of haldi at a time. And best news is, everything that happens in high school won't matter in the future. The world is a lot bigger than Arledge Prep."

"Maybe." I sigh. "But it's hard to think that when you're in it."

"Sure is. I spent all of high school caring about what other people think, too. Like, let's pretend I showed up to school back then and saw someone with a giant monkey sitting on their head. The logical reaction would've been to scream and ask what's going on, right?"

"Um, yeah . . ." Quentin eyes Seema like *she* has a monkey on her head.

"Well, all high schoolers are in panic mode. So instead, my first thought would have been, 'Wait, should I *also* have a monkey on my head? Did I forget my monkey at home?'"

I snicker. "Relatable."

"I'm just saying, don't try too hard to make high school great. I still have dreams that I forgot my locker combination, so I can't guarantee you'll be *totally* free, but . . ." Seema rests her hand on the top of my head. "You're going to be okay. Things will change. Keep that in mind for your manifestation."

"*Manifesto*," Quentin and I correct her, and Seema groans.

"Ugh, whatever."

Quentin and I exchange smiles, and we all return to our snacks in silence. I think about what I'd wish for if I had a penny to toss into the fountain. I wish I could say that I'm an enlightened monk, and that I wouldn't wish for getting into Stanford or Brian liking me back because that's for chumps, etcetera.

But I'm still me. I'm totally wishing for both of those things.

12
MY AMERICAN DREAM

✔ Get invited
to a cool party

Every state has a particular peak moment that's used in all advertising for that state forevermore. Vermont's is an autumn forest. California's is a beach sunset. Michigan's is a snowy cottage with a lake view.

There's something about the days before winter break that makes everyone cheery in Michigan. Although our windshields and driveways are freezing over, it's welcomed because it coincides with curling up with hot cider and cinnamon apples. The bus driver says hello when you get on the bus instead of grunting. The student council president starts wearing a Santa hat during announcements.

I've always loved the holidays, but this year feels like it's charged with even more possibility, especially after I acquired a cheap makeup collection from Walgreens. (When I got there, I texted Seema asking which makeup brand gives the biggest bang for your buck, and she replied, **Acrylic**. I almost searched for that brand until I realized she was messing with me and meant acrylic paint, but even *that* couldn't get me down.)

Now I'm humming a tune as I line my eyes with a dark blue eyeliner in the Arledge Prep girls' bathroom. I catapulted myself from the bus this morning to beat the crowd. I had also emptied my pencil pouch and put my makeup in it, a place Ma would never check. It's sometimes a whole CIA covert operation being an Indian kid.

As I struggle to zip my bulging pencil pouch over the blush brush, about to give up, I hear slow footsteps. Lily Perez. Her dark, straight hair falls over her shoulders like a shiny waterfall. She nods, barely acknowledging me as she slips into a stall. I was hoping for an "Oh, you look different," considering I spent hours watching online tutorials to re-create this look, but I shouldn't have expected anything from Lily.

The class sizes at Arledge are smaller for personalized instruction *and* all the nonwhite kids know each other by default, but Lily and I haven't spoken much. Marcy tells me I'm imagining it, but I'm convinced Lily secretly hates me. She gives me tight smiles and blank stares whenever I joke around at crochet club to lighten the mood. She takes crochet too seriously. It's not like our scarves are going to be sold at Anthropologie. They're going to end up in a memory box in the attic, so I don't get the serious looks. Maybe she dislikes me because I ran against her for president of crochet club, but I didn't win. Besides, I like to think of myself as so invisible that I can't be hated. It's like hating nitrogen—who has the energy for that?

I hear the first bell ring, and I finger-comb the wisps of my hair that frame my face before leaving the bathroom. Usually, I keep my head down when I wander the Arledge halls, but today, I manage to make eye contact with students as they amble by. I stand straighter. A few people smile at me, and Kevin waves as he passes. Sure, the crowd isn't parting for me, and there are no murmurs of, "Who's that girl? Is she new?" Still, I *feel* new. Now that my screaming chimples have been quieted with foundation, the leftover space can be filled with Quentin-y Zen vibes. If I rolled out a yoga mat right now, I'd magically be able to do the splits. If I joined a ballet class, I'd nail my pirouette.

When I get to Ms. Kavnick's classroom, I look for Brian, but he's not there yet. I take my usual seat next to Marcy, and as soon as she sees me, she shuts her textbook.

"Oh my."

"Don't look at me like that. I texted you last night that I bought some makeup, remember?"

Marcy leans in so close that I squirm. "I should've asked you to do my makeup for formal. When did you get so good at this?"

"It honestly wasn't too different from an AP Chem lab experiment." I can't stop my smile from spilling over my lips. Is this what school could have been like this whole time? With me *not* feeling like shoving myself into my locker for once?

As Ms. Kavnick pulls down the projector screen, Brian enters, right on time. My eyes meet his, and maybe I'm imagining it, but I think he smiles.

"All right, kiddos." Ms. Kavnick gathers her cardigan around her. "This is the last week before winter break. I'm not going to ask what your plans are, because I already know. Your plans will be completing a practice AP free-response question I'm going to assign today."

Moans ripple through the class, but Ms. Kavnick simply places a stack of paper on Lily's desk. In every class I've been in with Lily, she takes on the role of passing out paper handouts.

Considering there's no extra credit for it, I can't for the life of me understand why.

"This sample fiction prompt will have you analyze how an excerpt from *The Grapes of Wrath* depicts the American Dream. It's related to some of the themes we covered during our discussion of *The Great Gatsby*. And, because the holidays are coming up, I do have a little gift for you all."

Everyone leans forward.

"You can work in groups of up to four. And I'll give you all of class time today to work."

Collective sigh of relief.

"Before we get into groups, though, it's important that we define the American Dream as it's presented in the text. Can anyone explain the concept?" She uncaps her Expo marker and scans the room for victims.

Maybe it's the fact that I'm on a manifesto that feels like my version of the American Dream, or maybe it's that I'm hopped up on morning makeup energies, but I raise my arm. It's not a confident tree-branch arm. It's more of a tentative, bendy-twig arm, but Marcy gives me the proudest smile, like I've just volunteered for the Peace Corps. She often complains that I should've continued as staff writer for the *Antelope Times* because, and I quote, "on the off chance you say something, it's usually decent."

Ms. Kavnick nods at me. "Aisha?"

"It's the belief that all people should have equal opportunity. If you work hard, you can have a better life." My voice shakes, but at least it comes out audible.

Ms. Kavnick scribbles on the whiteboard. "That's right. It's the idea that upward mobility is available to everyone. Now, I want you all to think about your own opinions on that, and the idea of meritocracy in general. Do you believe that poverty is a choice? Do you believe hard work guarantees success, no matter what? Keep in mind the subjectivity of success we discussed in our last unit when we read *Gatsby*."

Making sacrifices, working hard. Those are the words people often use in relation to immigrant families. My parents were no exception. Maybe that's why I have no answers to the Stanford essay question—my parents left their comfort zone so I wouldn't have to.

I always thought the process of migrating to a new place was the toughest part, but considering our family drives an hour out of Arledge to get to a temple, I think settling here was toughest. It's the small things. My parents don't see their own parents more than once every few years since the flight is long and expensive. They still don't understand Halloween. Pa's always saying, *We clean our house and remove cobwebs to welcome Goddess Lakshmi on Diwali, while Americans add cobwebs to their homes on purpose!* They don't have any neighbors to speak Hindi with. Ma dropped out of her bioengineering program at Stanford to take care of my sister. That's the tapestry of our family, woven from sweat and tears, which is why I'm so obsessed with Stanford. I have to complete what Ma wasn't able to do.

Right then, Marcy's booming voice pulls me out of my thoughts.

"I think the American Dream is a hope, not a reality. Our generation has crippling student debt. Even if we go to college, it hardly means that we'll be financially secure. There are a lot of factors that influence whether you'll be successful, like the zip code you grow up in, the education you have access to, your family situation . . ."

Even though Marcy is a member of My Parents Can Afford My Tuition club, I like that she doesn't ignore the issues of the general populace.

"And your body," Lily adds. "You might be starting with a physical or learning disability, which can make it difficult to go to school or work."

Ms. Kavnick pens a summarized version on the whiteboard of what Marcy and Lily said.

"All great points. In the text, the Joad family was looking for a better life, but they realize the way they imagined California is far from reality. To them, the American Dream turned out to be a false promise. Some say college is also a false promise. But . . ." Ms. Kavnick faces the class. "The most important and interesting part of AP Literature is that these texts have nuance and support multiple interpretations. Is there anyone who believes in the concept of the American Dream? Or anyone who thinks poverty is a choice?"

From the corner of my eye, I see Brian raise his hand.

"Some people may have a head start, but I still believe America's structures allow you to grow your wealth even if you're starting with nothing. And I think there are people who are too lazy to try to change their situation, so they simply wait for government handouts or stay in a dead-end job."

I'm thinking Ms. Kavnick will ask Marcy or Lily for a rebuttal, but she simply writes his point on the board. Then she caps her marker. "Great discussion. Now let's form groups. Try to include people who have different opinions from yours. The prompt asks to explore both sides of the issue in the text, so multiple perspectives will make for the strongest essays."

Students scramble around the room. As expected, I cling to Marcy like Velcro. Lily is sitting behind me, so I ask her to join us, and she offers her usual curt nod. We're about to start writing when Ms. Kavnick ambles over to our pod of desks.

"Brian has a different opinion from you. It might add some layers to your essay, so I asked him to join your group."

We exchange looks. My pulse quickens as Brian appears from behind Ms. Kavnick's looming figure. He pushes a desk right against mine. As he sits, I take in a floral scent that reminds me of fresh laundry. It makes me want to bury my face in his Arledge sweater. I look down.

"Hey, groupies." He must be so close if I'm able to hear the vibrations of his voice this crisply.

"Hi, Brian," Marcy says, her eyes crinkling as she looks at me, like, *Boy, am I gonna enjoy this.*

"I'm thinking we can analyze the text for literary devices together, and then split up the devices we want to write about." Brian twirls his pencil in his hand. How does he spin it around his thumb like that? I wonder. Is that how he would've spun me at winter formal—confident, quick, passionate? Lily takes one tired look at Brian and pokes her earphones into her ears, burying her face in her wall of hair as she begins writing in her notebook without us. So much for group work.

"Sounds good," I squeak, keeping my eyes glued to my hands. Watching Brian spin his pencil is making *my* head spin.

Marcy bends forward. "I'm interested to see how the two

contenders for valedictorian work together on an assignment. Will there be sabotage?"

Brian rolls his eyes. "Aisha and I were project partners in middle school all the time." He gives me one of those tiny smiles of his, like we're sharing a secret, and my heart jumps.

"And I guess it's not necessarily down to both of us," I add. "There could be others in the running."

Marcy chews on the end of her pencil. "By the way, nice eyeliner, Aisha."

My eyes go wide. She must have a diabolical plan—she always does. Brian looks at me, and I shrink into my seat. "Th-Thanks."

"I'm loving the new look," Marcy presses on, and I notice from the corner of my eye that even Lily has punched out a single earphone to eavesdrop. "Is it part of the manifesto?"

"Manifesto?" Brian echoes, putting down his pencil. I notice his arm muscles. Smooth and sculpted. How will I get any work done with him in my group? "A manifesto for what?"

I bite my lip. There's no avoiding telling him now. "I'm just trying to get out of my comfort zone a little. The Stanford application essay asks about how you've gotten out of your comfort zone, and I realized I didn't have an answer. So I made a list of things to do that make me uncomfortable. I'm doing them so I can write a better essay, but also for me."

"Like a bucket list." He beams. "That's cool."

I shrug like it's no big deal.

"It's an ambitious list. I don't know how she's going to finish it all on her own." Marcy takes in a long breath, like she's grieving for her spouse who never came back from the war. She conveniently left out the fact that Quentin is helping me.

"What kind of stuff is on the list?" Brian looks intrigued,

and Marcy looks at me like *I got him now.*

"Well," she starts, brushing invisible fuzz balls from the sleeves of her monogrammed Arledge sweater, "there are a lot of simple things, like swimming and baking. But there are also harder ones, like going to a party with drinking and beer pong and everything . . ." She bats her eyelashes at Lily. "Maybe our resident crochet club president knows about a rager happening soon?" As Lily scowls, I can't help but chuckle. I'm surprised she was even listening for this long.

"Actually, you might not need Lily's help there." Brian's dark eyes lock with mine. "My friend Sanjay is throwing this New Year's Eve party at his parents' house. They'll be out of town for some conference. If you want to come, you're welcome to."

Ambulances go off in my brain, and all my thoughts pull over to clear the way for this moment. This *very* historic moment.

"Sanjay said I can invite whoever," Brian adds.

"*Whom*ever," Lily mumbles, and even in my shock, I manage to catch that.

"Really? We'd *love* to come." Marcy's sugary voice makes it sound like Brian volunteered to pay for her unborn child's college education.

"If it somehow helps with the Stanford essay, it's the least I could do. Especially after winter formal and . . . everything."

A few weeks ago, Brian and I were light-years away from each other's solar systems. Now he's a meteor hurtling toward the delicate balance of my planets. A million thoughts pop into my head, like tiny black holes erupting in the fabric of the universe:

1. Brian invited me to a party.
2. Marcy should be a war strategist.

3. There's no chance my parents will let me stay out much later than midnight, even if it is New Year's Eve.

4. Going to a party with alcohol sounded like a fun rite of passage in theory, but what if I get arrested for underage drinking and go to juvie?

5. I could wear the cutout dress I got from the mall.

6. This is my chance to cross off my *Kiss someone at midnight on New Year's* sticky note.

7. Brian invited *me* to a party?!

I'm so caught in the chutes and ladders inside my head that I have no idea what to say back to Brian. Of all people, Lily comes to my rescue.

"Can I come, too?" she asks, yanking out her other earphone. We all turn to look at her. For a moment, I think she's being sarcastic. Then I see her set lips, which look like a literal line segment, and I realize she's serious.

Brian looks surprised as he runs a hand through his hair. I swear, that is the shiny hair of a unicorn's mane. "Sure, Lily. Sanjay wouldn't mind."

"Does this Sanjay person go here?" Marcy asks. "And is he cute? Asking for a friend."

I glare at her, and she shrugs, like *What? I am.*

"I'd say he's an attractive guy, but no, he's a senior at Kresge," Brian answers, and my eyes widen.

Kresge High. That's where Quentin goes.

If I ask Quentin to come to the party, he'll probably know people there. Plus, I'll have someone to drive me home. Marcy is probably going to end up staying super late playing board games in another room. She brings Bananagrams with the expansion pack to every party and waits until the crowd thins to round up victims. *It's portable and approachable—everything you want in a game*, she claims.

"We'llbethere." I throw the words from my tongue before they drop back into my throat. "And can I bring a friend?"

Marcy mouths at me, *Quentin?* And I nod.

"Absolutely, bring anyone you like," Brian says, giving me a bright smile that reminds me of his fifth-grade yearbook photo. "An AP Lit reunion outside of school, huh?"

I'm hoping there's no dancing at this party because I look like a writhing fish out of water when I dance. With that comforting thought, the bell rings. As we all get up, I realize we got nothing done. I was too enchanted by Brian's pencil spins. It was Olympic figure skating as far as I'm concerned.

"We got nothing done," Marcy moans, as if reading my mind, and shuts her binder with a start. It's one of those rustic leather kinds that cost way more than binders should be allowed to cost. Marcy's financial situation doesn't drip from her like juice from a melting Popsicle. You'd only know if you noted the little things—unmarred binders and weighty Japanese mechanical pencils. (Besides, most days she forgets her pencil pouch at home and ends up using my cheap pencils with scratchy lead.)

"You want to work on the essay in the library after school?" Marcy asks us, and I'm about to answer when Lily mumbles that she has crochet club and then disappears into the herd of students stampeding to the cafeteria for lunch.

"I don't have practice today," Brian offers. "I'm in."

"Me too," I pipe up. I did have a crochet club meeting, but not anymore. No way I pass on this opportunity to watch more pencil spins. Besides, I doubt Lily will be *too* broken up if I don't show up this week. "Can you give me a ride home if we finish later, Marce? My family is going to an event at around five p.m."

I'm intentionally generic with *event*, but it's a puja at the Bhartiya Temple. Ever since college application season began, my parents have been going to the temple a lot.

I'm sure the two are unrelated.

"Well, I *would* drive you home, but I'm working on stuff for the yearbook club after. And Kevin and I have to finish the layout for next week's paper . . ." She sighs. "Speaking of, any update on finally writing me a guest op-ed?"

I bite my lip. "Sorry, Marce. You know my application essays come before the op-ed. But I'll wait at the library until you're done today."

"I might finish late. And I know your parents like you to be home for dinner." She looks at Brian like, *Now that you're paying for one of my children's college educations, you might as well pay for another, right?*

Brian gets the hint, pulling on the straps of his backpack. "Uh, I can give you a ride home, Aisha."

Marcy smiles. I know it to be a smile of unadulterated evil—the smiley on those "smile, you're on camera" signs at stores—but you have to know Marcy well to understand all her smiles and the level of evil associated with each.

In five minutes of intervening, she has accomplished more for my social life than I have in my seventeen years of trying.

13
LONG DRIVE HOME

✔ Invite Quentin over

After school, Marcy, Brian, and I meet at the library to finish the essay. I sit across from Brian, and Marcy sits next to him. I think she intentionally gave me the seat with the view.

"Lily texted me that she'll work on adding in examples from the text over winter break, so if we get the argument structure down today, we'll be pretty much done," Marcy says. "I marked some moments from the book that highlight the poignancy of the American Dream's failure. At the end, Rose of Sharon feeds a starving man her own breast milk, so there's that."

"I don't know," Brian says, leaning forward in his chair. "Rose doing that also shows that the community fabric is still intact. When I read that, I thought Steinbeck was conveying hope. Or implying that the community could come together and push for reform. Tom and Casy also fought against the system even though rebelling risked their lives."

"What about the turtle in chapter three? The turtle crossing the Oklahoma highway symbolizes the impossible journey of the migrant farmers, right?"

"Or their endurance."

Marcy lets out a sigh of exasperation. "Aisha, you love turtles. What do you think?"

"Uh . . ." They're both looking at me. Although I agree more with Marcy's take, I don't want to outright say so. "Maybe both of your thoughts aren't mutually exclusive. The turtle could mean both—it may be helpless, but it still endures. That's what the farmers did—they struggled, but they kept trying to find work and feed their families."

That's how the conversation goes on, and I let Brian and Marcy do most of the talking. Brian seems fired up about defending the government's shortcomings and unequal distribution of wealth in the book, and I can't quite understand why. I assumed anyone with parents who immigrated to the United States would know that the government doesn't make it easy for immigrants. And in middle school, he loved comic books about everyday people rising against a tyrannical force. Maybe he's playing devil's advocate?

When Marcy has to scurry off to yearbook club, I watch her leave in the panicked way I watched Pa remove the training wheels from my bike in fifth grade. Then Brian and I make our way to his car. I've often watched his car pulling out of school, imagining what it would be like to ride with him and talk like old times. I guess I've gotten into *two* cars I never thought I would get into recently.

"Do you need directions?" I'm ready to pluck my phone out of my skirt pocket.

"C'mon, Aisha. I remember your building. And your orange apartment door."

I play with the tips of my scarf. As Brian drives out of the school lot, I mine my brain for a conversation topic.

"How's the Stanford essay going?" Brian asks. One hand is on the steering wheel, and one hand is resting on the center console, inches away from mine. He's collected. When I drive, I'm choking the steering wheel with my hands, expecting flying red squirrels to parachute down from the trees at any moment.

"I've been writing, but it's all, um, terrible." I thought wearing makeup would change things, but it still feels like my words have migrated south of my brain for the winter when I'm around Brian. "How are things with your mom?"

"She's still on my case about college applications. Are your parents also panicking?"

"Not really. My mom said I should 'leave it up to God and that whatever happens now, happens for a reason.'"

I have that sentence memorized. If I had a nickel for every time that was said in my household, I would have at least a dozen of Marcy's fancy leather binders by now.

"Wonder if she means that."

"I think she'd be disappointed if I don't get into Stanford, but I'd be devastated."

"I'll bet. Any opportunity to get out of this town is a good opportunity."

"Exactly," I agree automatically, but I like Arledge and its fall pumpkin patches and springtime art fairs and quaint cafés.

Brian pulls up in front of my apartment building and stops the car. He turns to look at me, and my heart goes haywire, like pages of an open book in the wind. It's those eyes. Every time I think I'm in remission, his eyes bring me back to square one. It's the familiarity of his gaze that hasn't changed since we were kids, paired with his new, well, *hotness*.

"So, about your manifesto. Can I apply to participate?"

My eyes widen. "What do you mean?"

"I want to help you with your list. I owe you for winter formal, and I feel like it would take my mind off college apps. And Riley, to be honest. She's actually . . . dating someone new already."

All hail Queen Marcy. Her plan is working a little *too* well.

"Seriously? I'd *love* help." I imagine Quentin getting replaced by Brian in all the sticky note scenarios. Everything would turn romantic—a sepia filter for every experience.

"I'm at your service. Send me a picture of the notes later."

"I will!" My voice goes high. "You can decide which ones you might want to help with. No pressure, of course."

I intend to become a bit of an art director for that picture. I'll group the sticky notes to include ones that'll give me the most time with Brian. Maybe I can even leave the midnight kiss note in the picture, but a little cut off like, *Oops, didn't mean to put that one in!*

"Sounds like a plan. And can I ask you a question?"

Is he asking me out? Is he going to ask for a dance, the one that we couldn't have at winter formal? Is he—

"Who's that guy talking to your sister?"

I turn to see Quentin.

"*What the*—" I unbuckle my seat belt, resisting the urge to press my face to the car window for a better look. He's outside my redbrick apartment building making grand hand gestures at Seema, and Seema is teetering back and forth next to him, giggling. This moment feels like last week when I was listening to "Close to You" by the Carpenters, and then my earphones' wire caught on my doorknob, ripping the romance from my ears.

"Um, it's just someone I tutor sometimes."

I feel a twinge of guilt. I guess it's unfair to call Quentin *just* someone I tutor. And considering we've been meeting at least twice a week, *sometimes* isn't right, either.

"His wheels are ancient." Brian points to the Jetta parked a few paces ahead. "Is that his car?"

"Yep. It's old, but it runs."

"Jeez, not for long."

I'm struck by this curious gathering. How did Quentin get here? What secrets of mine are being divulged? Is my sister telling Quentin that I used to call the condensation on cups "cup sweat" as a kid? I'm about to bust open the door when Brian touches my shoulder.

"Hey, wait."

"Yeah?" He's awakened nerve endings in my shoulder I didn't even know existed.

"I also wanted to ask—what are your plans for winter break?"

"Same as you. Sanjay's New Year's Eve party, remember?" I turn my palms skyward and pulse my hands up and down.

Brian laughs. "Based on that dance move, I don't know if it's gonna be your scene." Whenever I make Brian laugh, I feel a *zing*—like I've just sent the ball flying upward in a game of pinball. "If you don't have plans for the rest of break, Kevin and I are going ice-skating on New Year's Day. I think Kevin's going to ask Marcy, and if you're not busy with your Stanford app, would you want to come, too?"

Omigod.

I don't know how to ice-skate. At all. Yet Brian's dark brown eyes are confusing me and dimming every trace of logic in my brain, the way cellular reception fades as you drive farther north in Michigan. This is the double-date dream.

"Sure! I mean, yes! I'd love to."

"You know how to ice-skate, yeah?" His eyes search mine.

"Yeah!"

Oh, Aisha, what have you done.

I jump out and wrestle my backpack from the back seat. It resists my pull at first, like a kid being dragged out of a candy shop. As I take one last look at Brian, my brain drops into a taffy pulling machine, twisting in ten thousand directions. "Thanks for the ride."

Brian doesn't look back as his car fires forward. When I turn around, Seema and Quentin are waving at me. I smile, but it comes out more as a grimace. My sister flies toward me, leaving Quentin standing alone in front of the door of my apartment building.

"My dear sister, how you've grown!" she sings, clamping her hands around my shoulders. "Aren't you overjoyed that I've officially returned from my studies to celebrate the holidays with you? To give you three weeks of *bliss*?"

I wriggle out of her viselike grip. "Yeah, so glad to have someone hogging the remote again. It just wasn't the same when I could watch whenever I wanted."

There's a beautiful space of silence, but I know it'll pass. Three, two—

"Why are you wearing your uniform skirt? I know the wool pants aren't sexy, but it's better than catching a cold. And don't forget to take off your makeup with the removal pads I gave you before going upstairs, or Ma will see and blow her top. Also, did Brian give you a ride? I haven't seen that kid in forever."

"We were just at the library."

"Wait, do you still like him?" She lowers her voice. "I'm pretty sure you used to be obsessed with him. Remember how you gave him the best valentines from our card packs, and you took Mandarin for your elective with Mr. Bore just because Brian took it?"

"I'm not *obsessed* with Brian! And it wasn't Mr. Bore, it was Mr. *Boris.*"

"Yeah, but everyone called him Mr. Bore since he went on tangents." She holds up her hands. "Just sayin'."

This is the usual mood when talking to Seema. My insides are revealed against my will and squashed. Delightful. Quentin saunters up to join us, his eyes flicking from my sour expression to my sister's self-congratulatory look.

"What are we talking about?"

"Nothing." How is he here, in his usual navy-blue winter jacket with the furry hood? It's a bizarre crossover episode between Home Life and Extracurricular Life. "What in the *world* are you doing here?"

"I told him he could hang out in our apartment building game room for a bit." Seema shrugs. "He apparently texted you earlier, but you didn't respond, so he texted me asking if he could come over."

"But *why* did you come over?" I insist.

He looks taken aback. "Hello to you, too."

I study him, knowing there must be more to this, but I have other pressing matters to address. "I texted you at lunch. About Brian driving me home and Sanjay's party. Did you see it?"

"Yeah, and I responded. It's funny, I used to be pretty close friends with Sanjay."

Upon hearing this, I bounce on the balls of my feet, almost jogging in place. "Really? So, will you come with me?"

"I'll ask my mom. I'm pretty sure I can go if—"

"Wait, there's more!" The words spew out before I register that I'm interrupting him. "Brian just asked me to go ice-skating with him, Kevin, and Marcy."

"*What?*" He holds up his hand for a high five, and as I slap it, he says, "This is amazing. Your manifesto is really taking off. *Go on a date*, check."

"Wait, wait." Seema turns to Quentin. "You're *helping* Aisha with Brian stuff? That's hilarious because I honestly thought *you* liked—"

"NO!" Quentin and I exclaim in unison, and then exchange looks.

I figured Quentin would never like me after everything he knows, but his vehement *NO* confirms it. I don't mind. The absence of romantic potential allows me to relax around him. Besides, I can't blame him. It's like when you watch a bad music video for a song that you originally thought was okay—you can't unsee the video. I'm sure he can't unsee me pathetically sobbing in his car and going on about my chimples at the mall, and I can't unsee the fact that he saw.

"O-kay. Sor-ray." Seema turns to me, and I know she's wondering if I'm lying. I shake my head at her, like *I don't like him, I swear.* And I mean it. My heartbeat is steady as a metronome around him.

"And you're going ice-skating with that boy?" she asks me.

Quentin's interest is piqued. "*That* boy? Do you not like him?"

"He has a checkered past. He didn't deserve to be forgiven so quickly after standing Aisha up like that for winter formal, either."

"He explained it!" I protest. "His mom is strict, so it's been hard for him. Deep down, he's a nice person."

"*Everyone* is nice deep down, Aish, but you hope it's not scuba-diving-in-the-Maldives deep down, you know?"

Quentin smirks, and I shoot paintballs at him with my eyes. "Well, *I* like him."

Seema raises her eyebrows. "It's cool you're admitting it. Even if it did mean an entire year with Mr. Bore." Her phone lights up. Must be her latest college heartthrob. She heads toward the door of our apartment building. "I'm gonna take this. You kids have fun."

"So, who's Mr. Bore?" Quentin asks brightly as soon as she's out of earshot, and I narrow my eyes.

"Why did you *really* come over? You did not come to say hi."

"I'll be honest. When you texted me that Brian was driving you home, I made this plan to show up at your house. So that he'd see me."

"*What?*"

"Jealousy is a foolproof strategy." He shrugs, like *Basic physics*.

"Did you *actually*—"

He laughs. "C'mon, don't flatter yourself. I forgot my house key. My mom wasn't going to be home from work for a while, so I needed a place to kill time. I thought you'd just be getting home from crochet club, so I texted you, but you didn't respond."

"*Then?*" I must know all about the events happening in every village corner of my kingdom.

"Then I had the idea to text Seema. She let me hang out in your apartment's game room. That's it, you didn't miss much."

I feel like that time in fifth grade when my parents took Seema and me to the Cedar Point amusement park and didn't let me go on half the rides because I was too young. "When did you and Seema even exchange numbers?"

"The day we went to the mall."

I don't know why my territorial tiger stripes are flashing. It's just, sometimes it feels like Seema already has everything: she's beautiful, she's studying premed, she has a million friends texting her. Hanging out with Quentin was the one thing that was *mine*.

He pulls up the hood of his coat, shivering from the icy wind. The fur frames his face, and a few of his curls spill out. "Congratulations on being asked out twice. It's like a double feature."

"Thanks . . ." I clear my throat. "About that. There's one more *tiny* thing I might need your help with."

He watches me for a few moments before groaning and clutching his head in his hands. "Fudge nuggets."

"Wow, do you even know what I'm going—"

"You can't ice-skate, can you?"

I give him the toothy grin of a kid hoping their crayon scribble drawing will be put on the fridge.

"All right, all right, I'll teach you. Stop looking at me like that. It's creeping me out."

My drawing-on-fridge smile pulls wider. "You're the best, you know that? And how about we make macarons together next Friday, after tutoring? We can cross that off the sticky note wall plus bring them to the party."

A smile tugs on the corner of his mouth. "You want to bring

homemade French macarons to a high school party? Just a thought, but I feel like they *might* not be appreciated by drunk seniors."

"They're for Brian. It'll be a poetic end to the Asian Tupperware War. I can put the macarons in the Tupperware that Brian's mom gave me and return it to him."

Considering Brian always looks so polished, I'm sure he'd appreciate neat-looking French macarons. Besides, everyone knows the best breakup remedy is sugar.

"Why, of course. *Tupperware.* The key element of every epic teen romance."

"Oh, shut it."

"Maybe we can make the macarons at your house. We're getting our bathroom walls repainted."

I gulp. I've never invited any of my Arledge friends over to my tiny apartment, much less a *boy.* Marcy drops me off outside my building whenever she gives me a ride home. Aside from the fact my apartment is cramped, I know my parents will say something embarrassing, and my friends might be put off by the smell of ghee and our Ganesha statue. I can imagine Lily turning her nose up at the faded couch cushions.

I guess Seema was right about living separate lives—at school, I walk by an expansive courtyard with a fountain every morning and eat American food for lunch, and at home, I'm eating rajma with jeera rice and trying to figure out how to fit my textbook and my laptop on my tiny desk at the same time.

"Is that okay?" Quentin asks, and I realize I've been standing there staring at him. "If not, we can make the macarons another time."

I know when Ma puts together that the boy I've been tutoring is my age, she'll look at Quentin a little too long without blinking for most of his visit, but she'll still offer chai and a snack. That's an Indian household must. Besides, I can't avoid inviting Quentin over if he's going to be helping me with my manifesto. He's seen so much of me I'd ordinarily hide that I might as well throw in my house, too.

"Of course," I manage. "Come on over."

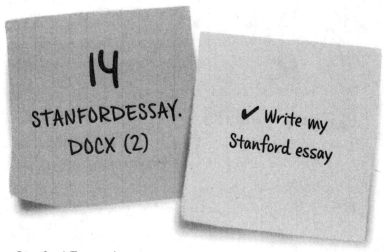

Stanford Essay.docx
Last Modified Friday, Dec 20, 9:49 p.m.

Share a time you left your comfort zone. (600 words)

~~Honestly, I have not personally gotten out of my comfort zone, but my parents have. My mother completed a degree at Stanford after immigrating here. Thus, my parents struggled to give my sister and me a better life . . . <insert more emotional details about struggles of Indian immigrant life. As I sit here and eat a bag of Flamin' Hot Cheetos??>~~

~~To me, getting out of my comfort zone equates to trying new things. Recently, I have tried two things I never thought I'd have time for: makeup and boys. I even invited a boy over to my house. Despite my foray into such subjects, I am a very focused student and would never sacrifice my academics for~~

~~Forget it, I don't even want to get into your DUMB SCHOOL aslsefjdlfjsdfldsfj~~

15
SANTA'S COOKIES

✔ Make (gluten-free) holiday-themed macarons from scratch

Winter break has begun. For Marcy, winter break means tree-shaped cookie cutters and hot cocoa in her dad's cabin up north. For me, it means curling up on my couch and color-coding my list of winter break to-dos—Stanford essay drafts, scholarship applications, AP Lit essay. But this year is different because there's a section dedicated to *fun*. So far, that section has *finish a watercolor painting* and *finish my crochet turtle*. I've been working on my turtle for weeks, while Lily has probably crocheted an animal farm by now.

I'm about to add *Sanjay's New Year's Eve party* to the fun section when my phone vibrates. I'm used to spam calls from so-called IRS representatives or calls from Seema asking me to get her water when she's too lazy to leave the couch. So, when I turn my phone over and see Quentin's name, I sit up. We've been following our tutoring plan for weeks now, but we've never actually spoken on the phone—we've stuck to texting. I smooth down my hair before I answer, even though he can't see me.

"Hello?"

"Aisha." His voice comes out breathy and quick. "Sorry for the late notice, but would you be all right with a cute eleven-year-old boy joining the gluten-free-macaron-making party tonight? His dad doesn't let him eat sugar, so he'd be very thrilled."

"Hmm, I dunno. Then we'll have *two* boys at my house with eleven-year-old mental capacities."

"Whoa, don't say that. I'm sure your dad is a smart guy."

"Very funny. Who's the kid?"

"Owen. He's my neighbor who I watch some days."

"Ah, right. The fudge nuggets kid."

"Yep. I was going to ask his dad to reschedule, but my shift at Divine Tea ended late, so I couldn't tell his dad in time. . . ."

I press the phone to my ear. "Wait a minute. You work at Divine Tea? You've been keeping this from me for *weeks*?"

Divine Tea is a tea shop in downtown Arledge that Marcy showed me. They give out fresh pots and painted teacups, no tea bags.

"Um, I didn't think it was breaking news. I only work there once or twice a week. Wait, so is it okay if Owen comes along?"

"Of course. Aren't you going to ask for the unit I live in? You've only been to my building game room."

"It's on the first floor and the only one with the orange door, right? And you used to write that on your birthday party invitations?"

I gasp. "You weren't even there when I told your mom that."

"Our walls are paper thin. Oh, and I was eavesdropping."

"Ugh. Bye."

For the next hour, I ready my apartment for Quentin's arrival, inspecting every inch except Seema's room, since she's napping and would chop my head off for waking her. My definition of "cleaning" is shoving all that is visible into cupboards. Ma peeks at me over the cover of *Emma* periodically, while Pa finishes making rice in the kitchen. I'm fluffing up the sofa pillows, trying to get the level of fluff just right, when Pa pokes his head around the corner.

"I love what you've done with the place."

"I can tell the difference, okay?"

"Look at her room. That's what she should be cleaning. People won't mind a little mess here," Ma says, like I'm not even there. "It's normal to have things after living in a place for some time."

"Or maybe our apartment is too small to hold all this clutter."

I immediately regret saying that as I watch Ma shield her face with *Emma* again, muttering under her breath about "ungrateful kids these days." I try to reassure myself that it's good that I'm not like the spoiled rich students at Arledge Prep, but sometimes it gets to me. No Starbucks lattes when you can just "make your own chai and control the sugar." Along with the "I could've made that at home" slogan, immigrant parents also tend to live by "always live in the cheapest house in the nicest neighborhood." We probably could've afforded a condo if we lived elsewhere, but my parents chose Arledge because of the safety and the schools. And the proximity to the Jai Ho grocery store.

The doorbell sings its tune. I glance at the oven clock. Seven sharp.

"Your student is right on time." Ma peels off her reading glasses. She seemed surprisingly pleased when I told her that I was going to bake today. Although Ma and Pa lecture me about making use of the stellar school system they moved here for, they also worry about me not knowing how to do anything *but* study. Ma keeps telling me I need to learn to keep my room clean and make a few basic dishes without burning the house down before I leave for college.

I rush through the kitchen, my fuzzy avocado-patterned socks sliding on the tile. I take a deep breath before opening the door. Quentin is standing upright, his face partially lit by the hallway light, one of his hands on Owen's shoulder, and the other hand holding a paper grocery bag. Owen is sporting circular glasses, short brown hair, and an argyle sweater. He looks like he walked out of a Banana Republic ad for kids.

"Hello, Owen." I wave. "I'm Aisha."

"Hi," he mumbles, and Quentin bops him on the head like *Be friendly.*

"Come on in." I have the sudden compulsion to slam the door shut and pretend they never arrived. I wonder how Ma and Pa will react when they see that Quentin isn't exactly an elementary schooler struggling with multiplication tables.

"It smells good in here," Quentin says, bending forward to pull off his shoes, revealing his usual long stripy socks. Darn it. Despite the frosty air, I opened the windows, hoping the smell of sizzling mustard and cumin seeds would dissipate. I take his winter jacket from him, but then I realize we don't have a coat closet. Should I hang it in my closet? How does one have guests?!

"Aisha, your dad just finished making some dal," Ma announces, coming around the corner. When she sees Owen, she bends down to get closer to his eye level and gives him a big smile. "Hello there. You must be Quentin. I heard you all are making dessert today."

Oh no.

"Ma . . ." I cough, wildly pointing upward. I'm practically jabbing the air. "Actually, this is Quentin. I'm tutoring *him*, and that's Owen, his neighbor."

Her smile fades, and she gives me an extra-long look, while I feign innocence. *It's not a thing unless you make it a thing*, Marcy always says.

"Did I not tell you? Quentin is a senior in high school, too." I say it like *What fate! Isn't that the darndest thing?*

"My mistake," Ma says, but she gives me an accusing look that means *your mistake*. Then she nods at Quentin. It's a wary nod of acknowledgment that she gives street-side vendors in India right before she starts to bargain for a lower price. "Hello, Quentin."

I wince. She's saying it more like *kwan-tin* instead of *kwen-tin*, but Quentin doesn't seem to notice.

"Hello, Mrs. Agarwal. Nice to meet you."

Pa appears, and I hug the coats I'm holding closer. More parents means higher probability of embarrassment. I follow Quentin's gaze. Is he noticing all our expired coupon books? The kitchen cluttered with steel pots? The fraying rug?

"Hello," Pa says, and he's looking at Owen, so I think he's making the same assumption as Ma.

"This is Quentin," I say in one breath, and I point. I've pointed at him twice already, like he's some kind of "bathrooms this way" sign.

Pa looks confused for a moment, but then he seems to get it. At least he's smiling. He's better at understanding the concept that "friend who is a boy" does not equate to "boyfriend."

"Hello, Mr. Agarwal," Quentin says. "Thank you both for having me."

"Of course. Aisha could use some company."

I glare at Pa.

"I mean, math-loving company like you," he amends as he meets my eye, his toothy smile unwavering.

"So, wanna start making macarons now?" I offer, rubbing my hands together so hard you'd think I'm trying to start a brush fire.

"Actually, before that . . ." Quentin digs into his paper grocery bag. He lifts out a plant and tilts it toward my mom. Its bulbous shape reminds me of a Twinkie. "This is for you. Hyacinth. Nanay heard you like plants, and she wouldn't let me come empty-handed."

I almost choke. I've come empty-handed to Quentin's house every time. It dawns on me that I mentioned my mom likes plants while talking to Quentin's mom the first day we met. I wonder how she remembered. Ma's stony expression warms, like lava glowing through cracks in the earth. She touches the hyacinth's leaves and appraises the terra-cotta pot.

"You did not need to bring anything but thank you. It is a pretty plant."

Quentin's eyes catch on my artificial Christmas tree plugged in on the floor near the kitchen. Well, *tree* is a strong word. It's basically a glorified party hat, and my sister and I had to negotiate for keeping it in the living room. I do my best to deck it out every year, but it doesn't compare to Quentin's seven-foot tree.

"Your tree?" Quentin asks, and we slowly trickle into a line behind him as he approaches it. "I like all the handmade ornaments."

I painted them. I love them even though my sister says they look like remnants from an attic box labeled *stuff I kept to not hurt my kid's feelings*. I notice Owen shaking off his jacket from the corner of my eye. Right as I'm about to take it, he pulls Quentin's jacket from under my arm. Then he marches to my couch and neatly lays both jackets on the armrest. After single-handedly solving my coat conundrum, he skips back.

Owen looks at all the ornaments and spends extra time on the foam photo frame hanging from one of the plastic green branches. It's an old photo of my parents, with glitter glue lining the edges. Ma has her arms wrapped around Pa, and she's smiling big, the apples of her cheeks as red as the bindi on her forehead. They look different now. Pa has packed on a few pounds (probably from all the ghee and Parle-G biscuits). Ma's hair is thinner.

"Your parents?" Owen asks me, his big green eyes peering at me from behind his glasses. I watch Quentin bend to match Owen's height, angling the photo to avoid the glare from our kitchen lamp.

"Yep," I say. "I made that in art class in fifth grade."

"This was taken a year before Kanta and I got married," Pa explains, pointing to the yellow date stamp in the corner. "In college."

"Did you meet in college?" Quentin asks. As soon as the question is in the air, he looks at me like *Is it okay that I asked your parents a personal question?* I shrug back like *It's your funeral.*

156

Ma smiles, but then seems to remember that she shouldn't be fraternizing too much with my male peers. "Yes, we met at the Birla Institute of Technology and Science in drama club. Akshay used to visit me outside the girls' hostel. Then we got married."

Ma loves telling this story, but she always skips the details in between meeting Pa and marriage. She says that's because there are no in-between events to tell, which worries me even more. I'd want to date someone for at least five years before marrying them to be sure. That's twenty seasons, five birthdays each, and five anniversaries.

"And then!" Seema's voice echoes through the hallway. "Two years after they got married, I came along. Lucky them."

Seema rubs her eyes and staggers toward us in her snowman pajamas. When she sees Owen, she raises her eyebrows at me, like *You invited two boys over? I'm impressed.* At least that's what I'd like to think her look means. It also could mean *You're so desperate for friends that you hang out with little kids now?*

"So, you boys like our tree?" Seema asks. Quentin nods, but Owen shrugs.

"It's nice," he says, sniffling, "but it's small."

You can always trust kids to be honest.

"Agreed. We ask our parents to get a bigger tree every year, but no luck."

"Hamaare ghar mein itanee jagah nahin hai, Seema," Ma sighs. "Vaise bhi, hum Christian nahin hai, aur agar tree dekhna hai, tho mall main dekho. Kitna acha ped hai mall mein."

We don't have enough space, and we're not Christian. If you want to see a tree, go to the mall. That one's so nice.

I understand that argument, but at the same time, my parents have been in the United States for twenty years. A little tradition never hurt anybody, especially if it involves milk and cookies.

I roll my eyes. "Ma, please. There's no danger of us forgetting our Hindu roots. We're literally having a puja in a few weeks."

"What's that? Sounds cool," Quentin says, turning to me. I don't know why he's so curious. None of my Arledge friends have ever shown much interest in Indian stuff. Alexander still can't pronounce my name. Marcy has asked about Ma's biryani when I bring it for lunch sometimes, but considering I usually eat Snickers bars for lunch, she hasn't seen much of my Indian side.

"Basically, a pandit is going to come to our house and perform a three-hour prayer ceremony to bless the home, and then we all eat Indian sweets. It's called the satyanar . . ." I can hear how terrible my Hindi pronunciation is.

"Satyanarayana Puja," Pa finishes.

I used to enjoy the ceremony as a kid knowing there would be halwa served while the soothing scent of incense filled our home. In recent years, I obsess about all the time lost that could've been spent sleeping or studying for my AP exams. Is that bad?

"Whatcha think, Quentin?" Seema asks, giving me a knowing smile. "Does it *still* sound cool?"

"Honestly, yeah. It sounds like a nice way to slow down. And there's dessert at the end? I'd totally wanna come."

Seema and I exchange panicked looks. A wave of acute distress passes over my mother's face as she clutches her potted plant.

I'd totally wanna come may sound like a harmless figure of speech, but it's not in this context. When it comes to prayer, Indian superstitions process words literally. If you say you're going to the temple on Saturday, you *must* go to the temple on Saturday, or something terrible will happen. You must always distribute your wealth by sharing the prayer prasad, or the food blessed by the prayer, with anyone in the vicinity. And finally, if anyone says they want to come to the prayer, well . . . you better invite them. Or Lord Shiva will strike you with his trident.

Or something like that.

Ma looks at Pa. Then she looks at Quentin, her voice strained. "Er, well then . . . you should come."

Poor, poor Quentin. He doesn't even know he's being invited out of pure, trident-invoked fear. I'm tapping my foot so fast I might make guacamole from my avocado socks.

He glances at me. "Really? Wow, I mean, if you would like me to, I'd be honored . . ."

"But Quentin isn't Hindu, so I doubt he'd want to be there for all that . . . you know, stuff," I blurt.

"My family's Catholic, but we're more spiritual than religious. My mom believes any spiritual practice is enriching."

"Then you're most welcome." Pa's voice is firm. "Come. It will be the second Saturday of January at nine a.m."

As my sister watches my befuddled expression, she bites back a smile. I imagine Quentin being there for something so *personal*—the chanting, rituals, and singing—and I want to scamper to the nearest manhole and free-fall to the core of the earth. I've survived by keeping my American school world and my Indian family world separate. The compartmentalizing is how I make sense of my life. Within only a few minutes of being inside my home, Quentin Santos has nuked all that work.

I rest a hand on Owen's shoulder. "All right, people. Let's get cooking."

As I herd Quentin and Owen into the kitchen, I sneak a look back at Ma. She's confused. I don't blame her. I imagined a lot of scenarios for tonight, but not one of them involved Quentin getting invited to our puja. You can always trust the universe to be creative with its havoc.

"Oh boy," I mutter once my family is out of earshot, and Quentin gives me a sweet, my-dog-ate-my-homework smile.

As it turns out, Quentin is a bungling baker. He accidentally uses our Costco bulk pack of baking powder instead of the almond flour for our first batch of macarons. I think he feels bad about it because after we start the second batch, he gets the same focused expression he gets when he does calculus and hardly says a word.

"You don't need to measure it *that* perfectly," I say, watching him run a knife across the top of a steel measuring cup to round out the flour.

His face is scrunched in concentration. "I don't want to mess these ones up. Are you sure I should be helping?"

"Of course. We need you."

Owen has the opposite progression, moving from shyly arranging utensils to barking orders. Quentin and I become the sous chefs, but I don't mind. Owen looks cute commanding us in his tiny knitted socks.

"It says to pipe out the batter into halves." Owen reads the recipe from my phone. "Can someone get a baking sheet?"

"On it, Chef." As I eye Quentin ever-so-carefully tearing a piece of parchment paper, the corners of my mouth rise. "Also, tell me the truth, Owen. Is Quentin a good babysitter?"

"Yeah. He helps me with my homework. And he sometimes makes enchiladas for me if my dad's late."

"How much did he pay you to say that?"

"Quentin's too poor to pay me. He doesn't make much at Divine Tea."

Quentin pokes Owen in the side, torturing him until the poor kid is howling like a coyote.

"*FUDGE NUGGETS!*" Owen screeches. "Stop it, Quentin!"

I can't help but join in, until we're all ducking each other. Owen has the good sense to escape to the living room couch, flopping onto the pile of coats. We let him catch his breath, and Quentin and I finish piping out the macaron halves, which look more like ovals than circles. I do the honors of putting them in the oven.

"This is the critical moment in which I always fail at baking," I say. "Waiting. I'm always so tempted to open the oven door to see how it's doing."

"Use the oven light to check," Quentin says as he starts to rinse the mixing bowls in the sink. I don't tell him that I forgot about that. Unlike me, he seems to know his way around the kitchen. I didn't even know there was a difference between dry and liquid measuring cups until today. After we're finished cleaning, I click on the oven light.

"They say the macarons are supposed to have *feet*," I murmur, bending down to peer through the oven door. My eyes are so close to the door that my eyelashes are almost touching it. "The feet are how you know they're well baked and not hollow inside. We're doomed. These have no feet. Look." I wave my arms at Quentin like a traffic controller. "No feet."

"Say *feet* one more time."

"I'm serious! I think I'm headed toward yet another cooking disaster. What if they turn—"

"Shh. They're gonna use their feet to run away from all your negativity. Straight off the baking sheet."

"Or they're gonna use their feet to stomp all over your face."

"When do you finish first grade again?"

"I finished. I simply cater to the level of my audience."

"*Captive* audience."

"And captive for at least seven more minutes until these finish."

"As long as I don't have to eat them." He leans in. "I mean, they don't even have *feet*. . . ."

"Shut up. They're gonna turn out great. Right, Owen?"

"What?" Owen calls, still sprawled on the couch. "I didn't follow any of that."

"We're too quick," I tell Quentin. "In fact, some might say that we're quick on our . . ."

I elbow him until he laughs. I've never felt so much like *myself* around someone before. If I knew sobbing in someone's car would allow me to be this comfortable around them, I would've sobbed in every vehicle I've been in.

By the time Quentin and I return to the living room bearing the cooled batch of macarons for Owen to taste, we hear soft snores. Quentin drapes my blanket over Owen, tucking the excess into the cushions. We settle at the foot of the couch, our legs pulled up to our chests, the cookie sheet on the carpet between us. The red and green macaron halves have cracked tops but passable feet.

"So," I start, watching cars snake down the street from the window, their headlights washing over the wall before disappearing.

"So. I'm really sorry I ruined the first batch of macarons."

"Oh, c'mon. It's fine. Whether it's math or macarons, it's okay to make mistakes."

"I get stressed out whenever I mess up. Not really because I'm embarrassed, but because I hate the feeling of disappointing people. I'm literally sweating through my shirt right now."

"Think like the red squirrels. They sure don't worry about disappointing their squirrel friends," I deadpan, and he laughs.

"Okay, you got me. At least Owen's a good pastry chef."

"How do you know Owen again?" I peel a red macaron half from the cookie sheet, trying to see if the inside is hollow. That means the batter was overmixed.

"He's my next-door neighbor's son. I've been watching him since I was in middle school."

"That's sweet of you."

"Nah. It's for me. If I say I do puzzles with an eleven-year-old on Friday nights, I'll be the sexiest boy on the block."

I snicker. "Well, you seem to really care about him."

"We have a lot in common. His dad's a single parent, too. On top of that, he's a nurse and works on-call sometimes, so he needs someone to check on Owen." He pauses, as if waiting for me to react. "Are you thinking that my mom could marry Owen's dad and then we could be a nice happy family?"

"Um, no. I didn't think that at all."

He grins. "*I* used to."

"Did you try to get them together?"

"Did I ever. Then I realized that people don't end up together because of proximity."

I know he isn't talking about us, but it sure is applicable. Quentin and I are spending so much time together, but Quentin would never be interested in me . . . and my heart is with Brian.

I reach for Quentin's math notebook. I'm supposed to correct one of his problem sets tonight. For encouragement, I've been drawing a big gold star on the first page of every set he finishes, regardless of how many problems he got right.

Quentin lies down on the carpet next to me, tossing an oven mitt into the air and catching it. I like that even when I'm correcting his work, he never reaches for his phone for a hit of mindless scrolling. He waits.

"Is that how you practice tennis during off-season?" I snatch the mitt out of the air, and then bop him on the forehead with it.

"I dunno. Is drawing stars in gel pen on my problem sets how you practice art?"

"Touché." I notice clumps of his hair sticking up in random places, like little evergreen trees. "You know, it's rare my house is this quiet. Seema's home for the holidays, so you can imagine how much quiet time *that* allows for. And my mom is always home."

"Your mom doesn't work?"

"No." My voice comes out sharper than I intended. I can't help it. When people around Arledge hear this, I bet they assume Ma is from a tiny Indian village and didn't get the chance to have a college education. They probably don't imagine she started a PhD. I always wondered how the decision was made that Ma would be the one to give up her career rather than Pa, but I never asked. I'm almost afraid of the answer.

"Full disclosure, I saw her Stanford acceptance letter hanging on that wall." He points to the wooden frame above the couch.

"Pa framed it for her, so she wouldn't forget. And it would sound all noble if applying there was just because of Ma, but it's not. I want to get in for myself, too." I've latched on to the idea of Stanford for so long that it's comforting, like a cereal box that tells you exactly what prize awaits you. I always hated when the box just said *Prizes inside!* "But enough about Stanford."

"And more about this New Year's Eve party." Quentin digs into his messenger bag and pulls out a pouch of almonds. He offers me some, but I shake my head. If I spy a half-eaten healthy snack, Quentin is not far away. His mom is very into WFPB, which I thought stood for Whole Foods peanut butter, but turns out it stands for whole foods, plant-based diet. Much less exciting.

"Did you check with your mom about the party?" I ask. "Can you go? I was able to convince my parents by playing the I-won't-ask-for-anything-else-all-year card."

"It's a yes from my mom, too."

I resist the urge to punch the air in triumph.

"We usually celebrate New Year's with sparkling apple juice and Owen's dad." He smiles. "But my mom understood this is more my age. And I can't believe Brian is friends with Sanjay. Small world. Sanjay's known at school for hosting parties, although having super-rich parents who are super busy probably helps."

"I've always wanted to host my own party, too. Except more of a homey dinner party. Music that's not too loud."

"I remember. You put that one on the sticky note wall, right?"

I nod. "And now that this baking thing didn't end up as bad as I thought, maybe I could even pull off a homemade dinner."

"My dad did that kind of stuff. He loved hosting these big ravioli dinners to keep our Italian roots alive. He used my grandpa's recipe every year."

The lights from the Christmas tree dance in Quentin's eyes, reminding me of a kaleidoscope. Like the day at the mall, I have an invasive personal question I should probably refrain from asking, but the darkness makes me braver.

"What happened to your dad?"

Quentin doesn't look away, but his hand tightens over the pouch of almonds he's holding. "He died when I was younger, from pancreatic cancer."

After I sensed Quentin's dad wasn't around, I was hoping his parents were divorced. The scenario would still suck, but at least Quentin would get a chance to see his dad.

"I'm really sorry . . ." My voice is almost a whisper. He's picking at the fibers of my carpet. "Was sorry the wrong thing to say? I'm sorry— I, oh my gosh, I said it again. I just mean that I—"

"You're fine. I do hate it when people say he *lost* his battle against cancer, though. That implies he wasn't strong enough, but that's not how illness works. It takes you whether you fight or not."

"Do you think about him a lot?"

"It hits me at random times. People think I'd feel bad at graduations or birthdays, and that stuff is hard, but it's not the worst. The worst is the stuff you don't expect, like the saying

That's such a dad joke. Then I remember what I've missed out on." He has a faraway look on his face. "That's why I really liked the idea of your manifesto. We think we have more time, but we don't always. Everything ends eventually."

I get the feeling that Quentin's perspective shifted after his dad passed. I see the world as opportunities for the taking if I work hard enough, but Quentin sees the world as unforgiving. Seeing Quentin's steely gaze, I decide to change the subject.

"Too bad the macarons will be all cold and hardened by the time I give them to Brian next week." I set down my golden gel pen to appraise our macaron halves.

"That's okay. Revenge is a dish best served cold."

I scowl. "They're not *that* bad."

They are, but we sit for a little longer and continue to eat them anyway.

16
ICE COLD

✔ Go ice-skating

"Omigod, omigod, omigod," I whisper, clenching the side of the wall. I'm kicking along in the ice skates while Quentin cruises beside me, wagging his head. It's the day after Christmas, so the rink is crowded with ice skaters who can actually skate.

"Step one. Let go of the wall." He tries to pry my fingers from the glass, and my eyes go wide.

"Stop that! I'm not ready."

"You've been here for almost an hour. Owen learned already, and he's eleven."

Owen is circling the rink. This does not inspire me to leave the wall in the slightest. Kids think they're invincible. If I fall, it'll hurt. And the moisture from the ice will undo all my hair straightening. I'm somehow more concerned by the second part. "I don't want to fall."

"I won't let you fall. How'd you even agree to go ice-skating with Brian anyway?" he grumbles.

"I dunno. I got nervous. And it's a romantic thing people do in the movies. The strong, tall man holds the woman as she learns to ice-skate."

He stares at me.

I swallow hard. "What?"

"You don't have to do stuff because you think everyone else does it. If you hate ice-skating, don't ice-skate."

"Right, because you're just doing all the things you love. Like studying *math*."

"O-kay. Uncalled for."

"Sorry."

"It's okay. Let's distract you from ice-skating. Ask me a question."

"What did you do on Christmas?"

He places a light hand on my back, guiding me as I clomp across the ice. "Christmas tends to be no joke for Filipinos, so it was *busy*. We did a gift exchange with some cousins who drove into town from Ohio, we ate a ton of my favorite desserts—bibingka, buko pandan salad—and we went to Houghton Lake for Christmas Eve to have dinner with my grandpa and Sophie. You know, the old lady you stole a ride home from."

"Whoa, whoa, whoa. I didn't *steal* the ride. I took an available opportunity. And how was dinner with your grandpa?"

"He likes to use mealtime to criticize me or talk about his son being gone, so not the best." Quentin pulls me farther from the wall. "What did you do for Christmas?"

My parents used to get us gifts on Christmas when my sister and I were younger, but that waned over the years. Now the only way our household is affected by Christmas Day is that Costco is closed, so Pa can't come back with random snacks, which Ma then scolds him for buying.

"Our family doesn't really do much. I listened to a ton of

Christmas songs while writing college application essays. Talked on the phone with Marcy. Ordered a few books online."

"What books? I've been reading *The Book Thief* during slow shifts at Divine Tea."

"Er, well, not those kinds of books. I ordered books to help me write my college essays."

It must've been quite a sight, me gobbling sugar cookies and singing "with a CORN-cob pipe and BUT-ton nose . . ." while adding *50 Successful Ivy League Application Essays* to my cart.

He sighs. "Give me your hand. I'm getting you off this wall if it's the last thing I do."

He peels me away from my safe zone, while my other arm rises to balance myself. As soon as we start moving, I lose my footing and fall backward with a sickening smack. Pain sears through my tailbone. When I open my eyes, I realize Quentin has fallen next to me, too. He's breathing hard. Our hands are still clasped together.

"YOU SAID YOU WOULDN'T LET ME FALL."

He suppresses a smile, the skin around his eyes crinkling. Those golden flecks in his irises are much nearer than they've ever been before. I thought being this close to someone would send me rolling away like a fire safety video. Yet I'm still.

Stop it, I tell myself. *Quentin is not a boy. He's a piece of platonic toast.*

Quentin breaks the spell by sitting up and kneeling beside me like a teacher about to give an edifying lecture to a misbehaving preschooler. "I wasn't finished. I meant I wouldn't let you fall *alone.* You have to fall in order to learn how to ice-skate. But I'll be there to help you up."

"Gee, how sweet."

I inch across the ice and begrudgingly take his hand to get to my feet. I skate a little bit before careening forward again. Although I know I'll relate to Marcy's back pain a little *too* well tomorrow, I gotta admit, he's right. Falling isn't so bad. After another full hour of flails and falls, I'm able to make a few loops around the rink by myself. To the outside eye, I look like a wobbly ice skater. In my head, I've been reincarnated with all the grace and agility of an Indian goddess. As I pass Owen, he calls, "Holy fudge nuggets! You finally did it, Aisha!" I give him a double thumbs-up and then exit the rink, kicking off my skates and rubbing my sore ankles. This calls for sugary celebration.

I fetch some overpriced hot chocolate for Quentin and me. I think it's old Swiss Miss powder mixed with lukewarm water. We perch ourselves on the aluminum scaffold, watching Owen and the other ice skaters. Owen gives us the occasional wave to make sure we're watching. I'm tired, but not in the way schoolwork wears me out. I'm tired in a day-well-spent, accomplished way. That moment when I finished my first lap around the rink, I forgot all about Stanford.

"Thank you for helping me," I say. "I can't believe I can kind of ice-skate now. I actually started enjoying it."

"You're a quick learner."

I know he's just saying that to be nice, considering I clung to the wall for an hour while a bunch of toddlers lapped me, but I'll take it. I think back to Quentin skillfully coming to a halt on the ice without so much as a wobble. He looked so free. "How did you get so good at ice-skating?"

"My dad. He's the one who taught me tennis, too."

"Right, you're on the team at Kresge! I've seen your hoodie. Junior varsity or varsity?"

He shakes his head. "Of course you'd ask this question."

I frown. "What's that supposed to mean?"

"Nothing." His voice is light. "But yeah, I'm on junior varsity. My coach did encourage me to try out for varsity since they could use another lefty player with a reliable T serve, but . . ."

"But?"

"Well, I wanted to, but I was worried about not doing well after the tryouts. The team's pretty serious about getting to regionals this year, so I wouldn't want to ruin their chances. I like how JV has no stakes."

When I hear about a way I can do more, it's like gravity. Inescapable. No matter what grade I get in a class, I'm compelled to do the extra credit. This is why I've accrued double the volunteer hours necessary in the National Honor Society.

"You could've at least *tried* if you wanted it. Isn't there a line between staying true to what you know you want, and limiting yourself? I say you must seize the opportunities within your reach."

He snorts. "You sound like a fortune cookie."

"Maybe . . ." I rotate the cardboard sleeve around my cup of hot chocolate, watching the stamped ice rink logo reappear and disappear. "But don't you ever *want* something? Want it so much that it hurts?"

"I used to. I remember begging my parents for years to visit my cousin in Spain, so they finally promised to take me when I turned twelve. My dad said twelve was special since it's the *first abundant integer.* I keep looking it up and then instantly forgetting what that means . . ." He sees my eyes widen and arches an eyebrow at me. "You want to say it so bad, don't you?"

"It means that the sum of its divisors is greater than the number itself!"

He laughs. "Right. That. But, as you know . . . my dad got cancer. And I found out life's greatest secret: you usually don't get what you want."

"I understand . . ." My voice softens. "But striving is a reason to wake up in the morning. I may be disappointed more, but I'd still pick wanting it every time."

He sets his cup down. It's almost full. "Can I ask you a question? You don't have to answer it."

"Ask away."

"Why do you want Brian? I guess . . ." He looks at me. "What about him is so special?"

Whenever Brian is near, my heart races, my tongue ties, and my hands get clammy. That doesn't happen to me around anyone else. But it's hard to articulate what exactly I like about him now, considering the last time we really spent time together was years ago.

"Well, to put it bluntly, he's cute. And he's super smart. We're actually competing . . ." I'm about to say *for valedictorian*, but then I realize I sound like I'm bragging. "Well, we compete for grades. And I know that he's funny and sweet, too, from when we talk."

"So you talk a lot?"

"We used to. In middle school. And sometimes now. Occasionally, if the situation arises."

"I see."

"Don't give me those judgy eyes." I take a long swig of my hot chocolate, turning to face the rink again. "Feelings can't be explained."

"But what if Brian isn't the same person you remember from back then? Wouldn't you be disappointed? Regret all the time you spent fantasizing about him?"

"If Brian Wu ends up liking me back, there is no *way* I could be disappointed. It'd be a miracle. I mean, he's hot, he's athletic, he's funny, he's smart—I guess most students at Arledge have smart going for them, but definitely not the other stuff. He has *all* the stuff. I can't imagine why Riley broke up with him. Meanwhile, I'm not sporty. I'm not the class clown. I dunno, I'm kind of . . . plain. Like that girl who walks across the stage on graduation day, and everyone's like, *Who's that?*"

"Aisha, are you secretly a bowl of topping-less oatmeal?"

"Huh?"

"Unless you are, I definitely don't think you're plain."

Maybe I don't know Quentin as well as I think. Sometimes, I believe I have him all figured out. Easygoing, undisturbed. Even his hand gestures are sweeping and free. Then there are moments like these that surprise me. His eyes burn with intensity, and his voice loses its playful ring. He takes on a decidedness that reminds me of Lily when she ran for crochet club president.

"Well, this manifesto feels like the most interesting thing about me right now," I say. "Brian even offered to help with it."

He looks offended. "I'm being *replaced*?"

"Not yet. All I've done so far is send him a picture of the sticky note wall. You know, the wide-angle picture I asked you to send me?"

"I thought that was for your records."

"Nope. I sent it to him. And I strategically cropped the photo so that the midnight kiss note is in there."

He rolls his eyes. "Why don't you, I dunno . . . *ask him out*?"

"It's not that simple for me. I know you don't care what people think—you're, like, the practical type." Even Quentin's winter jacket is *pillow packable*—it has a collar attachment that converts to a compact travel neck pillow. "You don't even have anything superfluous in your room."

"*Superfluous*? Nice SAT vocab word."

"I'm serious. You and I are on different planes. Besides, you asked me why I like Brian, but why don't you like anyone? That's much more surprising."

He leans back, resting his palms on the bench. "There's no specific reason. I just think there's no point in putting so much time and effort into a relationship that's not going to last beyond high school. And I don't want to be the reason someone's happy or sad. That's a lot of pressure."

"Like I said, the point is to *try*. You never know what could happen. And maybe you just haven't met the person who'd make you comfortable enough to show all your sides. Even this cynical side."

"So you're telling me to look out for someone who makes me comfortable, yet you're literally out here trying to hide everything about yourself?"

I stiffen. His words etch into me like skates on ice.

He's right.

With Brian, I always feel like I'm auditioning for a part in a play without ever having read my lines, but maybe I don't need to audition. I *am* the part. Brian and I get each other. We have history. We grew up in Arledge with protective parents. We're driven. We're from the same cutthroat world of AP classes and extracurriculars. We make sense, even if Brian hasn't seen it yet.

"Sorry," Quentin mumbles as he sees my glum expression. "I didn't mean that. It's just, you don't need to pretend to be good at everything. I'm happy to teach you, but part of the romance might have been to let Brian teach you how to skate."

"You think he would have let me fall like you did?"

"Probably not. But then you also wouldn't have learned."

I turn to him. "Man, I'm going to have to kill you at some point. You know too much."

"I'll take your secrets to my grave, comrade."

If Quentin was in the army, I'm certain he would guard all his comrade's secrets. As I watch him sipping his hot chocolate, I remember how Quentin and I will go our separate ways soon. Northeastern is on the opposite coast from Stanford. Graduation is just a few months away. We'll probably drift apart over time. My throat tightens as I imagine the home screen of my phone being almost bare once again, notification-less apart from my family group chat and Marcy's texts. But when I see Owen making funny faces at us as he circles the rink, I decide this—right now—is enough.

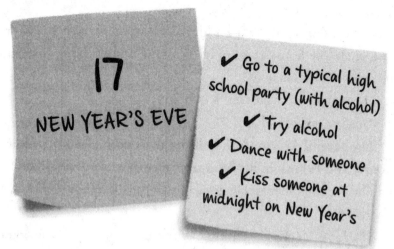

17
NEW YEAR'S EVE

✔ Go to a typical high
school party (with alcohol)
✔ Try alcohol
✔ Dance with someone
✔ Kiss someone at
midnight on New Year's

I run a brush through my freshly straightened hair, then smooth the skirt of my dress. I've been hogging the bathroom for a whole hour, since Seema is out with her friends at McGuire's Irish Pub. She told Ma she's having dinner at Rangoli Indian Cuisine.

My ratty crochet club sweatshirt has been replaced by the black cutout dress I got at the Lakeshore Mall. A strip of midriff peeks from the cutouts of my dress, like *heyooo*. I almost feel like it's Halloween, except instead of embodying a witch riding a kitchen broom, I'm a girl gone wild. "Girls Just Want to Have Fun" is my anthem.

I take one last look at myself in the mirror before shrugging on my knee-length winter coat and zipping it up to the tippy top. If my parents saw this outfit, they would probably ask why I forgot to wear pants. I flick the lights off in my room and shuffle into the corridor.

Pa yawns as he ambles across the hall. He jumps as he sees me. "Aish, turn on the light. Andhere mein kyun chalrahi ho?" *Why are you walking in the dark?* The hallway light flickers on, and he eyes my coat. I expect him to tell me to come home early and recite the house rules of no drinking and no boys. Instead, he calls, "Kantaaaaaa?"

I hear the covers rustle. "Kya hua?"

"Aisha's leaving."

The fearful knight doth call for the queen. Pa works long hours, and I think in his head, this means he's not qualified to handle these moments. He delegates all the disciplinary messaging to Ma.

Ma looks at me unblinking as she emerges, her beady eyes regarding me from behind her reading glasses. "So you're off to the party, then?"

"That's right," I reply cheerily, like *We're off to see the Wizard, the wonderful Wizard of—*

"Remember, we had a deal. You must come home by twelve thirty sharp and text me every hour. And you cannot make this a habit, Aisha. You can do these things when you're Seema's age, but I don't want you turning into—"

"I *know*, Ma. You already lectured me about the party last week. It's senior year, my last chance to have a little fun. And *all* my Arledge friends are going." Which means Marcy. And sort of Brian.

Ma recoils from "have a little fun" as if I've said "consume LSD." "You dressed warmly, right?"

The doorbell rings, and I almost sigh with relief. Saved by the bell. I feel my coat chafing against my upper thighs, which probably indicates how short the skirt of my dress is. Ma's making me second-guess myself, and now I'm half wondering if I should dive back into my room and change into a pair of roomy sweatpants. But Ma opens the door, her mouth set into a line, and I know it's too late.

Quentin appears, car keys jangling in his hands. He's wearing a big smile, and his hair is combed back instead of hanging over his forehead like usual. There's a fresh dusting of snowflakes on his scarf. "Good to see you, Mrs. Agarwal. Happy new year."

The lines on Ma's face soften. There's something about Quentin's disarming smile that pierces the toughest of Indian parent armor, I suppose. "Hello."

Quentin tries to make eye contact with Ma, but she's looking at me. Pa is camouflaging in the corner, watching the events unfold. Someone give the man opera glasses.

"Can you bring her home by half past midnight?" Ma turns to Quentin, her voice strained, like the whole ordeal had just shortened her life by a decade. She seems to trust Quentin with my safety now, which is why I asked him to give me a ride. Marcy's already driving Kevin, and I think Ma suspects she's a bad influence because she got me a set of nail polish for my birthday last year instead of a book on Ruth Bader Ginsburg or something. Ma or Pa would've jumped at the chance to drive me and come to the doorstep to make sure the party is safe, but every year on midnight, they call all their friends and family spread across the United States to wish them a happy new year. They also shout like they're using cup-and-string phones, as if yelling carries their voices to North Carolina directly.

"Of course, Mrs. Agarwal. I'll have her back right then, if not earlier."

Psh. Suck-up.

Satisfied, Ma and Pa retreat to their room, discussing in

conspiratorial murmurs how America spoils kids. I lock the front door behind me, and we head outside into the biting winter air. I pull the hood of my coat taut around my head, hoping no snowflakes zap my freshly straightened hair. Right as Quentin is about to take a turn toward his car, I yank him down the sidewalk that leads to my apartment building's game room.

"The game room has a bathroom," I say, as if that explains it all.

"Um, your house also has a bathroom."

"My *house* also has an Indian mom who doesn't approve of me wearing makeup or heels." As soon as we're inside, I point to a fake monstera floor plant next to the foosball table. "That's why I stashed everything in a tote bag and hid it behind that plant earlier today."

Quentin looks like he's about to say something, but he only sighs and sprawls onto the beanbag chair by the pool table, while I hurry into the bathroom, wriggle out of my coat, and pull my pencil pouch of makeup from my tote. I watched a "five-minute nighttime glam makeup" tutorial more than a few times yesterday, and the electronic music in the background got me in the party mood. I always feel like I could be studying more, crocheting more, exercising more. But New Year's Eve is the one night where it feels like all of that *more* is within reach. Maybe even my first kiss with Brian Wu is within reach, too.

After my dark eye shadow, winged liner, and red lip are complete, I lay my coat over my arm and pop out of the bathroom, like *Ta-da!*

Quentin's in the middle of a yawn when he hears the door squeaking open, but as soon as he sees me, he sits up. "Whoa, you . . . it's the pop-up card dress."

"And?" I know I'm fishing for a compliment, but I can't resist. I do a little spin. "How do I look?"

He blinks. ". . . Different."

I groan.

"Sorry, you look really pret—" He averts his eyes. "I mean, it looks pretty."

On the drive, Quentin is quiet. He's usually cruising with one hand hanging on the steering wheel and one hand on the gear-shift as he whistles a tune, but tonight, he has both his hands in perfect ten and two positions, and in the entire time we've been driving, he's hardly looked at me. He only meets my eye when we roll to a stop in front of Sanjay's.

It looks like a Beverly Hills mansion from reality TV, except switch out the sun and palm trees for snow and evergreen trees. The uplighting makes the brick look like it's glowing. I don't hear thumping music or see red Solo cups strewn all over the grass like I thought I would. There's a glass pool house attached to a garage that's visible from the street, but I don't see anyone cannonballing into the pool or lounging on the pool chairs.

"A shoebox of a house," Quentin says.

"A total dump," I agree, struggling to get out of the car while keeping the fabric of my dress over my thighs. Before we ring the doorbell, the porch light blinks on and the door swings open. Standing there is an Indian guy rocking an argyle sweater vest. The sleeves of the white button-up he's wearing underneath are rolled up, and his defined arms peek out. I wonder how he knew we were here.

"My man Quentin! What are you doing here?" He pulls

Quentin in for one of those half man-hugs that look more painful than comforting.

"Hey, Sanjay. I came with Aisha."

I'm trying to get a better look at Sanjay, but Quentin's blocking my view.

"Oh, Brian's friend! More esteemed Arledge Prep guests." Sanjay leans forward and extends his hand. "Pleasure to meet you, Aisha." I take it, blushing. With that chiseled jaw, I sure wouldn't mind my midnight kiss being from *him* as a backup. I almost feel giddy at the thought of having both a plan A *and* plan B for a kiss. A few weeks ago, I had no plans at all.

"Shoes on or off?" Quentin asks.

"Usually, I'd say off, but the floor is going to get pretty gross tonight, so you guys can keep 'em on."

"Sanjay!" a voice screeches. "Where are the cups? And we need more jungle juice!"

"Duty calls," Sanjay says. "But come on in and help yourself to snacks and drinks. I'll find you guys later. And Quentin, it's good to see you out and about, man."

What does that mean? I give Quentin a questioning glance, but he seems distracted.

Sanjay gets pulled away, and as I take a step inside, my heels wobble. Quentin sighs, holding out his arm. I give him a grateful look and latch on to his arm with one hand. As soon as we're in, my senses are overloaded with the stench of sweaty people and the sound of blaring music. I take it all in, my lips parting in awe. I look for Marcy's curtain of brown hair, but I don't see it in the crowd. When I identify a bowl of potato chips on a far countertop, I pull Quentin toward it.

"Man, I'm starving." I shove chips into my mouth. Cheeks full of chip mash is not the most attractive look, but at least only Quentin's watching. I'm a few inches taller than him with my heels, so I get a top view of his head.

"Didn't you eat dinner?" Quentin looks concerned, but I shrug.

"There were leftovers in the fridge, but I forgot. I was getting ready for the party."

"So your dinner is potato chips?"

I shrug again, and I'm about to ask Quentin if he knows anyone else here, but the music is too loud, and he keeps facing away from me. Every time I point something out, he gives me an unenthused nod. I knew this would probably not be his vibe. He's more of a sporty activities guy than a party guy.

"You want to try a drink with me?" I ask him brightly. "Some Mowgli juice?"

That earns me a smile. "I don't believe jungle juice is affiliated with *The Jungle Book*. And I'm driving you home, so no alcohol for me. And maybe you go easy, too, okay? I know it's part of your manifesto, but I promised your mom I'd bring you back safe. Besides, alcohol is overrated. It's an expensive headache."

I sigh, and we stand there watching the crowd for a while. I know I could go get some jungle juice by myself, but I'm feeling more and more like I don't belong. I'm overdressed in comparison to everyone else wearing jeans and sweaters, and they probably can tell that I just bought my dress this month and I don't know any of the music that's playing in—

Someone shoves into me, and I'm knocked against Quentin's

chest, the potato chip in my fingers crumbling against his coat. I rub my shoulder, groaning, and turn to see Lily.

Of course.

"Sorry about that." Lily's voice is barely audible over the music. Even here, her cool, apathetic vibe is in full swing. "I saw you, so I came to say hi, but I tripped."

I look down at her tennis shoes. Lily didn't dress up at all, either. She's wearing a crocheted scarf over an Arledge hoodie, and she looks beautiful. It's that silky hair that a hand could glide through without getting stuck. *It's okay*, I tell myself. *Some people like Lily are effortlessly pretty, but that doesn't mean I can't be effortfully . . . average.* My hand instinctively goes to my hair. I hope it's not curling up.

"I can't believe you came," I say. "I thought you were joking."

"I was curious about how these parties would be. And as I imagined, it sucks."

"You're not having fun?" I can't imagine Lily *ever* having fun. I can't even imagine her jumping in a bounce house as a kid. I bet she just stood in the center with her arms at her sides.

"Not even a little bit. I couldn't find water. There's only jungle juice."

"I know where the bottled water is. I'll get some for you," Quentin offers Lily, and as she notices him standing behind me, her eyes get starry. I can already tell she's imagining crocheting his face into a sweater. Lily nods, and as soon as Quentin disappears into the crowd, she flashes me a thumbs-up.

"What's that for?"

"Your boyfriend's cute."

"He's not my . . ." I gulp. Why am I having difficulty finishing this sentence? I could kiss anyone I wanted at this party, and that's how I want it to be, right? *Girls, they wanna have fu-un, oh, girls just*—ugh. This is killing my mood.

"He's not my boyfriend." I stare Lily square in the eye. "I don't like him like that."

And he would never like me like that.

She looks at me like she knows something I don't, her dark eyes boring holes into mine. When Quentin returns with her water, she takes the bottle and holds it up, as if toasting to my health.

"Thanks for the H_2O. I'm gonna say hi to some friends, so I'll see ya."

I nod at her. "See ya, Lily."

After Lily melts into the crowd, I notice Quentin has taken off his coat. Instead of his usual pocket tee or baseball tee, he's wearing a black polo, with the first two buttons undone. The sleeves hug his arms. He looks . . . good. I've never seen him in more dressy clothes before. My heart twists as I remember what I just said to Lily.

Quentin is not a boy, I tell myself. *He is a platonic igneous rock.*

My phone vibrates, a welcome distraction. It's Marcy.

Where you at? We're at beer pong.

I finally spot Brian, Kevin, and Marcy at the back corner of the room. Brian is throwing a Ping-Pong ball, and the group huddled around the table roars as it plops into one of the red cups. Marcy's wearing a plain red jumpsuit with black flats, which convinces me that I am indeed overdressed for this.

"Look, I see them!" I shake Quentin's arm like I've just seen a wild peacock on an animal safari.

He rolls his eyes. "Then you must make haste, Lady Aisha. Your midnight kiss awaits."

"It's not close to midnight yet. And you should say hi to Brian, too."

We make our way to the table, and as soon as Brian sees me, his face brightens. The collar of his button-up has a festive poinsettia print, and it fits like it was tailored to him. I pull down on my dress, giving him a small wave.

"Whoa, Aisha. You look *amazing*. I like your dress."

It feels like his words are on a ship crashing into my brain. *Amazing*. Brian just said *amazing*. Suddenly I'm glad I came overdressed. Kevin gives me a smile, and Marcy winks at me. Quentin looks like he's waiting for me to introduce him, but after one look at my dreamy expression, he waves at Brian.

"Hey, I'm Quentin. Aisha's friend."

"Nice to meet you." A beat passes. "Wait, you're the guy with the Jetta, right? I think I saw you outside Aisha's house a week or so ago."

"Yep, that was me."

"I hate to be the one to tell you this, but you might need a new car, man."

I wince, knowing how much Quentin loves his car, but Quentin doesn't look fazed.

"It looks old, but trust me, it's a trooper. When my grandpa gave it to me on my sixteenth birthday, he put a handwritten maintenance guide in the glove box that I've been following, and so far, no issues."

As much as Quentin fears his grandpa, I can tell he respects him. Even some of Quentin's habits remind me of a kind ol' grandpa: the way he offered to get water for Lily, or the way he tucked a blanket over Owen. I can imagine him lovingly power-washing his Jetta in his driveway for many summers to come.

"Hey, I got you something," I tell Brian, reaching into the tote bag I hid my heels in. I pull out the Tupperware of macarons, tied with pink ribbon. "I made these. As a thank-you for inviting me."

Brian holds up the container to look inside. "Aw, they're Christmas-themed. Thanks, Aisha."

My smile feels like it's tacked onto my face. "You're welcome."

"Where are my cookies?" Kevin jokes, holding out a hand, which Marcy swats down. I look at her for help, knowing she'll understand that I need her to throw sticks into this dwindling flame of a conversation.

"So, Aisha," she jumps in, "have you decided who you're gonna kiss at midnight for your manifesto?"

Quentin watches Marcy, wearing the same expression I do when I watch those made-for-TV holiday movies—entertained by plots so contrived that you can spot all the twists from a mile away. Unless you're Brian and Kevin, that is. They look intrigued.

Brian sets the macarons down on the Ping-Pong table. "Hey, I think I saw the midnight kiss sticky note in the picture you sent me—the one of your wall?"

I tuck my hair behind my ear like *How funny!* I notice Marcy whispering to Kevin, probably filling him in on my manifesto.

"*My* wall, actually," Quentin mutters, and I resist the urge to sock him in the arm. Not that I could sock him without falling over. Why did I wear heels tonight? Being *emotionally* unstable wasn't enough?

"Hope this isn't too crazy of a suggestion, but . . ." Brian looks at me. "I'd be honored to help with that one tonight."

How is Brian offering up his lips as casually as Quentin offering Lily a bottle of water?

"I mean, maybe we can help each other. I saw Riley here with someone else, so that way, I won't seem like a loner, either."

Kevin looks at me, curling his fingers and placing his hands over his head to give himself curved ears. I realize he's referencing our Build-A-Bear conversation from winter formal. I smile, and Kevin smiles back.

"Only if you feel comfortable," Brian adds. His gaze is steady. Confident. I suppose he thinks of me as his neighbor who he used to know well, so he's ready without warning.

I should be, too. I should be feeling the same joy I get from placing the last piece in a thousand-piece puzzle, but instead, I suddenly feel like someone just threw all my puzzle pieces into a blender. My chest is tightening, and my legs are quaking. I feel my breaths start to shorten. I wasn't prepared for this. It wasn't supposed to be this easy or happen this fast.

Brian doesn't know I've never kissed anyone before. What if I'm terrible at it, or worse, what if I just stand there like a dead fish? What if Riley sees us and laughs at my lack of kissing prowess while adjusting her perfect topknot?

Then again, if I say no, Brian will think I don't want to kiss him. Marcy will be disappointed that she helped me orchestrate this for nothing.

But I don't feel ready.

I can't.

"Actually . . ." I try to breathe, and I blurt, "Quentin volunteered to help me with that one!"

I feel Quentin's eyes on me, and I pray that the telepathy is working. Thankfully, he seems to get it, taking a small step closer to me.

"Right. I already, uh, offered my services."

I sigh with relief. My heart is nestled in the basket of a hot-air balloon: rising, rising, rising—

"Just as friends," he tacks on, and my heart balloon deflates.

"Oh." Brian's eyes move from me to Quentin. Kevin's eyes are wide, and Marcy is watching me. "Well, let me know how I can help with the other notes, Aisha. I'm gonna go say hi to some friends, but thanks for the macarons." He looks unbothered by how this turned out, the same way I look when there's only raspberry lemonade instead of regular.

"Of course," I squeak.

I planned this moment out for days leading up to the party, and I ruined it in one moment. Brian and I were supposed to share macarons and admit that we both liked each other before he moved away, and that was supposed to culminate in a passionate kiss. I was so close to stepping out of my comfort zone, and I stayed. Why did I stay?

As soon as Brian is gone, Marcy turns like a heavy revolving door—slow and stiff.

"Um, we're gonna go say hi, too. To Lily. And a few of Kevin's friends." She waves at Quentin. "But nice to meet you, Quentin."

How does everyone have friends at this party to say hi to but me?

"Yeah, nice to meet you, man," Kevin adds, glancing at Marcy.

Quentin gives them a big smile. Until tonight, I haven't seen Quentin smiling at other people so much. His attention is usually directed at me because there's no one else there. Marcy gives me a meaningful *we'll talk later* look, and she and Kevin disappear into the crowd.

I turn to him, biting my lip. "Thanks, Quentin. I don't know what happened, I freaked out. I'm sorry to make you lie."

Quentin's face darkens. "I didn't. I can, I mean . . . I can help. If there's no one else you feel comfortable with, I can totally—"

"You mean like a backup?" Our eyes catch.

He shoves his hands into his pockets. "Yeah, I guess you could call it that."

I've somehow turned kissing me for one microsecond into a bulletin board community service pamphlet.

No one wants you, a voice in my head whispers.

And maybe it's true. Brian was going to kiss me because smokin' hot Riley is here to see, and Quentin was going to kiss me for community service.

"I need some air," I say. "I'm going to go out for a sec."

Quentin's face falls. "Aish, did I do someth—"

"No, you didn't do anything." I swallow, feeling tears starting to well in my chest. "I just want to be alone."

He looks hurt, but I leave him there anyway. I can't be in here anymore. It's too loud, too much. I wade through the crowd without glancing back, toward the double French doors that lead out to Sanjay's pool deck. This is just like winter formal. I'm alone, and I'm leaving.

I'm relieved by how peaceful it is, the loud chatter and blaring music subdued to a muffled hum as I shut the glass door behind me. I lean over the pool, peering into the cerulean stillness, admiring the reflection of the dancing string lights. I imagine that the hazy bulbs are colored fish swimming through the water. It's quiet for now, but I know that when I go back in there, Marcy's going to grill me about what's going on between Quentin and me, and I'll have to explain that there's nothing. And how could there be?

I'm a bird, and Quentin's a fish, I realize.

He's cool and collected, swimming a safe distance from high school romances while not caring about what people think, and I'm anxious and frenzied, flitting toward straight As while trying to be liked by anyone and everyone. We're worlds apart.

"You're not supposed to be here, you know. Pool's off-limits."

I jump, whirling around. Sanjay. "Oh, I'm *so* sorry, I—"

"I'm just messing with you." He grins, approaching me with a red Solo cup in hand. His steps look wobbly, like he's balancing on a tightrope, so I can tell he's tipsy. "I just close this area off so people don't trash it."

I tug down on my dress, sneaking a glance at him. We're standing almost shoulder to shoulder. "Your house is really nice."

He takes a swig of his drink. "Thanks. My parents travel for work seminars around the holidays, so I've been hosting this party the past few years. They haven't found out yet."

"You have guts. I could never throw a party at my house.

And definitely not one as great as this." I say it like I'm some sort of seasoned party expert.

"If it's so great, why are you out here? Be honest, does my party suck?"

He's smiling now. His teasing is kind of disarming. It feels like he's not taking me too seriously, the way I've been taking myself all night.

"I noticed one of the chip options was Magic Masala, so this is unequivocally a great party. I just . . ." I suck in a breath. "I'm just bad at enjoying things sometimes."

"We're perfect for each other, then. I enjoy things a little too much. I'm trying to rein it in."

We're perfect for each other. I'm no flirting expert, but that sounds flirty even to my inexperienced ears. Then again, what do I know about flirting?

"So how long have you and Quentin known each other?" I ask.

"Years. We used to hang out all the time. We don't talk much anymore, though. He missed a lot of school after his dad passed, and when he came back, he shut me out. And everyone else, really. He said he didn't want to bring me down. I knew he was going through a lot. Dealing with anxiety, trying to be there for his mom. And he already had a counselor helping him through things, so I doubt he wanted my unprofessional consolation. But I did wonder why he did that for a long time. I could've helped distract him, or he could've just come over and done homework with me. We used to do that most of the time anyway."

So that's how Quentin knew where the water bottles were. And I can't imagine Quentin going to counseling for anxiety. It's like imagining your own therapist going to therapy.

He winces. "Sorry, I'm talking too much. I do that when I drink. Maybe you can help me finish this before I start talking even more." He thrusts his cup into my hand. "It's jungle juice."

I stare at the red liquid sloshing inside. It looks like fruit punch; how bad can it be? I put my lips to the rim and decide to commit to one big gulp. The bitterness tastes worse than cherry-flavored cough medicine, and as soon as it washes down my throat, it stings.

He watches me. "Safe to say you weren't a fan of that, huh?"

I give him a shy half smile. "Not so much."

He takes the cup back from me then, which makes me decide he's a good person, not like those actors in the peer pressure educational videos they made us watch in middle school.

"It's snowing," he says, setting his cup down on the tiled floor, and I look up to see snowflakes kissing the glass panes. "Will you dance with me? I always wanted to dance while it was snowing."

I'm thinking about how that's an oddly specific dream, but then I remember how much jungle juice this guy has probably had.

"I'm not very coordinated." I want to tell him it took me two hours to skate one lap around the ice rink, but then decide that might be oversharing. "I'm not very good at dancing in general."

"I'm not, either. But it'll be fun. One song." He nudges me. "Please?"

I find myself nodding under his pleading gaze as I remember one of the Great Wall notes: *dance with someone*. The clock hanging on the wall says 11:22 p.m., and dancing would be a perfect segue into a midnight kiss. I can get it over with, I can tell my friendly fish Quentin that I found someone else to kiss, and I won't ever have to see Sanjay again if I totally screw this up.

Commence plan B.

Sanjay plays a song on his phone I've never heard, and I can't hear the words well, but I can tell it's Hindi. Hindi reminds me of home, so I already feel closer to him somehow. I rest my hand on his shoulder, and he slides one hand on my waist. He's a few inches taller than me with my heels, but I can see over his shoulder. He steps backward, I step forward. *I'm doing it! I'm dancing!* And my dress is staying put.

"Thank you for this dance, m'lady." His words are slurred, but they make me smile. We dance, and I'm not thinking about anything. I'm . . . happy. The song ends, and the next one starts.

"Hey, I have an idea." Sanjay's breath tickles my ear.

"What is it?" I eye the door like I'm on a plane trying to identify the emergency exits.

"Can I twirl you?"

Phew. For a second I was worried he was going to pull the *Wanna check out my room?* move I saw in that peer pressure video.

"Um, probably not a good idea? I might slip in these heels."

"I'll catch you." He pulls away so I can see his pretty-please pouty lips.

"Oh, fine." I smile and he wraps his fingers around my wrist. I complete one slow twirl with my eyes fixed on my feet. All is well.

But then I hear Sanjay yelp.

Of course it didn't occur to me that *he* could slip.

His weight rams into me, and we meet the tile with a sickening smack. Pain spiders through my ankle.

"Oh man," Sanjay moans, and he rolls off me. He gets to his feet, but he's swaying like he might fall again.

I'm motionless for a few seconds, and then I sit up in a daze, trying to piece together what just happened. I almost fell into the deep end of the pool. The Hindi tunes are still playing. I try to get up, but I can't. I clutch my ankle as the pain starts again, worse this time.

Sanjay holds out a hand. "I'm so sorry. Are you okay? Let me—"

"Aisha, you okay?"

I crane my neck up. Blinking red and green lights dance across Quentin's face. He's angrier than I've ever seen him, eyes ablaze and hands balled into fists as he looms between Sanjay and me. Maybe it's because I'm on the ground, but he seems taller.

"Hey, what's up, man?" Sanjay's eyes are glossed over.

"What's up is that she can't swim, and she's a foot away from falling into the eight-feet side of this pool."

Sanjay is too drunk to understand what's going on. "Sorry, I didn't—"

"You can go inside. I got this."

"I—"

"Just go. Please."

The guy who is always cool as a cucumber, calm in the face of the hardest calculus problems, is upset. Because of me. As Sanjay goes back in, Quentin kneels next to me and wrangles my heels off.

"Is your ankle okay?" he asks, his face scrunched.

"I think so. It's not broken," I whisper.

"Let's get you home." He slides my heels back on, then drapes my arm over his shoulder, helping me to stand. I press into him, hobbling across the tiled floor in a daze. He pries open the glass door leading from the pool deck to the outside, and then we're cutting across the frosted lawn to his Jetta.

How is it that one moment, I was humming "Girls Just Want to Have Fun" in my head, and the next, I was on the floor?

The icy air on my skin sends shivers up my spine. It's almost a refreshing distraction from the burning pain in my ankle. Quentin unlocks his car and helps lower me down into the passenger's seat. He yanks my seat belt over me in one motion, shuts the door, and clomps around to get into the driver's seat. The car sputters to life, and the headlights illuminate the drifting snowflakes. He rests his forehead against his hand. I'm about to ask him if he's mad at me when I see Marcy. She's lifting the legs of her jumpsuit so they don't drag on the ground, and her flats are stamping prints in the snow.

"Hey, wait!" She taps on the window, her breath making little disappearing circles on the glass. I roll the window down. "It's not even midnight yet. Don't tell me your mom asked you to go home early."

"I . . . I twisted my ankle." I hope I don't look as miserable as I sound.

"Shit. Are you okay?"

"I think so."

"Oh. Okay." By the look on her face, I think she knows more than she's letting on. "Well, you forgot your coat. And I remembered your tote bag because of the turtles on it. I didn't know which coat was Quentin's, so I couldn't get his."

"Thanks, Marce." I reach through the window to take my things.

"Get home safe, guys. Happy new year."

"Happy new year," I mumble, cranking up the window. I wouldn't call this year *happy*. It's not even a new year yet. Right before Marcy disappears inside, she turns and flashes the *call me* signal.

"We don't have to go home yet," I offer, hovering my hands over the heating vents. "It's only 11:40, so if you want to stay, we can—"

"Aisha." His eyes are fixed on a fire hydrant in the distance.

I bite my lip. "I'm sorry, I really am. I didn't mean to worry you."

"I was looking for you *everywhere*, asking everyone if they'd seen you. And then I saw you and—" He falters. "I don't get it. I thought you wanted to be alone."

"I did, but then Sanjay came out to where I was, and he was really nice to me. And after I messed up my chance for a kiss with Brian, I thought—I thought he could help me. I'm just trying to have new experiences, even if they hurt." I point to my swollen ankle, which seems to have doubled in size in the last few minutes. "Literally."

"But I was right there. Did I not tell you that I—"

"I didn't want a pity kiss, Quentin. That would've made me feel pathetic."

"A *pity kiss*? That's what you—" He sighs. "Fine. Forget that, but what about the rest of the night? You weren't yourself at all."

Everyone wants me to be someone else. Marcy tells me to be

more adventurous, my parents tell me to be more careful, my sister tells me to be more chill, and now Quentin is telling me to be more *me*. Whatever that is.

"Well, maybe I don't wanna be myself. Maybe that's the idea." All my effort is going into holding back tears. If I cry in this car, it wouldn't be the first time.

"What about me, then? Your parents trusted me to be responsible for your safety. I'm supposed to watch you almost drown for your manifesto?"

"That's awfully dramatic."

"And your outfit?"

A tear frees itself, but I flick it away like it's a fly that landed on my cheek. "I can wear whatever I want!"

"I don't mean it that way. I'm all for wearing whatever you want. Even if it's nothing, for cryin' out loud. But my point is, you didn't seem comfortable at all. Didn't you say you don't like wearing a lot of lipstick? Didn't you say, and I quote, it turns your lips into prunes? And the entire night you were pulling on your dre—" He tightens his grip on the steering wheel. "I should stop."

"Yeah, you really *should* stop." I fire my words like bullets. "Because your way of staying comfortable isn't that great, either. You can't fail if you never try, so you just don't."

Quentin stiffens. "What's that supposed to mean?"

"You give up on calculus problems before even trying them. You didn't join the varsity tennis team even though you wanted to, because what? You were afraid of your team relying on you? The night we made macarons, you said you shouldn't help anymore just because you made a mistake on the first batch. And

Sanjay just told me that you shut him out. That's no way to live, either. To give up when things get hard. I'd rather make mistakes than not try."

"I'm trying. I'm learning math with you, aren't I?"

"It's not only about math. You're hiding from things with risk. That's not being content. That's complacent."

Quentin's gaze hardens. "If that's how you see me, fine. I'll stop interfering. My job is to help you complete the sticky notes, not give my opinion on them. And I'm probably some charity case you're tutoring for the community service section of your college application, right? Yet another thing on your list."

I turn toward him. "What's *with* you tonight? What happened to your whole go-with-the-flow thing?"

"My *thing*?" Quentin's eyebrows furrow. "Just because I'm taking a Buddhism elective doesn't mean I don't have feelings, Aisha. It doesn't mean I don't care if you're hurt."

"I'm *not* hurt. I can take care of myself."

"Okay, you *can* take care of yourself, but you choose not to. You had potato chips for dinner tonight. You disappeared, and then I find you sprawled on Sanjay's pool patio. It's like you're willing to put yourself through anything to get Stanford or Brian or whatever you decide is worth obsessing over." His voice rises. "What about *you*? Don't you matter?"

"Of course, but I need to—"

"You don't *need* to do anything. You can be proud of who you are already."

Although he sounds like an inspirational poster, his words hurt. I know I hide parts of myself: being lower income, being Indian. I've erased the parts of me that don't fit the idea of who

I want to be, but I sure don't need anyone pointing the erasure out.

"I *do* what I want already. I crochet. I paint."

"When's the last time you painted?"

"It's been a while, but I . . ." My voice cracks.

I'm the girl who brings macarons to parties. I do *more* in order to please. My succulent died because of overwatering. This is the first time in my life that someone wants me to do less. A few moments of silence pass, each striking my heart like a gong's mallet.

"C-Can you please just take me h-home?"

Quentin sees the tears spilling down my cheeks and instantly shifts his Jetta into first gear, his mouth clamping shut. How am I more hurt than the night Brian stood me up at winter formal? How could Quentin say he's another thing on my list? I lie awake nights thinking about how to help him understand calculus concepts better. I spend hours grading his problem sets and drawing a smiling gold star on the top of every one.

We're silent on the way back to my house. I wonder how the drifting snowflakes can be so beautiful while my mind is muck. The ride feels like an eternity.

When we pull up to my apartment, Quentin gets out of the car and comes around to my side. He offers his hand as I open the door, but I push it away, not bothering to put my hood up as I climb out. My hair can curl up all it wants. I'm expecting to hear the roar of his engine, but he doesn't leave. I suppose he's waiting to make sure I get inside. Annoyingly considerate. I'm limping along on a path drawn by his headlights when the sound of fireworks cracks in the air like a whip.

It's midnight.

I scan the spaces of sky between the trees for an afterglow, but nothing. Suddenly, Quentin's headlights flash at my feet. I turn back, squinting to see past the wash of light. They flash again, and a few moments later, Quentin's fuzzy silhouette grows bigger until he's right in front of me.

"Hey, wait." His cold fingers graze my hand. "I'm sorry. I don't want to leave things like this."

I blink to clear the spots in front of my eyes. "I don't, either, but I have a name, y'know. You didn't need to blind me with your high beams to get my attention."

"Actually, I did."

My vision clears. I see golden eyes and reddened cheeks. He's shivering in his polo, his hands glued to his sides as snowflakes fall and melt on his skin. He gives me the expectant look I usually give him when I'm waiting for him to catch his calculus mistake, and then raises his hands to my shoulders, pulling me closer. *Much* closer than the afternoon we went ice-skating.

As I see every shade of brown in his eyes, I remember. That afternoon we put up the manifesto wall, I told Quentin that the lead-up to a kiss scares me most. We joked that I'd need to be blinded beforehand if I have any chance.

He brushes my hair away from my face and dips closer. I feel his breath on my lips. I shut my eyes. I'm sure he's going to go for it, but after a few charged seconds, I sense he's waiting for me.

I don't question whether I should kiss Quentin, or what he'll think of my kissing skills, or what will happen afterward. I close the small space between us, and his lips press to mine. His hands rest on my waist, and my fingers settle around his shoulders. For a few electric moments, we stay like that. He pulls away.

"Happy new year, Aisha."

He walks to his car without so much as a glance back, leaving me standing in the snow while fireworks rain from the charcoal sky.

18
RADIO SILENCE

✔ Experience silent treatment

The next morning, Seema makes besan puda, crepes from chickpea flour. All throughout winter break, Seema has been asking Mom to teach her how to make Indian food. She claims she's sick of "deep-fried college campus sludge" and wants home-cooked meals.

"Mornin', sunshine." Seema plants a plate of puda in front of me, and I shovel forkfuls into my mouth. She then sits down across from me with her own plate in hand.

"I zon't banna talk."

"Weren't you supposed to go ice-skating with Marcy and Brian this afternoon?"

"And Kevin. Marcy wanted me to get to know him more. But I hurt my ankle last night."

"Ooh, you hurt your ankle? Doing what? Wink, wink."

Leave it to Seema to *say* "wink" instead of just winking.

"I'm not hungry, actually," I announce, slogging to my room without a look back. I'd rather eat my breakfast in peace later. As I shut the door behind me, I realize I left my phone at the table. But I suppose it doesn't matter—Quentin isn't texting me.

I can't figure out if he kissed me for the manifesto, or because he wanted to.

Technically speaking, I kissed him.

And it's not like I consciously went for it with pom-poms waving in my head like *Plan C commences!* For that minute, my brain went mysteriously offline.

I fold my legs into my crocheted blanket and drift off. In my half-asleep state, the kiss lingers in my mind like a floating cloud, brushing my senses. A loud knock at the door condenses the cloud into a raindrop.

"Ugh, what is it?"

"It's your favorite sister. Can I come in?"

"Fine."

Seema gets into bed next to me and drags some of my blanket away to pat around her legs. She holds out my half-eaten plate in one hand and my phone in the other. I take my phone from her and check my messages. Nothing. Then I snatch my plate, attacking my puda.

"Whab do you bahnt?"

"You seem down, Aish." Seema's face softens. "Did something happen last night?"

Seema and I may not have made blanket forts together or told each other about our crushes growing up, but if something's wrong, neither of us lets it slide. I take one more look at her, and the entire story busts out of me like a balloon popping. My almost kiss with Brian. My dance with Sanjay. Quentin accusing me of almost drowning for my manifesto. I tell her about everything but the kiss with Quentin. I can't tell her that part, or it becomes real. For once, she listens without interjecting.

"Hmm," she says finally. "Quentin has a solid point."

"You're supposed to be on *my* side!"

"Come on, Aish. You plan out every day so you're perfectly productive. I know you think that if you complete some life checklist, you'll be happier. But life doesn't work like that."

"What's wrong with having goals?"

"Nothing, but sometimes we run toward things to run from ourselves." She pauses. "Damn, that sounded wise. But my point is, running doesn't work. Being happy starts with *stopping*. No checklists. Just learning to be okay with yourself."

"I *am* okay with myself. I'm great with myself."

"Whenever any of my friends come over, you rush to the bathroom to straighten your hair. And you baked Brian dessert to get him to like you. I tried the leftover macarons, and let's just say I'd rather eat cat food."

I glare at her, but I know she's right. "I was trying to say yes more. I was trying to have, you know, swashbuckling adventures."

"Sure, but maybe you could stop trying so hard to mold yourself into someone you're not for this manifestation thing."

"Manifesto."

"Whatever. Point is, Sanjay probably wasn't the best pick for your first dance."

"What should I do about Quentin?"

She rolls her eyes. "Text him. I bet you're both waiting to hear from each other."

"He probably doesn't care. We haven't known each other that long. That's what makes our whole falling-out even stranger."

"Quentin cares about you. That day he came over when he was locked out, he told me that you're the best thing that happened to him this year. Technically, last year."

"Really?" I sit up. "He's never said that to me."

"I have that effect on people. They confide in me." I roll my eyes as she stands. "By the way, Brian called you while you were asleep, and I picked up. He wanted to know if you were okay. I guess he heard about last night."

I practically roll out of my bed. "*What?* How did you respond?"

"I said you were fine. But it gets crazier. Quentin called, too, at the very same time. So, I patched him in and made it a little three-way call, and—"

"*WHAT?!*"

"You are way too gullible, Aish." She snickers. "I worry about you. But to be clear, Brian did call. We got to talking, and I told him your birthday is coming up, so maybe he'll get you a gift. A portrait of himself, enlarged to show texture."

I never imagined that Brian would *call* me. Looks like the manifesto is working. Or maybe the macarons were so scrumptious that they cast a love spell on him.

Okay, it's probably the first one.

"Can you get out of my room now?"

"Fine, fine. I remember the days you'd follow me around the neighborhood on your training wheels. And now you're telling me to get out of your room—" She stops as she sees the books stacked on my floor. "Tell me those are not what I think."

"They're books on cracking the Ivy League essay. A lot of people are reading them now to understand how you can be a better storyteller with a small word count."

"Aisha, senior year free time is precious; it doesn't come back. Ask any old person like me."

She parts the curtains of my window before slamming the door shut behind her. I see our neighbor's kids playing in the street, stomping in the tire-tracked snow. *Learning to be okay with yourself* echoes in my head. I pick up my phone.

Hey Q, we good?

Too flippant. Backspace.

Quentin, I'm really sorry about last night.

Backspace.

I fling my phone into my essay book graveyard. A part of me is still raw from Quentin's words. If he thinks he's just a section on my college application, so be it. For his information, I have so much volunteer experience that tutoring him wouldn't even *fit* on my application.

The next week at school, I'm off-balance. Quentin and I are barely talking. The Stanford essay deadline is next Tuesday, and while I have a few passable drafts about wearing clothes I normally wouldn't and dancing with someone to a Hindi song, something's missing. I'm more shaken when Marcy, Brian, and I get our American Dream essay grade before independent writing time on Friday. Ms. Kavnick asks us to get into our groups and sets the paper facedown on my desk. I flip it over for all of us to see.

B-.

I haven't gotten a grade below an A- since sophomore year when I forgot to turn over a social studies pop quiz and complete the back.

Marcy grips the paper in her hands, whispering, "'The purpose of this assignment was to explore multiple perspectives on the idea of the American Dream and then craft a layered argument. While this essay is well written, it mostly supports the concept of the American Dream. There was little in-depth discussion of the flaws.'"

I remember the day we wrote the essay in the library together. I did think our essay felt one-sided. I was so wrapped up in Brian's enchanting pencil spins that I didn't speak up. Marcy tried debating with Brian, but she ultimately gave in, muttering to me, "I choose my battles."

Brian is quiet, rubbing at the circled B- on the page like it's a stain that will come out. Ms. Kavnick must've noticed our glum faces. She stops by our mourning circle while the rest of the groups are discussing the feedback they got.

"Do you need me to explain the feedback more?" Her voice is low.

"No, we understand," I say. I understand that this B- will lower my high A in the class to a borderline A. No more missteps if I want to keep myself in the running for valedictorian.

"Is there anything we can do?" Brian asks. "Rewrite the essay? I'm sure we'd all be happy to."

All of us nod, but Ms. Kavnick returns a sad smile.

"Unfortunately our grading policies don't allow for a rewrite." She sighs, her dangly owl earrings spinning every which way. "I'm on your side, though. I disagree with that policy. It's not fair to be stuck at the place you've been given, even if you're willing to work hard to change it, right?"

She taps my desk once before walking away, and I realize she's not talking about a flaw in the grading policy. She's referencing the American Dream. That's Ms. Kavnick, using every moment as a teachable moment.

I spend the rest of the period staring into space. I can't even enjoy lunch with Marcy. It's not just the grade—I'm ashamed that I didn't think to explore the flaws in the American Dream concept more in my essay. I'm sure Ma and Pa would have plenty to say on the subject.

Marcy unwraps her sandwich. "We missed you at ice-skating. Although Brian calling to check on you is a big deal. Things are coming along."

"I *think* they are." I sigh. "I've been confused lately about how much I like Brian. Or what liking someone means. I know I liked him in middle school, but he's different now, and . . ."

And I kissed Quentin.

I haven't been able to tell Marcy. Every time I'm about to, I imagine what Marcy will say: *A kiss means he likes you and you like him. You can date and see where it goes. So what's the problem?* Except there is a problem. I don't think Quentin likes me, and I've spent so much time thinking about Brian, which must mean something. It's all jumbled in my head.

"I think I know how you can clear this up," Marcy says. "Remember when I had a crush on that one singer who'd perform at Wooly's for live music night?"

"Of course. Ponytail girl." That was one of the first girl crushes Marcy ever told me about. She almost came out to her mom around that time, but then she decided to wait until her grandparents came back from vacation in Key West so she could tell everyone at once. She ended up chickening out. *I'll tell them if I start dating a girl*, she said, but I could tell she was disappointed in herself.

"And then remember how when I met her in person and got her autograph, I realized that she wasn't all that special and kind of smelled like stale jelly beans?" She dusts crumbs from her Arledge skirt. "Well, you need to get jelly-bean-close to Brian to see if your feelings are real. Maybe you haven't spent enough time getting close to him."

I unwrap my Snickers bar. Getting close to Quentin has only complicated things. Before that kiss, I could see Quentin as a friend. Nothing more, nothing less. But now, that shape-shifting magic is wearing off, and I still don't know why he got out of his Jetta that night. Was the kiss only for my manifesto, or were there feelings?

"Is that how you realized you have feelings for Kevin? Getting close?" I ask.

"Pretty much. Which reminds me, when are you finally going to hang out with us?"

"When I can bring *my* boyfriend instead of being a sad third wheel."

She sighs. "But I'm going to be swamped with yearbook stuff after this month. We're getting the votes in for the senior superlatives. I think Jayden will win Best Dressed; Brian is a high contender for Most Likely to Talk Himself out of a Parking Ticket. What do you think yours will be?"

"Most Likely to Not Be Noticed."

"C'mon, people know you. I told you everyone loved that social media op-ed you wrote freshman year. Anyway, let me know if you have time to hang, okay? I feel like I haven't seen you much lately, and I think if you got to know Kevin more, you'd really like—"

My phone vibrates.

"Quentin?" Marcy strains to see over her lunch tray.

"Nope. Spam." I nibble on my Snickers. "Quentin and I barely talked this week. Things are going to be extra weird when he comes over this Sunday."

"Wait, come over as in your *house*?" Her eyes are wide. "I didn't realize Quentin comes over for tutoring."

"Only once so far. This will be the second time because his mom's hosting her monthly book club meeting at his house, and she said it gets loud."

Marcy opens her sandwich and starts picking off the tomato slices. "You've never invited me over before. You always told me your mom doesn't like guests."

"It's for volunteer work, so she allows it," I lie. "Sorry, I do want you to come over, of course . . ."

I'm a terrible person. I just can't imagine Marcy with her perfect leather binders inside my house. She won't be able to eat without Lord Ganesha watching her every bite.

"If you're worried, you could ask Quentin to meet at Wooly's instead of your house. Then you can make an excuse and leave if things are awkward."

"That's a brilliant idea, I'll—" I freeze. "Marce, what's the date tomorrow?"

"January eighth." She looks up from her sandwich. "Why?"

Fudge nuggets. The date of our family prayer.

Quentin and I will be meeting earlier than I thought—amid a pandit, chanting, and, most worrisome of all, my entire family.

19
BLESSED BOOKS

✔ Have a friend over for a puja

The next morning, I sleep through my alarm. I have no time to straighten my hair before the pandit shows up. I wriggle into a hoodie and jeans and stomp to the living room. Pa is stirring the halwa nonstop to keep it from sticking to the pan, while Seema and Ma arrange puja materials on the floor—statues of Indian gods and goddesses, spice powders, quarters, incense, freshly cut marigold flowers, coconut, and fruit. I breathe in the fragrant sugar, cardamom, and saffron. Quentin hasn't texted. I wonder if he remembers. I want him to and don't want him to all at the same time.

"Kumbhakarna is here." Ma gestures toward me and pushes her hair out of her eyes. Her head is covered loosely with a red silk scarf. Kumbhakarna is a character from the famous Indian epic *The Ramayana*. His weakness is needing to sleep for six months. "I sent Seema to wake you, but she was kind enough to let you sleep longer."

"I took one look at Aisha and thought she *really* needed her beauty rest," Seema quips. I roll my eyes. Every Seema favor comes with a free side of wisecrack.

"Is your friend coming?" Ma asks. "We prepared some fruit for him to distribute, too."

Wow, she called him *friend* instead of *student*. Talk about moving up in the world.

"I think he forgot. I never reminded him, so he probably—"

The doorbell rings, and all eyes snap to me. *It's only weird if you make it weird*, I remind myself. Quentin's no boy I kissed. He's a cinder block.

I crack open the door the same way I do to collect a UPS delivery when my parents aren't home. There he is, in his usual navy coat and messenger bag. My heart jumps to my throat as our eyes catch. I'm trying to think of anything else, *anything*, but my mind is screaming *kisskisskiss* like those kiss cams at baseball games. My cinder-block plan has already failed.

"Hey." He doesn't look at me.

"Hey, come in."

He carefully unzips his coat. As it peels away, my nerves are eclipsed by amusement. Amusement *far* beyond watching Indian aunties and uncles sing karaoke at parties.

Quentin is wearing an embroidered white dhoti kurta, complete with wide-legged trouser pants and gaudy gold beading. Usually, simpler cotton kurtas are worn at home. My family has worn T-shirts and jeans during our prayer ceremonies for years. I've only seen flashy kurtas like these worn at Indian festivals or weddings.

I can't help it. I bust up laughing.

Quentin is startled, but I explain nothing. When his sneakers are off and his stripy socks unveiled, I pull him to the kitchen. He looks at me with confused doe eyes, and I feel a flash of Big

Bad Wolf guilt for turning him into a spectacle, but my life is rather dull. I need this.

"Pa, say hi to Quentin."

"Hello." Pa doesn't look up from his pot, but I poke his shoulder. His eyes wash over Quentin's clothes, and his face lights up. "You're wearing a kurta?"

Quentin looks like he wants to dig a hole and bury himself right there.

"It looks very nice," Pa assures Quentin.

Ma can't even maintain her usual icy demeanor when she sees Quentin, covering her smile with her hand. "It is looking nice on you."

Seema wastes no time. She sticks her phone up in the air and snaps a picture, giving me a cunning I'll-send-that-to-you-later smile.

"Where in the world did you find that, Quentin?" she coos. "There aren't many stores around here to buy Indian clothes."

"I borrowed it from a friend." He folds his arms over his chest in an attempt to hide the fabric.

"Which friend?" I ask, and as he clears his throat in response, it hits me. "Sanjay?"

His ears are turning red as chili powder, and I can tell his worst fears are coming to pass. "None of you are wearing traditional clothes today except me?"

Ma arranges fresh marigold flowers on a steel plate. "We don't wear them for pujas much anymore; I just wear a chunni to cover my head. But it is nice you wore this. You are following tradition best of us all."

"You need books to keep Ganesha on, right?" I ask Ma.

She pulls a spool of red thread out of a sandwich bag. "Pick out three big books. Quentin can help you carry them back."

As soon as we're in my room, he perches on the edge of my bed, head hanging in misery.

"Oh, lighten up, Aladdin. It looks good on you."

He sniffles, looking around. "Your room looks like buckets of paint exploded."

He's not wrong. I have watercolor swatches stuck all over the walls, like I'm testing paint chips from Home Depot.

I face my bookshelf, clasping my hands behind my back. "Help me pick out the three lucky books."

"What for?"

"We use them to prop up the statues of the gods and goddesses. My mom has been picking SAT books the past few years, since the puja apparently blesses the books and makes your studies in that area go well."

Quentin tilts his head to scan the titles. The smell of his pine aftershave gives me a sense of familiarity, the way the smell of sizzling cumin seeds takes me home. Quentin in traditional Indian garb is a collision of worlds. He looks . . . handsome. The golden beading on the fabric accentuates the warm brown of his eyes, and the cream-colored fabric pairs well with his skin tone. He turns my wrists so that my palms are facing up, and my skin tingles from the touch.

"Okay, I picked out *50 Successful Ivy League Application Essays* and *On Writing the College Application Essay* because I knew you'd want blessings in that area." He stacks the books onto my hands. "And I also will add one for myself. . . ."

He gently adds the third book. *The Joy of Watercolor: 40*

Happy Lessons for Painting the World Around You. I look up with a grin, but he's already shuffling out of the room. I don't need *two* doses of blessings for my essays. I replace *On Writing the College Application Essay* with *Precalculus: An Investigation of Functions*. Maybe this will help Quentin ace his midterm.

The puja starts as soon as the pandit arrives. He chants mantras while we feed a small fire with samagri, a mix of herbs. I suddenly feel silly for dreading today. Quentin seems to be having more fun than me, wearing the heck out of his kurta and eagerly tossing samagri into the flames. I've always thought of our annual puja as a ritual to be hidden, and Christmas as a holiday to be celebrated. But when I think about it, it's strange to leave cookies out for a fictional old man, too. I guess humans are universally strange.

The puja ends a few hours later, and the pandit leaves. Ma spoons halwa onto plates, and Pa distributes them. I can't help but notice that Ma gives Quentin the biggest helping with the most golden raisins. Somehow, Quentin has weaseled into her good graces. We eat quietly, gathered in a circle on the floor in the living room. It's the first moment of quiet I've had in my mind in a while, the crashing waves subdued to ripples.

"Thank you for having me," Quentin says. He finished every last crumb of his halwa in record time. "These drawstring pants are honestly the most comfortable I've ever worn."

Pa smiles. "India loves flowing cotton fabric. These skinny jeans and polyester leggings are a very Western concept."

"Well, I should probably call my mom to pick me up. She'll be excited to hear all about the puja." Quentin glances at me, then quickly looks away. "I have a shift at Divine Tea, but I'll be back tomorrow for tutoring."

"Your mother is coming to fetch you?" Ma asks him, setting down her plate. "You did not drive here?"

"My car needed an oil change."

"Aisha, why don't you drive him to Divine Tea instead?"

What? My own mother is volunteering me to spend time with my male non-Indian peer? What is happening to the rules of the universe? Quentin's looking at me now, and I bet he's expecting me to say I have studying to do. I *could* say that and get out of this, but I don't want to. After seeing him in my house in a kurta, I understand our friendship is deeper than a small argument.

And a short kiss.

"Sure. I'll drive."

I don't wait for Quentin's reaction. I get my backpack while he goes to the bathroom to change out of his kurta. We walk out together into the biting winter air, and I jingle my keys for comfort. Driving puts me on edge, especially when I'm driving someone new.

"Are you okay to drive with your ankle?" Quentin asks.

"It's all better. Healed up pretty good."

"This is the first time I'll be the passenger." Quentin points at the bumper sticker on Pa's baby-blue Chevy Spark. It says *bee nice, new driver* in a hippie font next to a gigantic yellow bee. "Now what do we have here?"

I groan. "My dad stuck that on there. I told him I get nervous driving, and he said, 'Why invest in more driving lessons when we can just invest in this sticker?'"

"My grandpa has a *beware of dog* sign that he bought for his house up in Houghton Lake. He said that's a whole lot cheaper than getting a guard dog."

Looks like miserly parent energy transcends all cultural differences.

"I've been to Houghton Lake for an eighth-grade field trip!" I remember. "I still have the Petoskey stone I got from the gift shop there."

"Yeah, it's just two-ish hours north. Pretty much a straight shot on I-75."

I notice Quentin's curls are more tamed. Okay, *tamed* is a strong word. It's more like appeased. But even the small amount his hair is wrestled back looks unlike the Quentin I know. He must style his hair like that for work.

As we ride in silence, I wonder how to bring up New Year's Eve. Maybe we've buried what happened under all our conversation today, making it too late to go back and dig it up. When we arrive at the strip mall, Quentin thanks me for the ride. I watch until he's swallowed by the doorway of Divine Tea. I can't let this happen.

I park the car.

"Can I get the jasmine green tea to go?"

The barista smacks her gum, her attention consumed by the order monitor. Quentin is arranging a tray of tea mugs in the back, but as soon as my voice breaks the air, he turns. He's wearing a brown canvas apron over his fitted button-up shirt.

He rushes to the counter. "I'll get this one, Keesha."

As soon as Keesha slinks to the baked goods shelf, I start. "ListenIcameheretosayI'msorryaboutNewYear'sEve."

His lips part.

"I should have been careful with Sanjay. And I shouldn't have said all that stuff about you not trying. I know you're trying."

"Aisha, I'm really sorry, too. I ended up not saying anything because I thought you might not want to talk about it." He nudges the handle of one of the teacups into alignment. "I have no right to tell you what to do. I was just supposed to be there supporting you. How I reacted was not okay."

"No, it's—"

"It came from a good place. When I saw you trying so hard, I got upset because I wanted . . . I just want you to see how great you are."

I pretend to toss my hair over my shoulder. "I already *know* I'm great."

I think he sees through me, but he doesn't push. "Well, I'm sorry. About that, and kissing you. I just thought, well—I felt—"

"You were helping me. It was for the manifesto." I feel like someone is holding candles up to my cheeks. "Right?"

He looks down. "Right."

I'm hating that he said that. I'm relieved he said that. I'm inconsistent. What of it.

"So you want some tea or what?"

"Of course. I'm a customer, sir."

"In that case, *ma'am*, are you part of our rewards program? You fill out your name, email, and birthday, and you get a free drink for every five hundred points." He tilts the monitor toward me, and I put in my information. "Thank you. You should be receiving the confirmation email shortly. Now, what can I get you today?"

I laugh. I'm not used to him being so matter-of-fact. "One small jasmine green tea for here, please."

As he inputs my order, Keesha mutters about him having to chat up every customer. Quentin presses his lips together

219

like *Thanks for getting me in trouble.* I point to my chest like *Who, me?*

"I can tell my parents I'm studying here until you close. I have my backpack."

He grins. "Of course you do."

I stick my tongue out at him, and with the certainty of our friendship restored, I'm free to focus on Brian again. If I'm brave enough to kiss Quentin *and* talk to him about it, my confidence must've grown. I'll use it to go all in with Brian.

I grab my backpack from the car and settle into a corner near the community bookshelf. I try to work on my AP Chem take-home practice test, but the words fly from the page and settle near Quentin. It's fascinating to watch him be so at home, unlike when he's studying calculus. He makes conversation with every customer, and Keesha brews the tea in between texting on her phone. I don't know how I thought for a moment that Quentin kissed me because he might like me. A fish could never love a bird. Of course the kiss was part of our exchange, the way ancient peoples bartered a bushel of wheat or a pair of shoes.

A few hours later, I'm finishing up my test, and Quentin gently tells the stragglers that the café is closing soon. I get up and put my mug in the bin near the counter. "Sorry for adding one more dish to your pile."

Quentin tosses an apron at me, the canvas covering my eyes. "If you're *really* sorry, you can help me dry these mugs."

"That's no way to treat your esteemed teacher." I drape the apron over my head, trying to tie it behind my waist.

Keesha stops tapping on her phone. "Is this some weird teacher and student role-playing thing you guys have?"

Quentin guffaws, and I smack him on the shoulder with a dish towel. "No way. Quentin's just my student."

Oh no. I sound like Ma.

"How nice. I feel so special. Like a plastic bag."

"Uh, my *special* student?" I correct him. I'm still struggling with the apron strings.

Quentin reaches behind me, tugging at the strings. I endure a few moments more before I jump back like a startled squirrel.

"Hey, I didn't finish."

"I can loop it to the front and tie it."

"O-kay, then."

Keesha watches us with interest. "You can close up by yourself, right, Quentin?"

Quentin's eyes are still on me. "Sure. Have a good evening."

Keesha pockets her phone and scuttles out. I lift a fresh towel from the washbasin.

"I'm not gonna lie," Quentin says. "I was shocked you came in here. Bold move."

"I remembered your midterm is soon, and I didn't want any awkwardness between us to get in the way of your learning."

"That's the reason?"

"I want you to pass. You're not just a section on my college app, contrary to popular belief." My voice lilts like it's a good-natured joke, but he turns off the sink with a frown.

"Aisha, I'm sorry for saying that. I know it's not true. I mean, you hand-draw gold stars on all my homework assignments. I was just being a jerk."

I start to dry one of the porcelain mugs. It's the size of a bowl. How much tea do people drink at this place? "It's okay. Besides, college apps are almost over. Now I'd use you as volunteer experience to get my college *internship*."

"She's back, ladies and gentlemen."

Quentin stacks the chairs and dims the lights. I've never been in a café when it's still. It's like being backstage at a concert.

He holds out my coat. "I'll walk you to your car."

"You don't need a ride?"

"My mom's picking me up on her way home from H Mart."

"I can walk to my car by myself. It's not even late."

"I'm worried about the other people on the street. *Especially* the people driving. Who knows what car you'll get into next."

As I follow him into the parking lot, I notice his steps have a spring. "You're in a good mood. You must love making people tea."

"It's kind of the only thing I never mess up. And I like how steeping takes its own sweet time. But if I'm being honest . . ." He slows his pace so our footfalls coincide. "I was happy to see you. I thought a lot about what happened on New Year's. I was so distraught that I almost asked my mom for advice on what to do."

"Asking her for advice is a big deal?"

"Me and my mom don't have emotional conversations much. We used to after my dad passed, but not anymore. I learned to sort out my stuff on my own, although I don't always do the best job. Besides, she'd kill me if she knew that I said anything to you."

I bat my eyelashes.

"You know she loves you," he says.

"Hey, Ma loves you, too, since you bought her affection with

222

a hydrangea plant. For the record, I *earned* my affection fair and square."

"For the zillionth time, it's hyacinth." He turns to me. "Wait a second. Did you end up going ice-skating?"

I gesture to my ankle, my open palm snapping up and down like a bungee cord. "My *party favor* was still bothering me. So no. Most people's heads hurt after a long night of partying, but for me . . ."

"It's just like you to put your own personal spin on everything."

"Gee, thanks. But it was all for the best." I kick at the frosty pavement. "I wasn't in the mood after everything. And Marcy and Kevin would have probably been all couple-y on the rink somewhere, so I'd be forced to talk to Brian alone."

"Isn't that a good thing?"

"Not when you're an awkward person. It'd be better if I had a few buffers. With more people, I don't have to do all the talking."

Quentin stops in front of Pa's car. You'd think I suggested spoon-feeding his organs to wolves. "Don't you even think about it."

"Don't you want to make a new friend?"

"I'd honestly rather do calculus."

"What if I—"

"Can you see the sun? Above the hill?"

"Nice change of subject." I balance on my tiptoes to see over the hill's crown. The sunlight is bathing the treetops in gold.

"Aisha, is this not the most beautiful sunset you've ever seen?"

"The *most* beautiful? I dunno." Hearing *most*, I'm reminded of the senior superlatives in the yearbook. "Hey, do you know what senior class superlatives are?"

"Nope. Sounds like an Arledge Prep sort of preppy thing."

"I thought most schools do it. Yours probably will, too. The yearbook team assigns each person in the senior graduating class some sort of title that starts with *most likely to*." I peek at him. "What do you think my senior superlative would be?"

"Most Likely to Go to Jail? For various crimes, most notably hijacking cars? Impersonation of an old lady by the name of Sophie?"

"I hereby forbid you from bringing that up again." I raise my arms, my face angled up to the sky. "Now dance for me, monkey!"

Quentin snorts. "Okay, fine. If I'm being serious . . ." My eyes have adjusted to the waning sunlight, so I can discern all the contours of his face. "Most Likely to Inspire a Revolution."

"*What?* Me, the quiet, shy person?"

"It's always the quiet ones who start revolutions."

"I'm asking for real."

"I am for real. You're the first person who has made me think math isn't so bad, which feels like a revolution already. And if there's something you want to do, you go for it. I admire that about you."

Our eyes lock for a moment before I look away. He pokes me in the side. "What's wrong?"

"Nothing. I just . . . never saw myself that way." I wish I could lie on a printing press that would stamp his words into my skin.

"So, what do you think mine would be?"

I lean on the car door. "Most Likely to Outdress an Indian Family at Their Puja."

"After all the meaningful things I said about you?"

On the drive home, the day replays. Even though none of the events were part of my sticky note manifesto, I had fun eating halwa with my family after the prayer and observing Quentin make tea. Maybe the list of notes that I put on Quentin's wall that cold afternoon weren't really mine at all. Maybe they were things I thought I *had* to do to have fun.

Suddenly, I know what's been missing from my Stanford essay.

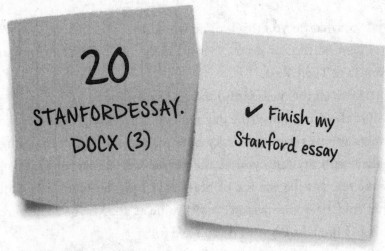

20

STANFORDESSAY.
DOCX (3)

✔ Finish my
Stanford essay

Stanford Essay.docx
Last Modified Monday, Jan 10, 5:49 p.m.

Share a time you left your comfort zone. (600 words)

When I first read this prompt, I honestly felt deep shame. I thought I had to swim with sharks to write a compelling response. I felt like I hadn't put myself in challenging situations, so my answer to that was creating a list of uncomfortable things to try. My friend called the list a manifesto, and at the time, it seemed like an effective way to hold myself accountable in my own growth. I didn't realize that ironically, I was trying to structure growth that is meant to be wild and spontaneous. As I completed classic items from my manifesto, such as dancing with someone, I found that the experiences that truly changed me were the ones that sounded bland on paper. I invited a friend to an Indian prayer ceremony, I went ice-skating for the first time, and I apologized to someone for a mistake I made. Those times were hard. Those times showed me how volunteering for an uncomfortable experience has no other requirements other than that it must be difficult for you. Taking on drastic endeavors, such as scaling Half Dome without a harness, is not the sole way to fulfill that requirement. For someone who's afraid of small spaces, riding in an elevator is excruciating. No one can decide the confines of comfort for another. The ways in which I challenged myself are just as, if not more, impactful. Those experiences showed me I'm capable of more than I think, and that the ceiling of how far I can go was one of my own making. . . .

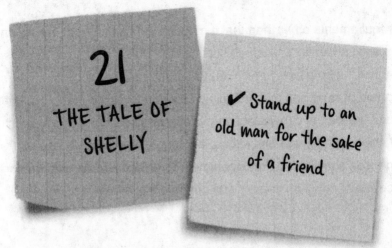

21

THE TALE OF SHELLY

✔ Stand up to an old man for the sake of a friend

After I submit my Stanford application, I do a dance in my room. I twirl so fast that my glasses fly clean off my face. I may not have been able to apply early action, but at least I submitted an application I'm proud of. And this marks my last application—I've already finished applying to a dozen other schools, including a few Ivies. After I rescue my glasses, I text Brian.

I did it! I submitted the Stanford app.

His response appears almost instantly.

Congratulations!!! Proud of you.

I don't know if it's the afterglow of submitting or my newfound confidence, but I reply asking if he wants to go to Pinball Basement. I add "in a group" because I'm not sure my nerves could take a one-on-one date yet. There's an unofficial countywide Senior Skip Day coming up this Friday, so it'd be the perfect day to go. Besides, *skip school and go to the arcade* is on my manifesto list, and Brian *did* offer to help with my manifesto.

After I dump my phone in my bag, I drive to Quentin's. He's working late at Divine Tea today, so Ms. Santos invited me over for snacks before tutoring.

"Quentin has a collection of candles he keeps under his bed,"

Ms. Santos tells Owen and me, setting a plate of lentil crackers in front of us. "I try to tell him, you're *literally* burning away the money you make at the tea shop."

I laugh. "I think you and my mom would be friends."

"It's the immigrant mindset. We like to conserve. Although we do splurge on some things." She points to her hair. "I pay a lot for the right shade of brown."

"My mom gets all the froyo toppings, too, even though she knows it's charged by weight."

"Froyo?" Owen sighs. "My dad doesn't let me eat sugar."

"We should all go out for froyo together," Ms. Santos says. "I would love to meet your parents, Aisha. Considering how wonderful you are, your family must be wonderful, too. A bunch of gentle souls."

"No way. My sister is anything but gentle. She's the critical type."

"Ah, well. Family cares most but also tends to be the most critical. Quentin has similar pressure from his grandpa. We all call him Grandpa Shelly because of his hard-shell personality."

"Grandpa Shelly is scary," Owen whispers to me.

"Not scary, just . . . harsh." A shadow crosses Ms. Santos's face. She pushes her empty bowl as if to ward away a memory. "For example, the day Grandpa Shelly heard that Quentin was failing math, he called, and the conversation didn't go well. He called Quentin a lazy bum."

I frown.

"It gets worse. The next day, Shelly asked Quentin to pick up a friend from some downtown jazz rehearsal."

I freeze midway through biting into a cracker. That was the night I met Quentin.

"And then?" I ask through a mouthful of cracker, although I already know.

"Quentin agreed, but he had a mix-up with the entrances and ended up just missing her. You can imagine how upset Shelly was. He called me and said it proves that Quentin should stay with him in Houghton Lake for winter break." She massages her temples. "I almost considered it, you know. Because despite me trying everything, Quentin hasn't really been able to recover since his father died."

"But he's on his way. He's making major progress in math."

"I'm worried that math is a symptom of the larger issue. Quentin used to be top of his class in math. He only fell behind after . . ." She sighs. "He feels a lot of pressure to not disappoint anyone. To not make a sound. I worry he's keeping everything inside."

Quentin can be hard to read at times, but I always thought his baseline energy was so *stable*. I'm the one flapping everywhere and almost falling into pools.

"But his overall grade has improved so much, so I can't thank you enough. We like having such a driven presence around." She nods at Owen. "It's good for this one, too."

Owen bobs his head. "Yeah, it's pretty cool having a girl around. I'm used to hanging out with girls more anyhow, because of my girlfriend, Yasmin."

Ms. Santos and I exchange looks.

"Thanks, Owen," I say. "And congratulations on being much further along in the romance department than I've ever been. I only recently started talking to my crush."

Ms. Santos whacks my arm. "They say the flower that blooms

late ends up being the most fragrant. Besides, you are an expert conversationalist. Even Shelly would like you."

"Doubt it. It seems like he hates everyone." Kind of like Lily.

"Shelly's . . . he's a bit of a prickly person, but he has a good heart. He's driving all the way from Houghton Lake to have dinner with us at Zola's tonight. I invited him. Quentin told me he was thinking of asking you to join, too."

I straighten like there's a plank of wood taped to my back. "Quentin *definitely* didn't mention this."

"He wanted someone there to divert the attention, since meals with his grandpa are always hard. If you do choose to come, you should trade him for something big."

Oh, I know *just* the favor to ask of Quentin in exchange, and I know he's going to hate it.

"So you asked Shelly to dinner," I summarize, half in surprise, half in admiration.

"He's my late husband's father. And we have a saying in the Philippines. Kung pukulin ka ng bato, tinapay ang iganti mo. That means . . . if someone throws stones at you, throw back bread."

I'm about to ask more about Grandpa Shelly and how to weasel into his good graces when the doorknob jiggles.

Quentin bursts through the door, keys jangling. "Aisha, I saw your car in the driveway. What are you doing here? I thought you were working on your essay."

"I wanted to tell you in person. I submitted. All done."

"Holy fu—" He glances at Owen. "Fudge nuggets. Congratulations! This calls for a celebration."

Ms. Santos rolls her eyes. "That's what this is, iho. I invited

231

Aisha for snacks and promised her some stories about you."

He looks from me to Owen to his mom. "Owen, what did my mom tell her?"

"Not much. Just that you have a secret obsession with scented candles."

He moans and rushes to the table, resting his hands on my shoulders. "Before more damage is done, let's go. I gotta earn more hand-drawn stars."

"But I'm not done talking to your—" I see him pout. "Fine."

Quentin walks my empty plate to the sink, and then he herds me up the stairs to his room. "Nanay, don't worry about the dishes," he calls. "I'll do them later."

I stare at him. "My parents can never get me to do my chores. I always use studying as an excuse."

Quentin flumps down into his chair. I sit at the foot of his bed. I plant a pillow on my lap and rest my elbows on it. "So, I heard you wanted to ask me for a favor."

"Huh?"

"It rhymes with belly and winner."

"Uh . . ."

I lean in like *wait for it* . . .

"Shelly and dinner?" Quentin groans. "She told you? I was just *considering* asking you and thought better of it. This is why I don't tell my mom anything. She has loose lips."

"Looks like we have an opportunity for an exchange here. You hang out with Brian, me, and Marcy at the arcade this Friday, and I will hang out with your grandpa and you tonight. It's perfect."

"It's so typical of you to make this a deal. Also, why in the world do you want third and fourth wheels for your arcade date? Don't you want it to be special?"

"Brian and I have been texting more, but texting is easier. I get nervous in one-on-one in-person situations. I need support, and four is the perfect size for a group. I already asked Marcy, and she's in. Kevin can't make it because he'll be at his little sister's volleyball game."

"Fine. I'll come. But you gotta stay for dinner *and* come out for ice cream with Owen and me."

"I'd do that anyway, silly. But why is ice cream part of this?"

"Because meeting Grandpa Shelly stresses me out, and I'll probably want some ice cream after."

"I thought you used candles to de-stress."

"Says the girl who makes to-do lists to de-stress. At least mine makes sense."

"Hey, my manifesto might be ending soon, now that my essay's done."

Even as I say it, I know it's not true. There are always more sticky notes.

Evening falls, and Ms. Santos drives us to Zola's.

"We're here, kids!" she trumpets, shifting the car into park. "Who's ready for pasta?"

"If I can get a bite down my throat without being criticized," Quentin mutters, climbing out of the car after me.

Owen gives Quentin a solemn nod. "It was nice knowing you."

We walk inside. I imagined Grandpa Shelly to be a grouchy old man with a handlebar mustache, an ironed pocket square, and a cane that he pokes people with. As he waves, I see he's in a plain sweater, a flat cap with a stiff brim at the front, and circular, gold-rimmed glasses.

"Ciao, Arianne." He kisses Ms. Santos on the cheek. He nods at Quentin and ruffles Owen's hair. His eyes move to me. They're Quentin's eyes, except they're more piercing than warm.

"Hi, I'm Aisha. A friend of Quentin's."

"She's helping him with math," Ms. Santos explains.

"You can call me Shelly. It's an honor to finally meet the math whiz. I got us a table in the back. I brought a friend, too."

"Didn't know you managed to keep any," Quentin mumbles.

As we skirt around the tables and looming plants, my eyes settle on a familiar face poking over a menu. Her long, silvery hair is unmistakable.

Sophie. Kevin's grandma. The person who was *supposed* to get into Quentin's car.

"Hey there." She sets down her menu and stands. Even by day, she's the swankiest old lady I've ever seen. Purple velvet pumps, a golden bangle, and a carved golden locket to match.

I peek at Quentin. He shrugs back like *She's ancient, she probably won't remember you.* I let everyone fill the seats first, so I can sit as far away from Sophie as I can. The last available spot is by Shelly. I have never understood the saying "between a rock and a hard place" better than this moment.

Sophie's eyes linger on me as we sit down. "Who is this, Jack? Introduce us."

"Of course." Grandpa Shelly rests a hand on the back of my chair. "This is Sophie, and this is a friend of Quentin's, Aisha. She's the town's Yoda, I hear."

"I'm Quentin's tutor," I explain. "And Quentin's been helping me, too."

"Quentin's helping you," Shelly repeats. "But you attend Arledge Preparatory, isn't that right? I doubt he could help you."

"He's been helping me with a bucket list of sorts. I spent a lot of time studying throughout school, and there was a lot of stuff I never got the chance to do. He's helping me complete my list."

"How . . . interesting."

I'm reminded of hanging out at Brian's house as a kid. Brian's mom was able to patronize anyone with one word. The time I sewed patches into my jeans jacket, it wasn't *adorable* or *creative*. It was *interesting*.

Quentin's looking at the menu for so long that I'm sure he's reread it at least four times.

Sophie is still sizing me up. "Have we met, dear? You look familiar. Maybe you came to one of my shows or something? I play the clarinet around town."

"No, ma'am. I probably just have one of those faces." I give her a big smile.

Quentin mouths *no, ma'am* at me from over his menu. As I glare at him, my phone buzzes on the table. A message from Brian. I assume Grandpa Shelly is a no-phones-at-the-table kinda guy, but I can't help it. I look.

Pinball Basement sounds awesome! I'm in.

This means I'll finally spend time with Brian. A *real* date. Well, with Quentin there as date monitor, and Marcy there as a conversation saver, but maybe it counts. I start typing back.

Marcy and Quentin are in, too! They wanted to check out the arcade.

When I look up from my phone, Quentin is looking at me.

"And how are you doing, Quentin?" Sophie asks. "Not breaking too many hearts?"

"More like breaking pencils in half as I study for my calculus midterm," he replies. "And working at Divine Tea. You should come by sometime."

"I'd love to! With you graduating and moving away, I better come soon."

"No rush," Shelly remarks. "At this rate, Quentin will be working there until he's old and gray like me."

Ms. Santos looks like she's about to say something, but the waiter arrives. I see why Quentin wanted me at this dinner. Even while attempting calculus problems, he must hear his grandpa's voice in his head. When the basket of bread arrives, I pray no one will ask me why I'm not eating any. I hate repeating the monologue of my late-onset gluten sensitivity woes.

"The bread isn't bad," Shelly remarks. "Wonder if the pasta will hold a candle to our homemade ravioli."

"Family recipe?" I ask.

"That's right. My son Emilio used our recipe to make ravioli every year around the holidays. He hosted a big gathering with friends and family, and many traveled far to come. The secret is olive oil. Most of the olive oil in this country is old and dead, like I will be soon—"

I notice Sophie shake her head from the corner of my eye.

"—but *real* olive oil is young. Sweet at the front of the mouth, spicy at the back."

"I'll keep that in mind. I've always wanted to host my own dinner party."

"I thought it was a wonderful tradition, although I did always nitpick at Emilio's four-cheese filling." Shelly wipes the corners of his mouth with his napkin. "Boy, I wish I had appreciated it more then. I'd give anything to relive those moments with him."

Ms. Santos peers into her plate of crumbs, her gaze glassy. Quentin busies himself by dunking his bread into the olive oil.

"Sorry, I didn't mean to—" I start, but Shelly puts his hand up.

"No, dear, I brought him up. It's nice to talk about Emilio and have his stories live on. Although the person who tells the best stories about him is probably my grandson. Likely because stories don't involve any math."

Quentin rolls his eyes. "Was that an attempt at a compliment, Grandpa?"

"I suppose it was."

I look at Quentin, jutting out my lower lip. "Can I hear a story, Quentin?"

Quentin looks at me like he wants to hurl a tub of salad forks at me one by one.

"I like stories," Owen adds.

"Me too," Sophie agrees.

Ms. Santos nods, and Quentin sighs. "I guess there's one favorite I could tell."

I feel that anticipatory tingle on my arms that I used to get before going to the library to check out new novels. Nowadays, the reading I do is college application how-to books or Princeton Review books.

"It was autumn in fifth grade in the town of Kresge. I had my heart set on being Superman for Halloween. Nanay was busy at an engineering conference, so my dad and I went to the costume shop. I knew what aisle everything was in. A12 for the red cape, C9 for the fabric paint to make the *S* emblem, and G4 for the blue shirt I'd wear underneath. I got the blue shirt, the fabric paint, and right as I walked down A12 after getting the cape, I saw him. Gary Mackens."

Ms. Santos rolls her eyes. "He never got over Gary."

"Gary Mackens was the school menace and my archrival. I was pretty sure he stole my sixty-four pack of crayons. And in this moment, I was mortified. Because I saw him with the exact same supplies: a cape, fabric paint, and a blue shirt."

"No," I gasp.

"How could I, who admired Superman for his utter goodness, wear the same costume as the school villain? I could not. So, as brave kids do . . . I ran to my dad in aisle C9 and cried."

Owen shakes his head, like *Kids*.

"My dad promised me that we would use those supplies to make an entirely different costume. A *better* costume. One that is the *real* hero of Halloween."

Ms. Santos smiles, murmuring, "That's just like Emilio."

"My dad disappeared into the study as soon as we came home. He didn't come out for a whole hour. Then he told me to close my eyes."

"What was it?" Owen demands.

"When I opened my eyes, I was an amazing, a *dazzling* . . ." Quentin looks at all of us. "BLUE SUPER M&M!"

I hear some groans.

I point in the air as I piece it together. "Your dad used the blue shirt as the blue M&M base, and then painted the white *m* on it, and then the cape for the 'super' part?"

"That's right, Aisha. He told me I was the real hero of Halloween, because Halloween's whole purpose is for kids to get chocolate. The end."

"And *now* . . ." Ms. Santos puts her arm around Quentin, squeezing him close. "Quentin's just as thoughtful as his father, isn't he?"

"Nanay, please." Quentin's ears go pink.

"Definitely," I agree, and I'm not agreeing out of politeness. When I speak, Quentin listens to every word before thoughtfully responding. It doesn't matter if I'm pontificating about math or complaining about how annoyingly perfect and swingy Seema's high ponytail looks all the time. Ms. Santos combs Quentin's hair back while he squirms.

"I suppose Quentin is similar to Emilio," Shelly says, and the ghost of a smile appears on Quentin's lips. "One key difference being, Emilio got into college without any trouble."

I can't look at Quentin's ashen expression. After a long, tense silence, I hear the screech of a chair scuttling back.

"Thanks for the bread. I think I'm going to go."

By the time I look up, Quentin is already gone, and his coat isn't hanging on the chair anymore. Ms. Santos's face is pale, but to my surprise, she's quiet. Sophie is watching Shelly with knitted eyebrows, but she's quiet, too. I look at Owen. He looks at me as if he's a toddler who just smashed his toy train, like *Fix it.*

"W-With all due respect, sir, that was an unfair statement."

I didn't expect to speak up. As Grandpa Shelly appraises me from behind his glasses, I'm reduced to a worm inching past him on the ground. I clear my throat, finding my voice again.

"Quentin is bright and hardworking. The only thing he needs is support. You said that you wish you would have appreciated the time with Emilio more, so why is Quentin any different?" I stand. "I'm going to go find Quentin. Owen, do you wanna—"

"Yes," Owen squeaks.

I head for the door, Owen at my heels. As soon as the winter air fills my lungs, I almost keel over. I hadn't been breathing. Neat.

"Holy fudge nuggets! That was *awesome*."

"Thanks, O-ster." I spot Quentin hunched over a small bench near the parking lot, heaps of half-melted snow on the cement next to him. I guide Owen along.

When Quentin sees us, he starts blinking so fast I think his eyelashes will stir up a snowstorm. "What are you guys doing out here? You should go back and eat dinner. I'll be fine."

I take a step closer. "You can't wait out here, it's freezing."

Owen bobs in his boots. "You know what Aisha just—"

I clap my hand over Owen's mouth. "We can walk to Wooly's. It's only a few blocks. I promised you ice cream, and we should let this poor kid have his fill of sugar, am I right?"

Quentin narrows his eyes. "What did you do, Aish?"

"Nothing, I swear. How about some chocolate chip cookie dough?"

He nods, and we plod down the sidewalk. Owen dawdles behind, plucking sticks of winterberry from a nearby shrub poking out of the frosted ground. I bet he's going to give the bouquet to his girlfriend on Monday or something.

I watch Quentin as we walk. He doesn't look angry. His expression is almost . . . *vacant*. "Are you all right?"

"Yeah. It's just hard to hear that stuff. It makes me wonder if I'd be disappointing my dad if he were alive."

"Not a chance. If I was your parent, I'd be super proud. You tell the best stories. You offer to do the dishes without being asked. You're a great babysitter. You help your friends when they almost fall into pools. In fact, I know your superlative. Most Likely to Be Brought Home to Meet the Parents."

That gets me a half smile.

"I don't know why Shelly's like that, but you don't need his approval. Look at all the stars on your problem sets. You know your stuff. You can do this."

"Thanks, Aisha. That means a lot."

I pretend to bow and blow kisses at the adoring crowd.

He eyes me. "You should take some of your own advice. I don't think you need me and Marcy to crash your date with Brian. He'd like you *without* buffers."

"Oh? You're not saying that to get out of it?"

"*No, ma'am*," he crows, and I laugh. "So what did you do at Zola's? Owen doesn't get excited for nothing."

"It's in the spirit of the manifesto, but not on the wall. I went off script."

I glance back, admiring Owen's serendipitous bouquet of winterberry twigs. Maybe I can learn to appreciate the unplanned, too.

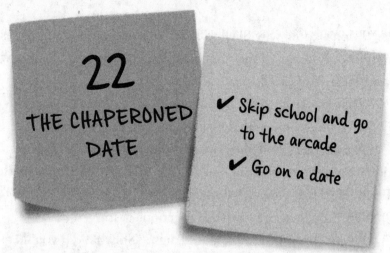

22
THE CHAPERONED DATE

✔ Skip school and go to the arcade
✔ Go on a date

I hop into Quentin's Jetta the same way I flop onto my couch at home after school. It's funny how comfortable I am in his car now compared to the night we first met.

"Seat belt, miss. And as your trusty driver, I put the *skip school and go to the arcade* sticky note in the glove box for you to cross off, along with the other notes from New Year's."

He always remembers. After I dig through the glove box, I bob my head to some tunes from the Bee Gees and bask in the sunshine warming my arms. The world is smiling upon me today. My chimples sank down a bit, it's not snowing even though the forecast guaranteed snowfall, and my birthday is tomorrow. That means Pa's gluten-free, homemade marble cake.

"Does Brian or Marcy need a ride, too?" Quentin asks.

"No, they live super close to the arcade. Brian drove, and Marcy's mom dropped her off."

"I can't believe I'm using Senior Skip Day on this."

"Considering our Senior Skip Days fell on the same day, I think it was fate." I bat my eyelashes at him, and he sighs.

"You don't find it strange that you asked me to crash your date with Brian, and now I'm driving you to Pinball Basement as your chaperone? Is this where I ask you for your signed permission slip?"

"Ma wouldn't sign the permission slip considering there are *two* boys. Getting her to let me skip school for today was hard enough. I'm excited to hear what you think of Brian after spending time with him today."

He veers to avoid a pothole. "I already overshared my opinion once, so I'm officially an opinion-less objective third-party bystander."

"What are you going to do there, then? Help me win enough tickets to get one of those pink teddy bears they hang from the ceiling?"

"That, and whenever the conversation dies, I'll ask a random question that makes you look good. *Hey, Aisha, remember that time you saved that dying cat from a tree?*"

There's a pit in my stomach, but I know the pit would have been much larger in radius without Quentin and Marcy. Besides, the four of us together will have a better chance of scoring enough tickets for a bear.

When we get to Pinball Basement, we find Brian sitting at the entrance, scrolling through his phone.

"Brian!" I wave.

He looks up. "Hey! Marcy's already inside. She's getting us some game tokens." His gaze moves to Quentin. "Good to see you again, man."

As soon as we all get inside, Marcy beelines toward us. She's wearing a red beanie and red high-top sneakers to match, shaking a big plastic cup of coins at us. "You're all here! I may have gone a little overboard with the tokens, but I couldn't resist." She slings her arm through mine. "Aisha, choose the first game."

The glowing arrow of the claw machine catches my eye. I point to it with a cheesy grin, and the group groans. Marcy drops a handful of tokens into my palm, and after I feed them into the machine, I position the claw right above a stuffed bunny with cloth ears and cute button eyes.

Quentin taps the glass. "A little to your left."

"Precision doesn't help here, silly."

As expected, the plunging claw comes up empty.

Quentin rolls up the sleeves of his green crewneck sweater. "I'm going to go for your little bunny, too."

"You're kidding. This is the *last* game I thought you'd use your tokens on."

"Someone wise told me that I should take more risks. That person also told me my room lacks character. This solves both."

"I don't get you guys." Brian shakes his head. "Why play something that's so obviously rigged against you?"

"Plus one," Marcy agrees.

Quentin shrugs. "For fun." He doesn't capture the bunny, so we make our way to the Whac-A-Mole game. I earn a whopping six tickets.

I peel them from the dispenser. "I blame my reflexes on sleep deprivation."

"I thought Arledge Prep would be more relaxed now with college apps done," Quentin says.

Marcy sighs. "You would think. Now we lose sleep thinking about which colleges we'll get into, until we find out in a few weeks. I'm praying for Northwestern, but I'm open to any college that has a reputable journalism program."

Quentin v. Moles commences. Moles lose. More and more tickets print from the machine as we look on in awe.

"Which college are you aiming for, Brian?" Quentin asks.

"Harvard."

Quentin raises his eyebrows. "Whoa. Pressure."

He nods. "If I don't get in now, grad school will be my mom's new project."

"Do you want to go? Or are you doing it for your mom?"

"I wish I could say it's my mom's dream and not mine, but I started wanting it for myself at some point, probably after watching all those college acceptance reaction videos. Your future depends on where you get your education. And who you know."

He's not wrong, but I wish he was. It's like the essay we wrote. The American Dream may advertise that background doesn't matter, but I know that being lower income and having parents who didn't grow up in America affects me. Some Arledge parents have access to bootlegged SAT exam booklets, while others have generational wealth that secures their child's admission to top institutions. My parents make a killer spiced mango pickle, but that doesn't help me much.

"That's not always true. Aisha got into Arledge Prep all on her own," Quentin says.

I stare at him. What happened to saying that I save cats from trees?

Brian drapes an arm over my shoulder, and I stiffen. "That's because she's the smartest person I know. We're going to be co-valedictorians."

"Um." Marcy puts a hand up. "Not so fast. There could be other perfect GPA holders wandering Arledge's halls."

"Well, even being in the running is awesome. Congratulations to you both." Quentin's voice is flat, unlike the lilt it had when he congratulated me for my first attempt at stovetop cooking a few days ago. I made broccoli cheese soup.

Okay, so it was mostly cheese soup.

After we wander to the multiplayer games, Quentin makes a joke here and there, but he hangs a few paces back. He's not playing. I'm about to ask him if everything is okay when his phone rings.

"Be right back," he murmurs. "My mom."

Marcy and I start a game of air hockey while Brian is in the bathroom, but my attention flits to Quentin. He's pacing by the claw machine as he talks. I can see the neon stripes of his socks poking out of his shoes, all the way from where I'm standing.

"Earth to Aisha." Marcy snaps her fingers. "I've scored six goals, and you've barely noticed."

"I've noticed, but my eyeballs have no peripheral vision at the moment." I point to my black-framed glasses. My eyes were too dry for contacts this morning, though I tried thrice.

"Your eyeballs look fine to me. Maybe they're just *preoccupied*."

My eyes narrow. "What do you mean?"

"I've noticed you watching Quentin a lot today. You can tell me, Aish. I'd like to know about your crush in a timelier fashion this go-round." She presses her lips together. "Do you like him?"

"Of *course* not." My voice is shrill. "I organized this arcade thing to spend more time with Brian."

She scowls. "Firstly, ouch. I thought you invited me to the arcade because you wanted to hang out. Secondly, you liking Quentin is not some outlandish idea. You guys have been spending a lot of time together, and for what it's worth, I approve. He said that thing about you getting into Arledge all on your own, and I can tell he—"

"Marce, he's not my type."

"Don't use that *type* thing, Aisha."

I fold my arms over my chest. "Just because I've never dated before, I can't have a type?"

"What would your type even be? Valedictorian who must be taller than you?"

"Maybe."

She frowns. "So, you can't go to college unless it's Stanford, and you can't go on a date unless it's Brian?"

"It's not like that."

My cheeks burn because it *is* like that. I aim for the top—top college, top of my class, top leadership position of crochet club. Without me realizing, maybe I'm also going for the boy who, in my eyes, is somehow at the *top*. Marcy is about to say more, but before she can, Brian jogs up.

"Who's winning?" he asks, a small smile poking a dimple into his cheek.

"Aisha is," Marcy replies sweetly. "Her concentration is astounding."

I sigh. What does Marcy know, anyway? She wouldn't understand that paralyzing *need* to strive for the best. If she doesn't do well in college, she can fall back on her mansion in the Arledge 'burbs.

"It's official, guys." Quentin's voice cuts into my thoughts. I didn't even notice him come up behind me. "I'm going away on a fishing trip with my grandpa tomorrow in nowheresville."

My face falls. "You're *leaving*?"

"It's an annual thing me, my dad, and my grandpa used to do. We'd fish and hang out for a few days. It's torture. And I don't have reception in Houghton Lake since my grandpa basically lives on a farm. The most popular attraction around there is the ice museum. I know more about the history of local ice harvesting than anyone should."

My throat tightens. "How long will you be gone?"

"Just the weekend. I'll keep up with the problem sets while I'm away. After things went south at dinner, my mom wants me to go patch things up."

I turn the air hockey puck over in my hand. A few days seem like an eternity. And he'll miss my birthday.

I need ice cream.

"Hey," I say. "Who's up to go to Wooly's? The forecast said it's supposed to snow, but it looks sunny enough for ice cream."

"I might head back now," Marcy says with a thin smile. "I have some stuff to work on for the yearbook."

Brian looks hesitant. "I was sorta trying to watch my diet for basketball. . . ."

I pout. "C'mon, guys, live a little. Can *I* at least get some?"

"Fine," Brian relents, giving me a half grin as he moves to stand beside me. "I can drive us."

"Quentin?" I purse my lips together. "Yeah?"

"Nah, you two go ahead. I should get going."

Quentin should come to Wooly's and then drive me home. That's how these events should go, like the starting position of a chessboard. But why am I hoping for that? My Brian-induced nerves have worn off, enough for me to win against Brian at Fruit Ninja *and* ask him to ice cream.

"But you love the chocolate chip cookie dough at Wooly's."

Quentin glances at his wooden watch. "It's already five, so I should study for my midterm, especially now that I'll be gone this weekend. But, Marcy, I can give you a ride home. Aisha mentioned your mom dropped you off today, right?"

She arches an eyebrow at me ever so slightly before turning to face him. "Yeah, thanks. That's super nice of you."

Quentin drives *me* home. Bishops can't move horizontally in chess.

"Aisha and I will carry on, then," Brian says, the tones of his deep voice sounding closer than ever. "And hey, Quentin, if you need some extra help on studying, let me know. I promise I'll make you love math."

Quentin's smile is stiff. "Thanks, but I'm more of a history guy myself."

"You *like* history?"

"Keeping a record of what's happened stops you from repeating mistakes. It's a sort of self-awareness mirror being held up to society that reflects both its cruelty and potential for change."

Huh. I never thought of history like that. Now I wish I added AP History to my sophomore year schedule.

Marcy clears her throat. "I drank an obscene amount of off-brand Sprite, so I'm gonna use the bathroom. I'll meet you at your car in five, Quentin. Which car is it?"

"Silver Volkswagen Jetta, close to the front."

"I'll walk you out," I blurt, stepping toward Quentin. "I . . . I left something in your car."

A look of surprise passes over Quentin's face, but he doesn't challenge the suggestion.

Brian shrugs. "Take your time. I'll shoot some hoops with the last few tokens."

Quentin and I walk to the parking lot together in silence. We stop in front of his car. I'm about to ask him if he had fun, but I think better of the question.

"Thank you," I say instead.

"Of course. It was part of the deal, and now that you'll be alone with Brian for ice cream, I think we can cross off *go on a date*."

"Even though I didn't technically ask him out?"

"I consulted the manifesto legal counsel, and they said it counts." He's smiling, but his usual intent look is gone. He presses his bouquet of tickets into my hand.

I look up at him, my eyes wide. "You're not going to redeem these for something?"

"Consider it an early birthday present. You can start saving up for your bear."

"How'd you know when my birthday is? I never told you, did I? Did Seema—"

"Remember how you signed up for the rewards program when you visited me at Divine Tea? You entered your birthday."

I grin. That's some sleuthing.

"I'm sorry I'll be gone for it. I can't even text you because I'll have no reception or Wi-Fi at Shelly's, but I'll be there in spirit. Save me a slice of cake, okay?"

There's this wavelike white noise filling my ears as Quentin gets into his Jetta. I watch as he leans over to poke his key into the ignition. He cranks down his window.

"By the way, I didn't know you had trouble sleeping lately. You're the one who told me that REM sleep is key to retaining the information we study. You okay?"

I bend so my eyes are level with his. "I'm fine. I think I was just anxious about the Stanford deadline. I applied regular decision, too, which lowers my chances."

"You need some of my scented candles."

I force a smile.

"Call me if you ever can't sleep. My dad used to read the encyclopedia to me as a kid, and it always worked." He pats the passenger's seat. "Also, what did you leave in my car? It looks all clear to me."

"Oh! Right. I thought I left my phone." I slap my jeans pocket. "But it's in here."

Liar, liar, jeans on fire.

"All right, well. Happy birthday, Aisha."

"Drive safe, Quentin."

I see Marcy pushing through the door of Pinball Basement. I wave at her as she approaches, but she doesn't give me her usual twenty-miles-per-hour wave. It's a tiny quarter wave. I don't know why, but it makes me feel like pond scum.

"Are you *sure* you don't want anything?" I ask Brian as the waitress sets my sundae in front of me. How does Brian look irresistible just sitting next to a window? The light is casting shadows across his biceps. I can even see the veins pulsing on his arms.

He spins his glass of water in his hands. "I'm sure. I can't get my mom's voice out of my head. She's always telling me that eating sugar will make me gain weight. You remember how chubby I used to be before high school. No one wants to see that again."

I do. I'd kill to spend time with the Brian I knew from middle school. It seems like his mom kept telling him that he wasn't enough, instead of loving him unconditionally like a parent should—like I did all those years ago.

"But then I lost a lot of weight, which involved a lot of caloric restriction and basketball. Honestly, it's not even the comments my mom makes that bother me anymore. It's her hypothetical comments I can't get out of my head."

The disapproving voices of parents always echo. My parents also tell me that I eat too many Snickers bars, use my computer too much, don't apply enough coconut oil to my dry scalp, and why, oh why, don't I try doing yoga with my grandma over video call?

"I need to get in shape for basketball anyhow," he adds.

He's already *plenty* in shape.

I know this is everything I wanted a few weeks ago when I was pasting the *go on a date* sticky note to Quentin's wall. Talking with Brian, relating to him, sitting with him at a real table instead of the depths of the library shelves. Yet how come when my wish is coming true, I can't stop thinking about—

"Quentin seems cool."

"He is." I imagine all the gold stars I won't be able to draw on his problem sets for the next few days.

"Are you and Quentin a thing? You guys seem close."

I freeze. To ask Brian a question like that, I'd need dim lighting and four a.m. timing. Bluntness is something he and Marcy have in common.

"No way." I force a short laugh. "My parents would kill me if they knew I was dating, just like yours. Besides, I actually like someone else. And Quentin isn't interested."

I can count every hair in Brian's eyebrows from here. That

alone is scrambling my brain like a Rubik's cube.

"And who is this mysterious *someone*? Do I know him?"

My feelings were supposed to live in obscurity until Brian's romantic confession of love for me after we continued spending time together. This wasn't the plan. "I—well . . ."

"You don't have to tell me if you don't want to." He fishes in his backpack. "But I can secretly hope my birthday gift is better than his, right?"

He slides a box across the table. I catch it with my hand.

Truffles. Each ball is dipped in glaze, the patterns intricate as stained-glass cathedral windows.

"They're chocolate truffles made in Los Angeles, from this place called Compartés. I thought, if you're going to eat chocolate for lunch, you might as well eat *good* chocolate."

These look expensive. Arledge Prep tuition expensive. And Brian ordered them all the way from the state of my dreams.

"They're gorgeous," I manage to choke out. "Thank you so much, Brian."

"It was only fair that I return the favor. You got me macarons for Christmas."

I look down. "I hope you liked them. It was my first time making them, and I know they were a little dry, so I—"

"They were really good."

The waitress pops in to see if we need anything. I shake my head, taping a smile to my face and stirring my melted, soupy ice cream like *This is just how I like it.*

When we leave Wooly's, I'm suddenly overcome with exhaustion. Brian's gift should have turned this into the coolest birthday ever. Instead, the sky-high hopes I had for today ended up draining my energy over time, like sand in an hourglass. I'm ready to hide in the gooey center of one of these truffles.

"Hey." I gently cut into Brian's monologue on basketball season. "Is it okay if I walk home? I have way too much energy after all that sugar."

"You sure? It's supposed to snow today. I'd be happy to drive you." He rests a hand on my shoulder. "I'll be quiet. I know I talk too much."

"Ha, no. There's not a cloud in the sky right now. And I might call Marcy to help her with yearbook stuff later." I take a small step back, and his hand slips. "Speaking of, what do you think my senior superlative will be? Any guesses?"

He takes a few moments to think before snapping his fingers. "Most Likely to Get into Every Ivy."

I thank him, but the answer feels like slicing open an avocado to find mushy brown. During my pilgrimage home, details of the day project into my mind like an old movie reel. Quentin asking why I wasn't sleeping well. Brian's truffles. Marcy's half wave. All of it swirls into a mixture of thoughts—soupy and messy, like my ice cream. The most important part of the soup being time alone with Brian not feeling like I'd hoped.

A snowflake kisses my wrist and disintegrates. I hadn't noticed the clouds gathering in the sky.

"Figures," I murmur as snow begins to fall.

23

HAPPY BIRTHDAY TO ME

✔ Get a cool birthday gift

"What do you want to eat, birthday girl?" Ma asks the next morning, squeezing me into a rib-crushing hug. "Papa is on cake duty, so I'll make breakfast."

"Anything's good."

Usually, when my birthday falls on a weekend, I sip a cup of hot cocoa, draw a bath, and wear my favorite sweater dress. Today, I towed myself out of bed as I tried to remember what I used to do before I messaged Quentin. He loses reception, and I'm acting like he burned up in the atmosphere on his journey into space. Marcy gave me one of those fancy pop-up greeting cards today before leaving for the weekend to visit her older brother in Chicago, so at least I have that to be grateful for. I called her yesterday to see if she needed help with yearbook stuff, but she said no, so I was worried things were still off between us. Then this morning, she stopped by with my card, and I figured we're okay. She kept looking at her shoes, though, so I can't be sure. . . .

"Sab teek tho hai, beta?" *Is everything okay?*

A few weeks ago, I had focus. Get Brian to fall in love with me, probably major in computer science at Stanford. Now it's all too much, like keeping ten tops spinning on a table without letting a single one wobble.

"Yes, Ma. Just tired."

"Pray to Shiva for energy. And Seema is driving over from college later to eat dinner with us. She says she got you a gift."

For someone who says college is *so* much better than high school, Seema visits home a lot. And she always gets me gifts she thinks I should want instead of stuff I need. Last year, she got me avocado-patterned socks and toast earrings. Gluten-free avocado toast. Har har.

My phone buzzes. Brian.

Happy birthday, Aisha!

Thank you 😊 How's your weekend been?

Good! Kevin and I might hang out later at the arcade. Maybe I'll win at Fruit Ninja this time 😊

Lol

Backspace. I'll reply to Brian later.

Pa appears in the kitchen right as I'm about to go hide out in my room like a rat skittering away from light. "Hello, birthday girl! What is this, now? You're not in your usual dress." He lowers his voice. "Baat kya hai? Are you worried about your admission to Stanford?"

"Sort of."

"Follow me. I found something you might like."

When we get inside my parents' room, he cracks open an old cardboard box and hands me a stack of wrinkled sheets of paper. The musty smell reminds me of the Arledge Prep library.

"I was organizing my papers a few weeks ago for taxes, and I found these."

A collection of artwork from when I was a kid. My parents discovered that a surefire way to tire me out was to make me draw a picture. I sift through the sheets filled with stick figures and unintelligible scribbles. The prompt-response style of the worksheets reminds me of Ms. Kavnick's journal assignments.

When I grow up, I want to be . . . ? Answer: *ARTIST.*

What's your best quality? Answer: *I NEVER give up.*

I continue flipping, coming to a painting of me and my elementary school crush, Cory, getting married. "Can't believe you kept these, Pa."

"Some of them are very clever. You drew a whole story about how we were a special family from outer space with powers." He rests his palm on my mass of unkempt hair. "Might I add, you made Seema the only human, and she had no powers at all."

"As it should be."

His smile fades. "You've been locked in your room a lot, beta. Stanford itni badi baat nahin hai, jaise tum soch rahi ho." *Stanford isn't as big of a deal as you think.*

That's what I'm afraid of. What if all the stuff I wanted for so long isn't all that great? Say, for example, what if I thought hanging out with my longtime crush would feel like plucking stars from the sky, but when it happened, it felt like eating ice cream soup at a diner?

Pa pulls the legs of his pants up as he sits in his desk chair. "You can always change your plans. I had a degree from back home that was in electrical engineering. Now I work in software, and we live in America."

"Living here wasn't the plan?" I thought my parents charted their course to America, marking maps and memorizing state abbreviations from childhood.

"Of course not. We didn't intend to stay here forever. We question if it was the right thing to do as our parents get older."

"Why did you stay, then?" I don't mean for it to sound like an accusation, but maybe my life would be easier if I was fully American or fully Indian, instead of in between. I always assumed my parents moved here for the same reason everyone does: the American Dream. But after Ms. Kavnick's unit, that started feeling overly simplified.

"My company sent me here, and we liked it. The opportunities, the comforts."

"Costco?"

He chuckles. "Costco. And if I had a job in Bangalore, the commute time would be crazy. There's a traffic light there called Sony World Signal, and the traffic pileup can last hours."

That sounds terrible, but think of how many audiobooks I'd be able to barrel through in that time. *50 Successful Ivy League Application Essays* hits the road.

"And then your mother got into Stanford for a wonderful engineering program."

"Yeah, but she didn't even finish."

Pa looks at me as if I've punched him in the gut. "That wasn't always the plan. Your mother didn't finish because Seema was born, and eventually we agreed that someone needed to be home to take care of her."

"But why'd it have to be Ma who took care of her?"

He rubs his scraggly beard. It has more flecks of gray than I remember. "Things were different back then. We didn't think so much. She chose to take care of the house; I went to work." He sees my scrunched face. "We discussed her returning to her PhD again after you both grew up, but she said no."

I rest my hip against Pa's desk, grasping my old drawings. Seven-year-old me was more self-aware than adult me. She knew she wanted to be an artist. She knew she wanted to marry Cory. I'm tending to a haphazard sticky note wall, unable to decipher what it means to like someone. I've regressed.

There's a gentle knock at the door. "Aisha?" Ma's voice is soft.

"Yeah? Did the oven timer go off?"

"Not yet. But you have a visitor."

"*What?*"

I'm not ready. I'm not even wearing a bra. I lift the scarf hanging over Pa's office chair and drape it around my chest, smoothing my tangled hair as I poke my head out of the room.

Owen.

He's holding a gift bag brimming with bright yellow tissue paper. "Happy birthday."

"Omigod, O-ster! How'd you get here?"

"Ms. Santos drove me. Quentin asked me to deliver this since he's gone fishing with Darth Vader." Owen jiggles the bag until I take it from him. "I have to go to my violin lesson now, but I wanted to tell you that I didn't add my name to the card on *purpose*. That's how bad this gift is."

I slide into my slippers and walk out with him. I watch as he finds his way through the overgrown, snow-topped bushes that our landlord hardly trims. They look like cake pops dipped in white chocolate.

I wave at the SUV parked outside, hoping Ms. Santos sees

me, and then I rush back into my room. I feel like I'm receiving word from a pen pal who's living on the moon, even though it's a gift from someone a few hours away. I pull out the card first. The outside has a print of watercolor macarons, and I'm surprised by how lengthy the message inside is. I thought he'd write a cake pun and leave it at that.

Dear Most Likely to Inspire a Revolution,

Although I never thought I'd say this, I'm glad you hijacked my car. You've taught me a lot, and I don't just mean the math. I've learned that with determination, you can do anything. (Just maybe not bake macarons. Those were pretty bad, not gonna lie. See front of card for a depiction of proper macaron feet.) I've had such a great time with you these past weeks. Stay in touch after graduation. If anything, I'll drop by for your annual prayer and wear a korta (spelling?).

I hope you like this small gift. It's so that you can never stop having adventures, no matter how small or silly. You're gonna do amazing things. If I'm lucky, I'll get to watch.

Happy birthday.

Sincerely,

Most Likely to Be Brought Home to Meet the Parents

PS The next sticky note you complete better be "learn to swim." You live in the Great Lakes State!!!

I tug away the yellow tissue paper. I laugh.

The bag is filled with individually wrapped packs of multi-colored sticky notes.

I pull out the packs one by one, my eyes tearing. Crying over sticky notes is a first for me, but despite them being blank, they contain a special message—cosmic reassurance that everything will be okay.

"Ai-sha, Seema is here." Pa's voice sings through the door.

"Coming!"

His footsteps grow fainter. My parents have gone through a lot on their own. Moving to a new country, raising children. But I'm not as alone as I thought. I have my family. I have a handful of (okay, two) good friends. As I imagine the adventure within each blank sticky note, I feel fortunate to have lived another year.

24
LOVESICK

✔ Visit an ailing friend

The next day, I'm listening to lo-fi beats on full volume while I finish my dinner and do homework. I can't figure out how to balance this chemistry equation, so I don't notice Seema is in my room until she pokes me in the arm.

"Yo. Did you sign up for the watercolor class yet?"

For my birthday, Seema got me a gift card to the neighborhood crafting store, Crafterina. The amount on the card is suspiciously close to the cost of the four-week watercolor painting class. I was touched she got me something I *wanted* this year, instead of continuing the toast earrings trend.

"Not yet. I've been balancing chemical equations."

She reclines on my bed, crossing one leg over the other. "You should sign up before the winter slots get taken." Her eyes catch the box of truffles on my nightstand. I already took a million pictures of the box in different lighting, from different angles. When she reaches for it, the pamphlet on top falls.

"You know the dessert is fancy when it comes with a guide. *Dark chocolate ganache infused with Vietnamese cinnamon.* Where'd you get these?"

"Brian. You can have them if you want. They have gluten."

She shakes off the lid and pops one into her mouth. "Doesn't Brian know you're gluten-free now?"

"I didn't tell him. I didn't want him to feel like I didn't appreciate the gift, and food allergies aren't exactly attractive."

"Dude." She smacks her lips as she finishes the chocolate. "You have issues."

My shoulders tighten. Why does she never have anything encouraging to say? Like *Hey, nice truffles. Hey, that's such a special gift. Lucky you.*

"I do, don't I? I'm the *worst*. And I'm just *so* sorry about my food allergies—I wish I could be as wonderful and perfect as you."

"Um." She sits up, her eyebrows rising. "Where'd that come from?"

"You always walk around like your life is better than mine, Seema." My voice rises. "But you don't know anything, okay? You don't get what it's like to be me. So, can I enjoy my music and solitude for once, without you reminding me what's wrong with me?"

"Aish, I'm just trying to—"

"Just leave me alone. Please."

Seema gets up to go, but not before turning her nose up at me, like *I'm leaving because I want to.* As soon as she's gone, I grab for my phone. I'm losing it, and there's only one person I know who balances my brain chemistry.

Q, are you back yet? Mind if I come over?

The response appears in seconds.

I just got home but I'm sick 😣 **If you're okay with the germs, come on over!**

I stick my spoon in my half-eaten bowl of lentils and eject myself from my room.

"Whoa there, speedy," Pa says, watching me slide toward the door. Seema is sitting at the dinner table. She doesn't look at me.

"JustgoingtogohelpQuentinstudy."

"Drive safely!" Pa calls. "And be back by nine. It's Sunday."

I make a stop at the local macaron shop. By the time I arrive at Quentin's, the sun is dipping, streaking the sky with pink. I wonder if Quentin can see the sunset from his window. Owen answers the door. He's wearing blue surgical gloves and a red paisley bandanna tied over his nose and mouth. I kick off my boots and set my box of macarons on the counter. "Where's Ms. Santos? And what's with the gear?"

"Ms. Santos is buying groceries to make Quentin more soup since there's only a little left. Quentin's in his room, so he doesn't get anyone sick. I have a violin recital on Tuesday I can't miss, plus I'm hanging out with Yasmin at the library after school tomorrow." His voice is muffled by his bandanna. "So, I really don't want whatever plague he has."

An eleven-year-old has way more of a social life than I will probably ever have. I scale the stairs and rap on Quentin's door. No answer.

"Quentiiiin?" I press my ear to the door.

"Come in," he croaks.

It's dark aside from pinpricks of orange light glowing through his blinds. He's splayed on his bed with only half his head visible, a stack of tissues next to him. He reminds me of a vase surrounded by packing peanuts. And for once, his room isn't tidy—there are some socks on the ground and a hoodie. Things must be bad.

"You're alive!" I go in for a hug.

He's still at first, but then his arms curl around me. His skin burns to the touch. I click on his bedside lamp.

"Omigod, you look terrible. Like you got run over by a bus. And then the bus, like, made a U-turn and ran over you again."

"Thank you." His eyes are rimmed with red. "I appreciate that."

My ears perk up as I hear Owen's violin through the door. "Whoa, he sounds good. He's improved a lot."

"That kid won't let me sleep. And side note, you don't need to ask to come over ever. Just come over."

"What if I drove here and you weren't home or something? Or you wanted alone time to rest?"

"Kids these days. Back in my day, we would wait hours on the porch on the off chance of seeing a friend. And now, y'all have your fancy smartphones and think—"

"O-kay. I think you spent too much time with Grandpa Shelly."

"I did," he moans. "I wanted to text you about how terrible Houghton Lake was. My grandpa still writes *letters*. He collects *stamps*. He thinks Wi-Fi is evil and that the radiation causes brain damage."

"Maybe he's on to something. I like the old-school way. *Especially* handwritten cards." I smile. "Thank you for that, Quentin. And the gift. It meant a lot."

"Of course. I almost got you a watercolor brush set, but then I figured you already have one."

"It was perfect." I trace the leaves on his bedspread with my finger. "So was it only the lack of Wi-Fi that made the trip terrible? Or was it your grandpa?"

265

"Surprisingly, my grandpa was *nice* to me. He even offered to take me to the ice museum. The whole time I was waiting for his usual jabs, but I got nothing. . . ." He coughs. "What about you? How was the rest of your date? I left the *go on a date* sticky note for you to cross off on my nightstand."

"It went . . . well."

Quentin holds up his hand for a high five for a second before retracting it. "Never mind. I'm contaminated. But that's awesome, Aish. I'm happy for you."

"Thanks."

He raises an eyebrow. "Okay, what gives?"

I hug my knees to my chest. "I'm not sure if Brian likes me. I can't really remember the date."

"What are you, a goldfish?"

"No, it's . . . you know that half-asleep state when you're not asleep but you dream of crazy stuff? That's how I feel with him. Like I'm not fully there. I'm always in my head."

"I get it." Quentin reaches for his mug. The tag of his tea bag jumps about. "Maybe you should go for a long drive. That helps me when I want to sort stuff out."

"Wanna come?"

"What? No. It's supposed to be an individual thing."

"But I hate being alone. I start thinking about all sorts of crazy things."

"That's the point."

"Fine." I get a sticky note from his desk, scrawl *go on a long solo drive to sort out my life* in Sharpie, and slap it to the wall. When I turn around, I see Quentin has slid farther beneath his covers. I touch his forehead with my palm.

"You're really warm."

"I believe the word you're looking for is *hot*."

I roll my eyes. "Owen told me there's some soup left. I'll go heat it up."

His eyelids flutter open, and he rasps, "Thank you, my child. Your kindness will never be forgotten. I am forever indebted to—"

"Shut up. I also brought you some macarons for when you're better."

Quentin makes a choking expression, and I glare at him.

"I *bought* them, okay?"

"Oh, thank goodness."

"Ugh. Bye."

I wander back to the living room. Owen's doing his homework.

"Is Quentin okay?" Owen asks.

"He is. By the way, you're shaping up to be a great violin player."

"You think so? Ms. Adeline said I'm a shoo-in for the spring solo concert coming up. Will you come to my show if I get picked?"

"I'd never miss a special day like that."

"Special day reminds me, how was your birthday? Did you open Quentin's weird gift?"

"I loved it. It was a little inside joke between us."

"Fudge nuggets." Owen gnaws on his pencil. "I should have put my name on the card, then."

"You being you is gift enough."

"That's nice. I try to say nice stuff like that to Yasmin, too."

I suppress a smile. "Oh yeah?"

"Yeah. I tell Quentin to tell you more nice stuff, too. That's how you get a girlfriend. But he's not the best with girls, which is probably why you like someone else instead."

I stare at him. He puts down his pencil.

"You didn't know that Quentin likes you?"

"That's not . . ." I fold my arms. "Quentin is *helping* me with Brian, and he doesn't believe in relationships in high school."

Of course there were times I considered the possibility. The New Year's kiss. Times when Quentin's eyes linger on me for an extra beat. Quentin laughing at my puns, while Seema looks on in disgust. But he said the kiss was for my manifesto. He left early from the arcade. Not dating in high school is one of his Philosophies with a capital *P.*

Owen leans in like he's going to tell me a secret. "Just ask Quentin if he likes you."

And let me also ask Kim Jong-Un for a cup of ginseng tea. Owen thinks it's simple. If I asked Quentin something like that, he'd assume I'm asking because *I* already like him. Which I don't. Even if I do, it's not that much. It's a manageable amount. This is exactly why I don't go on long drives by myself. My thoughts will fill the car and suffocate me.

"I should heat up some soup." I skulk there for another moment, envying how easily Owen returned to his fractions worksheet after exploding my universe into smithereens. As I pace in the kitchen, my head spins like the bowl of soup turning in the microwave. I've been trying my best to cherish the friendship with Quentin and get to know Brian. I was doing great until now.

The microwave dings. Trying to keep the soup from sloshing

in the bowl, I climb upstairs. Why does this all feel more *intimate* now?

I knock. No answer.

I go in and set the soup on his desk. He looks so serene while asleep. When I turn to leave, my hip rams into the nightstand. A small wooden box bounces onto the carpet, the lid hinging open. Luckily, Quentin doesn't stir. I kneel, reaching to gather the spilled contents. Tiny paper stars, colored with . . .

Colored with *my* gel pen.

These are the stars I drew on Quentin's problem sets.

The guy who has no room decor cut out worthless stars from me and kept them. I'm smiling as I hold one of the stars, but the warmth in my chest gives way to a sinking feeling. Why would Quentin keep these? To commemorate his learning journey, sure, but . . .

Owen is wrong. He must be.

I turn the box right-side up to put the stars back, but then I see that there's something else in there. I reach in. My hand closes over the crown of a pressed rose—the same rose I gave to Quentin the night we met.

25

ANTELOPE-
TIMES.ORG/NEWS/
VALEDICTORIAN-
ANNOUNCED/

✔ Become
valedictorian

Seniors Aisha Agarwal and Brian Wu have recently been selected as co-valedictorians, both earning a cumulative academic unweighted GPA of 4.0. This is the first time in eight years that Arledge Prep has selected two valedictorians, according to Principal Cornish. The valedictorians are chosen based on GPA and course rigor after a close review of the students' transcripts.

Agarwal has participated in crochet club, Youth For Tomorrow, the National Honor Society, and various volunteer projects. Agarwal attributed her success to many factors.

"I excelled because I tried so many different activities in school," Agarwal said. "I also had amazing teachers, like Ms. Kavnick, my AP Lit teacher."

Agarwal has plans to study mathematics and possibly minor in fine arts.

Meanwhile, Wu has participated in varsity basketball and the debate team. Wu said that he never chose his classes with the sole purpose of raising his GPA.

"I took classes I was really interested in," Wu said. "And playing basketball for four years has been awesome. I love my team." Wu plans to study medicine.

Wu and Agarwal will celebrate later this week with ice cream at local favorite, Wooly's.

"We're going to make our parents take us out," Wu said. "It's not every day you become valedictorian."

Both Wu and Agarwal said they have not yet written their speeches for graduation day. They will speak alongside senior class president Marissa Ringwold.

Sean Truwald, Staff Writer
Antelope Times

26
THE LAST DAY OF THE WAR

✔ End the Tupperware War

"Aisha, congratulations," Ms. Kavnick says, and I realize all the students have already trickled out of the classroom, including Marcy. Ever since the arcade, she hasn't been talking to me much. I thought she would've congratulated me about valedictorian after the announcement yesterday, but she hasn't texted me yet. "I heard about valedictorian. Do you know where you're headed for college yet?"

I approach her desk, slinging my backpack over my shoulder. "Not yet. I'm still waiting on some admission decisions."

"In that case, I hope I'm not too late." She hands me a creased brochure. I spot the big block *M* before anything else— the University of Michigan. I applied, but probably every kid in Michigan applies.

"I heard about this fellowship program in the Penny Stamps School of Art and Design, and I thought it sounded right up your alley. It's a dual-discipline program in generative art that admitted students can apply for. Basically, you paint using code."

It reminds me of the independent project I did last year on finding fractals in nature. I never imagined that art and math could be combined to create a major—I always thought you had to choose one.

"It sounds amazing." I swallow hard. "But aren't undergraduate fellowships hard to get?"

She winks. "That's why I gave *you* the brochure."

I appreciate Ms. Kavnick thinking of me, but now that I got valedictorian, I want Stanford even more. I got a taste of being able to have everything I want. I can't stop now.

As I trudge from Ms. Kavnick's classroom to my locker, shoulders buckling from the textbooks in my backpack, the office administrator begins summoning poor souls to the main office over the PA system. I'm convinced she takes a twisted satisfaction in divulging the details of students' personal lives if they don't get there in time.

When Lily got called to the office last week, it started with, "*Lily Perez, please report to the front office,*" but then it became, "*Lily Perez, please report to the front office. Your father is waiting to take you to your wisdom tooth extraction appointment.*" Today, I had my headphones on in between classes, so now I have the pleasure of hearing, "*Aisha Agarwal, please report to the front office. Your mother is waiting with your lunch.*" I abandon my backpack at my locker along with my dignity and race to the office.

There's Ma. She's wearing her puffy gray winter jacket and hugging a steel tin to her chest. The office administrator is typing away at her computer, a small smile frozen on her face, probably fed by the humiliation of Arledge students.

"Aisha, you should give yourself more time in the morning," Ma scolds, holding out the tin. "Lunch ghar pe rehgaya."

You left your lunch at home.

I don't have the heart to tell Ma that I eat Snickers bars for lunch. She believes I eat a balanced meal from the cafeteria with a perfect little food pyramid diagram smiling at me from the foam tray. I let her. But there are special days when my mom packs me a lunch. Today's lunch is in honor of becoming valedictorian. Ma didn't explicitly *say* that she believes I have the potential to come up with a solution to climate change, but her special biryani with caramelized onions is how I know she's proud of me.

"Thank you, Ma."

I wish I was proud of me, too. Yesterday when the valedictorians got announced, I walked the halls like a mariachi band was trailing behind me. I relished seeing my name on the school website alongside Brian's. I took a screenshot of the page in case Principal Cornish takes it all back. I called Quentin, forgetting all about those pesky star cutouts I found in his room. I got high fives from crochet club, even crotchety ol' Lily. It was my day. It was my world. Then the calendar page flipped. The mariachi band went back on tour. The guests trickled on home.

Ma puts a hand on my cheek. "Acha, main chalti hoon, lekin tumne Seema se baat kee? Usane ghar par phone nahin kiya, aur voh har hafte karti hai." *All right, I'll go, but have you talked to Seema? She hasn't called home yet like she does every week.*

Yikes. I wonder if my outburst has anything to do with that.

"She must be busy studying or something."

Like Quentin. His calculus midterm is tomorrow. I'm about to ask Ma if I can stay later at Quentin's to help him cram after school when Brian's mom steps into the waiting room. While Ma is wearing sweatpants and a faded shirt with Pa's company logo, Mrs. Wu looks like she just got off the air on *Good Morning America*. She's wearing black heels, pleated khaki pants, and a crane-patterned blouse. She hasn't aged a day. The office administrator gets one look at her and snatches up the phone for the intercom.

"Brian Wu, please report to the front office."

Yikes. Brian better get here stat, unless he wants the whole school to know his personal business. I pull out my phone to warn him.

"Kanta, is that really you?" Mrs. Wu takes quick and tiny steps toward Ma. *Clack. Clack. Clack.* "It's so good to see you."

Ma smiles. "It's been a long time. How are you?"

"All right. Work has been keeping me busy. And congratulations to you, Aisha. I heard about valedictorian from Brian. I can't say I was surprised."

"Thank you." The more attention I receive for valedictorian, the worse I'm starting to feel. I thought that becoming valedictorian would somehow turn me into a new person, but . . . it didn't. I feel like me, with the promise of wearing an extra medal at graduation.

"I was just here to drop off Brian's basketball shorts. He forgot them at home." She holds a tote bag in the air. "But I'm happy I ran into you both. Brian was suggesting that we all go out and celebrate together at Wooly's with ice cream. What do you think? Kanta, I know you watch your sugar."

Ma rests a hand on my shoulder. "I think sugar is reasonable for an occasion like this."

"It's settled, then. The girls plus the valedictorians. No husbands."

Ma laughs. "How about tomorrow evening? I'm going to

Costco today with Akshay. Have to make sure he doesn't buy that cookie assortment again."

"Hon, you might want to go eat what your mom brought you," the office administrator chimes in. "Lunch period is almost over."

"Oh, right. Thanks." I wave at Ma and Mrs. Wu before leaving the office, but they're lost in conversation. It's like a reunion of the estranged. Just as Brian and I are becoming friends again, Ma and Mrs. Wu are talking after years. I can't understand why they didn't keep in touch—they don't *seem* to be on bad terms.

As the office door closes behind me, I spot a stricken Brian half jogging through the hall. I want to assure him the whereabouts of his basketball shorts will not be announced, but I can't. I have ten minutes left of lunch, and I want to find Marcy. She hasn't sat with me at lunch in a while.

"Knock, knock," I call, and Marcy looks up from her computer. She's poring over an *Antelope Times* article at the media lab, as I expected her to be. I perch on the desk next to her, watching her drag and drop rectangles of text.

"Hey," she mumbles, her eyes flicking back to her screen.

"Where have you been? You didn't text me back. You probably heard, but I wanted to tell you that I—"

"Got valedictorian. I know. It was in the paper, which I am managing editor of."

My smile falls. "Is everything okay?"

"Yep."

I've never seen Marcy act so cold. It's . . . *scary*. She stands, stacking reference books onto the shelf, back turned.

"What's going on, Marce?"

"Nothing."

"Something is definitely up."

"Nope."

"Are you . . ." I stop.

"Am I what? Jealous of you?"

I'm quiet.

"*Seriously?*" She whirls around. "I knew you'd think something like that. Get over yourself, Aisha."

My cheeks color. "No! I just, I've never seen you so—"

"For your information, I was *happy* for you. Because that's what being friends means. You talk, you hang out, you root for each other."

"I *know* that. Where is this coming—"

"Aisha, after the arcade, I realized something." She sets her armful of books down before turning to me again. "We barely talk anymore. Like, *really* talk. You invited me to Pinball Basement because of Brian. Unless I'm somehow helping you with your manifesto, I don't exist. I've been trying to get you to hang out with Kevin more because I know you both would be really good friends if you gave him a chance, but you keep shooting me down. I'm not a switch you can turn on and off whenever you want."

The way she's looking at me is making me nauseous. Why is everything that held strong starting to break? Marcy is a constant, the person I count on for advice and listicles and laughs. And now, it's like I've lost her. She hates me.

"No! It's not like that. I don't think of you like that at all, Marcy," I plead. "It's just that I've been busy these days, so I—"

"It's not just that. You said your mom doesn't let you invite friends over, but Quentin is magically allowed? You expect me to believe that? I've been asking to come over for Indian food for *years*."

I figured Marcy wouldn't want to hear me go on about my Indian upbringing or hang out at my tiny apartment. I told myself she wouldn't relate and that I'm protecting her. I didn't realize that by assuming she didn't care about that stuff, I was making sure that she couldn't. I was protecting myself.

"The only cooking I've tried of yours are those rock-hard macarons."

My face pales. "What do you mean? The only box I made I gave to—"

"Brian. Which he left at Sanjay's house on New Year's. He didn't even open it. I took the box with me because I didn't want you to feel bad."

We have interference in the Asian Tupperware War by a peaceful non-Asian participant—neutral Switzerland has entered the ring. Why did Brian say he liked the macarons without trying them? I suppose he forgot the box and didn't want to hurt my feelings. Tears spring to my eyes as I imagine Marcy storing my little Tupperware box safely for weeks.

"I'm really sorry, Marce . . ." I take a step closer. "I am. I've just been going through a lot. You know it's hard for me at Arledge. I don't exactly fit in here."

"I know, and that sucks. But you can't say you're pulling yourself up by the bootstraps entirely. This is an Ivy feeder school, so everyone here has an edge by default. I at least try to remember that, but you only focus on how hard it is for you, or complain about Alexander not doing his share of your chem reports. You know you could try *talking* to him, right?"

"I did! Last week, I went over my name with him, and he finally got it!"

It sounds silly even to my ears, but I was proud of myself. I got the inspiration from Quentin's colleague at Divine Tea, Keesha. Her name tag said "key-sha" with a little key drawing next to it, so I drew an eye next to my name and told Alex to think of the eye and say "eye-sha." It worked.

"Well, I'm glad it only took you four years. Hopefully it doesn't take you another four to talk to him about proofreading his share of the report. And for the record, you're not the only one who feels different around here. I came out to my mom, and it's been . . ." Her voice cracks. "Really hard. She pretended like I never told her. I went to my brother's last weekend so I could get some space from her."

"Why didn't you tell me?"

"You didn't even have time to write an op-ed for the paper. As if you have time to listen to me talk about this."

"I *do* have time." I'm crying. "I didn't mean to forget about you. I just assumed you were fine. You're usually fine, so I—"

"Is anyone really ever fine?" She looks away. "Listen, you were my best friend, but I think that I was never yours. Let's just move on."

The lunch bell rings. Marcy unzips her backpack and sets my Tupperware container beside her computer before storming out. I stand there, plugging my snot waterfall with the arm of my Arledge sweater, not caring that I'm going to be late to class.

Marcy is right. I haven't been focusing on our friendship, and I know why. After what happened with Brian, I told myself that anyone who sees me up close—close enough to see all the splinters and the cracks—wouldn't want me anymore. That's why I chose Quentin to help me with my manifesto instead of Marcy. And throughout all the hiding and white lies, I've been comparing myself to Marcy, Brian, and all the other Arledge students. It's been *exhausting*.

And now Marcy's gone.

I slide the container into my backpack. I hear it rattle, so I pop open the lid. The container is filled with Snickers bars.

The Asian Tupperware War is over.

Almost right after school that day, I drive to Quentin's. I find him hunched over the desk in his room, all his summary sheets and old problem sets strewn about. We go over questions from sections of the textbook, but I can tell something's off, aside from his lingering cough. The hours are passing, but he's not warming up. He's making a lot of mistakes, some he's never made before. Finally, it's almost curfew, so I give him a practice exam to try. I light one of his candles, hoping the pleasant lavender smell will calm his nerves. When the timer dings, I take the packet.

Half of it is blank.

"I got stuck on one problem, and then I couldn't move past it. Every time I was trying to do another problem, I was thinking about that one." His face crumples. He's not looking at me. "I don't think I can do this, Aish."

"Hey, hey. You can do this. You've been studying for weeks."

"Tomorrow's midterm feels so important. It's a culmination of all the studying I did and all the work you put in . . ."

"It's not like that. I'm your friend before tutor."

"I know, but it feels like there's a lot of weight on one day. Like it's D-Day."

Even though I roughly know what happened on D-Day, I also know that asking Quentin to explain a history concept will make him feel better.

"Uh, what day?"

He sits up. "When Allied forces wanted to take back Europe from Nazi control. On D-Day, a bunch of soldiers invaded from France's Normandy region. One of the craziest military confrontations in history."

"Well, I'd say we have also extensively planned for M-Day." I punch the air. "Math Day!"

"That's the dorkiest thing I've seen in a while. But I'd expect nothing less from the girl who owns an annotated copy of *50 Successful Ivy League Application Essays*."

I look for a pillow to chuck at him, but all I see is the wooden box on his nightstand. Ever since I found those cursed stars, I've felt tension between Quentin and me. And I can't tell if it's real or my overactive imagination.

"You should go. You need your rest as Queen Valedictoria of Arledge."

"Don't remind me. It feels like everything's been going wrong since I became valedictorian. My sister hates me. Marcy hates me."

"That can't be true. And I'd ask more about this, but I don't want to add your mom to that list." Quentin angles his watch toward me. Almost nine o'clock. I have a half hour before I'm in deep trouble.

"Okay, I'll go. But good luck on M-Day." I hold out my hand. These days, I'm too jumpy for a hug, so a handshake will suffice.

He gives my hand a fervent shake. "Thank you, Lady Aisha. As your loyal subject, I'll try to make you proud."

"Indeed you shall! And then our kingdom will rejoice for a fortnight."

I let go of his hand and then practically swan dive down the stairs and jog to my car. I've driven a few blocks when I see a blue gift bag in my passenger's seat. Fudge nuggets. I forgot to give my good luck present to Quentin. If I go back, I'll be home late, but what's another life lecture from my parents in the grand scheme of things, right?

I turn back, and before I can ring Quentin's doorbell, Owen opens the door, violin in hand and a pencil tucked behind his ear. "I saw your car come back from the window."

"Ever the little detective. Can you get Quentin from—"

Quentin flies down the stairs two at a time. "You're back!"

"I forgot I had a good luck present for you." I hold out my sparkly surprise.

"Seriously? Best teacher *ever*."

Owen stands on his tiptoes to see inside the bag. Quentin peels away the tissue and pulls out a mason jar. He props the jar on his palm like he's modeling jewelry.

"HOLY SH—" He glances at Owen and coughs. "Shiitake mushrooms."

He suddenly wraps me in a hug. The heaviness stuck in my

chest from the fight with Marcy lifts. Realizing I might be lingering a few beats too long, I pull away.

"I *cannot* believe you got me a jar of all blue M&M's." He laughs, and the sound of it makes my heart do somersaults. "You went through the trouble of sorting the colors . . ."

"It's to remind you of the unique super blue M&M you are."

Owen wrinkles his nose. "You guys give each other *really* weird gifts."

Quentin and I think about it for a beat. When we realize how true that is, we crack up. As our laughter subsides, Quentin swipes his coat from the hanger. "I'll walk you out. I have to properly thank you."

"You already thanked me, silly." I say goodbye to Owen and we step outside and close the front door, our shoes squelching on the welcome mat still damp from the melting snow.

"Not for the jar." The light of the streetlamp reflects in his eyes as we walk to my car. "You were right about me, what you said on New Year's Eve. I stopped putting myself out there after my dad passed. I thought not trying is better than disappointing people, or even letting myself down. And after we met, I noticed how hard you try for everything."

"*Too* hard."

"Maybe, but it made me realize that not all battles are worth fighting, but some are. Even if you lose."

"Yep. Even if you twist your ankle, you get to keep the fond memory of what an idiot you were for dancing with Sanjay."

He clears his throat as we slow to a stop in front of my car. "I wouldn't say that was dancing. You guys were, like, swaying."

My jaw drops. "You were watching us?"

"Well, your mom had told me to keep an eye on you, and . . ."

"And what?"

"And I might have been a little jealous . . ." He looks at me, taking a step forward, and I take a step back, looking down at my shoes.

"I have a question for you, Aisha. I promise I won't ask again. And you don't have to answer if you don't want to." His voice is low, and I can feel the magnetism of his gaze. "Is that okay?"

I nod.

"Is Brian really the person you like?"

For years, I thought that being wanted by Brian would make me worthwhile. It was enough to be a moth, hovering near a light that shines, but lately, I've been wanting to make my own light—to be a person Most Likely to Inspire a Revolution.

And there's Quentin. Not at all like the person I had imagined, yet somehow more. It's the way he lends a listening ear, the way his eyes crinkle when he laughs, and the way he smiles when he knows something you don't. He feels different. Someone who doesn't grow on you, but grows within you, until their hold wraps every fiber of your being.

But I'm in high school. Maybe I think this is special because I don't know better. I want to go to Stanford, not anywhere near where Quentin will be. What if I'm great as a friend to Quentin, but not as anything beyond? I love how I can talk about anything with him, even my acne. I don't want to edit my words, but if I don't edit, Quentin will find out that I'm not Most Likely to Inspire a Revolution. He'll find out that I'm shallow, directionless me. Besides, Brian and I are birds—we belong. Quentin is a fish. Fish and birds can't be together.

"Yes."

I bring myself to look at him square in the eye.

"Yes, he is."

Quentin nods. As he takes a step back, I see the hurt in his eyes, but before I can say anything more, he turns. He doesn't look back as he walks away.

I'm left at the mercy of my thoughts, wondering if I will ever be able to understand the terrifying labyrinth of my own mind.

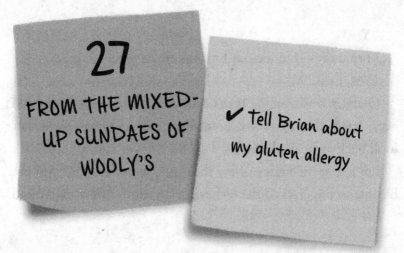

27

FROM THE MIXED-UP SUNDAES OF WOOLY'S

✔ tell Brian about my gluten allergy

On the drive from school to Wooly's with Ma, I'm sleepy. I'm so sleepy that I can't even scrounge up the energy to feel nervous about meeting Brian and his mom. I stayed up all night replaying what I said to Quentin over and over, like a terrifying, looping GIF. I'm not sure I told the truth. I hate that the conversation happened the night before Quentin's midterm.

"What's wrong?" Ma asks, running a hand through her freshly blow-dried hair as she turns into the parking lot of Wooly's. I haven't seen her get this dressed up in a while. I'm used to seeing Pa in work clothes and Ma in baggy knitted cardigans.

"I haven't been sleeping enough. And I have homework to do when I—"

"Aisha, be present. It is a big deal to become valedictorian. Even Tanuja Aunty called to congratulate you."

Tanuja Aunty lives a few miles away. Her son is three years younger than me, so she's always asking Ma for advice on when to start studying for the SAT and which advanced math class to enroll her son in. Looks like I'm hot stuff when it comes to the neighborhood Indian aunties.

Either way, Ma's right. Today should be about me. Forget Marcy and Quentin and Stanford. I deserve a stress-free sundae to celebrate the culmination of my life's work, don't I? Still, right before I get out of the car, I send a text to Quentin asking how his midterm went. The message says *sent*, not *delivered*. My chimples would scream that Quentin hates me and has blocked me forever. My more rational skin cells decide that Quentin's phone died.

As soon as I enter Wooly's behind Ma, I spot Brian and Mrs. Wu tucked into a corner booth at the far end. Mrs. Wu waves. Brian stands, which makes me feel like a bride entering a church.

This reminds me of old times. When we were kids, Brian and I would play at the park playground, while our parents sat and talked at the picnic tables. I wonder if Brian is basking in the nostalgia like I am. Maybe this will jog his memory, like an old newspaper clipping with the front-page headline, "BRIAN AND AISHA BELONG TOGETHER AND ALWAYS DID."

"Brian, I hardly recognized you," Ma remarks as she slides into the booth across from him. Her eyes sparkle with warmth. "You're taller than me now."

"I recognized you, Mrs. Agarwal. You look the same, not a day older."

Tonight, my choir of chimples has fallen silent. I don't feel like I'm auditioning for a role or waiting for a callback. I belong here, at this table with Brian. I'm valedictorian, too. I've been cast in the part.

"Congratulations to you both," Mrs. Wu says, putting her hand over Ma's. "You must be very proud, Kanta." Hearing

Ma's name in her voice again takes me back to fifth grade.

"I am proud. But I'm worried for how much time this girl spends on the computer. Her glasses get thicker every year. Soon, her nose will not be able to hold them up."

"Ma," I groan.

Mrs. Wu smiles. "I work long hours on the computer, so I can't say anything to you, Aisha."

"How is the job going?" Ma asks.

"It's difficult. I'm the only Chinese woman in my department, so at times I worry about my accent or not being able to make small talk with my colleagues. The bamboo ceiling is real, so we really need more smart Asian women leading companies. Like you, Aisha." Mrs. Wu winks. "But I'm grateful every day to have this opportunity. You know, when my mother was graduating from high school . . ."

Brian looks at me like *Here we go.*

"She got sent to a farming village in China. She was part of what people call 'China's Lost Generation,' or the young people sent to rural areas of China to work and help propel agriculture forward. Or that's what Chairman Mao Zedong intended. But the outcome was not so simple. Children were ripped from their families, and local officials and villagers often abused the children, especially women. Eventually my mother was sent home, and she was able to overcome her past and create a new life for my brother and me. I still don't know the details of what she went through. She refuses to speak about it."

Ma's nodding. "My mother also has early memories of the Partition that she doesn't like to discuss, and I can only imagine. They say that over one million people died when that border was drawn between India and Pakistan. To think so much blood was lost over invisible lines in the sand."

"The everyday citizens are the ones who suffer the consequences of decisions made by a select few. And that's why I always remember that we are some of the lucky everyday folks. We are safe, we had the opportunity to be educated, we can preserve our ancestors' stories by sharing them. I had to work for my seat at the table, but eventually, I got one." She gestures to her cozy corner of the booth with a smile. "And I like my seat."

Brian's mom had been frozen in my head as this villainous, controlling character, coaxing even the garden vines to grow her way. But now I get why she's so hard on Brian, and perhaps why she's willing to cross some lines to ensure his future. Maybe her own mother was hard on her after struggling to survive. And maybe that's why Brian argued for the American Dream so much. He probably has heard these stories from his mother a dozen times—how she built a new life for herself here in America. A good one.

Our sundaes arrive. Vanilla bean for me, low-fat pineapple for Brian and his mom, and chocolate banana-za for Ma. I steal a dollop from hers. It's been rough. Extra sugar is in order.

"What about you, Kanta?" Mrs. Wu asks. "Are you still doing interior design in your free time?"

"Oh, I wouldn't say I ever did interior design. I just liked painting our walls back then to make them look newer."

This is why Ma and Mrs. Wu grew apart. Mrs. Wu is a flitting bird, like me and Brian, and Ma is a gliding fish, like Quentin. Ma is content reading *Emma* on the sofa on Sundays, watching the rain drip from the window while sipping saffron tea. I wonder if Ma was always a fish. After all, she pursued a PhD. She's always telling me to focus on studying. She must have *some* ambitious feathers.

Mrs. Wu puts her arm around Brian, and he smiles. It's that same sweet smile from the fifth-grade yearbook. Brian had just won the Dream Career Day speech contest, and Mrs. Wu was fawning over him like he'd gotten a full scholarship to Harvard. As the evening goes on with chatter and laughter, I forget that I'm sitting across from Arledge's golden boy. I start sitting across from my friend again.

"By the way, Aisha," Mrs. Wu says as we all finish joking about the oxymoron that is *low-fat sundae.* "I want to apologize on behalf of Brian for the night of the winter formal dance."

Fudge nuggets. My throat tightens as Ma looks at me.

"What happened?" Ma asks me, two horizontal lines appearing on her forehead like cracks in a sidewalk. Those lines are always bad news.

I clear my throat. "Oh, um—"

"Aisha didn't tell you?" Mrs. Wu frowns. "Brian and Aisha were supposed to go to the dance together, but then Brian fell terribly sick. I felt so bad."

Guess she's still going with the Brian-was-sick story.

"Oh." I can see the gears in Ma's head grinding. "Aisha didn't tell me."

"I knew you wouldn't like me going with . . . anyone," I explain, and Brian nods. Based on his parted lips, I can tell he's about to rush to my defense.

"It was my fault, Mrs. Agarwal. I asked her to go with me, and I should have told Aisha earlier that I wasn't going to make it."

"Yes, you should have," Mrs. Wu says. I notice her demeanor

change suddenly, like how sunshine darkens to thunderstorm during Michigan summers. "But I am happy you both have been spending more time together. You might not remember, but you used to keep Brian out of trouble when he was a kid, Aisha."

"Unlike Seema, Aisha was a very obedient child." Ma pats my leg. "Although now I'm not so sure. . . ."

Mrs. Wu smiles. "I remember. That's why I told Brian, if you're going to take a girl to the dance, it has to be Aisha. Or else you're going alone."

I freeze for a moment. Then my spoon clatters back into my tulip-shaped sundae dish.

It all makes sense now—why Brian asked *me* instead of Lily or any other beautiful girl in our grade. Brian said that he asked me to winter formal "for old times' sake," but it was for his mother's sake. I suddenly feel sick, like I've eaten four sundaes instead of one.

"I want a cookie," I blurt. "I'll go buy one from the front."

Ma studies me. "Hungry?"

Mrs. Wu slides her credit card across the table to Brian. "Go buy it for her."

Ma starts to protest, but when Mrs. Wu gives her a withering look, Ma relents.

"Please, Kanta. Let me treat the kids this time. You can treat them next time."

With Brian's expression, you'd think he's being volunteered to be baked into a cookie. He doesn't meet my eye. I speed toward the glass shelves of cookies, past the tables full of Wooly's customers. When we're almost at the counter, he steps in front of me.

"Hey, I—"

"You *lied*." Every pore on my body is assembling for war. "You said that you wanted to go with me. You never said I was your only choice."

"Aisha, I swear it's not like that." His forehead creases. "I really did want to go with you."

"Just like how you really did try my macarons?"

He looks down. "Oh man, how did you—I just forgot the box at Sanjay's, and I didn't want to hurt your feelings."

As I watch him, I know. I don't have feelings for Brian. This whole time, I had feelings for the boy I remembered.

We may have lived in the same neighborhood and had the same woes of overprotective parents, but the "BRIAN AND AISHA BELONG TOGETHER AND ALWAYS DID" front-page headline is nothing but slander. I was nervous around him, but that was because I felt like I didn't measure up. I needed to get closer to understand that I love cozy sweatshirts and sketching turtles, and Brian loves aesthetic truffles and waxed basketball courts. I could've gotten into waxed courts, too, but I can't imagine Brian sketching for my sake. For the first time, I'm *seeing* him.

I have one burning question left.

"Did you know that I liked you in middle school?"

He looks down.

"So you knew."

". . . Maybe I had an idea. You took Mandarin with Mr. Bore as your elective, and no one would choose to suffer through that unless they—"

"Mandarin is one of the most spoken languages in the world."

"Why are you bringing this up? What does that have any-thing to do with this?"

"This is like Mr. Bore's class. You don't like me, but just like then, you're talking to me and getting my hopes up because it's something to do. You're not over Riley or you're bored or what-ever it is. And I'm just always there."

"That's not true, I—"

"Really? So you like me?"

His arms fall to his sides. "I . . . I mean, I haven't thought about—"

"You shouldn't have asked me to winter formal, Brian."

His eyes are bloodshot but there's only steeliness where my sympathy is supposed to be. This moment is mine.

"I'm really sorry," he whispers, his voice hoarse.

"No, you're not."

I never thought I'd feel sorry for someone like Brian. Some-one with perfect grades, chimple-less skin, and unyielding confidence. But I do. I thought he had it all figured out, but he doesn't.

I face the rows of cookies. This calls for a cookie on Brian's dime.

"Can I get a gluten-free chocolate chip cookie?"

The cute waiter is behind the counter today, staring at me openmouthed. I pluck Mrs. Wu's credit card out of Brian's hand. Seema would be proud. No matter how the reveal came about, I *finally* let Brian know I have a gluten sensitivity.

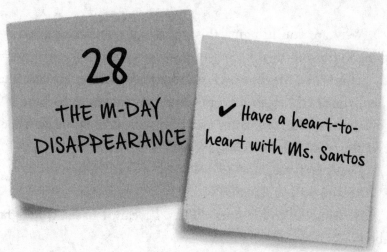

28
THE M-DAY DISAPPEARANCE

✔ Have a heart-to-heart with Ms. Santos

I'm ringing Quentin's doorbell. It's been one whole day, and my text message to Quentin is still underscored with *sent* and not *delivered*.

I'm not planning to tell Quentin about what happened with Brian yet. Or that I spent the entire day at school today avoiding both Brian and Marcy. With my life combusting, all I want is to anchor myself with those familiar brown eyes. I want nothing more than to hear Quentin talk about how his midterm went and what wisdom he's been absorbing from his Buddhism elective.

"Aisha, come on in," Ms. Santos calls. "It's unlocked."

I'm about to greet Ms. Santos with a smile, but I stop as I see her face. Her cheeks are splotchy, and her eyes are rimmed with red. My bag falls from my hand.

Car accident. Cancer. Black widow spider.

"Is Quentin okay?"

Meteor. Lightning strike. Landslide. Falling tree—

"He's okay." She puts a shaky hand on my arm. "I have some bad news, but let's sit down, Aisha. I'll get you a macaron. I got them fresh from the bakery up the street."

She plops a lone macaron on a tiny plate and sits down beside me, gathering her paisley scarf around her thin frame. Her hair dips over her face, revealing some strings of gray in the curtain of dark brown.

"Aisha, during yesterday's midterm, Quentin had an anxiety attack. He had to be taken to the emergency room."

My breath catches.

A series of images project in my mind, of Quentin sequestered behind a desk all by himself in a sterile white room, struggling to breathe. It can't be. Quentin's the one at ease, the composed one. The only variable that has been added to his life's equation recently is . . . *me.*

Did I put too much pressure on him?

Is this all my fault?

"Can I go see him?" I whisper. I want to sprint to the emergency room on foot, but I contain myself by smoothing the pleats of my Arledge skirt with my palms.

"I'm sorry, Aisha. His grandpa came to pick him up this afternoon from the hospital. Shelly said he thought it would be best that Quentin gets away to Houghton Lake. I was very worried about saying yes given the history, but after you left the dinner at Zola's, we had a long talk. Shelly assured me that he's going to behave more like a grandfather, less like a colonel. The doctor also mentioned a change of environment could do Quentin some good."

"How long will he be gone?"

"Only a couple of days. That's the maximum I could take. I let him go because I hadn't seen Quentin like this in so long, and it just brought me back to when . . ." Her eyes pool with tears. "When my husband passed away."

My throat tightens. "This isn't the first time something like this has happened?"

"Quentin started having anxiety attacks after his father passed away, and they continued throughout middle school, but this is the first time he's fainted. The doctor was saying anxiety-induced hyperventilation can cause the blood vessels to constrict, which reduces blood flow to the brain. It's rare, but it happens."

There's a bowling ball in my chest, knocking down all the pins in my heart. At the New Year's party, Sanjay had said that he and Quentin used to be friends before Quentin became distant. Was this why Quentin pulled away? The night I got into his car, I was struck by how he's so easy to be around. I never imagined that this whole time, although he was easy to be around, he found it difficult to be around others. I never thought there would be so much weight hiding behind his easy smiles.

"I thought the anxiety would improve with time. The grief counselor he was seeing said that there were triggers that caused the attacks, and with time, it would pass. It did, but I noticed Quentin distancing himself in the process." She brushes wisps of hair away from her face. "He stopped talking to me. He had friends, but he kept them at arm's length. He stopped working so hard in school. We tried medication, but then we weaned him off due to the side effects. I think he became so afraid of losing things after his father passed, he stopped engaging. I was actually the one who convinced him to take that Buddhism class when I saw it in his school catalog, hoping that some of the practices like meditation and observing your thoughts would help him."

The afternoon at the ice rink comes to mind. Quentin mentioned that he considered joining the varsity tennis team but didn't. Or how he doesn't believe in trying out a relationship if it's doomed to fail. Or how he hadn't added any decor to his room. He was prepared to erase himself at a moment's notice. I wrote that off as him not having enough motivation. Was the real reason that he was deeply afraid of losing important things in his life once he got them?

I look down at my hands. "I never imagined . . ."

"Of course you didn't. Before, I could hardly tell if Quentin was at home or at school—that's how quiet he was. After you started tutoring him, I noticed him changing. I started hearing laughter and voices through our old floorboards." She watches me from behind her tear-streaked glasses. "I'm sorry, Aisha. I feel as if we've disappointed you somehow. All the time you spent . . ."

"I don't care about any of that. I just want him to be okay."

I had always thought that closeness is associated with time passing, yet Quentin and I had become so close within just a few months. So close that I couldn't imagine my life without him. So close that I had started to fear it was *too* close.

Ms. Santos rummages through her purse for a pen. "You remember Sophie, right? Shelly's friend who came to dinner?"

The lady who started it all. As Principal Cornish described the butterfly effect ages ago, *Even if two things collide just once in space and time, they enter into a pattern of mutual influence forever.*

She scribbles on a napkin. "This is Sophie's number. There's horrible cell reception up in Houghton Lake, and Shelly isn't very responsive. You might have more luck calling Sophie if you'd like to get ahold of Shelly. He tends to stay in touch with her most. And you're welcome to come by here any time, Aisha. Even just to hang out with Owen and me."

I fold the napkin into quarters and slide it into my skirt pocket. I feel like it's going to burn a hole through the fabric.

"Thank you, Ms. Santos." My legs are numb. I've been sitting like a twisted pretzel. "Also, if Owen's dad needs someone to watch Owen, I'd be happy to fill in for Quentin."

She suddenly pops up from her chair and throws her arms around me. "Thank you, Aisha. You've not only helped Quentin. You standing up to Shelly gave me the space to talk to him that night. I was finally able to build a bridge."

When I step outside a few minutes later, I can't bend the hose-like pour of my thoughts. Does this mean Quentin will have to retake the exam? If I had made my lesson plans less intensive, would this have happened?

I think back to the night Quentin and I met. I complained that my life was uneventful. Soon after, the sticky note manifesto took off like a million race cars on a track—going to the mall, learning to ice-skate, applying to college, going to a New Year's party, tutoring Quentin, falling out with Marcy, confronting Brian, Quentin's anxiety attack. Well, I'm retiring my race cars.

It's time to park.

29

YOUR STANFORD APPLICATION STATUS HAS BEEN UPDATED

✔ Destroy my life

Dear Aisha,

Thank you for your application. I regret to inform you that we are unable to offer you admission to Stanford University. We were humbled by your talents and achievements and the commitment you demonstrated in your academic and extracurricular endeavors . . .

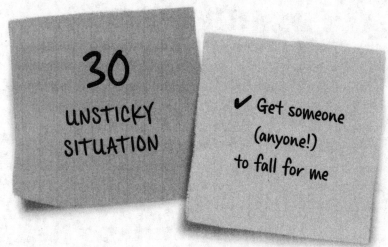

30
UNSTICKY
SITUATION

✔ Get someone
(anyone!)
to fall for me

My alarm blares, and I jump, feeling around for my phone.

Five thirty p.m.

The first lesson of the watercolor class I signed up for at Crafterina starts in thirty minutes. I'm in bed with no intention of leaving. For the first time since my strep throat incident in eighth grade, I skipped two days of school this week. My parents checked on me every so often, speaking in hushed whispers, but they mostly left me to my mourning. Even Seema stopped ignoring me during her home visits, instead observing me with sympathy. The only song I can stomach listening to now is "Everything Happens to Me" by Chet Baker.

I know bigger things are happening in the universe than my rejection from one of the world's leading teaching and research institutions. I know. But all these years through the itchy Arledge uniforms, Principal Cornish's lunch ramblings, standardized testing, and rigorous course schedule, I stayed sane due to one thought: it'd be worth it. I'd sip lemonade on the Golden Coast. I'd make up for my parents' toiling. I'd be rich beyond belief (as soon as I paid off my hefty student loans). All those buds were plucked from their roots. With one email.

It was pointless. The AP exams. Beefing up my extracurriculars. Rewriting the Stanford essay a dozen times. If the "hard work pays off" adage were true, I would've gotten into Stanford. Quentin would've finished calculus with an A. The world is unfair, and I refuse to participate. It's like what Brian said about the claw machines at Pinball Basement: *Why play something that's so obviously rigged against you?*

That's how I find myself watching the minutes creep by until my first watercolor class, which I am *not* attending. I have officially stopped playing.

There's a knock at my door.

"Beta, are you awake?" Ma asks.

"Kind of." I peel away the covers from over my head, strands of hair rising around my face from the static.

Ma comes in, her steel watering can in one hand, a stack of mail in the other. Her hair is pulled into a loose braid. She sets the can on the floor and the mail on my desk. She sits. I'm sure she's going to bring up the rejection and how "God wills everything to happen for a reason" for the millionth time, but she doesn't.

"Seema told me that Quentin wasn't able to clear his exam."

That's the one thing I've told Seema since our argument, and in response, I got a nod. No sardonic comeback like, "Well, it makes sense considering *you* were his tutor." The pity nod was somehow worse.

Ma studies me. "Do you like him?"

"Ma!" If she's trying to distract me, it's working.

"Remember, no boys in high school, Aisha. And maybe not even in college."

"You met Papa in college."

She brushes away the hair grazing my neck. That's the gesture that usually precedes a lecture. "That's different, beta. We hid our relationship until Akshay asked for my hand in marriage. He used to visit me outside the girls' hostel in the evening before curfew."

"Ma, you tell me this every week. And that's not how it works these days."

"I know. I just want to look out for you. No long faces." Ma pokes her fingers into my cheeks. "Your pa said you're starting a watercolor class?"

"I signed up for it with the gift card Seema got me. But I'm skipping today."

I signed up to distract myself from thinking about Quentin. Besides, *sign up for a watercolor painting class* is one of the manifesto sticky notes. Before he left, Quentin was taking the crossed-off notes I gave back to him and arranging them in a neat line on his wall. He said he'll create a brand-new row once I hit ten. With the watercolor one, I earn sticky note bingo—ten crossed-off notes in a row. I should go claim my official prize of a Werther's lozenge and a citrus-scented hand cream. At least, that's what they give out when I volunteer at the Sunrise Retirement Home.

I'm playing bingo with myself. Riveting.

"Good. Painting will be a good break from looking at your computer all the time."

"Ma, my glasses are already as thick as windows. It's too late."

"Eat more carrots. And ajwain seeds. Health begins in the gut."

I look at the lines framing Ma's mouth, like creases in an origami crane. She's still taking care of me. "Ma, have you ever considered working again? Or going back to school?"

"Why are you asking suddenly?"

"It's just . . . Seema and I are all grown up."

"I can see that."

"Don't you want to pick up where you left off? Focus on yourself?"

Ma frowns. "Is this what you've been thinking, Aisha? That I stopped focusing on myself?"

"You didn't get to finish your PhD. And I saw how interested you were in Mrs. Wu's work stories. I bet you could manage a team, too."

Ma watches me like *What's this really about?*

"I thought if I got into Stanford, or some Ivy League school . . . you'd at least feel like everything you gave up wasn't a waste . . ." I start to cry. "But now I didn't even get in. Not to Stanford, not to an Ivy."

Ma gathers me into a tight hug, stroking my hair and rocking me back and forth. "Meri pyaari bachi. What have you been thinking, Aisha? It's true I didn't finish my PhD or work. But I also got to spend so much time with you girls. I raised two strong daughters, and that is a much prouder achievement than a degree."

I press my face into her chest, taking in her familiar scent of cardamom and lavender. "But don't you want to be like Mrs. Wu?"

"I used to, but then I saw the toll work takes. The reason she and I stopped meeting is not because of any drama as such.

She didn't have time for me, beta. And you've seen the pressure on your papa. He's always being called into some meeting. So I realized what opportunity cost means, and while knowing I could complete my PhD, I chose not to. Then I got to watch you and Seema grow up. That is no lesser of a pursuit."

The familiar twang of her English and the rhythmic pat of her hand on my back makes me cry harder.

"Y-You don't r-regret it at all?"

She kisses the top of my head. "Not at all. I do sometimes wonder how my life would've been if I hadn't quit, but I always come to the same point—I'm happy with the decision I made, and I'd make it again. Even though I can work now that you and your didi are grown up, I've decided not to go back yet. I want to be here until you both go to college."

"*If* I get into college."

As someone who does the extra credit no matter what my grade is, I thought that if someone wasn't a frenzied bird flitting from one thing to the next, they secretly wanted to be. But here Ma is saying she's content giving up on work. She *chose* to be a fish. It's like the question I asked of Quentin at the ice rink— isn't there a line between staying true to what you know you want, and limiting yourself? I thought Ma had been limiting herself, but that's not true.

"Oh, you'll get into college, my little drama queen," a voice retorts.

Seema.

The door opens, and one eye peeks around the doorframe. "Am I permitted to enter your bedchamber, Your Highness?"

A chortle bubbles through my tears. "Come in."

Ma sighs. "What happened between you girls?"

"Nothing." Seema sits on my bed. "Aisha just recently went berserk on me for no reason."

I sniffle. "It wasn't for no reason. You pretend like you know everything. And I'll admit, you kinda do. But it's still annoying how perfect your life is."

"*What?*" The bewildered way she's looking at me, you'd think I suggested she's part of a traveling clown troupe. "My life is *not* perfect."

"You sure? Straight hair, perfect skin, good grades, no dietary restrictions, and you—"

"You think that equals a perfect life? *Straight hair?*" Seema plants her hand on top of my head. She moves my head back and forth like a bobblehead. "A question for you: Does having straight hair make butter chicken taste better?"

"No?"

"Does having straight hair give me the ability to not kill every plant I've ever owned?"

"No . . ."

"Straight hair isn't doing much for me, then, is it?"

"I mean—"

"Look up from your textbooks once in a while, Aish. You're not the only one with issues. Why do you think I come home almost every weekend?"

"I dunno." I shrug. "For the free food?"

"Aisha, *no*. It's because I've made no new friends at college. Most of my close friends went out of state, so I've been really lonely."

"Oh. Sorry."

She studies me for another moment before slapping me upside the head with her palm. I groan, rubbing my scalp.

"Apology accepted. Now can you stop your moping extravaganza? There are plenty of other amazing universities for you to attend, even if they weren't your first pick."

"I've gotten rejected from every Ivy so far, Seema. And most of the Public Ivies. Wait-listed at UCLA."

"Ivy-schmyvy. Besides, I think a little birdie might've seen a brochure on your desk for an exciting fellowship at U of M."

"What the f—" I glance at Ma and swallow. "Fudge nuggets? How'd you notice—"

"Like you said, I know everything, lil sis."

"Enough, girls." Ma places one hand on my shoulder, one hand on Seema's. "Aisha, get ready. Ms. Santos called, and she asked if you'd like to have dinner with her and Owen in an hour. I surprised myself and said yes."

She's surprising me, too. Ever since Ma realized how old Quentin is, she has grumbled about me going over to "boys' houses" and "getting into bad habits." I wonder what made her say yes.

"I don't want to," I say. Ms. Santos and Owen would remind me too much that Quentin is not a cinder block. He is a boy if I ever saw one, with his stupid lopsided grin and stupid stripy socks. Stupid, stupid—

"Ms. Santos said she made lentil soup." Pa's voice comes through the ajar door. We all exchange looks, grinning.

"Come in, Pa. Don't let total violation of my privacy stop you."

He bends his head into the doorway like a giraffe grazing on grass. "Privacy is a very American luxury, beta. And your ma is right. We're worried about you. We decided it'd be better for you to get out of the house. *Even* if it is a boy's house."

Ah, there it is.

"Pa will drive you." Ma gives me one last I'm-watching-you look as she slips out the door. As Seema follows her, I lie back on my bed.

All this time, I've been cramming everyone in my life into neat boxes. Bird or fish. Shy or outgoing. Indian or American. Brian is confident. Marcy is fun. Quentin is easygoing. Mrs. Wu is controlling. Ma is a victim of circumstance. Seema is perfect. I'm a nerd. I even crammed my *interests* into boxes. Painting is art, code is math, and the two could never mix.

None of those boxes turned out to fit. In fact, it seems no box—bird, fish, or otherwise—can fit a person. Turns out you can't reduce people like fractions. Who knew.

For the first time in two days, I'm not in my crochet club sweatshirt. I have to admit, combing my mass of tangled waves did lift my spirits a bit. Right as I'm about to ring the doorbell, Owen cannonballs into my stomach.

"I haven't seen you in forever. I wanted to tell you the news. I got the solo part in my spring violin concert!"

"That's *amazing*, Owen."

His enthusiasm reminds me of my own childhood, when I was excited by blue raspberry snow cones and watermelon-scented erasers. When did that turn into pining for college acceptance emails?

Ms. Santos appears. "Aisha, I'm so glad you could come."

As I step inside, I'm greeted by the sweet smell of chocolate. It brings me back to the first day I came over and began the sticky note wall. How can I be nostalgic for a feeling from a few months ago?

"Are you okay?" Ms. Santos appraises me from above her glasses. "Your mother told me you didn't get into Stanford."

"I'm doing okay."

"That's a lie. But there's nothing warm soup and chocolate pudding can't cure."

She serves us green lentil soup in painted bowls, and then she gabs about a tomato garden she was thinking of starting in the spring. Owen squints at his sheet music for his violin concert. I've about finished my soup when I ask The Question that has been on my tongue since I walked in.

"How's Quentin?"

She wipes the corners of her mouth with her napkin. "He's doing okay. It's been *so* tough to not go over there and check on him, but Quentin told me he needs a few days alone. I know if he was here, I would've been bringing him tea every few minutes. Shelly and I have worked out our roles. He's been taking him out fishing, and I've been emailing Quentin's teachers to let them know the situation. Other than that, Shelly tells me that Quentin's been spending a lot of time in bed."

Can't relate.

"Did you talk to him yet?" she asks.

I shake my head. One part of me is afraid to make Quentin anxious, and another part of me is hurt that he hasn't contacted me. A more shadowy part of me wonders if he isn't contacting me because I said I liked Brian. If I like Brian, is all the time we spent together meaningless to him?

"Not to worry," she says. "It'll happen."

I wish that were true, but almost everything I planned for didn't happen. I didn't go to winter formal. I didn't get into Stanford. I didn't fall in love with Brian. So many of my sticky notes remain incomplete. But hey, I did get sticky note bingo.

"Ms. Santos, would it be all right if I stopped by Quentin's room for a second? I have a few things I left there."

"Take your time. Your champorado will be waiting for you."

I go upstairs. The wooden door of Quentin's room is open. It's strange going inside without him ushering me in. The window is cracked open, so his hunter-green curtains are flying in a frenzy. Candles, the wooden box of star cutouts, the jar of blue M&M's I gave him, his Kresge tennis hoodie hanging on his closet doorknob, and his arranged set of mechanical pencils and loose-leaf paper. It's as if nothing has changed. I stop in front of the sticky note wall.

Learn to swim.

As Quentin wrote in my birthday card, I should be ashamed of leaving this one incomplete. Almost every Michigan kid swims in a lake during summer vacation. I was busy drowning myself in summer math workbooks instead.

Go on a long solo drive to sort out my life.

Quentin's suggestion. I thought I would, but then the Stanford rejection came.

Near the top of the wall, the completed sticky notes are arranged into an even row. I twist open a Sharpie from Quentin's desk and cross off **Sign up for a watercolor painting class.**

I move the note next to its predecessors.

~~Change up my look.~~
~~Go to a typical high school party (with alcohol).~~
~~Try alcohol.~~
~~Dance with someone.~~
~~Skip school and go to the arcade.~~
~~Make (gluten-free) holiday-themed macarons from scratch.~~
~~Kiss someone at midnight on New Year's.~~
~~Go on a date.~~

I step back to take a gander at the notes from afar, and I realize that now there are eleven crossed-off notes, not ten. My eyes catch on the extra sticky note in the row.

~~Get someone (anyone!) to fall for me.~~

I never crossed that one off.

I peel the sticky note away and hold it like it's precious. Like it's the last Snickers bar on earth. Owen was right, and I knew it, too.

Quentin has feelings for me.

I lie back on Quentin's bed, my hair splaying out onto his leaf-patterned covers. All this time, I believed that having a crush would be unsettling. But maybe falling for someone is going through a range of emotions. The day of Sanjay's party, I felt angry. The day Quentin told me I'm Most Likely to Inspire a Revolution, I felt powerful. The day of dinner with Grandpa Shelly, I felt protective. The day Quentin left early from the arcade, I felt disappointed. The days Quentin was gone fishing in Houghton Lake, I felt a yearning for his return. And finally, the night when Quentin asked me if I have feelings for Brian, I felt unable to face him. I was afraid. I didn't want to see the

310

truth in his eyes, and I didn't want him to find the truth in mine. The truth I had avoided admitting for much too long, even though probably everyone could see it but me.

The truth being, of course, that I had fallen for Quentin, too.

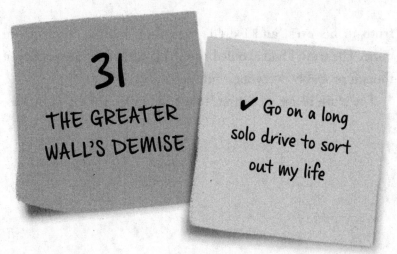

31
THE GREATER WALL'S DEMISE

✔ Go on a long solo drive to sort out my life

The more I look at the sea of yellow sticky notes, the more I decide that I may like Quentin, but I hate this wall. All of it.

I experienced so much, but this wall doesn't tell that story. This wall says there's a girl who created a list of to-dos to feel like she's worth something, only to complete a few. And if I'd added *Get into Stanford* to the wall, it would've lived in the mass of incomplete notes, discarded like an old receipt.

~~Change up my look.~~

I look down at my frumpy T-shirt I got free from a college visit. Okay, so the shine of that one faded quicker than the soles of my summer flip-flops.

~~Go on a date.~~

I did sort of go on a date with Brian at Wooly's, but one, he didn't know I was counting it as a date, and two, it sure didn't *feel* like a date. I let my ice cream melt to soup.

~~Dance with someone.~~

More like, danced with a tipsy boy who knocked me over.

Suddenly, I know what poetic justice means for this wall.

Peel. Whoosh. Flop.

Peel. Whoosh. Flop.

Yellow sticky notes litter the carpet en masse. This is my great wartime battle. L-Day, for List Day, with plenty of sticky note casualties in its wake.

As I think about Quentin, I remember the unplanned, noteworthy things that *did* happen these past few weeks. I open my bag, take out the brightly colored packs of sticky notes that he gifted me, and start to make a new wall.

~~Hijack a stranger's car.~~
~~Get a cool birthday gift.~~
~~Befriend a complete stranger.~~
~~Learn to ice-skate.~~
~~Draw gold stars on numerous problem sets.~~
~~Stand up to a grandpa at dinner.~~
~~Invite a friend to a family puja.~~
~~Watch Quentin make tea.~~
~~Go to the mall.~~
~~Sprain my ankle.~~
~~Get into a fight with my best friend.~~

I write and write. My notes aren't as evenly spaced as Quentin's, but it'll do. When I'm finished, I stand in front of the Greatest Wall: a wall of truth, containing the serendipitous experiences to the unseemly. Sure, spraining my ankle and getting into a fight with my best friend sucked, but I'm going to learn from both those things. I know it.

Ms. Santos is probably wondering if I'm holding a séance in here—dusk light has given way to darkness. As I throw the sticky-note pads in my bag, I see the napkin Ms. Santos gave me, poking from the zippered pocket.

Sophie Scott
1030 Pine St.
248-555-0190

It's seven p.m. Sophie shouldn't be asleep. My grandma does her evening yoga in India at seven thirty p.m. I punch Sophie's number into my phone.

"Hello?"

"Hello! It's, um, Aisha."

There's a pause and a crackle, and I pray she remembers me.

"Aisha! Quentin's friend."

"Right. I'm sorry for calling out of the blue, but Ms. Santos said you would know where Shelly is? I'm trying to reach Quentin."

"Of course. I can give you Shelly's home address, email, phone number, whatever you want." Her tone is chirpy. "I gotta say, though, terrible reception up there. And Shelly doesn't have Wi-Fi. He usually goes to the public library to write emails."

Sending Shelly an email confessing my feelings to Quentin is strange, but I also don't want to wait for some opportune time that never comes. If there's one thing I've learned from bingeing romance movies, it's that once you know you like someone, you shouldn't wait to tell them. Or else some childhood crush they had will pop up out of nowhere, steal your chance, and you'll never—

"Driving there is probably your best bet, hon."

"Huh?"

"The drive up north at night is beautiful. Lots of pretty roads cutting through the forest. I bet Quentin would love a visit from someone his own age. And you wouldn't need to warn Shelly you're coming. He loves surprise visits."

Would Shelly really *love* if I show up at his residence unannounced at night? What if Quentin doesn't want to see me? I'm about to politely decline and ask for Shelly's email, but then I remember what Quentin said the night he was sick.

Kids these days. Back in my day, we would wait hours on the porch on the off chance of seeing a friend. And now, y'all have your fancy smartphones . . .

Maybe I *should* make a grand gesture to show Quentin that he's not something on my list—he's so much more. I might be pedaling on the adrenaline of L-Day, but I feel invincible. Like that mother who was able to lift a car to save her baby.

Okay, maybe not quite at that level.

"It seems you're not fully convinced." I can almost hear Sophie smiling. "Perhaps I can sway you with a saying I've shared with you before. *Fortune favors the brave?*"

My mouth hangs open. "You remember m—"

"I'm not *that* old, honey."

"I'lldoit." The words parade from my mouth before I can stop them. "Can I have Shelly's home address?"

The phone call ends with Sophie wishing me luck, and as I zip my bag, I think of something. I sift through the pile of mangled sticky notes on the floor until I find it.

Go on a long solo drive to sort out my life.

I draw a line through it.

On my drive, trees on either side of the highway wave to and fro in the wind. They're the cheering crowd for the final stretch of my marathon. I've never driven this far north on my own before. I've never driven somewhere without telling my parents first before, either. I notice the details: lingering Christmas decorations, dice bobbing from an adjacent car's rearview mirror.

I'm playing 103.1 FM: Ozzy's jazz radio station, the station that Pa listens to on the way to Costco. Even with that soundtrack, this moment feels special—the kind of special that lasts. When I became valedictorian, it felt special for a few days, but then I craved more. Even if I got into Stanford, it wouldn't have been dipped in gold forever. Not too many things in life feel great soon after you get them. Maybe winter formal would've sucked, too.

After two and a half hours of pensive driving, I exit the highway. The GPS prompts me to turn onto a dark, winding road. The gravel crunches underneath the tires. My phone announces, *"Signal lost."*

So, it's true. A part of me wondered if the whole "no reception" thing was an excuse Grandpa Shelly used to be a hermit. I squint at the metal numbers nailed onto the mailboxes I'm passing: 124, 126 . . .

There it is—128.

I turn off my headlights, but I keep my car on like I'm on a stakeout mission. Clusters of twinkling stars are now visible through my windshield. If I didn't feel like such a stalker, I would stop to admire them.

When I make rash decisions, the rash appears later. The night I got into Quentin's car, I realized my mistake *after* he'd driven me halfway across town. This time, it's hitting me while parked outside Shelly's home. I'm a washed-up high school senior who drove over one hundred miles on a weeknight to her crush's grandfather's home—*without* being invited, mind you—in order to confess her feelings.

I silence the crackling radio and get out of my car. There's a fence lining the footpath, a big truck parked out front that has fishing gear strapped to it, and a yellow glow tracing the curtained window next to the door. I knock. Dishes clatter. The blinds near the door part. Two brown eyes peer at me. For a moment, I think it's Quentin, but then I notice creases around the eyes like the lines of winding rivers on a map.

The door opens. Shelly is in a fishing hat and sweater, wringing his hands on a dish towel. I wince from the flood of light.

"Aisha?" He looks surprised, but he's smiling. "What a lovely surprise."

"Hello-Shelly-I'm-here-to-see-Quentin-because-I-know-he-might-not-be-feeling-too-well-and-I-wanted-to-pay-him-a-surprise-visit-to-say-hello-I'm-sorry-for-showing-up-so-late-unannounced-and-I'm-sorry-for-what-I-said-at-dinner-it-was-not-my-place-um-would-it-be-possible-for-me-to-come-in-for-a-second-and-speak-to-Quentin?"

He steps aside, his arm propping the door open. "Oh dear. You have a thing for my grandson."

"Huh?" I squeak.

"Come in. You need some of my leftover holiday panettone. And some tea."

What's with this family and tea?

I follow Shelly inside, my fingers curled around the strap of my bag. His home feels like a cozy cabin. There's a crackling fire in the fireplace. Past the archway, there are fishing poles hanging on the walls and a gnarled ladder you can climb to reach the top floor. Wood everywhere. Even the table is a glossed log, the warped rings fanning out from the center.

I sit on one of the wicker chairs facing the fireplace, looking around.

"Looking for Quentin?" He holds out a mug of tea, and I gratefully accept, taking a long swig. Thank heavens for chamomile.

Shelly leans against the wooden archway. "I hope you won't mind, Aisha, but looks like you came all this way just to visit me."

I cough. "Pardon?"

"Quentin left a couple hours ago. He took one of my cars and drove home. Or he's *gone fishing*, as us fishermen like to call it."

Fudge nuggets.

This is too much, universe. I get the message—life doesn't always go as planned. But can I get just *one* plan to work out?

"I'm sorry." Shelly watches my face from over the rims of his glasses.

Well, I might as well make the most of this. I *did* just drive more than two hours to get here.

"Shelly, about what I said at dinner, I'm sorry about that. I usually, um, respect elders. Indian culture really loves their elders."

Is this helping? Why do I feel like it's not helping?

"Please, don't apologize." He sits in the wicker chair next to me, outstretching his spotted hands toward the fire. "It was a wake-up call. The truth is, I've always been a proud and impatient man. I'm glad it doesn't run in the family."

Quentin once waited thirty-five minutes for his sundae at Wooly's before asking the waitress if she had forgotten.

"And I'm not just talking about Quentin," he adds, as if to read my mind. "Quentin's father was the same, and I never understood. I thought a life needed money, ambition, and adventure, you know? The things I never had."

He curls his hand into a fist as he says *adventure*, the light of the flames dancing across his cheeks. His expression reminds me of Mrs. Wu at Wooly's, when she talked about Brian's future. It's a domineering kind of love—laced with a need for someone to live out your dreams for you. A love of a well-meaning puppeteer. I suddenly feel lucky that as protective as Ma and Pa are, they never try to be captain of my ship. It's hard when pirates seize your ship. Brian probably knows that best of anyone.

Shelly uncurls his fist with a sigh.

"You like adventure, but yet you love *fishing*?" I point to the fishing poles tacked to his wall. There are also two wooden oars making an X hanging next to them. I know I swore off cramming people in boxes, but Shelly is a bird if I ever saw one. I imagined him more as a marathon runner than a fisherman.

"Fishing was Emilio's favorite. I picked it up in his memory. And boy, when *Quentin* fishes? You should see that boy complain. He moans about 'taking Nemo from his natural habitat.' The only fishing he ever does is catch and release, so I always give him the barbless hook. And he gets sick with a fever *every* time we go on the lake."

I smile. Sounds like Quentin.

"But Quentin enjoyed fishing with his father. They would stay out into the night, catching fireflies at the creek. They both love the water. In fact, if Emilio could have been a fisherman for a living, I think he would have."

"What did Emilio do for a living?"

"High school math teacher. He made sure Quentin was always ahead."

Math? It can't be a coincidence that the subject Quentin fell behind in is the subject his father taught. I wonder if Quentin's anxiety is related.

"I'd want to teach math someday, too," I say. "Maybe a professor of computer science or something."

"That's wonderful. I wish I could say I was supportive of Emilio then. I thought his career as a schoolteacher was a waste of his grades—I always thought he could've gotten a doctorate or done research for the World Health Organization. Then, after his cancer . . ."

"None of that mattered," I finish, my voice soft.

"And I remember the week Emilio shared his diagnosis with his students. It was clear he already had success in its truest form. He got so many loving emails, letters, and one student even made a whole rap song. That student had spunk." He gives me a small smile. "Like you."

"What?"

"Yeah, kid. You got spunk. You remind me of myself when I was young."

I never thought of myself as having *spunk*, but I like the sound of it. "I don't know about that. Quentin was the one helping me try new things."

"As part of that *manifesto*, right? Quentin was explaining it yesterday, but I couldn't follow."

"It was more of a deal, modeled on FDR's New Deal. Reform for our lives, live the American Dream, that sort of thing. Although unlike FDR, I achieved next to nothing. Like ten things."

"Well, my dear, if it makes you feel better, the New Deal wasn't that great to begin with. It caused segregation of neighborhoods. The federal subsidy for home ownership wasn't divided fairly."

I stare at him. I know I romanticize a lot of stuff: straight hair, Stanford, Brian. And I've learned that nothing shiny is without flaws once you pick it apart. Yet, funnily enough, the one that has shocked me most is this. You too, New Deal?

"Anyway." He rests his palms on his knees. "Thank you for keeping my grandson company. He had a hard time losing his father so young, and I'm concerned. I'm hard on him because I want him to succeed. The world doesn't make excuses for you because your father passed away."

"I understand, but Quentin mastered a lot of math concepts that took me longer to learn at first. I think all he needs is to get back his . . ."

"Zest for life?"

I like the sound of it. "Yeah, that."

"I thought he might be going through stuff because he's swingin' for the other team." He chuckles. "Not that there's anything wrong with that. I've learned a thing or two over the years."

I freeze. Is Grandpa Shelly saying what I think he is?

"Um, pardon?"

"I thought he might be contending with being gay. That sort of thing."

"I dunno, I don't think—"

"Then I saw the way he looked at you. I wasn't sure if you felt the same, though, until you told me off at Zola's. That's one plus of being so old. You got your moanin' knees and crackin' bones, but you can catch on to stuff real quick, since chances are, you've been in a similar pickle."

I peer into my empty mug of tea like there's something interesting at the bottom.

"And," he continues, "seeing you here, I feel guilty, because I actually might be the reason you didn't get to meet him tonight."

"What do you mean?"

"Him and I got to talking this evening, and he said that he really liked you but wasn't sure how you felt about him. He seemed to think he's not smart enough for an Arledge Preparatory student like you. I felt like it was my civic duty to tell him about how you stood up to me at dinner and defended him like a queen protecting her royal subjects. You should've seen his face."

I cover my eyes with the pads of my fingers. "You told him about that?"

"Sì, I did. And looks like that's why he decided to drive home. As soon as I told him, he left without another word. Maybe you both had the same idea tonight."

I check the grandfather clock in the corner of the room. It's past ten p.m. on a weeknight. Ma's going to be pacing at the door like a prison warden while praying to the Ganesha statue on the mantel. I hadn't even texted her before leaving, and I can't text her now because I have no reception, and Shelly has no Wi-Fi.

"I should start driving back. Thank you for the chamomile tea."

"You didn't get to try the panettone. Next time." He puts our empty mugs on a bamboo tray. "Before you go, can I take a photo of you?" He looks at me as if the question is the most obvious one in the world for him to be asking now. "I have printed photos of everyone who visits my humble abode stuck up on the mantel there. It's a bit of a tradition."

On the wall above the stone fireplace, there's a bulletin board covered with photos, secured using colored thumbtacks. I don't know how I missed it.

"Of course." I smile at the collage. I wouldn't have pegged Shelly to be the memento type.

He disappears to the kitchen for a second and returns with an ancient digital camera. I bumble in front of the wall next to the fishing poles, and Shelly squints at the camera screen for a while before taking a photo. He snaps a few, murmuring about lighting issues. It's like when my nani visited from India and spent her months here taking a bajillion blurry photos with her decrepit Canon camera.

After he's done, I look at the photos pinned on the board. I recognize Quentin, Owen, Ms. Santos, and Sophie. There's a recipe in cramped cursive for homemade ravioli.

"Hey!" I tap on the card. "Is this the secret family recipe you talked about at Zola's? The one Quentin's dad made every year?"

Shelly looks up from his camera. "That's the one."

"Wow." I trace my finger across the cursive. "When I host a party, I'm gonna make ravioli from scratch, too. People will lose their minds."

"You should let them lose their mental faculties as soon as possible, dear. Don't delay."

I laugh. "I would, but I don't think there's enough room in my house for a dinner party. We have four chairs."

"For that ravioli, guests would pack themselves in like sardines."

A lot of fish references from this man, that's for sure.

"Do you mind if I take a picture of the recipe? I'll credit you when I make it, promise."

"No need, I'll text the picture to you. Got it backed up to iCloud already."

Backed up to iCloud?

I thought Shelly didn't know anything about technology. He pulls out his phone from his pocket, and my jaw drops. Brand-new iPhone. Top of the line.

"Wait, is that a—" I lean in, but he raises his arm into the air, straight as a flagpole.

"Before I let you see this, I have to ask. You can keep a secret, right?"

I nod, my eyes wide. "Of course."

He lowers his arm. "In that case, of course I have a phone. And of course I have Wi-Fi. I just unplug the router before Quentin visits. I also have a few social media accounts. You can follow me at fisherman-underscore-cottage. Don't forget the underscore, people always miss that."

"*What?*"

"C'mon. No one can get by without a cell phone these days. I just like to be present for my guests and for them to be present with me. People don't want to poke a conspiracy theory man, so I pretend that I think cell phones are the government's way to spy on us. Works every time. Anyway, Aisha, I'm glad you came by tonight." There's this twinkle in his eye, as if he knows something I don't. It's disconcerting, but I somehow know I'll never find what's turning behind those wise brown eyes. "Can I give you some unsolicited advice as you go?"

"Please do."

"Don't feel like you have to rush to sort everything out. Give yourselves time to find each other. As we say in Italy, the salt of patience seasons everything. If there's one thing I've learned about fishing, it's that if you're patient enough, the lunker always comes."

"Are you comparing your grandson to a giant fish?"

I can't say it's not a comparison I've made before.

Shelly throws his hands in the air. "If it gets the point across, then absolutely."

I grin. "Thank you, Shelly."

"No, thank *you*. I always love a surprise guest. It gets lonely here in Houghton Lake." He winks at me, sharing a secret between us. I know he means that he loves it up here by himself—his little cabin escape. I have to admit, I love it, too. The calm, the quiet, the absence of having to *do* something. I've been hurrying for too long. This time, I'll enjoy the wait.

32
WONDROUS WATERCOLOR

✔ Attend my first watercolor painting class

"You don't have to help clean up, Aisha," Sarah insists, but I continue scrubbing the table. I want to get into Sarah's good graces after missing the first watercolor class at Crafterina. My watercolor instructor can't think I'm lazy.

Okay, so that's not *really* it. I'm trying to delay my punishment. Because I got home so late from Houghton Lake, Ma told me pans with turmeric stains and dried rice would be awaiting me. Ma adopts bits of American culture that she likes, and one bit she thinks is most delightful is weekly chores. Along with doubling them for any curfew infraction. My plan is to drive to Quentin's tonight right after my sentence is complete.

Sarah leaves to fetch the keys and comes back a few minutes later.

"Aisha?" she asks. I only look up because her voice sounds a bit funny. "Are you expecting a visitor? There's a handsome someone outside waiting to see you. I told him we closed, but . . ."

"Who is it?" I might have an idea.

"See for yourself."

I start to leave, still hugging my canvas portfolio of water-color supplies to my chest. The class went better than I thought. After hearing everyone introduce themselves and explain why they're taking the class, I felt like I wasn't alone in being intimidated by sharing my paintings.

As soon as I'm through the automatic doors, I see him.

His hair is a little more tousled than usual, but sure enough, Quentin Santos is there, in his navy coat and his wooden watch and his long stripy socks peeking out from under his cropped pants. As soon as he sees me, he steps forward.

"Hey, Aisha."

I missed you. I'm glad you're okay. I'm sorry about your midterm. I can't believe you've been gone for four days. I went to your grandpa's house yesterday. You were right about painting again. It makes me feel like myself. I think I really like you.

"Hey."

"Sorry to just show up. Your dad told me you were here. Can we talk?"

I hadn't imagined our reunion would happen in this unromantic manner. I had imagined me, sitting on a park bench in a flowing dress. I would be wearing beautiful golden-strapped sandals and tapping my foot lightly on the pebbled pavement, my hair gathered into a braid. He would touch my shoulder. I'd pull off my sunglasses. Our eyes would meet.

Instead, we're in the parking lot of Crafterina, with packs of crayons stacked in the windows and cheesy decals advertising a "hello spring" sale. I'm wearing a smock streaked with paint.

"Sure." I look back to tell Sarah that I have to go, but she's already waving at me through the window of the workshop room. When we get to his car, I realize I forgot to leave my smock at the store. Great.

Quentin sees my portfolio flopping against my hip. He opens the door for me. I slide my portfolio into the back seat, and then I get into the passenger's seat. I breathe in the familiar musty scent of his car.

We look at each other and then look away.

He swallows hard. "I actually made a reservation for seven fifteen at Corelle's for dinner. Would you be up for going there to talk?"

A *reservation*? That's unusual. We've never made a reservation together before.

"Okay."

He peers over his shoulder to reverse. His eyes glow in the sun. I'm so close that I can see the slight flush of his cheeks and count his freckles. *If I wanted to, I could kiss him. I could lean over and just—*

I tug the hair tie on my wrist to reprimand myself. What am I thinking? I have always been comfortable in Quentin's car, but now I'm feeling this magnetic pull to touch him, to just rake my hands through his hair or bury my head in his chest. Sarah did say that watercolor has a way of revealing "wondrous thoughts" within our minds, since watercolor lends itself to organic experimentation. I didn't think it would be *these* kinds of thoughts.

Leave it to me to get embarrassed from thinking.

We're so quiet that I hear the rubber of the tires meeting the road. I don't look at him. I don't fiddle with the Jetta's old radio tuner. I feel awkward, like I'm carpooling in an Arledge parent's car for a crochet field trip. Suddenly, the car lurches forward. It's a traffic jam—cars stretching down the hill.

"We're not going to make it on time. Must be an accident blocking the road or something."

Quentin's fingers are drumming on the steering wheel, and not in the usual I'm-bopping-to-music way. Even with his stone-faced expression, I know he's nervous. For all the times Quentin admonished me to be myself, this time *he* is being unlike himself. I can't help it. I laugh.

"Wha . . . what is it?"

"Quentin, it's okay. We won't die if we don't make our reservation at Corelle's. We usually meet at Wooly's for sundaes every week. Not exactly Michelin-star stuff."

For a moment, Quentin looks stricken, but then he grins. We needed a reminder to restore the comfortable banter that is quintessentially us.

"You're right." He relaxes in his seat. "I just want to talk. I don't care about where we go."

"Lucky for you, I know *just* the spot for a dramatic conversation."

"Lead the way, Lady Aisha."

I try out my horrible British accent for a few turns, which earns me a smile. Finally, I direct him to turn into my neighborhood, and he gives me a once-over.

"Seriously, Aisha? Your grand plan is your house, with your dad watching us while he drinks his evening masala chai?"

"Not quite." When we're just one block south of my apartment building, I point outside. "There! Pull over right by that blue mailbox."

Quentin pulls over and takes the key out of the ignition. After a moment's pause, the headlights wink out. I see lines of orange in the sky, as if Lord Surya is driving his chariot of fire through the heavens.

"Uh, where are we?"

"Doesn't this look familiar?"

He looks at the house we're parked in front of, then the sky-blue mailbox, then the winterberry bush poking up from the frosty grass. "I know! This is the place we stopped to talk the night you hijacked—"

"*Joined* you in your car. I thought this is a tried and tested good conversation spot." I unbuckle my seat belt, untie my smock from around my waist, and toss it onto the back seat. "What is it that you want to talk about, now?"

Quentin starts with the details of his anxiety attack. He hadn't slept the night before his exam, and the morning of, he felt an ominous cloud following him. He was fine until he got to the more complex integrals. His thoughts spiraled into an I-can't-do-this vortex. He couldn't breathe. The world went black.

I'm quiet, interjecting with a nod every so often, so he knows I'm listening.

"It wasn't the first time. Ever since my dad passed, I've been living with this fear of doing anything. Like if I take a step, another tragedy will happen. But things were starting to change, thanks to you. You made me try new things. Like baking gluten-free macarons that taste like wood chips."

"They weren't *that* bad. But I do wonder if Marcy ate them. She ended up with the whole container."

I miss Marcy. School feels empty with us not talking. Lunch feels tasteless. AP Lit feels boring. I want to apologize, but

I'm afraid she won't forgive me. The apology has to be meaningful. I've been thinking of different ways—balloons, locker decorations—but none of it feels genuine enough. Or Marcy enough.

"I'm glad you're okay," I say. "I . . . missed you. Teasing Owen about his girlfriend wasn't the same."

"I missed you, too."

"I'm sure what you *really* missed was Wi-Fi."

"It wasn't so bad. I fished at the creek like my dad and I used to do. I thought about everything that happened this winter. Shelly was nicer than usual." He glances at me. "What did you do this week while I was away?"

"Nothin' much."

Oh, nothin'. Just realized I don't like Brian and that I'm basically in love with you, drove to your grandpa's home without telling him . . .

"C'mon. Stuff must have happened. I noticed you took down the sticky note wall in my room and replaced it."

"I signed up for the watercolor class."

"Yeah, your dad told me. I was happy to hear."

"Gotta keep myself occupied somehow in your absence, right?"

He looks down. "I'm sorry for not reaching out to you this week. I knew how disappointing it would be for you to hear that I screwed up, and I wasn't sure when the school would let me retake the midterm, or if the same thing would happen again when I did. . . ."

"Quentin, you don't have to apologize. I wasn't disappointed at all. I was *worried* about you. You ended up at the ER. Not like you wanted that to happen."

"I actually went to the ER on purpose," he deadpans. "So I could avoid you after the, er, conversation we had the night before my midterm."

"What conversation?"

"Shut up."

I laugh. "Please tell me you don't really hate me that much."

"Not gonna lie, these days I've been half wishing I did."

I look at him, *really* look at him, and I see how hard the past few days must have been for him. I want to scream *no, don't hate me, I like you, too*, but the words are wedged too far down my throat.

"Listen, Aisha. I don't mean to make things awkward between us, but I can't deny that I . . ." His voice turns soft. "I like you. A lot. I have for a while. Probably since before New Year's, but I didn't want to admit it."

Even though I know, hearing it from Quentin feels different. The day Brian asked me to winter formal, a part of me knew it was like a balloon—shiny and metallic on the outside, air on the inside. Quentin's confession makes me stir. It's the way his face is glowing in the purply dusk light. It's the way his words etch themselves into my heart. They feel precious—words I want to box up and take with me forever, to open when times get tough. My little Tupperware container of sweet macaron memories.

I have to tell him that I like him, too, that it has always been him, and—

"You don't have to say anything. The night my grandpa told me about how you stood up for me at Zola's, I had a realization."

Does he already know?

"I realized that you're an amazing friend."

What?

"You standing up for me like that is huge. Your friendship means a lot to me, so I just need some time to sort through this. I'm sorry if I made things weird, but it snuck up on me, and it got to a point where I had to tell you." He puts his hand on my shoulder. "But I really do want the best for you and Brian. I mean it."

I pretend to be transfixed by the blue mailbox outside the window. For Quentin, he was gone a few days, but for me, everything is different. I wonder if he'll understand.

"What's wrong?"

"I'm fine. I appreciate you saying that. I have some more news to share, too. . . ." I pause, breathing deeply.

In. Out.

I'm telling myself that it's not the right time, but I know that I'm scared. What happens when I tell Quentin I like him, too? Will he think I'm just jumping from boy to boy, without rhyme or reason? Do I have what it takes to face the consequences of my confession? I've never dated anyone, unless you count eating lunch in the library with a science project partner. What would Ma say about dating in high school, anyway? How does one even date?

Oh man. I'm like Pa trying to fix our broken showerhead last week. He said he knew how to fix it, and then he bent underneath it and went, "How do you get this thing off?" We all groaned because sometimes, if you have to even *ask* certain questions, it means you're not qualified to answer them. If I have to ask myself what dating means, then I'm not ready. I was talking a big game when I drove to Shelly's house, but a part of me was relieved when Quentin wasn't there. I'm not Most Likely to Inspire a Revolution.

I'm Most Likely to Be a Big Chicken.

"I didn't get into Stanford."

Bock bock.

Quentin folds me into a hug. His ear is warm against my cheek. I close my eyes.

"I'm so sorry, Aish. It's gonna be okay. You'll get into other great universities, I promise."

"Yeah, I did apply to this fellowship at U of M. My AP Lit teacher recommended it. But it's super selective, so I don't know if I'll get in. . . ."

He smells like the pine trees near Shelly's cabin. The weight of him reminds me that he's real. I know I can't just be his friend—every bone in my body is defying that notion. I've lost my words, but luckily, this isn't a Stanford essay or an *Antelope Times* op-ed. Like watercolor, there are ways to express myself besides words. I feel Quentin letting go, but before he can, I yank the collar of his button-up back toward me. He looks down at his bunched-up shirt clenched between my fingers, and then looks back at me. His eyes shine with the same chocolate-chip-cookie warmth I noted the night we met. We breathe.

In. Out.

In. Out.

I think about how I consider my every move. Thinking keeps me awake at night, even though I want to sleep so badly. What if I did what I felt without thinking for once? Would that be *so* bad?

I close the space between Quentin and me. My lips press

to his. He stiffens in surprise. After a few moments, he slides his hand around my waist, pulling me from my seat until I'm almost sitting in the center console of his Jetta, on top of the cupholders.

In. Out.

In. Out.

He kisses me again. I've watched him tousle his hair many times while doing calculus problems, but this time, it's my hands moving of their own accord. Our kiss grows deeper and more sure, as if we've done this many times before. My head bows and my arms bend, like a daisy angling to soak in the sunlight. The aches of daily frustrations and things gone wrong disappear. My mind goes still.

33
A MESSAGE FROM SAISHA WAGARWAL

✔ Write an apology email

Sent February 4, 5:56 p.m.
To: marcethefarce856@gmail.com
From: aisha.agarwal@gmail.com
Subject: !URGENT!

Hello, Ms. Coleman,

It has come to my attention recently that a student by the name of Aisha Agarwal is a total buffoon and took you for granted. Agarwal has requested that I relay that she is terribly apologetic. She never invited you over because she was embarrassed that she lives in a (very) humble apartment in Coral Tree, whilst you live in a larger home (read: mansion). However, she realizes now that you would never judge her for something as silly as the size of her dwelling. She also apologizes that she was not there for you when you came out to your mom. She wants to be there, and she will be now.

As part of her apology, she has attached two files. Firstly, she has enclosed an invitation for a dinner party at her home next week. She encourages you to bring your special plus-one, who she'd like to get to know more. She will make dinner from scratch, which she promises will be better than her macarons. To design the invitation, she used one of those e-card websites with a million pop-up ads for sexy singles near you. Please come if you feel a shred of pity. Secondly, she has attached a sample op-ed piece she'd like to publish in your esteemed newspaper, the *Antelope Times*. It contains the opinion that love matters most, above any valedictorian title or Stanford admission. As you will soon see, the piece has a level of cheese equivalent to the special homemade four-cheese ravioli Aisha will be serving at her dinner party. She, of course, would never dream of bribing you with four-cheese ravioli, but she hopes it serves as a tiny incentive.

Please accept this buffoon's sincerest apology. It came late because she wanted to apologize in the most genuine way she could think of.

Sincerely,
Saisha Wagarwal
Representative of Midwest Friendship Relations

Attachments:
dinner_invite_marcy.png
winter_op-ed_final_final2_finallyyy.pdf

34
THE BUTTERFLY EFFECT

✔ Host a dinner party at my home

The next week at school, Marcy still doesn't sit with me at lunch. I keep refreshing my email, but she hasn't replied, so I go to the library to eat alone like the socialite that I am. I'm parked on the carpet in between the biography shelves—the place that Brian and I had our conversation after winter formal. For the first time in months, I've packed myself a lunch. I used all my post-kiss adrenaline to make it. I say it's a feast fit for Goddess Parvati.

Okay, it's an apple and a paneer sandwich, but I'm proud of myself.

I'm about to unwrap my sandwich when a voice asks, "This seat taken?"

Lily. Her hair is brushed behind her shoulders, and her hands are curled over the straps of her backpack. I wonder how she found me.

"All yours."

She sits down, tugging her uniform skirt past her knees. My eyes are tethered to her every move. Maybe she found out about Stanford and wants to gloat. Or maybe she wants to tell me that because my crochet turtle has gone unfinished for months, I am no longer welcome as a member of crochet club.

"Aisha, I read your op-ed. I really liked it."

"Oh." How could she have read it? Marcy didn't reply to my email yet. "Did Marcy forward it to you for a second pair of eyes or something?"

"No, it got published in the school paper this morning. Didn't Marcy tell you?" She fishes in her backpack and hands me a crumpled sheet of paper. "I usually only read the *Antelope Times* online, but I printed your piece out using the library computers because I liked it so much."

Holding my breath, I take the paper from her.

INSIDE MY MANIFESTO TO HAVE IT ALL
By Aisha Agarwal

Marcy printed my piece.

Does this mean she forgives me? Or does this mean she wants to maintain a professional relationship?

"I didn't quite follow the bird and fish stuff at first, but then it came together. And for the parts about the American Dream and the Arledge scholarship, I related a lot." Lily waits for me to look up at her.

"I'm on scholarship, too. And since my parents aren't well-off, I didn't think I fit in with the Arledge students . . ." Her voice goes soft. "Including you."

"Hey, I'm a crochet turtle. Soft shell."

"I know. It's just, you and Brian both get the highest grades and were always trying to one-up each other, so I just categorized you as arrogant trust fund kids . . ." She bites her lip and leans against the bookshelf, dust raining down onto the carpet like confetti. "That wasn't fair. I'm sorry."

"It's okay, and I'm really glad you told me because I thought the same thing about you. In fact . . ." I blush. "I was kind of jealous of you always, honestly. Cool vibe, president of crochet club, super pretty . . ."

"Go on," she says, and I laugh.

I thought I was the only scholarship kid in the senior class. If I had told people earlier, Lily and I could've been friends.

But maybe it's not too late.

"Hey, I'm having a party at my house next Saturday night at seven. There's gonna be homemade gluten-free ravioli. You should come if you're free."

The party is brought to you by Shelly. At first, I thought it'd be too difficult to deep-clean every crevice of my apartment and stash our Ganesha statue in a drawer, but then Shelly's words came to mind. The focus of the night isn't me, or my apartment. It's ravioli featuring *real* olive oil. So, I asked Ma and Pa. They allowed me to host it as long as all my homework is done. And as long as the Ganesha statue stays upright and proud in the living room.

The apples of Lily's cheeks rise farther than I've ever seen them go. "I'll be there. I love ravioli."

With our last few minutes of lunch left, I'm tempted to ask about Brian. I know he should be far from my mind by now, like a boat adrift at sea, but the boat got yanked back to shore after I noticed Brian was absent from Ms. Kavnick's class today. He wouldn't ruin his perfect attendance record unless held hostage.

"Do you know why Brian was absent today?" I ask.

"No, but I did overhear that he didn't get into Harvard. Maybe it's related."

The co-valedictorians are 0 for 2 for college admissions. As I imagine Brian shouldering Mrs. Wu's disappointment, the hard feelings I had toward him fade like a plane's sky-written message. It's not easy untying the mental knots created by parents. Mrs. Wu demands perfection from Brian. My parents equate good grades to a good life, unaware of Seema's loneliness and my manifesto.

The lunch bell sounds. As Lily and I walk out of the library together, I decide to text Brian. I don't redraft the text a bunch of times or add a squillion emojis. I write from the heart.

Are you okay?

The evening of my party, my bedroom mirror reveals that I've grown a fresh chimple. It's more of a humble Mount Kilimanjaro than a Mount Everest. It's quieter than usual. It isn't barking that I'm a waste of space, or that my ravioli will taste like globs of earwax. I'm poking the toast earrings Seema gifted me into my ears and humming to Ozzy's jazz station when I hear a knock at the door.

"Yo, you in there?"

Seema. She promised to come home for the party, quipping, "I won't miss the opportunity to watch guests choke down your ravioli." For her information, I followed Shelly's recipe to a T, minus the wheat flour part. The ravioli has been covered in foil and placed on the dining table for Lord Ganesha to guard. I even hung paper rosettes from the living room ceiling and put our Diwali string lights up in the dining room.

"Come in."

"I have two topics to discuss." She sits on my bed. "One, I hear from Ma that you've been hanging out with Quentin a lot, to the point where she urged me to lecture you about how boys equal bad grades. So, I must ask, does this mean that Brian has fallen behind in the competition?"

"Disqualified, actually."

"I *knew* it!"

I grin, wrestling a wide-tooth comb through my damp curls. I watched a few videos on taking care of curly hair, and I've been trying not to straighten mine as much. It feels good to wake up without having to fry my hair after my eggs. I also bought a pair of Indian filigree earrings to wear on graduation day because I liked what Brian's mom said about preserving our stories.

And the earrings were on sale.

"The *second* big thing I have to discuss . . ." Seema pulls a letter from behind her back. I spot the yellow block *M* on the top as I nab it. "This came in the mail for you. Ma sent me to hand deliver it, since you got rejected the last time she was with you when you opened an admissions email."

"Indian superstitions," I mutter. I'm about to claw through the seal, but then I stop.

"Want some privacy?"

"Actually, I'm going to wait." I place the letter on my desk. "I haven't gotten a lot of good news lately. I don't want this week to be about college applications. That's why I didn't log in to the application portal when I saw my status had been updated, but looks like they sent a letter, too."

"Impressive restraint. My sister's letting go a little, huh?"

Seema leaves, and I linger at the mirror for a second, fingering my toast earrings. I've been trying to let go. Last night, I watched old cartoons with Pa instead of studying for my AP Chemistry quiz. Even Ma joined in for a few episodes before muttering about American TV lacking the twists and masala of Indian dramas.

The doorbell rings, and I scurry out of my room. I mustn't make my guests wait a second. I open the door, expecting Quentin to—

Marcy. Wearing a heavy black coat and a canvas tote bag. Kevin is standing behind her, waving.

"Omigod, you both came!" My hug sends Marcy careening backward.

"Hey." She smiles, and I pull back, bouncing around like a balloon in the wind.

"Sorry we're a bit late," Kevin says. "I had to drop off my grandma at the conservatory again."

"Sophie, right?"

His eyes go big. "Whoa, how do you—"

"A story I'll save for another time. But most important . . ." I look at Marcy. "Thank you for coming."

"I came for the ravioli and nothing more."

I know that smile. I know she came for me. And for Saisha Wagarwal, Representative of Midwest Friendship Relations.

"Marcy . . ." There's so much I want to say, but it's all word salad in my mind. I decide to start with the lettuce. "I'm sorry. And thank you for printing my op-ed."

"Will you invite us in or what?"

As soon as they come inside, Ma and Pa say hello and mill about awkwardly, their hands clasped behind their backs. Seema saves the day by introducing herself and starting a conversation about the *Antelope Times*. I busy myself by uncovering the foil from the little ravioli children I spent hours birthing this afternoon.

Okay, so maybe that's not the most appetizing comparison.

I'm about done warming my ravioli when the doorbell sounds again. It's fun playing the *who could it be?* game. I appear just as Seema gets the door.

Lily. She's already tugging off her sneakers.

I grin. "You made it."

Lily returns a shy smile, holding up a brown paper gift bag. "I brought some tiramisu from a bakery near my house. Thought it'd go well with the ravioli."

"Thanks, that's so thought—"

"Hey, we didn't come empty-handed, either," Marcy cuts in, reaching into her tote bag. "I brought you a never before seen, top-secret, unreleased . . ."

I press my lips together in anticipation.

"YEARBOOK DRAFT!" She slaps it into my chest.

"*Seriously?*" I trace my finger over the binder clip holding the stack of printed pages together. "I thought mere mortals aren't supposed to get an advance look at the yearbook."

"Being friends with the president of yearbook club makes you immortal."

I look up. She said *friends*. I intend to live up to that designation this time.

She winks. "By the way, I think you'll be pleased with your senior superlative. You're on page seventeen."

So, it's safe to say I didn't get Most Likely to Be Found in the Library During Lunch, although that wouldn't be untrue. There's another knock at the door—only one person it could be now. Seema hangs back and lets me answer.

Quentin's wearing his usual navy coat and wooden watch. The strap from his messenger bag cuts across his chest like a seat belt. Owen and Ms. Santos are standing next to him. She waves at me like she hasn't seen me in years.

"Aisha, so wonderful of you to invite us. Quentin tells me you made the same recipe Emilio used to make."

"I hope the gluten-free version does it justice. Ma also might have added a bit too many red chili flakes to the top."

There's chatter as we all gather around the table, set with two forks each because duplicate cutlery is how you know it's a real party. I also had to ask my neighbors if I could borrow a few dining table chairs, so I'd have enough seats for everyone. Once my neighbors saw my empty I-have-no-social-life eyes, they were happy to oblige.

I place the ravioli dish in Marcy's hands so gingerly you'd think it really did contain my children. She takes a scoop, passes it along. As soon as the first bite is had, the table comes alive. Everyone raves about the pesto. Ms. Santos talks to Ma about home gardens. Pa talks to Lily and Seema about crochet. Marcy and Kevin are wearing cunning grins, which leads me to believe they're grilling Quentin for Kresge High gossip. Owen tells me how thrilled he is about the tiramisu because the poor boy *still* isn't allowed sugar at home. The Ganesha statue isn't talking to anyone, but I think he's enjoying himself.

As I look at all the smiling faces, it occurs to me that this group looks like an obligatory diversity photo on a college website. Then it occurs to me that either Shelly's ravioli recipe is special, or the people in this room are. Or both.

When the last of the pesto is scraped from the pan, everyone proceeds to become players in the no-let-*me*-do-the-dishes game, which I half-heartedly participate in. I mean, I *did* make all the ravioli.

As soon as Quentin has shown off by washing the largest proportion of dishes, he joins me on the couch. The rest of the players are still in the kitchen drying and loading. Other than his signature stripy socks and hair running rogue as usual, his outfit isn't one I recognize. He's dressed in a floral button-up and a casual beige blazer. The yearbook draft pages are spread over my lap.

"Okay, so I haven't had time to ask this. When exactly did you fall madly in love with me?"

"*Shhh*, my parents might hear."

He leans over. "That's why you like me, then? My ill-timed questions?"

"There are a lot of reasons I like you."

"I'm listening."

"You have this warmth to you." I blush. "Like a star."

"A *star*, huh?"

"Just like the stars I drew on your problem sets, all of which you cut out and put into a wooden box."

He gawks at me. "How did you—"

"Besides, I never said I liked you. Explicitly."

"Well, if I remember right, *something* was rather explicit."

I giggle. "Shut up."

"It's funny Marcy brought you a book of sorts, because I also brought you one." He reaches into his messenger bag. "Close your eyes."

A weight falls on my lap. I open my eyes to *Precalculus: An Investigation of Functions.*

"I won't be needing it anymore."

I'm holding my breath. "Do you mean . . ."

"So you know how I retook the midterm? Grades came out yesterday, and I got a B. B minus, but I guess that's—"

"Omigod, Quentin!" I squeal, resisting the urge to launch from the couch to throw my arms around Quentin's neck. Looks like that family puja really did bless this book. I bet Grandpa Shelly will pin Quentin's transcript onto his bulletin board. And I'm *sure* he'll take a photo of it on his phone for iCloud backup.

"Well." Seema appears next to us, perching on the arm of the sofa. "What other stuff you got in that bag, Quentin? I hear that you gave Ma some roses while Aisha was busy fluffing her ravioli."

He shrugs.

I sputter into laughter. "You got Ma flowers on the night of *my* party?"

"Well, you see, at first I bought you flowers. But then, I thought, how did you even come into this world? Your mom. So, I gave her the bouquet instead, for a congratulations on a job well done."

I lift an eyebrow.

"I may have *also* realized the peril of an Indian girl in high school receiving a bouquet of flowers from a boy. With her strict mother watching."

"Got scared off, huh?"

"Not entirely." He pulls out a single rose from his blazer pocket and presses it into my hand.

I'm going to use *Precalculus: An Investigation of Functions* to press the rose, so it's preserved forever. I may have stolen the idea from a certain someone. "Didn't you say you didn't believe in relationships in high school?"

"Yes. *However*, in some months, we won't be in high school anymore." He looks so pleased with himself for finding a loophole.

"It took *this* long for you guys to happen, huh? Took longer than it did for me to learn violin." Owen. He's chomping on some Parle-G biscuits from the Indian grocery store. Where did he find those?

I tuck the rose into the middle of the yearbook draft and snap the binder clip back on. "My parents are gonna kill me if they find out about this."

Everyone trickles back into the living room. I'm about to haul some board games from our storage closet, but then I have a better idea.

"What do y'all think of a spontaneous trip to Wooly's for ice cream?"

There's a short pause before the room cheers. We assemble, hopping into our coats and punching into our mittens. As I look around for my bag, Ma rests her mittened hand on my shoulder. When I was a kid, Pa used to burst through the door after work and tell Seema and me that we were his diamonds. Ma never says stuff like that, but during moments like these, her look tells me all I need to know. In fact, that loving look is the one I've sketched out for my watercolor class project. I'm going to paint

Ma next to the gate of her college girls' hostel in India, her head cocked to the side. Pa will be next to her, his hands cupped around his mouth like he's about to tell her a secret.

I hope painting that scene will help me remember the butterfly effect, the one Principal Cornish mentioned during lunch months ago. *Even if two things collide just once in space and time, they enter into a pattern of mutual influence forever.* My parents' chance meeting is the reason I'm here, and I don't want to forget what a miracle that is—to be made of stars and earth and love and ravioli and rejection.

I know I'll forget. Some days I'll be hopeless again, curled up in bed with Snickers bars and Skittles. But I'm beginning to trust myself more. I chose to get into Quentin's car. I chose to start a sticky note manifesto. I chose to sign up for a watercolor class. I even chose to apply to Stanford. I survived after making choices that scared me. And tonight, I think I can make one more.

"Wait a minute," I say to Ma as she slips the car keys into her purse.

"Kya hua?"

"I forgot something in my room. I'll be just a second!"

I kick off my boots and make a dash to my bedroom, my toast earrings jumping about. The soft light of my desk lamp shines on the sealed University of Michigan envelope. This time, it's different. I'm nervous about the result, but I'm no longer afraid of it.

Dear Aisha . . .

35

GRANDPA SHELLY'S RAVIOLI (MODIFIED GLUTEN FREE)

DOUGH

- 1 pack parchment paper
- 4 cups Bob's Red Mill Gluten Free All-Purpose Baking Flour
- 10 egg yolks
- 1 teaspoon salt
- 1 egg, reserved for egg wash

FILLING

- 2 medium butternut squash
- 2 tablespoons *real* extra virgin olive oil
- 1½ cups goat cheese
- ½ cup grated Parmesan cheese
- ¼ cup cashews
- 1 teaspoon brown sugar
- ½ teaspoon salt
- ½ teaspoon black pepper
- 2 teaspoons red chili flakes (Ma's Indian touch)
- Large serving of love

PESTO

- ½ cup fresh thyme leaves (remove stems)
- 1 cup arugula
- 1 cup grated Parmesan cheese
- ½ cup fresh rosemary (remove stems)
- 5 garlic cloves
- 1 cup *real* extra virgin olive oil
- ½ cup roasted pine nuts, almonds, pecans, or walnuts
- Salt, to taste

PESTO

1. Add all ingredients to a blender or food processor and blend until smooth.
2. Store in refrigerator until ready to use.

FILLING

1. Preheat oven to 415 degrees F. If using uncut squash, peel and cube squash (remove seeds). Mix cubed squash, olive oil, and add a dash of salt and pepper. Add squash to greased baking sheet. Bake for 30 minutes, or until squash is tender. You can use a fork to check if the squash is cooked all the way through. If the fork easily pierces through the squash, it's cooked!
2. Add cooked squash, goat cheese, Parmesan cheese, cashews, and brown sugar to a blender or food processor. Blend until smooth. Season with salt, pepper, and red chili flakes.

DOUGH

1. Make egg wash by beating an egg with approximately 1 teaspoon of water.
2. Dust a large piece of parchment paper with flour. This parchment will be used to shape your ravioli.
3. Whisk together flour and salt, then add egg yolks and mix. Once mixed well, knead dough with your hands until it forms a ball.
4. Move ball to parchment paper. Keep kneading dough until smooth, then break the ball apart into approximately 8 smaller balls. Keep dough you're not using covered at all times so it doesn't dry out.
5. Take each dough ball and roll it out with a rolling pin. Try to roll each ball into a sheet that is $\frac{1}{8}$ to $\frac{1}{16}$ inch thick, or as thin as possible. Cut squares from the dough (approximately 2 inches by 2 inches) using a knife or pizza cutter. Repeat with all dough balls until all dough has been cut into squares.

ASSEMBLY

1. Place 1 heaping tablespoon of filling in the center of a square. Add another dough square on top to cover. Then brush around the edges of the ravioli with egg wash, press down around the edges with your fingers to seal, and crimp edges with a fork.
2. Bring a large pot of salted water to a boil. Boil ravioli in batches for 2 minutes until the pasta is al dente (ravioli should float to the top). Drain water.

3. Add the homemade pesto on top of the ravioli. Sprinkle with a large serving of love and chili flakes for spice. Enjoy!

Note: this recipe yields approximately ten servings.

Acknowledgments

If you're reading this, you have been inducted into a Very Special Top-Secret Club that reads the acknowledgments section instead of immediately shutting the book on completion and waddling to the fridge for a snack. Considering these pages have won out against hummus, I'm deeply honored.

Even with the snacks I had at my disposal throughout this process, I have to say: writing this book was the hardest thing I've ever done in my life (yes, even harder than surviving high school! Imagine!). But what made it equally as wondrous and magical were the hands that nudged me along the way, and if there's one thing I've learned as a debut author, it's that books (or any creative body of work for that matter) are never made alone. My book is composed of the books I've read over the years, the movies I've seen, the songs I've listened to on repeat, the conversations I've had, and the efforts of so many.

None of this would've been possible without my Pitch Wars 2021 cohort and mentors, Liz Lawson and Dante Medema. Your feedback on craft, line edits, and query letters transformed my manuscript and made it agent-showcase ready. And thank you to 2020 Pitch Wars mentors Chloe Gong and Tashie Bhuiyan for pointing out that my book probably needs some stakes (who knew).

To my previous agents, Alex Rice and Lola Bellier, thank you for believing in Aisha's story from the beginning. I'll never forget how seen I felt after our first phone call. You took me patiently through the submissions process, through the highs and lows, while allowing me to lean on your keen eyes and ears. And to my current agents, Tia Ikemoto and Sindhu Vegesena, thank you for jumping on board with such care, enthusiasm, and honesty, and guiding me through marketing and launching my book. Your expertise got me to the finish line.

To my editor, Alyssa Miele—thank you for choosing my book, and thank you for the countless hours you've spent hanging out with Quentin and Aisha, through drafts and drafts. I imagine they felt a bit like visitors in your house that wouldn't leave, no matter how openly you yawned or cast glances at the door, but still you offered them hummus, tirelessly listened to them, and gently pushed them to grow until they were ready for the world.

Much like the crucial role that no-show socks play in a prosperous shoe game, there are so many invisible hands that nurture a book to completion. I'm so grateful to the whole team at Quill Tree, including my cover designer, Molly, who rendered the cutest washi tape ever, and to Alexandra and the copyediting team who caught every inconsistency (how did Quentin go from wearing a button-up to a hoodie within one page? We'll never know, and thanks to you, readers will not have to ask). A special thank-you to the authenticity readers who gave me feedback on an early copy of *Aisha*. You made this book more representative of the mosaic of cultures and histories it contains.

To all the wonderful teachers and mentors I've had the pleasure of learning from—including Liza Pagano, Florence Lee, Philip Schweiger, Dr. Toyama, Mr. Zwolinski, Ms. Kuslits, Ms. East, Ms. Burke, and Ms. Taylor—you taught me things I could never find in a textbook: how to keep going and how to strive for quality.

This story was inspired by my story, except none of *my* crushes in high school liked me back (if you went to high school with me and I'm wrong, please let me know). Like Aisha, I lacked self-confidence and felt behind in life, and although I still grapple with those things today, I feel lucky to have people in my life who embody the qualities of Quentin: encouraging, loving (and cute, too).

To Pallavi: Thank you generally for being my family away from home (and at times my band manager and fellow spider exterminator) and for being the first (!) reader and listener of my story. Your support made me believe that this book could be on a shelf someday, and our silly kitchen conversations always put a smile on my face. I am so lucky to have you.

Thank you to my other dear friends for your encouragement and feedback during this intensive process—Aubrey, Neha & Rajat (your words and delicious chocolate cakes motivated me to keep going), Pranita (I'll try to finish Zenoria for you someday), Jed (thank you for letting me borrow some of our college memories as inspiration for this book), Justine, Maahirah & Bilqees, the lovely Epics & Goldens crew of Kuan, Xindi and Qin Yu, Shikhar, Baula, Danica, Akhil, Kushal, Vishal, Siddharth, and all my friends from San Francisco, Rochester, and beyond who make me feel at home. I'm eternally grateful.

I wouldn't be where I am without the love of my family. Anjana, you are my real-life Seema (with the wisdom and quips and all). If a zombie apocalypse hit, you'd be the first person I'd call to ask for advice, and I mean that very seriously. Thank you to my parents, who although have no idea how publication works still, are always in the audience, clapping and cheering me on. Your decision to let me buy books from the Scholastic Book Fair every year led me here.

To Ananth. Through all the good news, bad news, early drafts, and edit rounds, you were there with kind words, mochas, and dark chocolate. This trifecta was more helpful than you will ever know. Your support got me through the toughest parts of this process. Thank you for being my #1 fan.

Thank you to those involved in maintaining green spaces and parks—without you, I'd have 95 percent fewer ideas.

Finally, I want to thank *you*. I know there are a squillion books in the world being published every day, and it means so much to me that you chose mine and stuck with it long enough to reach this page. The reason I wrote this book is to remind myself and all of you that we cannot be reduced to our to-do lists or how many cones we hit on a driver's test or the job titles we hold. We are infinite, and at any time, we can begin again. As you go forth in the world and eat all the hummus you desire, I want you to know that truly, this book is for you.